the UNSEEN

CELESTE

book 2

First Trade Paperback Edition: July 2015

For information on subsidiary rights, please contact the publisher at rights@jollyfishpress.com.

For information, write us at Jolly Fish Press, PO Box 1773, Provo, UT 84603-1773, or visit us at www.jollyfishpress.com.

Printed in the United States of America
THIS TITLE IS ALSO AVAILABLE AS AN EBOOK.

Library of Congress Cataloging-in-Publication Data

Worthen, Johnny, 1966-
Celeste / by Johnny Worthen. -- First paperback edition.
    pages cm. -- (The unseen ; book 2)
Summary: "Sixteen-year-old Eleanor, a shapeshifter dealing with her new body, finds herself targeted by rumors, superstition, and religion, forcing her to decide if she should cling to hope, or follow her instincts and run"-- Provided by publisher.
ISBN 978-1-63163-022-4 (paperback)
[1. Shapeshifting--Fiction. 2. Wyoming--Fiction.] I. Title.
PZ7.W887876Ce 2015
[Fic]--dc23
                                                        2015008780

10 9 8 7 6 5 4 3 2 1

Til Familien Frederiksen

Praises for *The Unseen* Series

"Worthen's handling of the volatile issues of racism, societal inequalities, gossip mongering, peer pressure, bullying, death, and abandonment will provide readers with numerous opportunities for in-depth discussion."
—*School Library Journal*

"Worthen deftly sketches a flawed and enthralling character in Eleanor . . . A riveting supernatural character study wrought with the pains of first love and the struggles of self-acceptance."
—*Kirkus Reviews*

"This book is full with everything a novel should have to entertain and intrigue its reader."
—*Deseret News*

"Worthen captures emotion in words, which is a difficult feat for authors."
—*Tentacle Books*

the UNSEEN
CELESTE
book 2

a novel by
johnny worthen

JOLLY
FISH
PRESS
Provo, Utah

CHAPTER ONE

Eleanor glanced behind her, wishing she could see the highway, knowing David was there. He sat in his little car a half-mile away at the end of the Batton's dirt road waiting for her. She thought of her mother, Tabitha, parked in the same place in a borrowed car just two years before, waiting, like him, for this strange ritual that kept Eleanor alive and invisible.

A white wooden lattice hung against the house and tamed a climbing white rosebush. She worked her way to the wall. Thorns tugged at her clothes, but she moved slowly and methodically, patient and eager. She reached the trellis and began to climb it like a ladder as she had in past years.

Anyone looking couldn't help but see her. In the August moonlight, she was as exposed on the trellis as if she were a target on a wall. But the window was open, and her life had new meaning. She was excited to see what lay inside the room, what new image she would take from the girl inside.

She reached up to grasp the windowsill just above her head and felt the betrayal beneath her. The rains that had made the Nebraska corn tall had also weakened the woodwork. The plains were still alien to Eleanor and she struggled to identify the subtle odors and pollens her senses delivered to her. Different or dangerous, she realized too late. The trellis had rotted since she had last clambered up. All at once, in a splintering crash, it crumbled like a house of cards and dropped Eleanor to the ground, wrapped in clinging rose vines.

The noise bounced off the barns and rolled across the cornfields like thunder. Inside the house, a dog went wild, barking and snarling through a window, trying to see into the bush where Eleanor lay trapped.

Hours before, she'd crept from the cornfield to a parked tractor and then scurried between outbuildings and silos, ever watchful of danger. A bright half moon shone clear in the late summer sky. A steady, southeast, night breeze carried earthy scents of tilled and irrigated land; corn, horses, and ripening fruit. It had been welcoming and lovely and, she thought, portentous of good things to come.

She'd seen no movement in the house for hours. The corn, tall and lush, promised of a healthy harvest. They'd had the good water year Jamesford had not. She'd waited until she was sure no one was awake and then she'd begun her spirals around the house.

Inside she'd seen the father, the mother, a young boy around five years, a baby still under a year, and Celeste Batton, the girl whom she'd come to visit. Celeste still had the room in the front corner on the second floor, the one above the rose bush. She'd left her window open.

Because they had seen it in a movie, Eleanor had worn black clothes for the affair: dark jeans, a long sleeved black turtleneck, and a wool cap to hold her hair. She'd balked at the shoe polish for her face and complained of looking stupid. David had said she looked like a burglar and so was appropriately attired. "To hide in the dark, look like the dark," David had said sagaciously. But against the white roses, beneath the shattered white trellis, and under glowing moonlight, the black outfit did anything but hide her.

Lights blinked on inside the house. Noise of movement, alarmed and hurried. Voices in shades of worry, surprise, and anger. Clatter, shouts, footsteps. Eleanor struggled against the vines, but the thorns gripped her stupid outfit like Velcro. The thousand scrapes and cuts she suffered were nothing to the anguish she felt over her stupid carelessness. She'd been incautious and optimistic; too convinced that her run of recent good luck would continue through this annual ritual.

From upstairs in the far back, to the middle of the house, to the front, Eleanor watched with rising panic as the lights approached ever nearer the porch.

Suddenly, the door flew open, casting light onto the porch like a net. A yipping dog shot out of the house like a homing missile and ran right at Eleanor.

Following the dog, silhouetted against the porch light, framed in the threshold, came a man. The glimmer of steel in his hands was unmistakable and final.

He stepped off the porch and, led by the baying dog, quickly found Eleanor struggling for escape in the broken roses under the window.

He flicked off the safety, chambered a round, and lifted the rifle to his shoulder. Eleanor froze, feral memories of guns and fear paralyzing her. The dog fell silent in anticipation. The man lined up the sights in the moonlight, steadied the barrel, and took aim at the trapped and helpless prowler.

CHAPTER TWO

"Goddammit, Celeste. Not enough you break our hearts, you've got to break your neck?"

Eleanor blinked. The man lowered his rifle.

"I ought to tan your hide for this. You know how close you came to getting shot? What were you thinking, girl?"

"Uhm," she said.

"What is wrong with you? Where were you going? What do you think is out there? See? This is exactly the kind of stupidity I was talking about. You don't know anything."

"What is it, Wayne?" A woman with a flashlight stood on the porch in a flannel robe and curlers.

"Our daughter is playing *Mission Impossible* down the rose trellis. Trying to escape, like this is some kind of prison."

"Is she hurt?"

"Probably," he said. "Hopefully. Maybe it'll teach her something." Eleanor could sense his anger rise instead of ebb with each syllable.

"Don't be so hard on her," the woman said. "Help her out of there."

"She can get herself out. She's so independent."

"Wayne!"

The dog hopped and yipped excitedly. Eleanor was surprised to see that the dog, for all its loud and raucous barking, was no bigger than a cat. It was a dachshund, a wiener dog. It darted forward and licked her face like they were old friends.

The man laid the gun down and offered a hand to Eleanor. She reached up and took it. He pulled her out none too gently, and thorns ripped her shirt and cut into her side.

"Are you all right?" he demanded.

"I guess so," she said, addressing the comment to the ground.

Had she been looking at him she could have ducked. His hand came up so fast, so unexpectedly, that the slap caught her full across the jaw. She heard it before she felt it. It knocked her to the ground.

"Wayne!" cried the woman.

The man stood over Eleanor, a towering shadow in the moonlight.

"You're an ungrateful little girl," he yelled at her, emphasizing his words with a finger in her face. "After all we've done for you. I knew you'd try something like this. You ungrateful brat!"

The woman tried to get to Eleanor, but the man held her back.

"Desiree, you've got to back me in this. This is what your daughter thinks of us, thinks of the things we give her, the life—the good life—we've given her."

The woman stayed back.

"I should just let you go," the man roared at Eleanor. "You'd learn quickly how cruel the world is, how good you've had it. You think because we've put up with you, that because we've loved you, that the world will? Do you think the world will care about you the way we do?"

Eleanor stood up but was unsteady on her feet. The blow had dazed her, the situation more so.

"That's enough, Wayne," the woman said sternly. "We'll talk about this in the morning, and Celeste won't be the only one offering an apology."

The woman slid her arm around Eleanor's waist and ushered her forward into the house. The little dog followed, tail flipping like a whip. The man remained outside, standing slump-shouldered in the yard, bathed in cold moonlight.

The smack had nearly sent her running, not from fear of the man, but from fear of what she might do in retaliation. The thing inside her had stirred from the blow, awoken, and began to edge itself into her mind and skin with claw and hide and survival fury. She'd fought it back, but it had scared her more than she'd admit.

The woman marched her through a hallway up a flight of stairs, not speaking a word. She steered her to the left then opened a door.

"Go to bed, dear," she said. "Your father isn't himself right now. We love you. He'll regret what he's done."

Eleanor looked inside and saw a dark room and an empty bed. Among the odors of perfume and dust came familiar smells: her breath and sweat, her borrowed skin. Hers, but not hers. Moonlight streamed in the open window, and pale lace curtains rustled in the night breeze. She stepped inside, and the woman pulled the door closed behind her.

Eleanor turned around. Standing against the wall, hidden by the door, stood a tall, auburn-haired girl. The face that stared at her with wonder and excitement she knew very well, because it was the face she wore.

When the girl didn't cry out or move, but only watched, Eleanor raised her hand and made an awkward little finger wave.

"Hello, Celeste," she said. "How ya been?"

Celeste's finger shot to her lips. Her eyes grew even wider, which Eleanor didn't think was possible. She gestured her to move. Eleanor heard it then in the hall, someone approaching the door. She moved as directed. Celeste stepped forward just as there came a timid little knock.

"Ceely?" It was a small voice, a young boy's. "Ceely, you okay?"

"I'm fine, Nugget," she said, opening the door a crack and peering out. "You go to bed. You'll get in trouble for being up so late."

"But I heard noise, and everyone else is up."

"Go to bed," she said sternly.

"Can I sleep with you tonight?"

"No. Now go to bed."

Celeste gave the boy a hard glare, and then Eleanor heard him leave.

Eleanor studied Celeste in the light from the hall. She had changed so much from last year. She had grown inches taller, filled out in all the right places, and added six inches to her hair. She noticed the traces of eyeliner, painted fingernails, and a mark on her arm. She wondered if her father had given her that bruise.

Celeste closed the door, and the finger returned to her lips. Staring at each other in the moonlight, they waited and listened. In a few minutes, they heard the heavy tread of the man coming up the stairs and going into a room on the other side of the house.

"Not now, Desiree," Eleanor heard him say. "Save it 'til tomorrow. Just don't."

"Humph," the woman snorted.

The two girls regarded each other in silence for several minutes, then Eleanor heard a low snore from across the house. Celeste pulled a robe on over her pajamas, opened the door, and beckoned Eleanor to follow.

Eleanor glanced at the window. She knew she could survive the fall. She'd done so once already, and for a long moment, she thought of jumping to escape. But she wasn't so afraid. Celeste hadn't revealed her. Celeste seemed excited, surprised—happy even—to see her. As much as she could at that moment, Eleanor felt welcome. Besides, she still didn't have what she came for.

When Eleanor didn't immediately follow her, Celeste rolled her eyes and waved her over. Finally, she grabbed Eleanor's hand and pulled her out the door.

Celeste led Eleanor out of the room and down the stairs. She deliberately stepped over the fifth step and made sure Eleanor did the same. Together they went to the back of the house through the kitchen. The little dog looked up, wagged its tail, and curled up in its basket. They left through the back door.

Outside, Celeste let go of Eleanor's hand and walked quickly away from the house. She stopped several times to look back to make sure Eleanor was following her and that no one else was. She made a beeline for the barn and opened the small man-sized door in the side. The barn was as big as an aircraft hangar and needed motors to operate the big doors. The little one on the side was unlocked.

Inside, Eleanor saw a yellow combine harvester, its engine splayed open, black oily parts set out on plastic tables among tools and lubricants. Celeste closed the door and switched on a light. It was a single bare bulb above the door, a porch light, but on the inside. It would be undetectable from the house. It offered just enough light to lead someone to another light switch farther on, perhaps to the switch that would ignite the rows of fluorescents hanging high above the floor.

Eleanor didn't like being inside and lingered close to the door in case she needed to bolt. She didn't want to be trapped. There were windows in the barn, but they were high up, and it would require serious effort to reach them.

Outside, Eleanor heard the sounds of the quiet farm, the sounds she had listened to all night before she'd tried the trellis. She heard the wind rustle the corn stalks, bending them gracefully in waves with a sound not unlike the folding of tissue paper. A frog croaked, a cricket chirped, an owl hooted far away.

"Who are you?" The question was asked so suddenly, so loudly, that Eleanor jumped. "I thought you were make-believe!" Celeste said. "I can't believe this is real. That you're real. Are you my twin? Does my mom know? Who are you?"

Celeste was shaking in excitement. Her face was flushed, and she even hopped up and down.

"I'm your twin," Eleanor stammered.

"No, you're not," said Celeste. "You're lying. My God, I can tell you're lying because you did that thing with your eyes like I do, where you look up just for a second. You did that same thing."

"Um," Eleanor said, pulling off her wool cap.

"You look just like me," said Celeste. "Or at least like I used to. I haven't had my hair that short since last year. You look like I did last year when you came. What are you?"

"Celeste—" Eleanor started.

"You're about to lie again," she said, pointing at Eleanor's eye.

Since she was very little, Eleanor had always approached Celeste at night, in the dark, usually without even waking her. She'd steal a kiss and be gone. Occasionally Celeste stirred, came half awake and even said hello once. It had never been bad. Eleanor deliberately made the visits as brief as possible, just long enough for her to sample the growing Celeste, to gather the pattern she needed to change so she could appear to age. She'd always felt a deep kinship with Celeste, but it was distant and secret.

Celeste bounced on her heels impatiently, waiting for Eleanor to speak.

Eleanor felt the familiar pangs of fear and confusion, the urge to fight or flight. She tensed her legs and shuffled her feet. Her eyes flickered around, searching for dangers and escapes. She looked at Celeste and bit her lip, struggling to remain, forcing herself to stay upon the new path of trust that David had led her to.

"I'm not sure what I am," Eleanor said finally. "I look like you because I can look like anything. Sometimes I think that means I'm nothing."

"Whoa," she said. "Do I sound like that? Hey, you've visited me before, right? I wasn't dreaming it?"

"Every year about this time," Eleanor admitted.

"I saw you in a bathroom once."

"Yes, that was the second time."

"When was the first?"

"Yellowstone," Eleanor said.

"I don't remember that time."

"Yes, you do," she said glumly.

"When?"

"I was the coyote who licked you."

"That was you?" she said slowly, taking a step backwards as if shoved by the words. "Seriously?"

"I needed to be human again. I found you. You were so sweet. I kissed you and became you. I'd still look exactly like you did then if I hadn't come back and found you later."

"Are you dangerous?"

"Not to you," she said.

"Because we're connected somehow and you can't hurt the person you look like?"

"No," Eleanor said, amused. "I'm not dangerous to you because I like you."

"So, no supernatural thing? No psychic connections and all that?"

Eleanor shrugged her shoulders. "I may be a supernatural thing. I mean, what else can I be? But I'm not a vampire or werewolf, though I suspect my kind were once identified as those."

"Your kind? There're more of you?"

"I had a family once," she said. "They're all dead, but my mother talked like we were a clan. Like there were more of us. Or had been at least."

Celeste finally tired and slumped onto a bale of straw, shaking her head. Eleanor sat next to her. She let the silence settle over them like a shroud.

Celeste, almost talking to herself, said, "You come every year, sneak into my room, and give me a kiss."

"I need to taste you," Eleanor said. "That sample and my observations are what I use to make the pattern to change."

"Show me," she said.

"It can take a long time," she said. "And it hurts."

"Oh. Okay," she said.

Eleanor heard the disappointment in her voice but left it unattended.

After a while, Celeste said, again, almost to herself, "I honestly thought I had imagined you. No one I told ever believed me. I stopped trying ages ago. You were my special twin."

"You've grown so much this last year," Eleanor said, studying her.

"You just want a kiss?" Celeste asked.

Eleanor nodded.

"Did I really look like this?" Celeste said.

"You did a year ago."

"And now you'll look like me again?"

"If you'll let me."

"What if I don't?"

"I don't know," Eleanor said. "I can't believe it's worked this long."

"What would you do if you couldn't sample me?" Celeste asked.

"I don't know," she said. "Before, I've always been ready to run. Every other time I came here I had a plan to disappear and start again somewhere else if I failed. But this time, I didn't. If I had, I'd be long gone by now. I can't believe I let your mother walk me into your house."

"And you let my dad hit you," she said. "I saw it all from my window."

"I didn't have much choice in that," Eleanor admitted. "I wasn't looking."

"So what changed? How come you didn't run?"

"I have a life now. I've put something together, something I probably don't deserve. I have it because I have you. If I didn't have you, if I lost you, I'd lose that too. It's so fragile that just thinking about it can paralyze me with fear."

"And you have your life because once a year you kiss me?"

Eleanor nodded. "It's allowed me to look like a . . ." she paused and then forced herself to say it. "To look human," she finished.

"Where do you live?"

"I shouldn't tell you."

"Why? Don't you trust me?"

She hesitated.

"You don't trust easily, do you?"

"No," said Eleanor. "I can't afford to."

"You can trust me," she said earnestly. Eleanor wanted to believe her and looked for guile and deceit in the familiar face and saw none. She meant to keep whatever confidence they'd share, but still Eleanor hesitated. She'd already said too much. It had all come out too easily. She realized she'd spoken so frankly to Celeste because she felt she owed this girl a debt she could never repay. As payment or penance, she'd given her a deserved peek at the most valuable thing she possessed.

"I can tell you're scared," Celeste said. "I've always sensed it. From the beginning, I've sensed you were afraid. I never thought you were dangerous, but I always knew you were scared."

"It's a terrible way to be," said Eleanor. "I feel like I'm on borrowed time. Any second I'm going to be found out and then . . . then I'll be dead or I'll have to run."

Celeste leaned over and kissed Eleanor on the cheek.

"There," she said. "We got that out of the way. You can relax."

"*I've* got to kiss you," Eleanor said ashamed.

Celeste puckered up her lips and leaned in to her. It made Eleanor laugh. "Go on," Celeste said.

Eleanor kissed her. It was just a peck, a taste of her lip that let her sample the skin before drawing it back to deposit a cluster of molecules in a pocket in her throat.

"Thank you," Eleanor said.

"I'm Celeste Batton. What's your name?"

Eleanor looked at her, studied her face in the dim light, subconsciously memorizing scars and lines, smells and feelings.

"Your hair is so long," she said.

Celeste stared at her pleasantly. Eleanor recognized the expression, knew it intimately.

"Yes, I was avoiding the question." She laughed. "I call myself Eleanor. Eleanor Anders. It's not my real name, not my original name. I don't remember my original name. I got this one from a woman named Tabitha who died last year. She was my mother. My foster mother."

"She knew about you?"

"Yes," she said.

"And you can change into other people?"

Eleanor nodded.

"And animals? Birds? Fish?"

"I think so," she admitted.

Because she knew that face so well, its expressions and tics, she knew Celeste's mind was whizzing in a million directions. A dark expression passed her face and made Eleanor look away.

"I know I'm a monster," Eleanor said. "It's why I never wanted to talk to you. I didn't want you to know."

"I didn't say that."

"You're thinking it," Eleanor said.

"No I wasn't. I was thinking how cool it would be to be you."

"It's lonely," she said.

"How many people know?"

"It was just Tabitha. Now there's a boy named David. He's wonderful. He's the real reason I came tonight. I'm afraid of losing him."

"And now there's me. That's two people in the whole world besides you."

"Just two people," Eleanor said. "I'm not a person."

"No. You're better," Celeste said. "I'm glad you trust me."

"You won't tell?"

"What are friends for?"

"We're friends?" Eleanor asked.

"I'd say we're more than that." Celeste giggled. "Sisters at the very least. Where do you live?"

"I live in a little town in Wyoming. It's called Jamesford. It's tiny."

"Can't be smaller than this."

"Okay, it's bigger than this, but I think I'd do better in a bigger city. Easier to hide. It's hard to keep a big secret in a small town."

"I can see that," Celeste said. "So what's keeping you?"

"David," she said. "And I'm—we're still young. When we're eighteen, we can go places."

"So next year?"

"I'm sixteen," Eleanor said.

"Well I'm seventeen," Celeste said. "How does that work?"

"I only look like you," she said sheepishly.

"Yeah, of course," she said. "Still, you're freakin' amazing. I wish I were you. I'd be so gone from here. Sometimes I feel like all this corn. Planted and stuck. I'd rather be an owl, or a hawk, or an eastbound train. This place is a dead end. Nothing happens here. How is it in Jamesford?"

"Things happen there, and I wish they wouldn't."

"I met this guy who's a gypsy," Celeste said excitedly. "His family lives out of an RV, and they just move from place to place. Doesn't that sound great? When you get sick of somewhere, you just turn on the engine and go? See new things all the time."

"Freedom's just another word for nothing left to lose," Eleanor said, quoting an old song Tabitha had liked.

"Maybe," she said. "But I'm not going to be another corn stalk."

The first rays of sunrise appeared as a yellow glow in the high windows.

"I should go," Eleanor said. "David's waiting down the road. Doesn't your family get up early?"

"Yeah, but I don't want to—"

"We can't let anyone see us together," said Eleanor.

"No, I guess not," sighed Celeste.

"Celeste, I can't thank you enough."

"You know, when I get really sick of this place I sometimes think of you and think that I'm actually living two lives: one interesting and rewarding, the other in Nebraska. I find it comforting."

"Glad you're getting something out of it," Eleanor said.

In the distance, in the house, muffled by walls and distance, Eleanor could just make out the sound of an alarm clock going off.

"Your dad's getting up," Eleanor said.

"Yeah, it's five," Celeste said suddenly in a hurry to get back. "I'm sorry my dad hit you."

"I'm more sorry he hit you," said Eleanor. "He was trying to hit you."

"Well I was being a dork, trying to climb the rose trellis. What was I thinking?"

They both laughed.

"My dad will cool off," Celeste said, looking at the house as they walked. "But he'll be in a fury if I'm not in my room when he checks."

Light appeared in a small window, a bathroom Eleanor figured.

The moon was still up, but the ground was aglow in predawn light. They walked together slowly to the back door. Eleanor knew it was time to go, but she lingered. She saw Celeste felt the same, saw on her face how she looked when one side of her tugged her away while another tried to stay rooted. It was surreal, she thought, seeing herself like that.

"You'll come back?" Celeste said.

"If I can," Eleanor promised.

A light came on in Celeste's room and a half beat later came the roar, "Goddammit, Celeste!"

They ran for the house. Celeste opened the door to the kitchen and stepped inside. She stopped and looked back at Eleanor. Before running into the cornfield, without a word or a sound, Eleanor waved good-bye, and Celeste blew her a kiss.

CHAPTER THREE

"She's so tall now. And her hair. I don't think she cut it all year." Eleanor sat in the passenger seat as David scanned storefronts of early-morning Minden, looking for a motel.

"We saw that coming. We knew she'd be different," David said, his voice casual, but Eleanor could sense some residual anxiety lingering. He'd had a frightful night of worry and dread waiting for her. Her tale of near capture and physical harm did little to ease his mood. He couldn't leave the Batton farm fast enough.

"I'm going to need clothes," she said.

"Hey, there's a place we can stay."

Eleanor looked out at a downtown hotel and shook her head. "Someplace farther away. More private."

"Okay. We'll try another town."

"Go to Lexington. They have a secondhand shop. I know the area."

David drove west. "And she was okay with it?"

"She was," Eleanor said. "It was surreal, I admit, but we connected. She wasn't afraid of me. I am her special secret friend."

"Shame you couldn't have talked longer," said David.

"No," Eleanor said. "I'm glad it was short."

"Yeah," David agreed.

She looked at David, at his thick hair, so dark brown it bordered on black. The wind jabbed at it through his open window, making it even fuller and richer. Occasionally, he'd dart his similarly dark brown eyes at her and smile, just to say how happy he was to have her back, and her heart would skip a beat. She loved those eyes. At one time, they had been the only friendly eyes she knew. She'd had a mother whose eyes were love to depths beyond understanding, but David's eyes, even as a child, were friendly and warm, and she'd loved them then. Now, years later, with secrets spoken and crises shared and the kisses. She melted in those eyes. He was beautiful. He looked much the same as he did the year before, when he came back to Jamesford, but now to her, he was truly beautiful.

"I don't know about the hair," Eleanor said, remembering the moment and what lay ahead.

"What's the deal with the hair? Can't you make it any length?"

"I don't know," she said. "I think it's possible, but I haven't had a lot of luck with it. It's usually all or nothing."

"How does the DNA indicate hair length?" he said.

"I'm not sure it is DNA," Eleanor said. She and David had theorized on the mechanics of her talent, but it was all conjecture. "I told you. I think that's a lot of it, but there's more. I get a complete picture of the donor. It's what I see and smell and hear and sense. Subconscious stuff I can't quantify or describe. Everything. It all goes into the recipe. It just happens. I can't control it. At least, not much."

"Okay, then we'll cut your hair when you're done. That's an easy one. I think the height jump will be more of a problem."

"I'm used to that one," she said. Eleanor had stayed hidden in her little house for two weeks before the trip, only coming out for necessities and purposefully avoiding as many people as possible. It was the system her mother, Tabitha, had invented to conceal the sudden change her Nebraska trips invariably brought. When people saw Eleanor again, they'd all comment on her sudden growth, but realize they hadn't seen her in weeks and leave it at that. Karen Venn, David's mother, would be another matter. She'd seen Eleanor regularly during the past month. She was Eleanor's legal guardian, and though Eleanor was allowed to live in her old house pretty much independently, she had regular contact with David's family. David's sister Wendy was also close. There'd be some explaining to do with them.

"Man, it's so flat here," David said.

"Hard to hide," said Eleanor.

"You don't have to," he said putting his hand on Eleanor's. He sped to Lexington.

They found a cheap motel off I-80. The clerk raised an eyebrow but took David's money and gave them a private room "away from other guests" as requested. David walked Eleanor to the room, but Eleanor stopped him at the door.

"I need you to go get me some food. Protein. Cooked if possible. Ham is good. Spam is okay. Whole milk. Buttermilk if you can find it." She dug a bottle of children's chewable vitamins from her purse and turned the door handle. She took the "Do Not Disturb" sign off the inner doorknob and hung it facing the hall.

"Leave the food on the floor, knock on the door, and then leave," she said.

"What? I want to help you."

"You are," she said. "But I don't want you seeing this."

"Why?" he asked.

"I don't want you to see me this way."

"Don't be silly," he said. "You let Tabitha help."

"She was my mother. And a girl. Now go get me food. When I'm ready for you, I'll take down the sign. Please," she said.

He knitted his brow, looked hurt and insulted. Angry. "After all this, you don't trust me?"

There was a temper in him she'd not seen before, physical and tense, a bowstring pulled taut in defense of an ideal. In another, it would frighten her, but in David, it worried her.

"You have to trust me," she said. "Please. I'm not ready for that yet." She met his eyes and saw them soften.

As quickly as it had come, his temper faded, and he said, "Okay. How long will this take?"

She remembered Celeste in the moonlight and the inches she'd grown. "Half a day at most, if I have enough to eat. Go see a movie."

Eleanor could see that he wasn't pleased with the arrangement, but he agreed and left Eleanor alone in the room.

The room had a single queen bed that dominated the space. There was a single nightstand and a blocky TV on a cheap chest of drawers built from a kit. The carpet was new but brown and muted, able to match anything from the faux oak paneling on one wall, to the tattered harvest orange drapes over the single-paned window on the other.

The bathroom was small and bright and had a tub. She ran hot water, undressed, turned the TV to a loud channel and cranked up the volume. Then she ate a mouthful of vitamins and took a deep breath.

She flexed her throat and tasted Celeste, absorbing her in a flash of electric fluid. Her hands shook, and her head ached. She lowered herself into the tub, turned on the shower, and opened the drain.

The pain began in her back, and she groaned. Her legs went numb for a while and then her arms. It crept up her spine in inches until she heard a break under one ear and passed out.

When she came to, her flesh was burning, her legs ached, and her spine felt like it was being pulled out of her body. She grabbed a washcloth and bit it, stifling a scream. There was a knock on the door.

She listened and waited for David to go before she pulled herself out of the tub and crawled out of the bathroom. She paused before opening the door, listening to make sure no one was outside.

Still on the floor, she cracked open the door and pulled in a box of supplies. She dragged it into the bathroom and set upon the luncheon meat and quarts of milk like a starving castaway. When she had eaten all she could, she returned to the tub and braced herself for another round of metamorphosis and pain.

When it was over, she let herself rest. Her body had changed, but her mind needed more time. By the clock, it had taken her four hours from the first shock to the final muscle pull. It was not the worst transformation she'd ever had. From the old shape of Celeste to the new shape of Celeste was a simple upgrade, and she'd gone as slowly as she could to make it easier. She probably could have done it in half the time if she'd had the courage to face it all without rest. She slept for an hour curled up in the bedspread.

When she got up, none of her clothes fit right. The best she could do was a skirt with an elastic waistband that would stretch to go around her new, bigger hips. She had a T-shirt that would work, though it exposed her belly button when she reached up and was a little tight for modesty. She put them on after another long shower where she used an entire bar of soap and all the shampoo the little room offered.

Her hair was long, a match to Celeste's long, straight auburn tresses. She truly didn't understand how any of it worked, only that it did. She studied herself in the mirror while brushing her hair. Was she Celeste become Eleanor, or Eleanor become Celeste? Not for the first time, she wondered how much of her own personality, her own soul, and the things that made her the individual she thought she was, were actually inherited from Celeste. The idea disturbed her. She was glad she had not spent more time in the barn with Celeste. She feared contracting her personality, copying her soul from too much exposure. She only wanted the shape.

She thought back on Jamesford, remembered Tabitha, David, and the years in the woods as the coyote, and knew these things were hers; the experiences, the lessons, the imprints were all hers. She told herself that the total of her life added to a different sum than Celeste's. She was not just a copy of Celeste Batton. She had to believe that.

Still, she felt changes that were not wholly physical. Only the coyote did she know better than this form, or versions of it anyway. She noted a new excitement that was not there before, a new energy that might not be her own. Maybe she had sensed it when talking to Celeste on the straw, or maybe it was another hormonal characteristic of a growing girl as Tabitha had warned her, but there was something new. She understood in a new way Celeste's discontent with the flat plains and her desire to see more. Eleanor looked out her little window across the unbroken horizon and thought it was an empty place.

She sipped the last of the buttermilk and then remembered to turn the sign back. She was in the hallway turning it when David came up the stairs. He stopped and watched. Eleanor waved him in. He ran to her.

"Look at you," he said excitedly. "You're right. Long hair and tall." He grasped her hands in both of his and looked her up and down.

"How was it?" he asked.

"It wasn't so bad." She let go of him and went to the little window and opened it to clear the air. She was aware of a lingering musk beneath the odors of shampoo and soap. She didn't know if David could detect it, but she could.

"So are we going to cut your hair?" he asked.

"Do you think I have to? It feels right."

"Wear it up for a while. In a couple of weeks you can drop it down."

"Do you like it?"

"You look different, but I can get used to it. I like it. It is still you under there, isn't it?"

"Yeah, it's still me," said Eleanor.

"Do you think it'll still happen?" he asked clearing his throat. She knew what he meant and blushed. They'd discovered the year before that their kisses were electric. For her, it was a volatile charge, not unlike the pre-stages of a shape-shift.

David had described something similar. Whatever it was, it took their breaths away and linked them.

"I guess we better check," she said.

David leaned in close and looked at her face and then deep in her eyes. "Yes," he said. "I see you in there."

She saw herself in his eyes, reflected and embraced. They hypnotized her and sent her blood rushing. He closed them and leaned forward. She inhaled his breath, felt his heat and the scents of his body and her skin tingled.

Then they kissed.

The charge came as before. If anything, it had grown stronger. Eleanor felt it from her toes to her forehead. It was euphoric, dreamlike, and intoxicating. She lost track of time and felt her heart beat in sync with David's as if they shared a single circulation, each heartbeat sharing life between the two, as it had been before. But now with her new body, her new, matured body, the sensation was more primal and compelling than ever.

She reached her hands up and under David's shirt, feeling the gooseflesh erupt under her fingers as she did. She absorbed the heat from his flesh and returned it with her own.

It took all she had to pull away from him, but she knew she had to. There were promises to keep and dangers of trust. Even with David, there were dangers of trust.

They came apart, and David fell back onto the bed.

Swaying on her feet she watched him fall, her heart going with him. He grinned and tried to open his eyes. She admired his long eyelashes as he blinked against the light, watched them flicker like butterfly wings, delicate and wonderful.

"I can't focus my eyes," he gasped.

"It's different," said Eleanor, falling onto the bed beside him.

"Wow," he said and suddenly started to laugh. It was contagious, and soon both of them were rolling on the bed in tears of hysterics.

After a while he said, "It's going to be hard to keep this to once a week."

"We have to," Eleanor said. It had been the one thing they'd allowed themselves after promising David's mother that they would behave as brother and sister; she would not act as Eleanor's guardian if they did not. They'd kept their promise, but had allowed themselves a kiss about once a week to remind themselves of their special connection. It was that kiss that kept Eleanor in Jamesford against her instincts.

It was a sacrifice, but Eleanor gladly accepted it for Karen's sake. David's mother had done so much for her. She did not want to cause more trouble for her, and Eleanor knew she was trouble.

Though she confided all to David, there were things that frightened her, and things she knew but had no words for. She did not want her relationship to David or the Venns to grow too quickly or too strongly. She was dangerous. She knew this as well as she knew the breeze or the rocks. She could bring ruin upon the fragile little family and to David as well.

The only sure way to protect them was for her to leave, and much of her wanted to do just that. Be it fear or instinct—and she wondered if they weren't the same thing—she yearned to be away. She wanted to run from the storm clouds she smelled over the horizon. The animal in her wanted shelter and distance. But the human in her, the girl she was, did not want to leave the little family that had adopted her and the boy with the untamed hair and chocolate brown eyes who loved her and whom she loved.

So she maintained a distance that kept the lovers close but apart; she lived in a house on her own but remained part of the Venn family. She stayed in Jamesford with people, but she hid among them.

"Did you find any clothes?" she asked him.

"Are you kidding? I am in no way qualified to buy you clothes. We'll go now. You look fine."

She didn't think she did, but there was little alternative. She showed David where the secondhand store was, and they shopped together for an hour before it closed. Eleanor came out with four new outfits, pants, shirts, and a coat, plus three pairs of shoes and a handbag she liked. The rest of her new essentials she bought at a drugstore on the way back to the motel while David got them cheeseburgers.

"You should have seen that place," he said. "You ever see *American Graffiti*? It's an old movie from the fifties or something. That burger stand looks like one of the sets. It's like a time warp here."

Back in the room, David counted their money. "After paying for the motel, we should make it back home with fifty or so to spare, provided we don't have lobsters."

"Maybe we shouldn't go back," Eleanor said. "Maybe we should just keep going."

David looked up.

"Why now?"

"I don't know," she said. "Going home seems risky."

"No, it'll blow over. It's all just rumors. Rumors are just words and words can't hurt you."

"I'm not so sure."

"Besides, we promised my mom," David said.

"Of course," she said. "I'm sorry. I guess I have the new-body jitters."

"Let's see how things go," he said. "There's no hurry. We bought ourselves some more time today, didn't we?"

"Yeah, we did," she said.

She felt tired. She'd made this trip eight times. Each time she'd bought another year of blending in. But it was always borrowed time, and today, with her new long hair and taller body, fuller hips and chest, she felt more than ever that it was time to stop hiding and start running. She had managed to survive the previous year with all its terrible hazards. But she'd been lucky. To go back to Jamesford now would be to press that luck.

"We could just run away," she said.

"What? No. There's no need for that. We're golden. It's going to be a great year. You'll see. Really." His smile reached to his eyes.

"Okay. We'll go back in the morning," Eleanor said. "Call Karen and tell her."

"I already did," he said.

"That's good," she said. "Give me a burger. I'm still hungry."

"Where do you put it all?" he said jokingly.

"In my hair," she said.

CHAPTER FOUR

Eleanor sat in front of her mother's old bureau, playing with her hair. She tucked and folded, wrapped and pinned it into knots that could hide the six inches of new growth. Once she picked up a pair of scissors and took aim, but decided she'd only mess it up and put them down. She twisted her hair into a braid and craned her neck in the mirror to see if she'd managed to cinch it up into something subtle.

With a start, she noticed the bruise on her arm. It was a pale blue blemish she'd seen on Celeste in her bedroom. She'd duplicated it. It was just above her elbow on her right arm.

She gingerly touched the place and it felt a little sore. It was nothing that would hinder her in any way, but Eleanor remembered her mother's cancer. When she had taken her shape, the cancer had come along. The pain of that wicked disease was devastating, unendurable, and perpetual. She looked at the bruise in the mirror and thought with dread that she'd have it for a year.

She had to get going. She'd avoided seeing Karen and Wendy for another weekend by saying she'd had a bad cold, but today she had to face them and Stephanie Pearce, her social worker. Stephanie had suffered badly under the story that David and Eleanor had concocted to keep Eleanor in Jamesford and explain, or rather, not explain the strange things happening around her. Eleanor's case with Child Protection Services was still open. She was supposed to have been put out to a foster family, but thanks to Karen's offer of temporary guardianship and general confusion around the case, she'd not had to go to strangers.

Eleanor dressed in her best clothes, the new skirt she'd picked up and a nice blouse. She left her house before noon. The day was warm and dry. It hadn't rained in months and the streets were dusty. She kept to the side roads, careful to avoid people when she could. She was aware of her new size when ducking under branches and squeezing through torn fences. She wished she'd known before that Celeste was seventeen, a year older than Eleanor claimed to be. She might be a year closer to emancipation and away from Stephanie Pearce.

Crossing the yard of an abandoned house on Ash Street, Eleanor stumbled across Ramos. He was sleeping in a make-shift tent fabricated from cardboard and shopping bags. Ramos was a hobo. Some people called him worse, but hobo fit him as well as anything. He'd been in Jamesford for a couple of years. He lived off begging and the help of local churches. Sometimes, in the height of the tourist season, the town might put him on a bus and send him away, but he invariably found his way back to Jamesford. Eleanor would have avoided him if she'd known he was there, but the wind was blowing the wrong way and she'd assumed the tent was a garbage pile.

Ramos rolled over and looked at her as she veered away. He blinked and squinted, and then sneered. The look was accusatory and malicious and made Eleanor hurry her steps.

He watched her until she slipped through a fence and disappeared around a house.

Though she'd never been in a position to offer him anything, Eleanor had never been unkind to Ramos. They knew each other by sight, both frequenting the unseen places in the town and had always just ignored each other. Today, however, Ramos recognized her and actively disliked her.

She hastened her steps for half a block and then stopped. Eleanor was used to avoiding confrontation or any notice at all, but somehow today, in the warm summer Wyoming sunlight on her way to the Venns and Stephanie, in her new body of Celeste at seventeen, this was not good enough. Perhaps it was her new size, perhaps she had inherited something intangible and courageous from the older Celeste, or maybe she'd remembered something her mother had told her. Maybe she was just growing up. Eleanor turned around and marched back to the lot. The bum watched her approach.

"What's your problem?" she demanded of him. "Why do you look at me like that?"

"I've heard stories about you," he slurred. He smelled of alcohol and was as dirty as a gas station gutter. "Slut. Witch," he said.

"I've heard things about you too, Ramos. Should I be unkind to you because of them?"

"Me?" he said.

"You," she said. "They say you steal beer from the grocery and break into trucks at Cowboy Bob's. They call you a mean, loathsome, foul-mouthed scum who should be driven into the woods to freeze to death before next summer's tourists come. That's what they say. Should I drive you out of town to freeze to death because that's what people say?" She took a step forward for emphasis, but Ramos saw it as aggression and scampered behind a broken barrel trough.

"I didn't do nothing to you," he said.

"Nor I to you," she said. "I have as much right to be here as anyone else. Don't you forget it."

She stormed off angry but satisfied. It felt good to say that. She'd needed to say something like that for a long time, she realized. Pity she'd only said it to Ramos, the vagabond.

The Venns lived in a mobile home in a small trailer park toward the center of town. A gravel road split the park in two halves and a chain-link fence surrounded it to keep the tumbleweeds out. Out of habit, Eleanor ducked behind the left trailers as soon as she entered the gate and followed the fence to the Venns' trailer to avoid being seen. She walked up the little wooden porch and knocked on the door.

"Why you knocking, silly?" said Wendy, throwing open the door. "You're family."

"That's right," Eleanor said. "I keep forgetting."

Eleanor could smell the remnants of breakfast inside. They'd had toast and eggs. Some half eaten strawberries and a mound of pink sugar showed Wendy's after-breakfast snack in front of the television. Eleanor could hear Karen in the back of the trailer with a hair dryer and David moving in his room.

"You want some berries?" Wendy asked. "They're good but not the leaves."

Eleanor sat down on the sofa and hunched her shoulders to help conceal her height.

"I like your hair," Wendy said admiring her half-braided bun. "Can you show me how?"

"I'm not very good at it," she said.

Just then Karen came in. "Eleanor," she said. "Have you eaten?"

"Yes, ma'am."

"You're not going to start that again, are you?" she said.

"Sorry," said Eleanor, then corrected herself. "Karen."

"A new outfit? Stand up, let's have a look at you. I like your hair."

Eleanor hesitated and then reluctantly stood up. She tried to hunch her shoulders but realized it just made her look guilty. She put on a pleasant, casual smile and stood up straight.

Karen's mouth fell open and her eyes grew wide. She made to phrase a word, offer a question, an exclamation perhaps, but it never came. She stared at Eleanor from the kitchen, unspeaking, her eyes darting from her hair to her hips, her legs to her face.

There came a knock on the door. David walked into the living room and saw his mother.

"You want me to get that?" he asked. When Karen didn't speak, he crossed to the door and let in Stephanie Pearce.

Stephanie was a large woman and the only social field worker in Jamesford. She carried her burden of troubled youths and broken families like her extra pounds, with resigned endurance. She smiled when David let her in and went straight to a chair and sat down. Eleanor sat down quickly herself.

"Mom?" said David.

Snapped out of her reverie, Karen said, "Would you like some iced tea, Miss Pearce?"

"Yes, that would be great."

Karen had learned from experience, and from Eleanor's

stories, that Stephanie's mood could be partially controlled with offerings of food and drink. She had a thankless job and appreciated anything that wasn't hostile.

"So how have you been getting on, Eleanor?" she asked, looking at her papers. "You ready for school next week?"

"Yes," she said. "I hear Mr. Graham finally retired."

"Yes, you have a new science teacher. His name is Mr. Gurreno. He's nice. Comes from Riverton originally, though he's been in California for a while." She looked up from her papers then and around the trailer. It was her practice to measure how well a child was doing by the state of the house they lived in. Eleanor didn't live in the Venns' trailer and Stephanie knew it, but she nonetheless noticed the strawberries and Wendy's toy pile in the corner and the half-finished dishes in the sink.

Karen brought over a tray of iced tea and sat down with David on the sofa beside Eleanor.

"You've grown," Stephanie said and sipped her drink. "And your hair is different."

"I'm trying something new," Eleanor said.

"You can tell she's eating better, can't you?" David said. "I swear she's grown a foot this summer with us."

Stephanie looked at Eleanor for a moment, taking in the changes since her last visit. Strangely, Eleanor saw her eyes moisten as if she were about to cry. Then she shrugged and went back to her papers.

"No decision has been made about Eleanor yet," she said. "Things seem to be working out here, but the committee doesn't want to make it permanent."

"Why not?" said David. Karen put a hand on his arm to calm him. His tone was not gentle.

"Honestly?" asked Stephanie.

"No, lie to us," David said. "We like that."

"David," cautioned Karen.

He looked at Eleanor. Eleanor looked back with beseeching eyes. David didn't understand how hard this woman could make their lives.

"Sorry," he said.

"David is protective of me, Miss Pearce," said Eleanor. "He's afraid you're going to send me away to strangers. We've all heard such horror stories about foster families."

"Don't believe everything you hear," she said. "But truth be told, they don't have anyone willing to take you, Eleanor. The committee asked for alternatives, but we don't have any. So you're here for at least another quarter."

"That's not long," David said.

"She said 'at least,'" explained Karen. "But Stephanie, I don't understand. What's the problem?"

She sighed. "The stories about Eleanor have gotten around. No families are interested in her. Not with her past."

"So leave her with us," said David. "Problem solved."

"It's not that easy," said Pearce. "The stories are why the committee wants her moved. I'm trying, but they think that Eleanor needs a change. Jamesford is full of rumors and whispers about her. It can't be good for her."

"Don't you think she should make that decision?" asked David.

Karen shot David another look.

"Eleanor," said Stephanie. "What do you think?"

Eleanor looked at her expecting to see a malevolent, accusing stare like Ramos' across the little table. But it wasn't there. Stephanie had every right to dislike Eleanor. She'd come out looking bad after Tabitha's death. She'd been painted as a home-wrecking brute to justify Eleanor's inexcusable behavior. It had made the papers, and it was publicly known that she'd had a drubbing from her superiors who now put all her decisions before a committee while she was on probation. Her career was nearly finished. And yet, when Eleanor looked at her now, she didn't see hatred, but true conviction and caring. Curiosity. Perhaps even affection. Eleanor sensed that she truly wanted to do what was best for her.

She'd been afraid of Stephanie for so long, seeing her as the monster that would tear apart her family, her life, her loves. But she no longer seemed like that. Eleanor wondered if she was seeing a change in Stephanie or if she'd simply been misreading her for years. Whatever she might have been to her before, now she didn't strike Eleanor as a monster, but as a hero keeping a monster at bay. Had Stephanie changed or had she?

"I don't know," Eleanor said. "I see what you mean, but I don't have anyone else. The Venns are the closest thing to family I have left."

"You're not making things easy for them," Stephanie said.

When Karen didn't speak up to contradict her, David did. "The extra money helps, and she's no bother at all. She minds her own business, has her own house. What's the problem?"

"Let's not get into the housing issue right now, okay?" Pearce said. "I was talking about the stories. Eleanor's toxic in some circles. I'm sorry, but that's the only word I can think of. It can't be easy for the rest of you to be her champions. It isn't for me."

"I have no problem with it," David said.

"Paulina said she's a witch," said Wendy, silencing the room.

After a moment, and a draught of iced tea, Stephanie said,

"How about you, Karen? Have you noticed anything because of this?"

"It's a small town," she said. "People are going to talk. Ghost stories in summertime. Who'd have thought?"

She paused and looked out a window. She hadn't glanced at Eleanor since the interview began. When the silence stretched out, Karen added, "The extra money's been nice though. It's working out. These rumors will pass. It's all too far-fetched not to."

"Well," Pearce said, "there's nothing we can do about it now unless we take her to Honor Farm."

"What?" said David. "You'd lock her up in jail if we don't want her?"

"It's not all a jail. There's housing there for youth who have nowhere else to go. It's an alternative. It might not be so bad; a new start in Riverton."

"No," said David.

"We'll keep her," Karen said. "Thanks just the same."

"Hooray!" said Wendy.

"Thanks," said Eleanor, but recalling Ramos, she worried about how bad things had gotten over the summer: "Slut." "Witch."

CHAPTER FIVE

School began a week after Stephanie's visit. The junior class was welcomed back with the seniors on Tuesday. The sophomores had Monday all to themselves to wander the halls and find their way around without the older students. It was an old tradition, but totally unnecessary. The entire high school student body was less than a hundred and shrinking.

Though it was out of his way, David walked Eleanor to school the first day back. Eleanor would have preferred to sneak into school and vanish in a back row of a classroom rather than promenade with David, but he insisted they hold their heads up. She felt the stares of the other students as they walked into the building.

"Hello, David," said Barbara Pennon as they came in. She was flanked by Alexi, Crystal, and Penelope. Their clothes were bright and new, their perfumes thick and expensive. They each cast a sad, distrustful look at Eleanor.

"How was your summer?" Barbara said to David. "I didn't see you at all during August."

"I was busy," he said. "You remember Eleanor, don't you?"

"Of course," said Crystal. "The witch of Jamesford High."

"That's not funny," David said.

"Why? Is it true?" asked Penelope. "Tell me about the ghost stories. Is it true her dead mother walked the town trying to cash a check?"

Eleanor felt her cheeks blush and flicked her hair to cover her face. The longer tresses made this more difficult since it was so much more obvious.

"I like that story too," said David. "I really like the one where aliens come down and teleport her to Seattle for a rock festival."

"I hadn't heard that one," said Crystal.

"Well I just made it up. It's as good as the others, don't you think?"

"No," said Barbara.

"Here comes Russell," said Crystal.

Russell Liddle strutted down the hallway flanked by Tanner Nelson. They took up the entire hall and pushed anyone out of their way who didn't move for them. Tanner had grown a couple of inches himself over the summer. Russell looked about the same but wore the remnants of a black eye under his close-cut hair.

"Venn," said Russell.

"Russell," said David.

"Screw you," he said and walked by.

Barbara's face blanched a little, and she hurried after Russell. She stopped him a few steps down the hall, looked around to see they were alone. Eleanor fixed her senses on them, trying to isolate their voices from all the noise of the hallway and the conversation around her.

"Russell," Barbara said, "You promised. You've got to try."

"It's not my problem," he said.

"No, it's ours," she said, and her face went a little paler. A glistening in her eye suggested a tear.

Eleanor was confused. She'd hated this girl, had nearly killed her, but now, for a moment anyway, she felt sorry for her.

Russell turned and stormed down the hall. Barbara put a smile on her face and returned to the group.

"Show me your hand," Penelope asked David. "Where Russell cut you."

David showed his thumb. The stitches were out, but it was still red and sore.

"You know he thinks you're a coward for not doing anything about it," Crystal said. "He said if you were a real man, you'd try to get even."

"There's still time," said Alexi. "I bet David's got a plan."

"So where'd he get the black eye?" Eleanor said to remind everyone she was there, a thing she'd never dreamed of doing a year before. It shocked her to hear herself doing it, a reaction to how the other girls fawned over David.

"From his dad," said Crystal. "That's what Barbara said."

"I'm only guessing," Barbara said quickly. "It might have been a fight with Tanner for all I know."

Eleanor sensed she was lying; she was covering up for Russell, and it made her happy. For all Barbara's advances on David, she was still Russell's girl. As long as she thought so, she was safe. As long as Russell thought so, David was safe. It was when Barbara went after David that Russell did the same.

Eleanor caught the smell then. It was a familiar odor underneath the floral fragrances. It was a smell she'd gone to some lengths to banish from her home. It was the smell of cancer. Eleanor leaned in and tried to place it. It wasn't as she'd smelled it on Tabitha's breath, but as it had been on Eleanor's clothes after she'd cared for her mother. It was subtle but unmistakable. It was on Penelope.

Penelope was bulimic. She thought herself beautiful, but Eleanor found her ghastly. For years, Eleanor had known that she snuck away into the school bathroom and threw up after lunch. She surely did the same at home. Her bones poked through her skin like branches in a pillowcase. Her cheeks were sharp and her eyes were sunken in murky caves under her brow. Her teeth were bleached and straight, her hair sculpted in the latest style, her clothes expensive and tight fitting. She looked like a scarecrow. Eleanor would feel sorry for her if she wasn't such a stuck-up snob. She was particularly cruel to Midge Felton, who had a weight problem in the other direction.

Eleanor noticed Midge standing at her locker two rows down. She pretended to be busy, but Eleanor could tell that she was waiting for the other girls to leave before coming over. The previous year, Midge had shown herself to be Eleanor's secret friend, warning her of trouble. She was shy and overweight and, like Eleanor, spent most of her school career trying to be invisible.

The girls demanded an explanation of David's decision to sell his Mercedes for the little Honda they'd seen him driving. Eleanor knew the story and wasn't in the mood for the girls' shallow pity.

In keeping with the part of sibling rather than jealous girlfriend, Eleanor left the group and went over to Midge. David followed her with his eyes, wanting to get away from the girls too. She was happy of that.

"You look good," said Midge.

"You look good too," she said. "How was your summer?"

"It was okay. Things are better between Henry and me. He doesn't talk about you so much."

"You spend much time on the reservation with Henry?"

"Actually I have," she said. "I helped his family run a little shop selling Indian things to tourists all summer. I'm an honorary Shoshone, they say."

Eleanor didn't trust Henry Crow, Midge's boyfriend. He was a pureblood Shoshone, and how he and Midge hooked up she couldn't guess. Eleanor had a long-held distrust of Indians, a hatred that her mother tried to break her from but never could. Henry particularly had bothered Eleanor. He'd watched her dance with David at Christmas with the most penetrating and accusing eyes. He'd told Robby Guide, the only Indian in Eleanor's high school class, that Eleanor was a *Nimirika,* a supernatural creature, an ogre and cannibal. Robby had tried to keep her away from David. Henry wouldn't even come close to her.

"Does Henry still think I'm a witch?" Eleanor asked.

"I'm sorry Eleanor," Midge said.

"He does then?" she said.

Midge nodded.

"Do you?"

Midge hadn't expected the question and took a moment to think about it. "Not if you don't want me to," she said.

"Eleanor!" said Aubrey Ingram, running up and throwing her arms around her. "Look at you. I leave town for two months and you grow a foot."

"Yeah, David's mom cooks a lot of pasta," she said.

"You've got to tell me all about your summer," she said. "Hey Midge, you lose weight?"

"A little," she said.

"Did you hear about Barbara?" Aubrey said in whispers. "She got in such trouble for hanging out with Russell. Her parents threatened to send her away. They hate him. They grounded her for like a month, took away her credit card and everything. My neighbors said they heard a scream-out fight that lasted a couple of days."

"A lot happened during the summer," said Eleanor. "She doesn't seem any different."

"Those kind of people never change, do they?" said Aubrey.

Eleanor caught Jennifer Hutton's gaze from down the hall. Their eyes locked, then Jennifer stopped, turned, and walked the other direction.

Eleanor's friends followed her gaze down the hall.

"Is that Jennifer?" Aubrey asked.

"Yes," said Eleanor. "Is she mad at me or something? I thought we were friends."

"I haven't talked to her since David's birthday party," Midge said.

Eleanor's heart sank. She'd been foolish to think that she'd keep all her friends after everything that'd happened. Even if the rumors were ignored and they only listened to the official story, Eleanor was a ghoul. She'd buried her own mother in the garden and then ran away. Eleanor took a deep breath and wondered how she was going to survive another week in Jamesford, let alone two years.

Mr. Gurenno was their new homeroom teacher. He took Mr. Graham's position as science and math instructor. A distinguished man with grey temples and a slender build, he wore slacks with a black belt and a short sleeve button-down shirt over a white T-shirt.

"I haven't taught in a while," he admitted. "I've been doing research work at Cal Tech. If I go too fast, let me know and I'll slow down."

Eleanor sat in the back of the class as far from the other students as possible—out of habit as much as anything else. David had tried to sit with her, but she shook him off. "Brother and sister," she reminded him. He didn't like it, but went up beside Robby in the second row.

"My forte is biology. Last year you had physics, pulleys and ramps. This year you'll get cells and frogs. But we start out with math."

Mr. Gurenno was the only new teacher the juniors had. Mr. Blake was still their Spanish teacher. Mrs. Hart would teach them English when she returned from her sabbatical. Their substitute humanities teacher explained how she'd taken some time off to take classes out of state. Physical education was no longer required and most students went into an elective subject such as computer science or stenography to round out their education in an effort to meet minimum state standards. Eleanor went to home economics because there were so few people who did.

The home economics teacher was Mrs. Westlake. Eleanor had suffered under her teaching in eighth grade. She was a religious fanatic and had finally been pulled from her humanities classes in favor of less controversial topics. She gave Eleanor a long, cold stare as she found a seat in the back of the class. Jennifer took a seat in the front with several seniors.

"I like to start each school year out with a prayer," Mrs. Westlake said. "It's totally voluntary. It'll just take a moment."

The seniors snickered. Jennifer's head went down.

"Lord, keep us from evil, deliver us from the devil in all its forms, and give us blessing and light. Amen."

"Amen," said Jennifer.

Mrs. Westlake explained that students would be required to bring their own ingredients for the class, and each had a cabinet and a bin in the fridge to keep their things. She looked right at Eleanor when she explained that if they could not afford to buy their own things, they could apply to the school for a cooking scholarship.

"How was it?" David asked after school.

"It was okay. How was computers?"

"Easy. I could teach the class. It's so basic it's lame."

Eleanor saw Jennifer putting up a poster by the office. "You talk to Jennifer lately?"

"No," he said. "Not since my birthday."

When Jennifer was gone, Eleanor walked over to the poster and read it.

Christian Club Prayer Meeting Every Morning Before School.
Room 31.
All welcome.
Sponsored by the New Church of Christ Revealed.

"New Church of Christ Revealed," said Eleanor. "Who are they?"

"They sound familiar," said David.

"They do," she agreed. "I thought I knew all the churches in Jamesford, but I don't remember them."

"Who cares?" he said.

"Room 31. That's the cooking classroom."

"So, Mrs. Westlake," said David. "Figures. I heard she's a Jesus freak."

"Jennifer Hutton hung it up," said Eleanor. "What do you think that means?"

"That she's found Jesus," he said. "Why? What do you think it means?"

"Jennifer's been avoiding me," said Eleanor.

"That's lame," he said. "I thought she was a friend."

"I've precious few of those."

"You have me," he said. "And Aubrey and Midge looked genuinely glad to see you."

"I think they were. And Barbara seemed pleased to see you."

"Oh, you're not going there are you? You're the one who said we have to be like brother and sister all the time. If I ignored her, it'd look bad."

"I know," she said. "She just bothers me."

"Still? She seems different to me. More grown up."

Eleanor understood what he meant, but didn't like him paying her any kind of compliment and so pouted.

"Don't let it get to you," he said.

"Don't let her get to you," she said.

"Har har," he said.

They left the school, crossed the highway, and walked past the artists' galleries luring in the last of the season's tourists with sales on leather coats and blown-glass bison.

"What's new with Penelope?" asked Eleanor.

"What do you mean? She seemed fine."

"I could smell cancer on her."

"You could? Cancer has a smell?"

"Oh yes, a terrible smell."

"I don't know anything about Penelope. You think she's sick?"

"I don't think it's her, but someone she knows."

"You should be a doctor," David said.

"Never. They're dangerous."

"You're just saying that because of what happened to Tabitha. They did their best."

"I know," she said. But her feelings about doctors had little to do with Tabitha's death.

CHAPTER SIX

Jamesford High settled into a new school year routine of schedules, classes, books, and lockers. Familiar groups met at their usual tables for lunch. Russell and Tanner hung with their group of petty thugs and shared stories of summer exploits the sheriff and game warden would both be interested to hear.

Barbara sat with Crystal and Alexi, comparing vacations. Alexi talked about France, Crystal about Florida, and Barbara about Mexico. Their tans were identical, their clothes close matches, their laughter haughty, and their conversation prone to fall into sudden whispering. Eleanor's keen ears caught snippets of gossip deriding Midge's weight, Aubrey's clothes, and Eleanor's hair. She'd heard it all before. Not much had changed with that clique in three months except Eleanor's tolerance of them.

"Eleanor, I thought you didn't like Indians," Barbara said, carrying Eleanor's tray past her table. "Now you look like a squaw with that lame braid."

Eleanor was alone at the table when the three girls came by.

"You used to be so lanky and ugly," said Penelope. "Now you're ugly and lanky."

Eleanor looked up at the three girls. Sensing a scene developing, the remnants of the lunch crowd looked over.

Eleanor felt her face burn but knew it wasn't a blush. Something was happening to her face, her eyes and teeth. It was small, but she felt it and it hurt.

Her voice deepened slightly, a growl in the vowels.

"You are never to speak to me like that again," she said. "I won't have it. I'm sick of it. I'm done with it. And so are you."

Alexi looked scandalized. Penelope laughed uncomfortably. Barbara's eyes went big and looked at Eleanor with an expression not unlike respect.

"You can go now," Eleanor snarled, and they did.

Eleanor waited all week for a backlash, but it never came.

That weekend Stephanie Pearce visited Eleanor at home. Eleanor saw her coming up her steps and thought immediately that this was how the girls had retaliated. Alexi had money, lots of money. Her father was a big deal in Jamesford. He could make things happen. This would be just the kind of petty influence-pandering blow Alexi could engineer to put Eleanor back in her place.

"What's wrong, Miss Pearce?" Eleanor asked at the door.

"Nothing," she said. "I'm not actually working right now. This is a social visit. Can I come in?"

Eleanor regarded her suspiciously. She wished Tabitha were there to help her, wished the Venns were there to represent her, wished David was there to comfort her, but she was alone. If there'd been a boogeyman in Eleanor's life, it was this woman. She wanted to run, felt the urge—the necessity—to avoid her, but she stayed. She straightened her back, felt her new height, her new body, her new life, and opened the door for Stephanie, bracing herself as best she could.

"You have the cleanest house in town," Stephanie said. "And I've seen them all, or most of them. You keep a very neat house, Eleanor."

"My mother showed me how," she said. "I'd offer you a snack, but I haven't been to the grocery this week."

"No, thanks," Stephanie said sheepishly. "Actually, it's about your mother that I came today."

Eleanor steeled herself. She had options, whatever happened. She would listen calmly to whatever was said today. She would not be afraid. Concealing her terror as she was so used to doing, she forced a pleasant expression on her face and sat down across from Miss Pearce.

"Eleanor," Stephanie began with a sigh. "My mother died when I was fifteen. I wasn't with her. She died in a car accident after dropping me at school." She dug in her purse and found a tissue and barely had it to her face before tears flowed down her cheeks.

"There was a moment," she said. "A moment in the hall before my first class." She gasped, hesitated, and then lost control. She fell into heaving sobs for several uncomfortable minutes. She dabbed her face with the tissue now colored black and beige with melted makeup.

"There was a moment that I thought my mother was standing in the hallway beside me. I didn't see her, but I felt she was there. And I knew she loved me. I felt her saying she loved me and everything would be all right."

She coughed and gasped.

"I'd forgotten about that. Everyone said I'd made it up, that that kind of thing was always made up, just a reaction from my grief. After a while, I believed them and forgot about the hallway. For years, I had completely forgotten about my mother's last gift to me."

Eleanor shifted awkwardly in her chair. She smelled for alcohol or chemicals that might explain what was happening, but detected nothing.

"Then," she went on. "Then I saw your mother. She sat in my office and talked to me. It was impossible. She'd already passed."

"I can't explain it, Miss Pearce," Eleanor said reflexively.

"You don't have to. I know what it means. It means my mother was there. It means so much. It means everything. It means what happened to me was real. It means my mother loved me. It means your mother loved you."

Eleanor didn't know what to say.

"A lot of people saw her and some are afraid, but I'm not. I know it was a miracle. It finally came to me and I remembered the hallway, my mother, the farewell. It was all real. I just wanted to tell you that."

Eleanor kept still, but she was not immune to the emotional confession and found a tear rolling down her own face.

They sat together for a while, neither one speaking, as if words had lost all relevance. Finally, Stephanie got up and said good-bye with an air of new intimacy that Eleanor found strangely comforting.

At the door, Stephanie turned to her. "Your mother wanted me to help you," she said. "Count on it." And she kissed Eleanor on the forehead as her mother had done.

That weekend, alone in her house, Eleanor did not feel so lonely. In fact, she felt safe in Jamesford for the first time in years.

The looks and gossip were still there, distant mutterings and judgments she'd grown accustomed to hearing because she was poor or homely or strange. It was normal for her, had been for years, but in her newfound happiness, she allowed herself to ignore it all and relish a newfound feeling of hope.

The feeling lasted until late September.

"Jennifer Hutton asked me to go with her on Sunday to the Revealer meeting," Midge said. "Do you think I should go? I don't think she really likes me. I don't know why she invited me."

"Who are the Revealers?" asked Eleanor.

"The Church of Christ Revealed," she said. "Jennifer is a member. She joined last summer. Mrs. Westlake is a member too. Jennifer's really religious now. She says she's worried about my soul."

"Stay away," Aubrey said direly.

"Why would she worry about your soul?" asked Eleanor.

"I think because I'm friends with you," Midge said.

That day after school Eleanor stopped by the drugstore to look at the message board.

"Hello, Eleanor," said the pharmacist. "My, how you've grown. How have you been?"

The pharmacist knew Eleanor from her monthly trips to pick up her mother's medicine. He'd always been kind to her, and she'd never been able to understand why. Her mother had suggested that perhaps he was just a kind man.

"I've been all right," she said. "Can you sell me this?" She'd picked up a coloring book for Wendy as an excuse while she read the board.

"Sure thing," he said. Eleanor scanned the flyers stapled to the wall.

"I want you to know something," said the pharmacist. "I know why you did what you did. I know you loved your mother. I think you should have been able to plant her at home where she belongs."

Eleanor regarded him. He was old, his scalp looked of hair dye poorly applied. His wrinkled eyes were not accusing. There was no deceit there, only a kindness she couldn't figure.

"Thank you," she said. "I miss her."

"I know you do," he said.

The Revealers had a flyer on the bulletin board as she thought they might. It listed the time and place of their weekly prayer meeting as well as their planned protests. There was a military funeral on Thursday and they planned to picket there. A new suicide crisis center was opening in Riverton and they planned to be there for the ribbon cutting on Saturday. Their letter-writing campaign against "gay Muslim influence in the mainstream media" was ongoing. A website offered a template to send to your congressman.

Eleanor remembered then where she knew the name. The Church of Christ Revealed was a mobile hate factory. Led by the Pastor Francis Lugner, they picketed funerals and weddings and anywhere that might get some attention. They had a long list of grievances, which they boiled down to "combatting evil." They cast exorcisms in front of schools, summoned angels to influence political contests, and arranged boycotts of offensive products like Israeli olives and movie premiers.

There'd been some rumor of their involvement in a series of hate crimes before their home church in Kansas had burned to the ground the previous year. After that, they'd taken to the road in Winnebagos to spread the word of "Christ Revealed" like a traveling carnival. They'd put stakes down in Jamesford.

"You thinking of going to a meeting?" asked the pharmacist.

"No. Why?"

"I'd stay away from them," he said, taking Eleanor's bank card.

"Why are they here?"

"They're hounding some rich guy who built a house up the canyon. They hold vigils for his soul. Today they're up Carter Canyon counter-protesting against an environmental group. Something about hydraulic fracking for natural gas up there."

"What does religion have to do with fracking?"

"Beats me, but they're doing it." The machine beeped. Eleanor hadn't heard it make that sound before. He swiped the card again, and the same final sound came from it.

"Uhm," he said. "It looks like your card is denied. Must be some misunderstanding. You can have the book. Pay for it next time."

"No," she said. "I'll figure it out."

Eleanor left the store empty-handed and felt the other clerks stare at her as she went. They were not pleasant looks.

Outside, she crossed the road to the bank. Again she felt eyes upon her. She would have waited for the bank to empty before going in, but two men she didn't know stared at her from a bus stop on the corner.

She went in and saw familiar faces of the long-time bank employees. They saw her and busied themselves. She approached a teller.

"I'd like to check my balance," she said.

"Let me get the manager," the teller said and immediately left.

Eleanor felt the stares like spiders on her skin.

"I'm the manager. How can I help you, Miss Anders?" The man was in a blue business suit. Eleanor had seen him before but had never talked to him. She had never needed to.

"I'd like to check my balance," she said.

"There is a hold on your account, I'm afraid," he said.

"Why?"

"Uhm, I'm not entirely sure," he said but did nothing to find out.

"Can you remove the hold please," Eleanor said. She felt her ears get hot.

"I suppose I can put in a request."

"Where was the hold done?" she asked.

"I can't be sure," he said, finally looking at the computer. "Oh, it appears it was done here."

"By whom? I know you keep that record. Who did it?'

"I'm not at liberty to say," he said.

"Take it off or I'll bring in the law," Eleanor said coldly. The banker looked at her across the counter, condescension dripping from his face. It faded suddenly and then he grew wide-eyed as Eleanor stared daggers back at him. She didn't know what she looked like, but she felt her face tighten into a painful visage she suspected was not wholly human.

"I'll get it done right away," he stammered. "Must have been a mistake. Sorry for the inconvenience."

As he drummed the keyboard, the woman teller behind him spoke. "You know with service like this, you might want to try another bank," she said.

"I hear the credit union has low standards," another employee said. "You might have fewer problems there."

"There's no credit union in Jamesford," Eleanor said.

"I was talking about Riverton."

"Or Cheyenne," said the bank manager under his breath.

Eleanor's hands clenched at her sides. Her arms began to shake and her legs flex. She had a sudden urge to strike the bank manager and each teller across the face, to tear their heads off. She felt she could do it. She felt she was about to do it.

She turned and walked out of the bank. She hurried through traffic and ran toward the park. It was away from her home, but it was also away from the bank and the stares in the drugstore and the men on the bench.

She was halfway up the tree-lined road to the park when she became aware of a car coming up behind her. She veered onto the sidewalk and slowed her pace. She wiped a useless tear from her face and tried to look as normal as possible.

The car slowed behind her. At first she thought it was David, but the sound wasn't right. Then she thought it had to be Sheriff Hannon. She expected another visit from him sometime. There'd been no decision yet about charging her with "improper disposal of a body." She kept walking, waiting for the siren to stop her. Behind her, the car matched her speed. Finally, she stopped and turned around.

The can hit her on the forehead and dropped her to the ground.

How long she lay on the sidewalk she didn't know. When she opened her eyes, she was looking at a blue Wyoming sky through the leafy canopy of a hundred-year-old cottonwood. A ruptured beer can lay beside her in a warm yellow pool. She had a lump on her forehead the size of a golf ball.

She sat up and looked around. She saw no one. She'd seen a light-colored truck before the can hit her, but she wasn't even sure of the color. It could have been tan, white, or baby blue. It had happened so fast. She got to her feet and nearly fell over. She was dizzy. Her head ached and her vision was blurry. She had a concussion and she knew it. But it would pass. For her, it would pass. She staggered to the tree and leaned against it. She slid down it and then sat on the ground.

She should have known. She'd heard the rumors all summer and ignored them. She heard the whispers in the grocery store, the mention of Tabitha buying food weeks after she was said to be dead in the ground. She heard other people, crueler people, suggest that Eleanor had killed her mother. Some remembered the food poisoning at school and made tenuous links to Eleanor's involvement. Miss Church, the lunch lady, had been fired, all the while claiming that Eleanor was responsible for nearly killing half the kids in Jamesford. Some recalled the rumors of her promiscuity, citing a midnight trip to a truck stop and something unseemly at the winter dance. All of it painted Eleanor as a pariah. The newest rumors, the ones she couldn't have foreseen, blamed her for the drought and the strange taste in the drinking water. She had become the scapegoat.

Her instinct was to run. Sitting alone on the dusty street, waiting for her eldritch metabolism to repair her skull, she knew it was only a matter of time. Borrowed time.

She closed her eyes and waited for the dizziness to pass. Some time after dark, she got up and found her way home.

CHAPTER SEVEN

"Eleanor, why didn't you go to school today? They called me. I said you were sick."

"That's right. I don't feel well. I've been sleeping all day. I should have called you. I'm sorry."

"Do you need anything?" asked Karen. "Should we see a doctor?"

"No, it's just cramps," Eleanor said into the phone. "I'll be fine tomorrow."

"I'll bring you some dinner," she said. "David's worried too. You really should have called."

"I know," she said into the phone. "I'm sorry."

She could have gone to school. She was well enough. She wore no marks from the attack, not a bruise or scratch or hair out of place. But inside, she felt a thick, ugly scar forming in her mind. No, more than a scar. It was a cancer. She felt it permeate into her dreams and threaten to kill hopes she'd only just allowed herself to have.

She sat in the chair her mother had occupied for so many days and looked out the window that had been her view of the world the last year of her life. Tabitha had chosen this little town because "nothing ever happened here." She had been right until last year when Eleanor had become careless and brazen and messed things up in a thousand different ways.

Just half a year before, she had thought of setting a match to this chair and burning down the house as a final gesture of exodus from this life. But her courage had failed her—or saved her, depending on her mood. Things had worked out so well with David that she was sure for a while that she'd been right to stay. She'd got everything she could imagine, more than she could hope for, but as yesterday showed her, it was an illusion.

She needed two years from Jamesford. She'd be eighteen then, an adult by legal definition, and free. But free to do what? Today she didn't know, but she'd hoped to have two years to figure it out.

She cleaned the house as she had when her mother was alive, when she had to present a more-than-perfect home for the visiting social worker. She swept, vacuumed, dusted, polished and washed. She presented her mother's room as if she'd be home any minute, but made it a more hopeful scene than before by throwing out the medicines, wigs, and pamphlets that reminded Eleanor of the cancer that'd killed her. Eleanor had been unable to move from her loft bedroom to her mother's old room or even rearrange the furniture. It just didn't feel right to change anything. Besides, she liked her loft bedroom with the low ceilings and high window. It'd been her space for a long time, and she cherished it.

She struggled over whether to tell David about the attack and her treatment at the bank. In the end, she decided that honesty would be best. When she was finally forced to leave, he'd need to know all of it if he was to ever understand why.

She decided to tell him after dinner. She didn't want to ruin the occasion. It wasn't often she got to host the Venns at her place.

At six o'clock, the doorbell rang. Eleanor recognized Wendy's enthusiastic button-pushing and opened the door.

Karen carried a chicken from Sherman's Grocery's deli and a bag of salads. David carried a six-pack of Pepsi while Wendy had already started on a sleeve of chocolate chip cookies.

"How're you feeling?" asked Karen.

"I'm fine," she said. David looked at her in a way that asked the same question but with a different tone.

"I'm fine," she said again.

"Is that a bruise on your arm?" asked Karen.

"It's nothing. I sleep funny sometimes. I always seem to have a bruise there."

David raised an eyebrow.

"Let's eat," said Wendy, "so I can have a cookie."

Eleanor had already set the table. They put down the food, took their seats, and dug in.

"When does rodeo practice begin?" asked Karen as she scooped macaroni salad onto Wendy's plate.

"Next week. First of October," David said.

"And when's the rodeo?"

"October twenty-fifth, I think," he said.

"So your dad will be here to see it," said Karen.

It took a moment, a beat, but then the table fell silent. Everyone stopped eating. Karen smiled.

"Dad's coming home on the twentieth," she said.

"What?" said David.

Wendy squealed and clapped her hands. David forced a smile. Eleanor nibbled her chicken.

"How long have you known?" David asked.

"I found out today," she said.

"How long this time? Just a week or what?"

"No, he's back now," Karen said. "He's done. He's being discharged."

"Yay! Daddy's coming home!" squealed Wendy.

"This is great news," David said, but Eleanor knew he didn't mean it. "You'll get to meet my dad, Eleanor."

"Great," she said and smiled for Karen.

She couldn't tell them about the bank or the beer can. Not that day.

The next day, Eleanor entered the school early before the buses arrived and slipped into science class before anyone else.

Mr. Gurenno came in shortly afterwards and set about putting his lecture together. He had a big Styrofoam box that jittered and scratched. Eleanor recognized a familiar amphibian smell: frogs. Copying from a book, he drew a frog on the board and labeled its different interior parts in colored chalk. He was halfway through before he noticed Eleanor sitting in the back of his class.

"Eleanor," he said, surprised. "I didn't see you there."

"Sorry," she said.

"Mr. Graham told me about you," he said.

"What did he say?"

"He said you hid your potential. Is that true?"

"Who am I to know my potential?"

"Good answer," he said. "Why do you sit so far back?"

"You haven't been here long enough to hear, then?"

"The ghost stories?"

She nodded.

"I've heard some dumb things. I thought this was the twenty-first century, but maybe my clock's a little fast."

"I don't like attention," she said.

He weighed her words as if solving a complex problem in his head. "Okay," he said finally and returned to his drawing.

The class filtered in and the day began. After the usual homeroom announcements, which mostly had to do with the coming rodeo, Mr. Gurenno began his lecture.

"No math today," he said. "We're going to have two hours of biology so we can finish the assignment. Today we're going to dissect frogs."

The class groaned.

"Ewww."

"Gross."

"Cool," said Russell.

"Everyone will have their own specimen, and we'll take this step by step as a group." Mr. Gurenno opened a jar and poured a vaporous liquid into the Styrofoam box and closed the lid. Soon the noise within it stopped. "Line up for your supplies," he said.

He had a box of tools, a pile of cork slates, sponges, swabs, and exam gloves. Everyone lined up and took their supplies. Mr. Gurenno served up euthanized frogs with a pair of tongs. David looked peaked and averted his eyes when the animal was plopped on his slate.

"Using the pins in your kit, pin your frog to your slate on its back as I've illustrated." The room was a clatter of snapping rubber gloves and repellent sighs.

"I know there's a debate about the efficacy of doing actual dissection versus merely reading about it. I don't think you can learn half as much from a theoretical approach as you can from a practical one. To learn something, it must be *studied*. It should be studied as deeply and completely as possible—from all angles. It's always the best way."

"Not the best way for the frog," said Brian, and the class chortled.

"Ah, yes, the debate about animal testing. Is it moral to kill the frog so we can study it? It's a good question," he said. "Let's discuss that. But first, after the frog is pinned down, you'll need to make an incision from the base of the throat to the crotch. Do not cut deeply. Cut just the skin. Make several shallow cuts if you have to. We don't want you to injure the organs. Follow this line here." He gestured to the drawing. "The scalpel is very sharp. Be careful. Make horizontal incisions here and here, like a book. Then open the cavity carefully. Stretch the skin back and pin it down, exposing the insides."

More groans from the class, but blades flashed. Eleanor did as she was told. She watched her classmates, noting with some interest Russell's enthusiasm for the exercise and David's aversion to it. David was white as a sheet. He was sweating.

"It's a question of priority," Mr. Gurenno went on. "Is it okay to kill one person to save two? To kill one to save a thousand? A million? Mathematically, such a sacrifice makes perfect sense. It's the basis for all armed conflict. Now, extend that to other species. Is it okay to kill a mouse to determine if a medicine is effective or poisonous to people? How about a guinea pig? A cat? A dog or a horse? These are all animals we breed for the purpose of testing. It's their function. Like these frogs. They were bred, raised, and sold for this experiment today. Their lives are given for the betterment of our species."

"What if they were endangered?" asked Robby.

"Well be assured these aren't," said Mr. Gurenno, "but it's

a good question." He looked out over the class and saw that most had their frogs opened up. "Now, I want you all to find the frog's stomach. It should be right here." He pointed to a pink shape on his drawing. "Use your probe to pull it out. Look for the liver next. It should be around here near the neck. Remove it, and we'll look for the gallbladder.

"*This* is the probe, Mr. Venn," said Mr. Gurenno, holding up the instrument so the whole class could see which it was.

"Now, about endangered animals," he said. "There is good reason to protect diversity as far as we can. But what if a species is dangerous to humans and our way of life? On the one hand, we have wolves and tigers, predators to our species and our agriculture. We control them now, but if they become dangerous again, like that pack of wolves that came down from Canada last year, they won't be tolerated."

"We don't experiment on wolves," said Robby.

"No, but we try to understand them. Sometimes the experiment is not to find a cure, but merely to gain understanding. That's what we're doing here today. No one is going to find a cure for baldness in these frogs, but you will understand how things are put together. Sometimes we find something very unusual, say a new kind of slug or a variation of finch on an island. In those cases, we are obliged to learn as much about it as possible. Say the slug has a venom that numbs its prey. That would be useful to understand. We could spend a lifetime watching it eat grass and never learn a thing, but if we cut it open, examine its biology under a microscope and extract the glands, we might come up with a new anesthesia."

"What if the slug was the last of its kind?" Eleanor asked and was shocked to hear her own voice.

"Well, then we absolutely have to know all we can about

the slug while we can. We study it alive until we've learned all we can, and then we study it deeper."

Eleanor's stomach knotted.

Mr. Gurenno walked between the tables and looked at each student's progress. "Now let's determine the sex of your frog," he said. "Mr. Venn, you haven't even pinned the skin back."

He presented David with a pair of forceps. David swallowed and took the tool. He grabbed the skin and revealed the right side of the frog. David turned suddenly and threw up on the floor with a retch. The class laughed as David vomited scrambled eggs and orange juice down his table onto the floor.

"Mr. Venn, you're excused," said Mr. Gurenno, throwing a handful of towels on the mess. "Clean up in the bathroom and come back when you feel better."

Ashen and staggering, David left.

"What a sissy," said Russell. "This ain't nothin'. I've cleaned whole elk. This isn't even as bad as a fish."

Eleanor looked for David during the break, anxious to get away from the dissecting table herself. David was still in the bathroom. Robby came out after a moment and glanced at Eleanor. He was about to walk past her back into the classroom when he stopped and addressed her.

"He's okay," he said. "He's queasy, but he's okay."

"Thanks," she said.

Mr. Gurenno didn't require David to come back. Eleanor learned at lunch that David had actually checked himself out of school. She overheard the girls talking about it in line.

"I don't know what was grosser," said Penelope, "the frog guts or David's puke."

"The puke, for sure," said Alexi.

"I can't stand that kind of thing," said Penelope. "I wish I'd have thought to throw up—I could be home now too. I can't stand sick people. Hospitals are gross."

"Your grandma's at the hospital, isn't she?"

"She'll be dead soon," said Penelope.

"No hope?" asked Barbara, selecting a salad.

"She's old and has all kinds of sick in her. She should have died ages ago. She's a cranky old bitch. At least when she dies I'll get some money. Can't wait. I can't stand her. She smells."

"She came down here to be with your mother, didn't she?"

"To mooch, you mean."

"You said she has money," said Crystal.

"Not mooch money, mooch affection. She wants to be doted on. She wants me to see her in the hospital. I went once and that was it. Talk about depressing. If she wants to see me, she can come to my house. It's too gross there."

Eleanor collected some pasta and a carton of milk. She stopped at the girls' table on the way to hers and stood over them with her tray until they looked up.

"Penelope," she said. "You should see your grandmother while you have the chance."

"Mind your own business, slut," she spat.

Eleanor retreated to her usual table. Midge tried to talk to her, but her mood was too foul for even a polite response to questions about David. Naturally, she was concerned about him, but that wasn't why she was so upset. It was the thought of a woman dying in a hospital of cancer, wanting only to see her granddaughter before the end, and the snobby girl refusing to visit. She couldn't imagine such shallowness, even from Penelope, the skeleton girl. She looked like death herself and yet she wouldn't deign to visit her dying grandmother because it offended her sensibilities. Eleanor remembered

Tabitha, recalled the precious moments she'd spent with her before the end, the love, the caring, the silent understanding of generations of love. Though they shared no blood, their bonds were the steel of mother and daughter, friends and companions. Eleanor would give anything for another moment with her, and she knew what it had meant to Tabitha that she had been there. In the end, Tabitha had dismissed Eleanor to face death alone as all must do, but she did not do so forsaken, as Penelope's grandmother would now.

The thought of it, of such a simple request—a dying request—being ignored, enraged Eleanor. Penelope knew nothing. She valued nothing. Eleanor tried to tell herself that it was a good thing that the dying old woman was spared the company of such a beast, but it didn't help. It was beyond callous. It was cruel.

CHAPTER EIGHT

"I couldn't handle the guts," said David. "I didn't know I was so squeamish, but there I was ralphing up breakfast."

"I can't believe he killed the frogs," Wendy moaned.

"They were probably sick frogs," said Karen.

Eleanor appreciated Karen's efforts to mollify the grisly tale. The conversation was hardly something to share at dinner, let alone with a six-year-old.

Eleanor had a standing invitation to eat with the Venns, and ate with them at least twice a week.

The urgency Eleanor had felt to tell David about her terrible day in town had vanished in the excitement about his father's return. The last of it dissolved completely after witnessing his embarrassment in class. Eleanor could deal with Jamesford's unkindness on her own. She'd survived worse. This was all just a small thing, a thing to be endured, a thing that would pass eventually. She only had to be careful.

"I'll never be a doctor, Mom. Sorry," said David jokingly. "Law then?"

"How about a soldier? Like Dad?" said Wendy.

"No," said Karen. "Law is fine."

"Was he hurt?" asked David. "Is that why he's coming home early?"

"No," said Karen carefully. "Just tired."

"Are there frogs around here?" asked Wendy. "Let's go catch some."

"Wrong time of year," said Eleanor. "In the spring, I'll show you a place."

The next day, Eleanor set off for the hospital after school. She didn't know what she'd do when she got there or even what to expect, but she felt she had to go anyway. She felt she needed to see the dying old woman if only to clear her mind of the image that was Tabitha in that room.

Eleanor moved parallel to Highway 26. This time of year it was mostly a secondary corridor for northwest trucking. The familiar smells of diesel exhaust and the sounds of shifting gears and rattling trucks had a calming effect on her. It was the promise of other places. She avoided the highway because it was the main artery through town, and she was not in the mood to face another idiot with a beer can, but she liked knowing it was there.

She knew the paths through Jamesford that would keep her hidden. She knew the paths the animals followed and the shortcuts the kids made. It wasn't hard to be unseen in such a little town even on a bright Friday afternoon.

She circled around a vacant lot where she smelled a cooking fire and heard voices. She recognized Ramos, the homeless man who'd stared at her, along with several other vagrants she'd seen in the back alleys and dumpsters around town.

"They said I couldn't hold a sign unless I cleaned up. I still got food though."

"Fed me too. Wasn't bad neither," said Ramos.

"I think they'll give you a place to stay if you wash and walk with them."

"I'll take their food but I won't go to jail for nobody," said another.

When she got to the hospital, Eleanor thought she knew what the vagrants had been talking about. There was a crowd of about a dozen people milling around the main entrance. Eleanor recognized Sheriff Hannon among them directing the others to one side with the help of some other officers.

Eleanor instinctively held back and watched.

"You're Eleanor Anders, aren't you?" said a woman. Eleanor recognized Miss Lamb, or rather, Agent Lamb. She'd met her the previous year. She worked for Homeland Security. She'd been on the panel investigating the food-poisoning incident. Like her, the agent watched the crowd from a safe distance.

"You have a good memory," Eleanor said. "You're Agent Lamb, aren't you?"

"You have a good memory too. Call me Shannon." She smiled warmly. Eleanor wished she hadn't. It put her at ease, and she knew that would be a mistake. The last time she'd felt safe she'd been clobbered with a beer can.

"What's going on?" Eleanor asked. "Why are you here?"

"Have you heard of the Revealers?" she asked. Eleanor nodded. "That's what's going on. I drew the short straw and get to babysit a bunch of backward haters on their merry journey of publicity seeking. It brought me back to this insufferable berg."

"You don't like Jamesford?"

"Oh, it's okay," she said. "I'm sorry, I was insensitive. Maybe that's why I got assigned to Wyoming. No, Jamesford is a fine little town. It's just not the kind of place one can get noticed."

"That's its strength," Eleanor said.

"Not if you're looking for a promotion," she said.

The protestors moved from the main door and hoisted their signs onto their shoulders. Their signs proclaimed that "Evil is bred of evil people," "God smiles when wicked people die," and "Obey God's Laws or Burn!"

"What are they so mad about?" asked Eleanor.

"Ever hear of Dr. Zalarnik? No? How about BioTech Innovations Inc., BTII on the exchange? Well that's what got the Revealers in an uproar. Zalarnik is a big name in medical research. He built a cabin and is living here part time. He's studying mold in Yellowstone and says he likes the isolation. Good on him. He had the audacity to buy everyone at the hospital lunch after they wrapped a sprained ankle. He's in there now. Pastor Lugner got wind of it and here he is. Oh balls, there's the press."

Just then, a boxy van fitted with a satellite dish and the words "Live Action News 6" painted across its side turned the corner. Before it had stopped moving, cameras and cables spilled out its doors and a woman with tissues in her collar and a wireless microphone jogged toward the hospital.

"Here comes the show," said Agent Lamb.

The sheriff had nearly moved everyone out of the way when the Revealers saw the news team. Suddenly they surged forward and started screaming. They pushed the sheriff, and when he grabbed someone to keep his balance, a sign-toting protestor threw himself to the ground and screamed police brutality.

The camera followed the action as the crowd broke into chants, then yells, then a skirmish between a deputy and a kicking housewife, which led to a momentary melee as officers linked arms and pushed them all back. Agent Lamb checked her gun under her coat and trotted across the street to help.

Eleanor stayed back. She circled around the mayhem and made sure to stay out of the view of the camera. She was shocked at how quickly things had escalated and how ugly they'd become. A horrific picture of a dead, three-headed cow suddenly appeared on a sign over a battling crowd and proclaimed "Zalarnik mocks nature." Several protesters rolled their eyes back into their heads and spouted unintelligible gibberish while shaking as if electrocuted. Some fell to the ground in seizures; others remained on their feet but flailed like napkins in the wind.

An ambulance, with its lights flashing, circled the building once and then sped south toward Riverton ninety minutes away.

Eleanor recognized several faces in the crowd. Mrs. Westlake stood with a sign proclaiming God's power over the hubris of science. She looked for Jennifer and found her pushing pamphlets into the hands of onlookers across the street. She caught the eye of Betty Church, Jamesford High's former cafeteria director. She gave Eleanor such a malignant stare that a cold chill went down her back.

The news crew set up for an on-camera interview and the crowd quieted. A tall, thin man in a flat black suit and white cravat stepped up to talk to the reporter. He had boney, age-spotted hands, and his long, gray hair flowed over his shoulders in an anachronistic style which made Eleanor think of Puritans. If he'd had buckles on his boots he couldn't have looked more out of time. He had big, white, square teeth and smiled with them in a way that made Eleanor think of a crocodile.

"Why are you protesting today, Pastor Lugner?" asked the bubbly reporter.

"*Doctor* Zalarnik," he slurred in a way that made the title sound like a disease, "commits crimes against man and God. He goes against nature. He is an evil man and all evil must be fought. It is our Christian obligation to do so."

"What specifically are you upset about? Is it Zalarnik's support of stem cells? His theories of extraterrestrial bacteria? Or his work with AIDS research?"

"All that and more. You see how he's subverting God's will and teachings at every step. AIDS is God's punishment. To fight against a righteous punishment is a sin. Such punishment is deserved and should bring about contrition, not cross-species contamination. Zalarnik experiments with animal cells in human beings. Frankenstein never conceived of such terrible crimes as Zalarnik gets government funding for. He needs to be stopped."

"How far are you willing to go to stop him?"

"Evil is real. It is around us all the time. It may look like a doctor or a teenage girl, but it is there. It must be fought and cast out. Evil begets more evil. It is a weed. We are, of course, a peaceful sect, but we would understand—as any God-fearing Christian would understand—if someone's faith led them to follow the Old Testament in such things."

Eleanor could hear the interview clearly from her vantage point at the corner, but still she couldn't believe her ears. Had Pastor Lugner just mentioned evil in the form of a teenage girl? Was he talking about her?

Eleanor watched the scene play out for another hour until the news crew left. When their van was out of sight, the protestors packed up. There'd been several arrests. Lugner argued with Sheriff Hannon, but he backed down when he was threatened with arrest as well. With no cameras to witness it, he wasn't in a hurry to be cuffed.

Eleanor scurried across the street. She paused on the sidewalk feeling suddenly exposed. She turned and saw Miss Church talking to Pastor Lugner by his car. She gestured toward Eleanor, and the gray-haired man looked at her contemptuously. Eleanor fled into the hospital.

Inside, orderlies in green scrubs and nurses in blue had seen enough of the tumult in front of their clinic and were returning to work. Several uniformed private security officers remained in the waiting room and eyed Eleanor suspiciously as she approached the counter. Sheriff Hannon was nowhere to be seen.

"Hello," Eleanor said. "I'd like to know about the condition of Mrs. Lange."

The woman consulted a computer and shook her head. "No one by that name here," she said in a south Texas accent.

"Do you know Penelope Lange? She's a junior at Jamesford High School? A skinny girl. It's her grandmother."

"No, I don't," she said.

"No, of course not," said Eleanor remembering that she wouldn't visit. "She's an old woman. With cancer. I think it's terminal."

"You might mean Mrs. Chapman. Room 36," she said. "She's the only one here that matches that description."

"Can I see her?"

"Sorry. Family only."

"Can you tell me how she's doing?"

"Why do you care?" she asked.

"My mother died of cancer last year," she said. "I was curious."

Sudden recognition flashed across the woman's face. "You're the girl that buried her mother in the yard, aren't you?"

Eleanor froze.

"Hey Bill," called the receptionist over shoulder. "Guess who I got out here."

Eleanor turned around and walked out of the hospital before the gawkers could assemble.

CHAPTER NINE

"I know I should have said something earlier," Eleanor told David the next day, "But it's really no big deal."

"No big deal? You could have been killed."

"I don't think they meant to kill me," she said. "It was just a lucky throw."

Wendy called for them to watch her on the slide. She slid down with her hands held up like on a roller coaster.

The park wasn't crowded. Cold weather kept the locals away and the tourists had mostly gone home. Still, there was a jogger, several dog walkers, and a pack of kids trying to start a baseball game with only seven players. Eleanor had mentioned the attack by way of association as they walked up the lane for a Saturday excursion.

"Do you think it was Russell? He hangs out with Greg Findlay. Greg has a truck."

"His is different," Eleanor said. "I don't think it was them."

"When my dad gets here and settles in, I bet he won't tolerate this place long. We'll move someplace civilized."

"You say that like you're sure he'll take me along."

"Of course he will. Wherever I go, you go," said David. "And if not, then we'll go to Canada like you said."

"It's not so bad here," Eleanor said halfheartedly.

"I can tell it is," David said. "But you can't let them get to you. They want to wear you down because they're jerks. You always talk about fight or flight. Fight a little. You're twice what these people are—ten times better. Believe it. What you did at the bank, standing up to that jerk, is just what you needed to do. They didn't expect that you'd come in and make a scene or they wouldn't have done it. You fought back, and it worked. Good for you. Keep fighting."

"I don't know. Maybe I made it worse."

"No way," he said. "And another thing: stop thinking that you're alone in this. You're not. You have friends. My mom would have stormed in there with a baseball bat if you'd told her about it."

"I don't know. She's got a lot on her mind right now."

"Dad? I guess so, but she's not in a coma. She'd have helped. She might even be upset that you didn't ask her to."

"Great," Eleanor said. "Now I'm making your mom angry."

He gave her a little shove. "You're a pill sometimes," he said.

"Push me on the swings," called Wendy.

"Pump your legs. You know how," called David, annoyed.

"I'll do it," said Eleanor getting up. David followed her.

"I'm an eagle," cried Wendy. "Caw, caw!"

"That's a crow," said David.

"What does an eagle sound like?" she asked.

David looked at Eleanor. Eleanor looked around. No one was near. She closed her eyes and remembered. Then she let out a high-pitched stuttering whistle from deep in her throat. She repeated it and made an inflection.

"That's not what an eagle sounds like," said Wendy.

"Yes it is," said David admiringly.

Mr. Gurenno allowed David to copy the frog assignment from other students as a makeup. "I didn't know you were so sensitive," he said apologetically.

"Neither did I," said David.

The dissecting kits were put away, and biology returned to lectures and diagrams, though Mr. Gurenno promised more hands-on work later.

Mrs. Hart was still on leave, so their substitute humanities teacher led them through a prepared syllabus of the First World War and college essay skills. Literature was put aside for thesis paragraphs and compound sentences, the kind of things that impress college admission scorers.

Class schedules were juggled to allow students time to practice for the annual County High School Rodeo. David was excited about it having done so well the year before, and Mrs. Westlake admonished the cooking students that "this is your time to shine."

Eleanor felt uneasy in cooking class. Jennifer ignored her with an air of pious pity, like a pedestrian avoiding a carcass on the road. This was nothing new. It was how Jennifer treated her in all their shared classes, but in such a small class as cooking, Eleanor was acutely aware of it.

It was similar with Mrs. Westlake. Though she couldn't avoid talking to Eleanor the way Jennifer did, she nevertheless displayed a similar bearing. Sometimes Eleanor felt a revulsion from the teacher and a decided unwillingness to approach her, let alone help her fold dough or squeeze rose petals from a frosting sleeve. Luckily, Eleanor didn't need much supervision.

She was a quick study, and if she saw another student doing the task correctly, she could mimic the maneuvers. Besides, the class was only pass/fail. Little was expected of her but attendance and a minimum of effort. She kept her mouth shut and learned to separate egg whites and whip meringue without supervision.

The second week of October the school was abuzz with the news of a dead foreign hitchhiker. His body had been found on the highway just this side of Cowboy Bob's Truck Stop, so, officially within Jamesford city limits.

"I think I saw that guy at my dad's restaurant," said Eric Collins at lunch.

"You talked to him?" asked Midge.

"Yeah, I think so. He was from Germany. He was hitching across the country. He was funny. He had this silver bottle of peppermint schnapps. He said he needed it to make American coffee drinkable. He had some stories. I hope it's not him."

"Who did it?" asked Eleanor.

"They haven't caught anyone yet," said Brian.

"Is this kind of thing common in Jamesford?" asked David.

"Last time I heard talk of a murder around here, there was a manhunt for Eleanor." Barbara had sidled up to their table.

"No," said Brian, glaring at Barbara. "Not common at all."

"What brings you to the cheap seats?" asked Eleanor.

Barbara smiled at her. It was not a malicious smile, more of impressed surprise. It made Eleanor blush.

"Penelope is pissing me off," she said, stealing a french fry from David's tray. "All she can talk about is how much money she's going to get when her grandmother dies. It's morbid."

It was Eleanor's turn to wear a look of impressed surprise.

"I heard her grandmother was sick," said Midge.

"Penelope says she's got days left is all."

"Has she visited her?" asked Eleanor.

"Nah. Her mother stopped going too. She's on life support and barely conscious. Penelope says she couldn't communicate even if she went, so what's the point?"

"This is great lunch conversation," said Robby. "Murder and death. Anyone have any stories of locusts to round us out?"

His point was made, and the talk went to the rodeo, Barbara's borrowed saddle for the barrels, and Robby's bet that the Wild River Shoshone School would take all the roping trophies again. No one took the wager.

"At least the Revealers have gone," said Eric.

"For now," said Midge.

"Where'd they go?" asked Eleanor.

"Yellowstone. They're hounding that doctor. He's set up a field thingy to study geyser moss or something."

"Glad they're gone," said Barbara. "So pushy."

Later that week, Mr. Gurenno announced that Dr. Zalarnik and BTII had donated twenty microscopes to the high school. He distributed them and explained their use. He was visibly excited with the new toys.

"These are expensive," he said. "We're lucky to have them. We can thank Dr. Zalarnik for the donation. In fact we will. Everyone has to write a thank-you letter as a homework assignment."

"So, they were free?" said Tanner.

"Not if you break one," the teacher cautioned. "Then they cost you five hundred dollars. Wholesale."

There were enough scopes for everyone to have their own, but Mr. Gurenno had them pair up, perhaps not wanting to risk all his new toys at once. David appeared beside Eleanor right on cue.

"What are we doing exactly?" asked David.

"Today, something easy," Gurenno said. "We're just going to get used to them. We'll set up a petri dish experiment for next week. We'll start them tomorrow and let them grow over the weekend."

"We don't have biology tomorrow," said Brian. "Rodeo practice."

"Oh. Right," he said. "Okay, we'll start today."

He handed out sterilized cotton swabs and clean petri dishes and glanced at his watch. "We'll go a little late today," he said.

When everyone had a dish and a couple of swabs, he explained the experiment.

"Let's look at our spit," he said and waited for quiet before continuing.

"Use a swab and collect some saliva and study it under the microscope. Make detailed drawings and notes. Then, take another sample and seed it on the dish. Next week we'll see what happens when the saliva has a nice place to germinate."

"Gross," said Alexi.

"Decide whose spit to use. Use the same person's saliva on both the slide and the dish. If someone's had a cold recently, use them. It'll be more interesting."

Eleanor grabbed David's sleeve.

"I know," he said. "We'll use mine. Don't worry."

"No," she said. "Get Penelope's swab for me."

"What?"

"You said to fight," she said. "I'm fighting. I need her swab."

David shook his head not understanding. She glared at him.

"Okay," he said. "We'll talk about this later?"

"Yeah," she said.

David nonchalantly strolled up to Penelope and Crystal's table.

"You're doing it wrong," he said.

"What?" said Crystal. "You know how to do this?"

"Yeah, I used one of these in Georgia."

He tore open a swab package and turned to Penelope. "Open up," he said.

"But I was going to—" began Crystal.

"Open big," he said, putting himself between the two girls.

Penelope opened her mouth and David slid the swab under her tongue.

"Hold the slide there," David said to Crystal.

She held the slide while David dabbed the swab on it. He slid the swab back into the paper sleeve and put it aside. He grabbed another swab and ripped it open while Crystal fitted the slide into the microscope.

"Now one for the dish," he said, and Penelope stuck out her tongue for another sample.

David smeared the swab across the bottom of the dish and snapped the lid shut. He slid the used swab back into its sleeve and tossed it in the trash.

"Don't forget to write your name on it," he said. "Hate to have it confused with Russell's."

"What are you talking about, Venn?" said Russell.

"I just don't want Penelope thinking she has rabies," he said. The class chortled.

"Mr. Venn, return to your seat," Mr. Gurenno said. David dutifully went back to Eleanor's table. He slid a paper sleeve with Penelope's used swab onto the table and winked.

When no one was looking, Eleanor stuck the swab in her mouth. David involuntarily turned away.

She navigated the molecules and identified Penelope among the toothpaste and Diet Coke. She felt a shudder of half absorption before it slid into the pocket of her throat. She tossed the swab in the garbage and opened a dish to accept David's sample.

"Thanks," she whispered.

"Penelope?" he said, his face pale.

"It's something I've got to do," she said.

"Not for long, okay? I can't stand that scarecrow."

"No, not long," she said and squeezed his hand affectionately beneath the table.

CHAPTER TEN

"Why do you need so much food?" David asked, putting another bag in his trunk. "Penelope is a stick."

"I need it. I think I can do with less, but it hurts more and takes longer. Plus, I'll need to recover."

"You should add fiber, don't you think."

"Protein and fat. I don't think sugars and grains work as well."

"You don't know?"

"Not really," she said. "No one taught me and I haven't had much practice."

"Man, I'd be all over this," he said. "I'd be changing into all kinds of things if I could be you."

"You wouldn't," she said and got in the car. "It hurts."

Eleanor put the groceries away and put the frozen stuff on the counter to thaw overnight. David flopped in a chair and picked up a dog-eared copy of *Anne of Green Gables* and thumbed through it.

"Penelope's grandmother?" he said, not for the first time. "Seems like a lot of risk for little reward."

"You mean because she's going to die soon?"

"That and she is nothing to you. For a girl who likes to fly beneath the radar, you're going out of your way to make ripples."

"You're mixing your metaphors," she said.

He dropped the book on the table. "Seriously? Are you sure you want to do this? Need to do this?"

"You're the one who said to fight. This is how I fight," she said.

"I meant for yourself," he said. "Stick up for yourself."

Eleanor looked out the kitchen window at her tomato garden and sighed. She tried to think of words to explain it. If she found any, she wondered if they'd be for him or for her. Finally, she said, "You don't have to help me."

"Hey, don't be like that," he said. "I'll help. I want to help. I meant it when I said you weren't alone. What do you need me to do?"

"I wish I knew more about her," she said.

"Then put it off," he said. "Or don't do it."

She shot him a look.

"Just kidding," he said. "Chill out."

"You can drive me to the hospital tomorrow night," she said. "After dark."

"Okay," he said. "Mom has a list of chores for me to do to get ready for my dad." David was not excited about his father's return. He hadn't spoken to her about it, and she hadn't pressed. She knew something of their strained relationship and hoped David would confide in her eventually. But now was not the time.

"Tell Karen I'm sorry I can't help now. Tell her I'll be there next week to help out after school. Every day if she needs me."

"What should I say to her about this weekend?"

"Personal stuff."

She knew eventually he'd be involved in this part of her life, but not now. She'd discussed her "talent" with him of course. They'd had months together during the summer and he was naturally curious. She didn't want to talk about it. She couldn't share David's enthusiasm. Though she didn't say it was a curse, she thought it a closer description than "gift," which he used. Maybe she should have been flattered that David considered her biggest flaw to be her greatest asset, but to her, it meant that she'd never be able to be anything but a copy and a lie.

The next morning, she began the day with a big breakfast. She would use the entire day to gradually transform, hoping to alleviate the pain by taking it slowly. She wasn't sure she could control the transformation that much, but she sensed she could. In the last year she'd found herself accidentally changing to suit the situation and then being able to consciously reverse it. It took a lot of effort, but she had done it. Although it still repulsed her, she knew she had to understand the event better for her own survival.

So much of the transformation was microscopic and reflexive. She could do little more than resist, delay, and study the order of events and note the intervals of searing pain versus the moments of stabbing agony.

She eased into it. Going slow helped, but only insofar as giving her a chance to catch her breath. She'd read stories of childbirth and labor and imagined she faced something similar during transformation. After a while, she thought it better that she just bear down and get it over with rather than extend the ordeal.

Still it took an excruciatingly long time. At one point, she stepped out of the shower for a cloth and made the mistake of looking into a mirror. She saw her bald head and twisted half face and threw herself back into the tub screaming. It took her some time to calm down.

The running water helped sooth her searing flesh and wash off the sloughing skin so she didn't have to pull at it as much. But there was so much of it that it clogged the drain and if she didn't want to sit in blood, she had to scoop it out into a bucket on the floor.

Her new shape would be about the same height. Still, she felt her bones break and mend in odd places to alter proportion. Her head rang in pain as bone and teeth were either dropped out and remade or absorbed and reformed.

The base of her neck shuttered, and she lay down in the tub, knowing that for a moment at least, she'd be unconscious as nerve endings ripped and regrew. As she was sliding into unconsciousness down a shoot of slippery blackness, just for an instant, she thought she saw David watching her from the doorway. She began to call out when the darkness hit and drew her away.

When she came to he wasn't there. With a voice that wasn't her own, she called for him but no sound came back.

She bore down and hurried the change, felt the billion pinpricks of a billion morphing cells, felt the chemical heat of biological alchemy in her flesh and felt a flash of alien personality conjured from her imagination and the biological clues contained in the sample she'd swallowed.

By six o'clock she was done and dressed. Hungry from the change and caged in an emaciated body, she was ravenous. She dug into the cache she and David had assembled and savored the milk fats and proteins like it was candy at Christmas. She felt her body strengthen as if every one of her cells had been an empty container, holding its shape without contents, a skeleton without muscle, a frame without walls. She laughed to think what her schoolmates would say if they saw Penelope eat like this and then not disappear into the bathroom to throw it all up.

At ten o'clock, David knocked on the door. A wind cast tree-shadows from a streetlamp across her window. Crickets sang in the yard. A nearby cat called for a friend.

Eleanor opened the door and was met with David's blanched face.

"It's me, David," she said. "Are you okay?"

He looked away. "Uhm," he began.

"I know," she said. "It's only for tonight."

He nodded and led the way to the car without looking at her.

Half and hour later, Penelope Lange signed her name in a strained and shaky hand at the reception desk. Hospital visiting hours ran officially until eleven o'clock but they were lax, especially for the terminal cases, and Mrs. Chapman, Room 36, was most definitely terminal.

"I'm glad someone came down," said the nurse leading her down the hall. "We called this morning, but you're the first to come. I don't think I've seen you here before."

"No," she said. "I haven't visited much."

"It's good you came," she said, opening the door for her. "As I said on the phone, this is probably your last chance."

Penelope stepped into the room and breathed in the smell of antiseptics and medicines, decay and cancer. She knew that smell well, too well. It was a slightly different scent than she remembered, but unmistakable and wicked. The woman on the bed was in her late eighties. Her skin was pale as tissue paper. Her hair was white and silken, fine as gossamer and recently brushed. Her hands were knots of gnarled knuckles and age spots, bruises and scabs. A clear hose, like the one under her nose, stuck out the back of one hand and from the crux of her other arm. The low hum of electric fans nearly drowned out the sound of her soft shallow breathing. She was asleep.

Penelope stood by the door and wondered at the years this woman had seen. The woman had a strong jaw and short nails that spoke of work before failing under arthritis.

There was a chair next to the bed, and Penelope sat in it and watched the old woman sleep. Drapes had been pulled across the window, but she could see the stars through a break in them. The moon would be up soon. She was glad the room was on this side of the hospital. Less noise.

Suddenly the old woman opened her eyes and blinked. Penelope's heart raced, and she felt an urge to leave. Instead, she reached out and took the old woman's hand. It was light and frail, bony, like her own starved hand. She held it warmly.

The woman turned and blinked. Penelope smelled the strong painkillers in her breath and wondered if she'd be clear enough to recognize her, but knew it didn't matter. She'd come here to hold the woman's hand and that was what she was doing.

The woman smiled. Her teeth were bright, her smile genuine.

"I didn't think I'd see you," she rasped.

"I'm here," Penelope said and smiled back.

"My God, child," she said. "You're thinner than I am."

"Don't worry about me."

"Let Nanna worry about who she worries about," she said.

"Do you want something? Can I get you anything?"

"Penny," she said, her eyes rolling back in their sockets as she swallowed a blast of pain. "Death is coming. He's coming soon. Listen to me. This is what I know. You can't rush to him. You've got to fight him at every step. He'll win eventually, and that's okay. But don't give him a head start. Darling, look at you. You're giving him a head start with this eating nonsense. You didn't used to be like this."

"I don't know what to say, Nanna," she said.

"Darling, if you don't like who you are, changing the outside won't fix it. I know you're still that sweet little girl who played with puppies. Do you remember that? That was a day. Oh yes, what a day. You've just got lost in the divorce. Forgive your parents. Love everyone. Be beautiful on the inside, and the outside will take care of itself."

"Nanna," she said. "I'll try."

"And you'll do it, Penny. You came to see me. I didn't think you would, but you did. You're my special Penny, my shiny Penny. You're the only person I wanted to see today. Today, the last day."

"Don't say that Nanna," Penelope said.

"It's okay. I'm ready. Lord knows I'm ready. I'm glad I had a chance to see you. To say what I did. Do you understand what I meant? It's the only thing I know, the only thing I learned in ninety years. It's the only real thing of value I can give my granddaughter. Do you understand?"

"Yes, Nanna," she said.

"Please eat. Be strong. Live a long, loving life. It's all you can do. Nothing else matters. Nothing else. I wish I had done more of it," she said. "But I must have done enough because you're here with me now."

"I love you, Nanna," she said.

"And I love you," she said, but her smile changed to a grimace. She reached over for a chord and pressed a button.

"It's getting bad again," she grunted. "If I fall asleep don't take it personal."

"I won't," Penelope said, then leaned over and kissed the old woman on her cheek.

"Love, Penny," she said, sliding into dreams. "It's all that mattered."

She slipped into sleep. Penelope held her hand and listened to her breathe. She heard it go slight and stutter and then stop. Somewhere in the hospital, beyond the door, behind Penelope, an alarm sounded, and she knew it was over.

The nurse who'd shown her in opened the door.

"Are you going to do something?" asked Penelope.

"DNR," she said sympathetically. "She didn't want us to try and revive her."

"I understand," she said and wiped a tear from her eye.

The nurse checked the machines and recorded information on a clipboard. Penelope stood up to leave.

"Will you call the family about this?" asked Penelope.

"You don't want to?"

"No. You do it. I was never here," she said.

The nurse raised an eyebrow but didn't get a chance to say more before Penelope was gone.

She crossed the street to a dark parking lot and found

the burgundy Honda. David was in the driver's seat, his ears plugged with earphones. He still looked sick. She knocked on the window, and he unlocked the door for her.

"How'd it go?" he said. "You've been crying. That bad?"

"No," she said. "It was good. How are you doing?"

"I'm better," he said. "Get in. I'll take you home."

"No," she said suddenly. "I have to do something first. Do you have Penelope's number?"

"Actually, I think I do," he said and reached into his wallet.

"Barbara gave it to you?" she asked.

"Uhm, yeah," he said not looking at her. He passed her a folded piece of paper with a half dozen names and numbers on it. It was in Barbara's handwriting. She recognized the names and immediately set them all to memory.

"I'll be right back," she said.

She had an idea, and she knew she had very little time to do anything before it would be too late. It might already be too late.

Back in the hospital, she quickly crossed the waiting room and ducked behind a nurse's desk. She picked up the phone. She called the number. On the eighth ring, Penelope answered.

"Hello," she said impatiently.

"Penny," she said in a harsh, raspy voice, "Penny, my shiny Penny, this is Nanna."

"Nanna?" she said softly.

"I need to tell you something. I don't have long, death is here, my granddaughter. It's the only thing of real value I have to give you. Will you listen to me? Will you hear me? This one time? This last time?"

"Yes, Nanna, I'll listen," she said, and her voice was weak.

And in the borrowed voice of a dead woman, she told her.

CHAPTER ELEVEN

"Her mother was on the phone talking to the hospital at the same time," said Barbara. "Her grandmother was already dead."

"No way," said Alexi.

"Nice try," said Crystal. "A little early for Halloween isn't it?"

"No, I'm telling you. It happened. It's why we haven't seen Penelope. She's left Jamesford. Her parents sent her away. She had a breakdown."

Mr. Gurenno had set them all to studying leaves under their new microscopes. He didn't mind a little conversation while they worked, provided they stayed on task and didn't disrupt anyone.

The conversation picked up when Barbara broke the news. "Penelope called me in tears the day after it happened and told me," she explained. "I haven't heard from her since. I called her house and all her mother will say is that she's gone for a while. She's even going to miss the funeral."

The entire class was listening.

"Doesn't surprise me," said Crystal. "She wouldn't have gone anyway. She hated her grandmother."

"That's a sin," said Jennifer. "She broke the fifth commandment; honor thy mother and father."

"Jennifer," said Aubrey. "Give it a rest."

"Whatever," said Alexi.

Barbara went on, "A nurse said she saw Penelope at the hospital—described her to a T. Saw her visiting her grandmother just before she died. Before the phone call, when Penelope was home asleep."

"No way," said Brian.

"When I talked to her, Penelope was crying so hard, saying how her grandmother's ghost had reached out to her. She said it was a miracle. She was hysterical."

"Sorcery is what it was," said Jennifer.

"How about you shut your ignorant mouth?" said Aubrey.

Jennifer's face went crimson. Aubrey had the least patience of anyone for Jennifer's fanaticism.

"Is she going to be all right?" Eleanor asked Barbara.

"I think so," she said without derision.

David ignored them and studied his leaf. He had not been the same since that night. He'd dropped Eleanor off around midnight and then didn't call or see her all weekend. He'd been brusque and distracted with her before class. Eleanor figured something had happened at home. She would wait until he was ready to talk about it. Give him his space. It's what friends did.

"It's a great ghost story," said Robby.

"Sounds like more than a story," said Crystal.

"Only a witch, the devil's agent, can raise the dead," said Jennifer.

"Jennifer, leave it alone," said Robby.

"Quiet down, class," said Mr. Gurenno.

Rumors spread about the phone call and ghostly visitation, and soon the entire town was discussing it. She heard also the mention of the similarities between Penelope's relative returning and her own. The old stories rose like Halloween ghosts to haunt the town of Jamesford that October.

Eleanor didn't like the stories. They weren't as threatening as she could imagine, but it still worried her. Earlier, she'd overheard Mrs. Westlake talking on her cell phone. "It's because of that Anders girl and that unhallowed burial that all this is happening. Tell the pastor he needs to get down here quick."

And David was a distant friend. He avoided her all week, finding excuses to stay away at lunch, hurriedly rushing away after school. She imagined he was setting up a surprise for her, a sudden reappearance for their overdue kiss. But it didn't come.

His sullenness was intentional and universal. He shunned everyone and at the odd moments when she caught him unawares, he looked pensive and worried.

She'd kept a distance between them, a safety barrier she thought, a moat to keep everyone safe, but this was too much. This was more than she could bear. She missed him and worried for him. She pulled on a coat and set out for David's house looking for answers.

She entered the trailer park like a whisper and automatically walked the fence to his house. As she approached the trailer, she heard raised voices. She melted into the shadow of the front porch, sat down, and listened.

"It'll be different," Karen said.

"How? What's happened to change him?"

"He's out of the army now. That's how."

Eleanor could hear Wendy crying softly in her room.

"Being out of the army didn't help last time. All he could do was talk about getting back. How will never being able to get back be better?"

"It will be," Karen said. "Don't be like this. He's coming home tomorrow." Eleanor heard tears in her voice.

"He lit the house on fire, Mom. Why are you letting him back here?"

"We don't know that," she said.

"Mom," challenged David.

"He's gotten help. Or he'll get it," she said. "He's got nowhere else to go. He's your father, David. Try and remember that. Try to forgive. Give him a chance."

"I don't understand you," he said. "Why do I have to put up with him? Do you like being hit? Because I don't."

"I took Eleanor in for you. You can do this for me."

There was silence.

"Okay, you tell Dad to take a hike, and I'll dump Eleanor. We were doing fine without them. I don't need her. I'm better off without her, like you were better off without Dad. There are other fish in the sea, Mom. Think about it."

"David, you don't mean that. You two are fighting now," Karen said. "Eleanor is a nice girl. You two will make up. Your dad and I always make up."

"Stop comparing us. Don't pretend you understand me or Eleanor. I'm not simple and she's . . ." He faltered. In the space of that unfinished sentence whatever was left of Eleanor's life collapsed. She began to cry.

It was time to leave Jamesford.

She found a picnic table three trailers down and sat down in the darkness to think. She could not imagine living in James-ford without David, had not even considered the possibility since her mother died.

She heard a rustling in the grass and saw Odin, David's cat, trot up to her. He mewed, and she reached out a hand. He brushed his face against her and purred like a power saw. She picked him up.

The cat had lost an eye to a BB gun, and David had saved it as a lesson to Eleanor. She'd seen too much cruelty to think the cat would survive but, thanks to David, he had. Odin was an excellent mouser. He hadn't been neutered, and he was the tom of the neighborhood, defending his territory and his harem successfully all summer in loud midnight fights that woke the neighbors.

Mean as he was, he stretched out on Eleanor's lap wanting to be petted. It calmed her, feeling the purring cat in her arms. He had a white patch on his tummy that he showed only to special friends. Eleanor picked burrs out of it carefully while he stretched.

She recalled how she'd eaten cat. Those days were so far away that they seemed like a dream now. She couldn't imagine eating Odin or any pet, but they'd been her prized prey when crossing Colorado so many lifetimes ago.

Alone in the cold night, the cat looking at her with its one bright eye, Eleanor saw herself again on all fours, struggling to find food, shelter, safety, a host of predators and terrors stalking her for her flesh or just to test a new gun. It was a ter-rible existence, but it was also simpler, and she longed for it in the way she longed for sleep after her mother died. An escape. She had to survive, but she might choose the conditions of her existence. Her instinct would let her do that. She could leave humanity behind—cruel, uncertain, and betraying humanity—for the simple, honest existence of an animal.

The cat rolled over, wanting its back scratched. She obliged, and Odin contentedly kneaded his claws into her thigh.

David had been the reason she'd stayed in Jamesford last spring. He had been everything to her: her world, her hope. She thought of his face, the taste of his lips, the depths of his eyes, and felt hollow, thinking they were gone.

There was the problem. Though her attraction for him, and her need for him, was greater than ever, it could not be the only thing that defined her, and kept her, and gave her hope.

Her thoughts turned to school and the easy conversations she'd had with Aubrey and Brian, Midge, and Barbara—yes, even Barbara. She was accepted. It might just be a teenage vanity, but it meant something to her.

Tabitha had pushed her at the end to do more than exist. She'd wanted Eleanor to participate in the pageant of human life. And she had. She was. She was part of a community. She may not have been the most popular, but she was involved now.

She'd been alone for so long—an animal in the wild. Then she'd had only her mother as she hid in Jamesford. Just last year, she had opened her circle to include David. Now she had Wendy and Karen and teachers and friends, and she was a part of the group. Good, bad, or ugly, she was in the pageant now. She liked her life. As hard and challenging as the road ahead might be, the road was hers, and she was not alone. Even without David, she was not alone.

She was not ready to return to the days in the wilderness,

without speech, without friends, without a future. She'd made something here. It was tentative and small and fragile, but it was hers, authentic and real. Not a copy. Not stolen. She was going to keep it as long as she could. For herself.

Still cradling the cat, she walked back to David's trailer and knocked on the door. She heard no voices inside but the lights were on. Karen answered.

"Eleanor," she said, surprised. "And Odin. Come in."

David was in his room; Eleanor could hear low music from his computer.

"How are you doing, Karen?" Eleanor said.

"Raising teenagers," she said. "Have you been crying?"

"We're a pair," she said, and Karen didn't deny it.

"David's in his room. I'll get him."

The house was clean and neat. On the table in a paper bag from Sherman's Grocery, where Karen worked, was a collection of colorful streamers, American flags, and Scotch tape.

"Eleanor," David said. "What are you doing here?"

"I thought we should talk," she said.

Karen watched from the hall. "Sounds like a good idea," she said.

"Put on your coat. We'll go for a walk," said Eleanor.

Reluctantly, David donned his jacket and left the trailer. Karen gave Eleanor a warm smile that cheered her more than she'd thought it could.

"He's had a bad day," she whispered. "Don't be too hard on him."

"I won't," Eleanor said with a wave and followed him outside.

David left the trailer park with his hands in his pockets.

Eleanor followed and let the stillness of the night soften David's mood before speaking. They turned toward the highway and the flashing neon lights of the tourist cafes.

"So, what do we need to talk about?" he said.

"Why does your mother think we're fighting?" she asked.

David stopped. "You heard that? You were eavesdropping on me?"

His voice was like a slap, but if a one-eyed cat could survive in this town, so could she. "It's what I do. I can't help it. I was outside. You've been weird all week."

"You calling me weird?" David said bitterly, and the slap was doubly hard.

"Is it about your dad?" she said, keeping her composure.

"That's part of it," he said, walking again. He stared at the ground.

"What is it, David?" she said. "I'm only asking because you told me to."

"What? How did I tell you to meddle?"

Another slap. She bit her lip. "You told me to fight. You said I shouldn't run, but fight. Well, I'm fighting. My best friend told me to fight for what I want and that's what I'm doing. You're my best friend and I'm fighting to keep you."

He slowed his steps and sighed.

"My friend also told me that I wasn't alone in my fight," she said. "I've felt pretty alone this week, but the advice is still sound. And David, you're not alone either. Let me help."

They came to a frosted bench and sat down.

"How can you help when you're the problem?" he asked.

"What?"

"My dad coming back is scary. I am worried about that."

"He hit you? And your mother?"

"Yeah. And burned down our house, and the neighbor's house. They haven't finished investigating yet, but I know he did it. I don't know him anymore, if I ever did. The war killed him. He's still dying."

"Can't he get help? He's a veteran."

"You'd think so, but no. The wait is longer than his tour was. And he's proud. It's a mess."

"I'm sorry, David."

"It's nothing new," he said.

"So that's what's bothering you," she said, relieved.

"No," he said to his shoes. "It's you. I don't know how I feel about you anymore."

The air was sucked out of her chest.

"I saw you Saturday," he said. "I know I should have stayed away. You told me to, but I wanted to help. And I saw you."

"David, you've seen me as other people before. You saw me as you."

"I didn't see you in-between. You weren't human. You weren't animal. You weren't anything. You were all guts and blood. You were like the frog on the board, only alive. It was horrible."

Her stomach clenched and her heart skipped a beat. She'd have let it stop entirely if she could have. She was light-headed. Tears poured down her face.

"I can't look at you now without thinking about that, without seeing you shedding skin like a snake, all blood and gunk."

"Oh, God," she whispered.

"I don't know what else to say. I don't know what to think."

"The kisses?" she said. "What about the kisses?"

"I can't," he said. "My mind knows it's you. My eyes see you, but my imagination colors it all now."

She began to cry.

"And what did you do to Penelope?" he said.

"What?"

"You did something, didn't you? You called her and scared her."

"I called her to deliver a message from her grandmother. It was a gift."

"It doesn't look that way."

"So, you think I'm a monster?" she said.

"I don't know. Penelope might not have been the nicest girl, but she didn't deserve that."

"She was a jerk," Eleanor said. "But I didn't do anything but convey her loving grandmother's dying words to her. How is that so bad?"

"But it was," he said.

"You said fight!" she yelled and then dropped her head into her hands and sobbed for all she was worth. She was in free fall. The ground was gone. Her head spun, she wailed and despaired. It was a bottomless chasm. She saw everyone she knew, everyone she ever loved whirl by her in anguish and judgment. She reached out to them, but no one could catch her. She clawed and fought, but on she fell. Suddenly, an arm reached out and rescued her. The hand that caught her, the face that saved her, was her own.

She snorted and wiped her eyes.

"I'm sorry, Eleanor," he said. "It's me. I'm squeamish. I once saw my mom change Wendy's diaper and couldn't look at her for a month. It's like that."

"You think I'm crap?" she said.

"No. No. It's just . . . I'm squeamish." Eleanor could hear

the confusion and despair in his voice, the struggle he was having, but it was no comfort to her.

Her face was wet with tears, cold from the wind, and stolen from a girl in Nebraska. David looked at her and, though he flinched, he kept his eyes locked on hers apologetically.

"I'll work on it," he said.

"Don't be nice to me because you feel you have to."

"Eleanor . . ."

"I can't blame you," she said. "I'm a thief, and a fraud, and a monster. I don't like what I am any better than you do."

Now David began to cry.

"Eleanor, I'm sorry," he pleaded. "I don't want to lose you. I shouldn't have said anything. Forget I said anything. Give me a little time."

She stood up, and, without looking back for fear of falling, she walked home.

CHAPTER TWELVE

David had gone to Cheyenne with his family to pick up his father when Dr. Zalarnik came to the school for a science assembly. Mr. Gurenno had arranged it and drew the entire high school to the auditorium to hear him speak.

Eleanor's mood was sour. She kept to herself trying to remake the distance that used to protect her and simplify her life. But her friends were having none of it.

Barbara and Robby found her first in Zalarnik's assembly followed by Midge. Then came Alexi, Crystal, and Aubrey. Eric, Brian and even Russell and Tanner decided that the place to sit that day was beside Eleanor. She scowled, but inside, she was happy to see them.

"What do you guys want?" she said.

"Where's your boyfriend, Anders?" Russell asked.

"He's picking up his dad," she said. "Now that you know, will you leave?"

Midge drew a breath. Barbara raised an eyebrow.

"Just asking," he said.

"I thought you were brother and sister," said Alexi. "How's that work?"

"Can you bully me another time?" Eleanor said. "I'm not in the mood."

"I was just kidding," said Alexi. "Sheesh."

There was activity on stage. The last of the sophomores took their seats. A microphone was plugged in. Barbara leaned in to Eleanor.

"Eleanor," said Barbara, "I've got a message."

She wheeled on her, ready to slap her face if she said anything vulgar.

"It's not from me," she said.

"What is it?"

"I got a call from Penelope. She wanted me to tell you that you were right. She should have visited her grandmother."

"Is she still going on about the phantom phone call?" asked Russell.

Barbara didn't react to him but watched Eleanor for an answer, but Eleanor hadn't heard a question.

"She was adamant that I tell you this. It meant a lot to her that I do it, that you know she's sorry."

Eleanor studied her face, memorized the lines, the scars, the pores, the color, assessing her as she had last summer but seeing a different person than before.

She thought she understood the change in the group then, how she was suddenly more popular, why her secluded seat had attracted her entire class. Penelope's apology had changed her status. She felt embarrassed about how rude she had been.

"I'm glad she got the call," Eleanor said.

"And her grandmother got the visit," added Robby.

Eleanor wondered if she was being baited, but Robby's expression was as sincere as Barbara's.

"Students of Jamesford High, please welcome Dr. Dimitri

Zalarnik," said Principal Curtz, applauding at the microphone. Eleanor expected the famous scientist to be more memorable, or at least more clinical. He looked ordinary. He was middle-aged, middle-height, with a conservative haircut, slightly sunburned face, and a plain but tailored suit. His face was angular but not distractingly so. Outside of the expensive suit, he'd be invisible in any middle-class corporation.

"I'm here to talk to you burgeoning scientists about biological technology," he said.

"Boo!" yelled Jennifer. "Heretic!"

"What is wrong with that chick?" said Russell.

"She's gotten all religious again," said Aubrey.

Mr. Blake worked his way into the bleachers to personally escort Jennifer out of the room while the school waited. Several other students were also removed to cries of "Sinner!" and "Satanist!"

"Again?" said Eleanor.

"Her family used to be in a cult," said Aubrey.

"How do you know?" asked Robby.

"I was taken out of the same one," she said. Everyone looked at her. Eleanor suddenly understood.

"The scars," she said.

"Yeah, that's where I got them," she said. "My parents gave them to me when I tried to run."

"Your parents seem so nice," said Midge.

"Not them. My real parents," she said. "When I was rescued, they adopted me."

"Jennifer's a wack job," said Russell.

Dr. Zalarnik continued. "Yes, biotechnology has its

deterrents, but I think they're wrong. Biotechnology is just a modern name for an ancient practice of making the world what we want it to be, to make nature do our bidding."

He let this settle in.

"How many of you have dogs?" High schoolers didn't react to that kind of participatory question easily. "Okay, raise your hands if you've never had a dog. So all of you have had one," he said, grinning.

"Dogs are domesticated wolves, bred over the centuries for certain characteristics, be it guarding, herding, or just as companions. That's biotechnology.

"The food we eat is all the product of biotechnology. Ears of corn are bigger because we made them so. Chickens are bigger and tomatoes last longer on the shelf because of science.

"Similarly, medicine comes from nature. Penicillin is just one example of how science has bred, nurtured, and adapted the natural world into lifesaving cures.

"My company, BioTech Innovations Inc., is looking at nature to find ways to help the body regenerate." He paused for dramatic effect. "We might even be on the trail to immortality."

"Stem cells," whispered Brian. "He's selling stem cell research."

"We've made wonderful finds in the geyser basins of Yellowstone," said Dr. Zalarnik, "and in the cell walls of deep-sea sponges." A projector flicked on and the lights dimmed.

"It's an exciting time to be a scientist," he said.

His corporate speech over, he proceeded to a corporate slide show of the adventurous places they'd found interesting plants and animals. From the arctic seas, to Yellowstone, to the Amazonian rainforest, BioTech Innovations was aggressively seeking to sample the disappearing flora and fauna for the betterment of all mankind.

It was a professional presentation with video clips, interviews, microscopic germs, and plenty of clean-room laboratories producing white pills for happy, smiling, everyday people.

Eleanor noticed several men in suits watching the crowd from doorways and corners. Though the speech and the speaker were casual enough, their subtle presence gave Zalarnik an air of power and prestige, if not danger. Eleanor could even see earphones tucked in their collars. One of them, a large, square-mouthed man with a crew cut, was particularly unnerving in his watchfulness. He panned over the students like a strafing machine gun sweeping a beach.

The bell rang to end the day just as Zalarnik was wrapping up. No one heard him over the clamor of bored students making their exit.

It was that noise that kept Eleanor from noticing the protestors until she walked outside.

Pastor Lugner and a score of his church members picketed the school. They were loud and shouted at the same news crew who'd been at the hospital. Eleanor thought the Revealers had left Jamesford but figured since they were following Dr. Zalarnik, it made sense they were back.

"Don't believe the lies, children," Lugner yelled through a bullhorn. "Truth comes not from abomination but from salvation!"

Suddenly Eleanor heard a familiar voice cry, "Witch!" She looked up and saw Miss Church pointing at her. She screamed it again. Several others picked up the insult and cast it at her with enthusiastic loathing. Lugner heard the change in the crowd and looked for the cause. His eyes landed on Church and then Eleanor.

"There is evil in Jamesford," he preached. "Satan has sent his minions here to test the faithful and punish the blasphemer who lets evil thrive. Ghosts walk the streets, poison our children, and terrorize the bereaved. Wise up, Jamesford. A reckoning is upon you!"

Eleanor retreated into the school. She hid in a bathroom and waited for them to leave. Forty minutes later, she could still hear them, still smell them, so she snuck out the back and found her way home through out-of-the-way neighborhoods and roundabout dirt roads. It took her hours.

David drove up just as she arrived and sat down to rest. She recognized the engine but didn't rise immediately when he knocked.

"Eleanor," he called. "Eleanor. Please."

She got up and opened the door for him and then immediately returned to the rocking chair. He stepped inside and closed the door.

"Why is it so dark in here?" he asked.

"I like it dark sometimes," she said. "I think better in the dark."

He sighed and sat down.

"Eleanor," he began.

"Don't," she said. "I've already had a bad day. I don't need more."

"That's not what I meant. Not why I'm here," he said. "My mom sent me to get you."

"So your mom wants to see me and you don't?" she said petulantly.

"She wants you to meet my dad," he said. "We're having

burgers. You're invited. You should come. Please come. Let's not fight."

"We're not fighting," she said. "We're not anything."

"We're something," he said. "I'm just muddled. It's me, okay? Not you, but me." She rolled her eyes. "I'm confused. You can understand that, can't you? You've been confused before, haven't you?"

The sun was falling fast, but even in the twilight through the half-drawn drapes, she saw his pained face clearly. She knew confusion. She'd asked a lot of David, and he'd given her more. He was trying. He was rightfully confused. She needed to be patient.

"I'll come if *you* want me to," she said.

"Good," he said.

"You won't throw up if you look at me?" she said and immediately regretted it.

"No, Eleanor, I won't."

She saw the hurt in his eyes. "Sorry," she said. "I've had a bad day. Wait a second while I change."

She turned on a lamp and then scampered up the ladder to her loft where she changed into her best dress and shoes. She put a ribbon in her hair and applied the faintest makeup. She was getting better with makeup, but still she used it very sparingly, having discovered the line between attractive and ridiculous to be razor thin.

"You look nice," David said when she came down. He looked at her and smiled awkwardly.

"Let's go meet your father," she said.

A few minutes later, David pulled his little car in front of his trailer. Eleanor could smell meat cooking on the barbecue behind the trailer and heard the low conversation as they approached.

"I wanted him to have the car," Eleanor heard a man say.

"We needed the money more than the car," said Karen.

They stopped when David brought Eleanor close.

"Dad, this is Eleanor. Eleanor, this is my father," David said.

Eleanor recognized David's father from his photos, but in person he was a presence. He offered Eleanor his hand and shook hers. His were rough and strong, big enough to crush nuts. The overhead spotlight cast shadows from his brow down his face, but even in the bad light she saw a welcoming smile. He turned to the grill and flipped a patty. Flames erupted from the grease and lit up his eyes in bizarre orange reflections that made Eleanor remember the fate of David's last home.

"How you like your burger?" he asked her.

"However you're having them," she said.

"Medium-burned for everyone," he said.

"You must be cold, dear," said Karen to Eleanor. "You should have worn a coat. We'll eat inside, Jim."

"Okay," he said. "Make your buns."

The decorations she'd seen before were hung festively in the living room and kitchen. "Welcome Home Daddy!" in green, glittery letters hung just inside the door. Red, white, and blue balloons littered the floor. Wendy sat among them in front of the TV, playing with Odin. The cat ran purring to Eleanor when she came in and stared up at her with his one good eye before rubbing his chin on her ankle.

"I thought I was his favorite," complained Wendy.

"You are," Eleanor said, scratching the cat. "He just never sees me."

Karen set a bowl of potato salad on the table. Eleanor smelled cherry pie in the oven.

"It's a little late for a barbecue," David explained, "but this is what Dad wanted."

"Smells wonderful."

Mr. Venn came inside carrying a tray of cheeseburgers. He put it on the table and took the head seat. The others sat down.

"Dig in," he said. "I know I am."

David took a rare one on accident and bit into it before he noticed. The look of sudden revulsion on his face made Eleanor wince. She'd seen that face in biology and also in the doorway of her bathroom.

"They're not done, Jim," said Karen. David spit his food out on his plate.

"Mine's done," he said and took a big bite. Eleanor ate some salad. Hers was a little rare, but that didn't bother her.

"Don't be such a child, David," his father said. "Eat."

"I'll just throw it on for another minute," David said getting up.

His father's expression turned hard and angry but he didn't say anything. He watched David carry his plate outside and devoured his own burger with renewed enthusiasm.

He took a deep breath and turned to Eleanor. "So I hear you're my new daughter," he said. "What's your story?"

"Jim," chided Karen.

"I'm just asking. She has a tongue. I want to hear what she has to say."

"My mother died," she said. "Karen is acting as my legal guardian until the social service people decide what to do with me."

"Or she's eighteen," added Wendy, proud to make a contribution.

"But you don't live here," Mr. Venn said. "You have your own place?"

"Officially, she lives here, Jim," Karen said carefully. "Her mother had a place on Cedar Street. She stays there most days. There's more room there."

"Sounds like an easy arrangement," he said.

"I don't know what would have happened to me if it hadn't been for Karen and your family helping me. They're very kind."

"I remember you from before. David's had a crush on you forever," he said laughing.

"Don't embarrass David. He's not even here," said Karen.

"I'm sure Eleanor has figured it out by now, Karen. She's not blind."

"David looks out for me," she said.

"We look out for each other," David said from the doorway.

"That's the way it should be," Mr. Venn said. "Responsibility is what it's all about. You might not want to get your hands dirty, but your friends are your family, and your family is all that matters. To do any less is disloyal. To let them down is treason. That's what the army taught me, and I'm glad David learned it too."

Eleanor liked the sentiment but didn't understand why he'd said it.

"How's your burger, Eleanor? Too raw?" he asked.

"No, it's good," she said. "I can't wait for pie though."

"And ice cream!" squealed Wendy.

"I bet you're happy to be home, Mr. Venn. Must have been hard over there."

He thought for a moment. "It is good to be home," he said, "but it doesn't feel right."

"You'll get used to it, dear," said Karen. "This is your first night home."

"Feels like I left my buddies in a lurch," he said. "One day I was there at the front, the next, I was on a plane to Germany. Weird."

Karen put her sandwich down. "You were at the front? I thought you were administrative support?"

He spoke to his plate. "I volunteered for front-line combat," he said. "That's where I got the money for David's car."

After a long, uncomfortable moment Karen said, "You volunteered?"

"My duty," he said. "I was glad to do it. Got David his car."

"You volunteered for combat?" Karen said disbelievingly.

"And you went and sold the car, Davie. I swear times have changed since I was a teenager."

"We live in a trailer, Dad," David said. "We needed groceries more than a luxury car."

Eleanor saw the veins in his neck pulse and his face grow hot again, but after a glance at her, he relaxed.

"Looking out for the family," he said firmly. "Smart boy, David."

They went back to eating, but silent tension hung over the table. Eleanor tried to help.

"So it's good you're home now," she said. "Safe and sound."

"Exactly," Mr. Venn said. "I'm ready for pie."

The family cleared the table. While Karen cut the pie and

Wendy shoveled vanilla scoops onto little plates, the others settled in on the couches.

"Turn to the news, David," said his father. "Let's see what this hick town does for information."

He switched channels on the remote until he found one with a scrolling chyron, and a woman standing in front of Jamesford High with a microphone. Beside her stood Pastor Lugner, spouting about hellfire and devils, blasphemy, and unnatural experiments. The interview cut to scenes of the picketers and the school letting out. In horror Eleanor saw herself on the screen, a close-up of her face right after she'd been called a witch. Luckily the sound was of Lugner's interview and not the curses cast at her. Nevertheless, Eleanor's surprised and frightened face was a powerful counter-image to the confident preacher, and the screen held it there for five long seconds.

"Hey, look, that's Eleanor," said Wendy. "You're on TV. You're famous!"

CHAPTER THIRTEEN

A week before the rodeo, Mrs. Westlake was put on administrative leave for picketing with the Revealers on school property. Jennifer's punishment for her outburst during the assembly kept her out of school for a day.

Mrs. Westlake had never been particularly kind to Eleanor, and things had gotten worse since the Revealers started picketing in Jamesford, but Eleanor wished she'd been there those days before the rodeo. With only three days until the school would travel to Dubois, she had yet to perfect her maple spice recipe. She wouldn't have liked it, but Mrs. Westlake might have been able to tell her where her problem lay. The ingredients were expensive, and she hated wasting them in failed attempts to isolate the problem flavor. The substitute teacher, Ms. Moore, didn't know much about cooking beyond following a recipe, and Eleanor was far beyond that. Her homemade maple spice was an evolved pastry and a real contender for a ribbon.

While David practiced at the pistol range with his father, Eleanor stayed late every day after school trying different baking powders and spices until she thought she'd never be able to look at another piece of maple spice cake again. But finally, aided by her uncanny sense of smell, she found a recipe that pleased her and had three cakes ready in time for Friday's rodeo.

The day before the rodeo, she waited outside the school for David and his father to drive her home. She couldn't manage the cakes alone. She left them in the school office and sat on a bench in the front enjoying the last of the fall scents, leaves and hay, fresh carved pumpkins and fallen apples. Eleanor liked fall. It was the most sensual of seasons.

Ramos walked up to the school. He wore new clothes: several new layers of grimy wool sweaters and fresh cargo pants. His stuttering steps caused him to zigzag off the sidewalk and into the street, but he made slow, steady progress toward the school. He still needed a bath. Students waiting for rides whispered and giggled as he approached. Eleanor thought to retreat into the office but didn't. She was training herself not to be so afraid.

He staggered to a lamppost and held on to it for a moment. He blinked across the courtyard, and taking aim at the flagpole, shuffled forward. Before reaching the pole, however, he veered off and sat on a bench.

"You don't know what you're talking about," he slurred to no one.

David's Honda pulled into the parking lot. Eleanor stood up and waved, then went inside for a cake before meeting the car on the curb.

"I have two more just inside the door," she said. David got out to fetch them. His father was behind the wheel.

"You're that skank who picks up guys at gas stations," Ramos said at her.

"What did you say?" David said.

"Leave it," she said. "He's drunk."

"She caused the drought," said the hobo. "She's poison."

"I ought to smash your grubby face in," David said.

"You're a sniveling, snotty brat," he slurred. "You're crap on my boot."

David stepped toward him.

"Hold on, David," said Principal Curtz. Eleanor saw Mr. Venn get out of the car and stand in the open door.

"Someone gotta say it," Ramos said. "Bad genes. Probably got webbed toes and a missing rib. Shoulda tossed this kid in a dumpster."

"You're trespassing," the principal said. "Leave now, or I'll have you arrested."

"He's nearly as ugly as that slut over there." He pointed an unsteady finger at Eleanor then turned it on David. "Not surprising since your mother's probably a sow." David rushed him. He crashed into him shoulder-first and leveled Ramos to the pavement. The bum yelled in pain and surprise. Curtz dashed forward and pulled David off him, but not before he had landed a solid punch into Ramos's nose and a kick in his side.

"David, calm down," called his father running up. "He's not worth it."

"You trash! I hope you die!" yelled David.

Ramos got to his feet and glared at David. David's father took a step toward him and that made him run. They all watched him trip down the road toward the highway as fast as he could.

David stormed into the school, Eleanor followed, and together they brought the cakes out.

No one spoke until they were nearly to Eleanor's house when Mr. Venn said, "What was that all about?"

"That guy called Karen a pig," said Eleanor when David didn't speak.

"And he called you a . . ." spluttered David.

"So, a battle of honor," grinned Mr. Venn. "Well done, son. Well done." He slapped David on the knee with pride. David looked up as if he'd been shocked.

"You think so, Dad?"

"He had it coming," he said. "That he did. If you get any flack for this, let me know and I'll go in guns ablazing. So to speak."

"I think you hurt him," said Eleanor.

"You taught him a lesson, Dave. That's what matters."

From the backseat, Eleanor saw David look at his father in a new way.

"That was a pretty good tackle, son," said Mr. Venn.

"You should have seen me on Russell last year. I really smashed him up."

"I assume he had it coming?"

"He fought dirty, Mr. Venn. Tried to kick David when he was down," said Eleanor.

"But you won? Great! Always put up the good fight. Stick up for your family. I'm proud of you."

Eleanor was glad some of the frost had melted between them, but she couldn't join in the *esprit de corps*. David's temper unsettled her. It hadn't been necessary to hit the homeless man. The problem could have been solved another way.

They helped her inside with her cakes and promised to pick her up early the next morning.

The day of the rodeo, schools from all over the county and the Wild River Reservation descended upon the little town of

Dubois, Wyoming. It was their turn to host. The little town showed its pride with banners and picnic tables, tents, flags, free coffee, and plenty of parking.

At the Jamesford tents, excitement over the rodeo ebbed long enough to hear how David had sent away the foul-mouthed drunkard. The story had permeated the entire town but they wanted to hear David tell it.

"He's a creep," said Alexi. "The things he said to me I can't repeat."

"So David Venn is a hero for punching that bum," said Russell, "and Sheriff Hannon locks me up for doing the same last month. That's justice for you."

"Maybe you should have hit him in front of a teacher instead of in an alley," said Crystal.

He shot her a dirty look.

"He had it coming then too," said Barbara in his defense.

"Were you there?" Eric asked.

"Did I have to be?" said Barbara.

"Nuts," said David, looking at a clock. "Russell, we gotta book. Pistols in ten minutes." The shooters collected their things and hurried off to the range. Everyone who didn't have practice time followed them. Eleanor and the other cooks had already dropped their food off in the cafeteria for judging. The riders disappeared to the stables to prepare their mounts.

Eleanor found the Venns huddled in blankets on a berm overlooking the contest.

"Can't see much from up here," said Karen.

"Couldn't see anything down there either," said Mr. Venn, "but up here, David can see us, know we're rooting for him."

"He's a good shot, Mr. Venn," said Eleanor. "I'd be surprised if he didn't finish toward the top."

"Call me Jim. I saw last year's trophy," he said. "Hey what's going on down there now?"

Eleanor heard Russell arguing with the judge.

"Russell Liddle is trying to get David disqualified for using that kind of gun," she said.

"But they're on the same team?" he said getting up.

Eleanor tugged his coat. "It's over now," she said. "David gets to shoot."

"Little punk. Has he no sense of loyalty?" he said. "Hey, how did you know what was happening?"

"He tried the same thing last year."

The rest of the shooting came off without incident.

David took first place again, and his dad was there to join in the celebration and hold the trophy for a picture. Eleanor stayed away. She'd been photographed enough for one week.

At lunchtime, Eleanor carried her tray of food to Midge's table. She had a bowl of venison chili, milk, salad, and a selection of desserts that'd been judged against hers. She almost turned around when she saw Henry Creek sit down at the table a moment before she arrived. She took a deep breath and sat down anyway.

"Hello, Henry," she said. "Mind if I sit here?"

"Of course not," Midge said.

Eleanor tasted a cream pie that hadn't bothered to use real lemons, a chocolate cake that was too sweet, and a decent peach pie.

Henry kept his gaze on his plate. Midge shifted uncomfortably in her chair but smiled brightly when Eleanor looked at her.

Eleanor looked at Henry, "So, you think I'm a witch?" she said. "I'm getting pretty sick of hearing that."

Henry sighed.

"I heard about that stupid homeless guy, Eleanor," Midge said. "Glad David socked him."

Henry met Eleanor's stare. "I've been rude," he said. "You've done nothing to me and I'm sorry."

"Why the change of heart?" she asked bitterly, not believing the contrition in his tone. "Do you still think I'm *Nimirika?*"

"If you are, then I should respect you as a part of my people's history. If you aren't, then I shouldn't call you one."

It was a sincere answer but didn't address her question.

"So, you don't know?" she asked him.

"No," he said softly.

"Eleanor, you won!" It was Barbara. "You won best dish. Not only best dessert, but best dish! You got a trophy!"

"Don't tease her," said Midge.

Barbara grabbed Eleanor's arm from behind and pulled her up. She led her across the cafeteria to the dessert table. A tall, gold trophy stood behind the last slice of Eleanor's maple spice cake, declaring it best dish of the day. Eleanor scanned the large buffet table and saw ribbons for best dishes in each category, but only she had a trophy.

Jamesford pride transcended personal rivalry and Eleanor found herself hugged by Barbara. The rest of the team came up and congratulated her. The ones who hadn't been quick enough to get a piece of cake begged her to make another when they got back.

Eleanor couldn't help but get caught up in the excitement. Her pulse raced with pride as people she didn't know stepped forward to congratulate her and rain praises on her work. Jamesford people spoke her name with admiration. If she'd had any doubts about her acceptance among her peers, it dissolved that day in their smiles and applause, with Henry Creek's strange apology still echoing in her mind.

Eleanor sat with friends at the horsemanship competition and found herself not only rooting for her fellow classmates, but actually cheering Alexi and Barbara in their events.

At the ending ceremonies, Eleanor joined her school in the Cowboy Fight Song, including the traditional wolf whoop at the end of it. If anyone noticed the strangely authentic wolf howl mixed in with the other voices, no one said anything.

Though the Shoshone dominated all the riding contests, Jamesford's kids brought home several trophies and a dozen ribbons. The riding contests were the most esteemed, but that didn't detract from Eleanor's pride in her own accomplishment.

Driving back to Jamesford that evening in Karen's van, Eleanor sat next to David in the back seat. While he dozed in the long straightaways, Eleanor looked out the windows. The moonlit winter landscape didn't seem so cold any more. She cradled her trophy in her lap. It was an inexpensive, simple thing: a plastic base with a brass plaque, a gold cup atop a broad pillar, but Eleanor held it like it was hope itself.

CHAPTER FOURTEEN

Saturday, Eleanor woke up feeling light. She looked around her little room and saw her trophy on her trunk. It touched the ceiling where it slanted down, making it look bigger than it was. The morning sun made it shine, and the memories of winning it made her happy.

After breakfast, she decided to bake another round of her cakes to give as gifts. She didn't know who'd get one, but she felt a desire to share, and the feeling was too good to ignore.

She cheerfully assembled the ingredients, happy she hadn't taken them all to school. Her little oven meant she'd need to bake them one at a time, but that was all right. She had all day.

David called just after she'd put the first one in the oven.

"What's wrong?" she asked. She heard the stress in the first word he spoke.

"Eleanor, do you know where my gun is?"

"Your pistol? Didn't you put in the car after shooting?"

"I thought I did, but I can't find it now."

"Does she know?" It was David's father in the background. Eleanor could hear anger in his voice and fear in David's.

"Let me think," she said. "I remember seeing it on the judge's table. Have you called Dubois? Maybe they found it."

"They didn't," he said miserably. "Do you remember anything at all?"

Eleanor's memory was good, but yesterday's events were all a jumble of joyous emotions.

"We separated after the shooting contest," she said. "I went to the cafeteria tent, and you went with your dad somewhere."

"The gun's really expensive," he said. "My dad's really mad."

"Did you search the van?"

"Of course," he said.

"Get in the car," Eleanor heard Mr. Venn say. "We better go look for it."

"I gotta go, Eleanor," he said. "If you think of anything, call me, okay?"

"Sure," she said.

"And don't tell anyone it's missing."

"Why?"

"It's an embarrassment. And there might be a legal thing too. Dad says to keep it quiet until we've had a chance to look for it."

"Come on, David. Get in the car. Now." Jim's voice was menacing and cross.

"I gotta go."

Eleanor remembered David having the gun after the competition. It was in a black metal case. He didn't have it when she saw him again, but that was nearly an hour later.

The rodeo excitement paled in Eleanor's thoughts as she imagined someone stealing David's prized gun from the back of his mom's van while she took congratulations about her cake. Her suspicions went to Russell, but there were hundreds of people who could have grabbed it. She was sure it was lost. The best she could hope for was that Mr. Venn would understand it hadn't been David's fault. He was the victim.

David called later that night. Still no gun. He'd ask around at school on Monday.

Sunday morning, Sheriff Hannon knocked on Eleanor's door at eight o'clock. She had woken at the sound of the car pulling up. From her bedroom window, she watched the sheriff get out and walk to her door.

She quickly threw on some clothes and climbed down the ladder. Before answering the knock, she put on her shoes, unlatched the back door, and put some money in her pocket.

She left the chain on and peered out the narrow crack at her visitor.

"What's wrong, Sheriff?" Eleanor asked.

"I'd like you to come with me," he said.

"Am I under arrest? What did I do?"

"No, nothing like that," he said. "It'll just be easier if you come with me. You're in no trouble. It'll just be easier if you come."

Eleanor searched his face for clues and threats. She was afraid. A year ago, she'd never have answered the door. She'd be over the fence and up the river before the sheriff got back in his car. But she was trying on a new persona, a confident fighter who didn't balk at her own shadow. It wasn't an easy shift, but she was trying. Besides, she thought she knew what this was about.

"You'd be doing me a favor," he said, "if you just come along."

His face was sincere. He'd been kind to Eleanor when he

hadn't needed to be. She'd been suspicious of his motives, as she was of any kindness, but he had done her favors.

"Let me get my coat," she said.

Eleanor climbed into the backseat of the sheriff's SUV and felt a surge of panic when she realized there were no handles on the inside of the doors and a wire mesh stood between the front and back seats. She was trapped.

Sudden, cold sweat trickled down her back, and her heart raced to catch up to her frightened breathing. She felt vulnerable. She looked at the cage and the glass windows and wondered how hard it would be to break the glass, rip away the mesh with her bare hands, and crawl away. With a start, she felt her hands harden. Pinpricks and deep aching signaled the beginnings of a change. Her hands were turning into weapons. Once before this had happened, once before had she felt an unknown shape take control of her body. It would turn her into a beast, a lethal weapon, savage and strong. A fingernail fell off her right hand and tumbled to the floor. In its place a thick claw, catlike and sharp, tried to form at her bleeding and blackening fingertip.

"David," she said out loud, forcing herself to think of him. "David," she said.

"He's in no trouble," said the sheriff. "Don't worry about him."

"I'm hungry," she said just to say words, human words, a mantra of reason against what her body was doing. "I'm hungry."

"We have donuts at the station," he said. "I'll send out for a breakfast burrito if you like. Least I can do for taking up your Sunday morning."

"Protein, vitamins, salt," she said.

"Hey, I heard you did real good in Dubois. Way to go. First cooking trophy we ever got. Don't forget to bring it to school on Monday so Principal Curtz can display it in the window."

"Maple spice cake," she said. She recalled ingredients: cinnamon, maple, sugar, and yeast. She remembered the three cakes on her counter, the ones she'd share with her friends at school tomorrow. That thought stayed her transformation.

"Ouch," she said as her hands began to reverse the change and her breathing slowed to near normal.

"Those seats aren't made for comfort," he said. "But we're here now."

He pulled into the station and quickly got out to open Eleanor's door. She tried to exit calmly and gracefully, but dashed out just the same.

"Claustrophobic?" Hannon asked.

"I guess so," she said. She concealed her finger in her other hand and gritted her teeth against the pain.

"Can I use the bathroom real quick?" she asked.

"Oh, yeah, sure," he said and opened the door for her. "There on the left."

Eleanor scurried into the lavatory and checked her face. It was flushed, but not different. Her usual worried expression looked back at her. She searched the walls for windows, just in case, but found none. Again she was trapped. She studied her hands, clenching and opening her fingers slowly and deliberately until they no longer felt like clubs or knives.

She studied her finger where the nail had fallen off. It looked unnatural and blunt, pinched and pink. It wouldn't do. She focused her attention to it. She stared at it, willing the nail to come back. She felt the tremor start at her shoulder and run down her elbow, then up her wrist, and into her finger. It hurt. She let it.

Her finger grew hot, and then a milky slab slid out of her skin like a playing card pushed from a deck. She pushed it out of her hand with muscles that would disintegrate painfully when the task was complete. The nail stopped suddenly when it was uniform with her others, but there was a moment, a brief moment before the muscles relaxed, when she felt she could have done more, make her nail longer, thicker, shorter, color it even. It was a moment of potential that went beyond mimicry. But then it was gone and her hand ached as muscles realigned and dissolved.

She could do this, she told herself. The sheriff said she was in no danger and she had to believe him. She owed him a debt. He'd believed her about her mother's death, but then again, she'd lied.

She drank from the tap. She was hungry, and the water helped. She washed her hands, fixed her hair, and flushed a toilet before meeting the sheriff in the lobby.

"So when do I find out what this is all about?"

"Right now," he said. A deputy pushed a button that opened a lock to a door leading deeper into the building. Passing through it, she chuckled to herself when she realized she was again trapped. Everything was a trap here. She had to stay calm.

He led her down a narrow hall to an interrogation room. Inside, Ms. Lamb from Homeland Security was sitting at a table reading a file.

"Is this about the Revealers?" Eleanor asked.

"Nothing that creepy," she said. "I'm just helping out another agency."

Eleanor sat down in a chair, but the sheriff stayed standing. Eleanor kept her hands in her lap, her face up, and tried to keep her wits about her.

She watched Ms. Lamb turn a page and then look at Eleanor. She studied her face and then went back to the folder.

"It's weird," said Agent Lamb.

"So what do we do?" asked the sheriff.

"Might as well bring them in," she said.

He nodded and left.

"Really," Eleanor said. "Someone better tell me what's going on right now."

"How long have you lived in Jamesford?"

"My mom and I moved here ten years ago," she said.

"Where before that?"

"Utah," she said.

"You were born in Utah?"

"Yes," she said, proud that her voice sounded sure and unbroken while her belly did cartwheels. "What's this about, Agent Lamb?"

Sheriff Hannon returned with two people. There was a woman in her fifties, a little plump, bobbed hair, and tanned. She wore a sensible floral blouse and cotton slacks with comfortable shoes. She'd been crying. The man wore jeans and a flannel shirt, work boots, and a scuffed belt. His face was tanned and wrinkled from years in the sun so Eleanor could only guess at his age, but she put it near the woman's, in his mid to late fifties. His hands were gnarled and strong from work.

The policeman fell silent and watched. Eleanor studied the strangers' faces and they studied hers. Suddenly, she recognized the eyes of the woman, the chin of the man, the auburn hair they both shared.

Eleanor screamed and sprang to her feet.

The woman was on her in a second. She threw herself forward and pinned Eleanor against the wall. She held her in a strangling embrace, buried her face in Eleanor's shoulder and cried, "Celeste! Celeste! Thank God, we've found you!"

CHAPTER FIFTEEN

"Get away from me!" screamed Eleanor, struggling against the woman. "I don't know you!"

Agent Lamb jumped up and tried to pull her off. The woman held tight and peppered Eleanor's thrashing head with weeping kisses.

"Celeste! Celeste," she moaned. "We were so worried."

"Get her away from me," said Eleanor, finally freeing herself. She scurried into the corner as far as she could go. Sheriff Hannon and the man blocked the door or she'd have made for it and tried her luck with the locks and the deputies.

In the woman's face Eleanor saw much of her own. She recognized it, but it was different in the light. The man Eleanor knew well. She remembered him standing over her, pointing a rifle at her chest. She remembered him striking her in the moonlight. She remembered him from nearly a decade before aiming another gun at her while she ran from the laughing Celeste. She remembered waiting for the sound of that gun, the burn of the bullet in her side as she ran into the woods, ready to start a new life, afraid he would end it before she had the chance to begin.

Fighting against Agent Lamb, the woman reached out to Eleanor as if touching her again meant the difference between her living and dying. Eleanor cringed back as if she were on fire.

"I don't know these people," Eleanor said. She knew she looked scared. She was scared. She was literally cornered. Her body wanted to arm itself, create thick primeval hide, scales of armor, fat and bone, claw and tooth, but she fought it. She turned the seething energies aside. Though her head swam and throbbed with ubiquitous pain—the punishment for the stuttering collapse of her reflexive change—she forced herself to focus. She had to think her way out of this nightmare, bluff her way through. Think and escape, or all would be lost.

"Sheriff Hannon," Eleanor said. "Please explain."

"Eleanor," he began. "These people—"

"Eleanor?" interrupted the man. "Her name is Celeste. Your name is Celeste. What are you trying to do? What are you doing to your mother?"

"Mr. Batton," the sheriff said. "I know this girl. Her name is Eleanor Anders. I think you have the wrong person."

"Don't you think a mother would know her own daughter?" demanded Mrs. Batton between garbled sobs. "What are you trying to do, daughter? Tell him, Celeste. Stop this game. Come home now."

"I'm Eleanor," she said. "I live on Ceder Street. I live in Jamesford, Wyoming. My mother died last spring. I won a trophy on Friday. I've never been to Nebraska."

"Goddammit Celeste, this isn't funny," the man said. "Stop this nonsense this minute. Do you know how much trouble you've caused?"

"I am not Celeste," Eleanor said.

"Stop it, Celeste. Why are you so cruel?" the mother cried.

"Sheriff," said the man, "this is our daughter. I don't know what lies she's told you, but this is Celeste Batton, age seventeen from Nebraska."

"I'm sixteen," Eleanor said. "Look, here's my school ID." She took the card from her pocket and tossed it to Ms. Lamb who looked at it before passing it on.

"What is this?" she said.

"I think it's a case of mistaken identity, Mr. Batton," said Sheriff Hannon, "and you're scaring the wits out of this girl."

"That's my Celeste. You can see the family resemblance," said the man. "We gave you pictures. Look at the pictures."

The sheriff leaned over Ms. Lamb's shoulder, and together they studied a photo. Eleanor didn't like the uncertainty in their faces.

"Can I go home?" Eleanor said.

"Not just yet," said Ms. Lamb.

"What are you doing here?" she said to Lamb. "Am I being accused of terrorism again?"

"What?" said Mr. Batton.

"No, Eleanor," Ms. Lamb said.

"Celeste," the man corrected her.

"It's a missing person case," she said to Eleanor. "My agency is assisting the FBI. They don't have an agent here."

"It's a found person case, you mean," the man said. "Get in the car, Celeste. We're going home." He moved around to grab Eleanor. The sheriff stepped in front of him.

Hannon said, "She says she's not your daughter."

"We know our daughter. I'm looking at her. She's playing some game. She's mad at us. She's punishing us. It's a game. That's Celeste. This is nuts."

"If you won't let me go home, call Karen and Jim. I want them here," Eleanor said.

"Who're Karen and Jim?" asked Mrs. Batton.

"Eleanor's legal guardians," said the sheriff.

"This is nuts," repeated the man.

"Mr. and Mrs. Batton, I suggest you wait in the other room."

"Nuts. Just nuts."

Sheriff Hannon opened the door and led them out.

When the room was cleared, and it was just Eleanor and Agent Lamb, Eleanor crept out of her corner and retook her chair.

"There're no windows in here," she said. "I have claustrophobia."

"It's an interview room," Lamb said. "They never have windows. You're lucky there's a clock."

"Can I go home?"

"Not just yet," she said. "Those people think you're their daughter. I think it's best that we settle this now one way or the other, don't you?"

"No," Eleanor said. "I want to go home. Am I under arrest?"

"I said no."

"Then why can't I leave?"

"Suspect in a missing persons case," she said.

She swallowed and tried to focus. She felt every muscle, every fiber, every cell in her body fighting to become something else, something more useful. Something dangerous.

"So, what's their story?" she asked. "Who's Celeste?"

Lamb looked at her stack of papers, several boxy official forms with handwritten check marks and descriptions, a long typewritten report with the title "Statement" at the top, and a few photos of Celeste Batton—some old, some new, some that looked exactly like Eleanor Anders did today.

"Celeste Batton is a young woman who lives, or rather lived, with her family on a farm not far from Minden, Nebraska," she said. "Last August, she and her parents got in a fight, a real screamer by the sound of it. Two days later, Celeste was gone. For reasons above my pay grade, they're not calling it a runaway. They called an Amber Alert and have been looking for her ever since."

"That's sad. Why are they in Jamesford?"

"Looking for their daughter," she said.

"This some kind of career opportunity for you?" Eleanor said. "Harassing me like this?"

"I don't remember you being this insolent."

"I want to go home," she said.

"How'd you know they were from Nebraska?" she asked.

"I saw a license plate coming in," she lied quickly.

"You look an awful lot like her, you know," she said. "It's uncanny really. Practically twins." She slid a picture of Celeste across the table. It was a large color photograph. It had a gold monograph in the corner with a year stamp. It was Celeste's most recent yearbook picture. The face looking out at the camera was Eleanor's own. It might have been a mirror. Agent Lamb watched Eleanor as she studied the picture.

"You don't look surprised," she said.

She should have gasped. She should have reacted. She'd been too calm.

"I've seen Photoshop before," she said.

"Let me see that again," Lamb said. Eleanor flipped the photo back to her.

"Eleanor, the Venns will be here in a minute," the sheriff said, coming in.

"Listen, I'm sorry to hear about those people's sad situation, but they've made a mistake. You told them that right?"

"Yeah, I told them," he said. "But they're convinced you're their daughter."

"Not my problem," Eleanor said.

"Fingerprints," said Ms. Lamb. "We could clear this up with a comparison of fingerprints. I could even do it."

Eleanor felt a scream form in her throat but choked it back.

"They don't have any," the sheriff said. "I already thought of that."

"DNA then," said Lamb. "We have the parents and we have her," she gestured to Eleanor like she was a bloodstain on the floor. "Cost maybe a hundred bucks. Take about a week if we have to send it out."

"Or you could cut me open and count the rings," said Eleanor. "This is stupid. Agent Lamb might not know me, but, Sheriff, you've known me for years. Check my school record. This is stupid, and you're scaring me. Haven't I endured enough official harassment?"

Miss Lamb regarded her skeptically. The sheriff, however, nodded.

"Yeah," he said. "Just a weird coincidence. Let's get you home."

"Sheriff," Ms. Lamb said. "Look at this photo. Look at the arm. They have the same bruise."

"Looks just like you, Eleanor," he said.

"I don't own a dress that nice," she said in her defense.

"How'd you get that bruise?"

"I don't know. I think I got it sleeping."

He bent in close to scrutinize the photo. Maybe he'd seen a scar or a blemish. Would he notice Eleanor's pierced ears and remember never having seen her wear earrings before?

"Isn't that supposed to be an old photo?" Eleanor asked. "Looks like the kind of thing you get on the first day of school. It's practically November now. You're comparing an old photo of her to a new me. It's an illusion. You're scaring me again. Let me go or give me a lawyer."

It was something she'd seen on TV and didn't know if it would mean anything, but desperation was bubbling like a boiling pot inside her. She felt the panicked animal inside trying to get out, wanting to try its clawing, biting, running solution to this terrible problem.

When the sheriff hesitated, Eleanor began to cry. It was a tightrope letting the tears come and not the rest of it, but she held it together enough to play on his sympathy until he led her out of the room and down the hall.

From behind an office door, a young boy peeked out. Eleanor didn't know the child, but the cheekbones, eyes, and tawny hair could belong to none other than Celeste's brother.

"Ceely?" he said. "Ceely, come back."

Eleanor flashed back to another five-year-old brother, a tan boy with jet-black hair and eyes deep enough to swim in. She couldn't remember his name, but after years of trying, she could summon the emotions around him. She missed the little boy, her brother, her murdered brother. She could just recall his lively smile and dead stare in the same thought. He told her from the past to be careful; he showed her what trusting people can get you. He warned her. She wondered if it was already too late. She hurried her step to the door, to the sunshine, and the open air where she still might dash to Canada and hide for another half century. Maybe longer, maybe forever.

She could be anything. Why human? She'd encountered no dangers so terrible, so insidious or painful in nature as she'd met as a person among people. Never as a golden-brown coyote in the wilds of the mountains, chased by dogs, hunted by men, frozen in blizzards, and wracked by thirst did she suffer and fear the way she did as a quiet girl in sleepy Jamesford. Friend or enemy, it was cut and dried in the wild. Among people, there were shifting shades of faithfulness, and betrayal was always just a word away.

Eleanor felt the stares of the deputies as she was marched out of the secure areas and into the reception room.

"I can't give you a ride home," the sheriff explained. "Not right now. But the Venns will be here soon."

"Maybe I'll walk," she said, meaning run, but why stop lying now? "Sheriff Hannon, how did they ever land on me?"

"One of their friends saw you on television. They showed up last night with a photo of you, uhm, I mean their daughter, and asked for our help. Lamb is here as a favor to the FBI. It's their case."

"She thinks I'm Celeste," Eleanor said.

"You do look like her."

"But you know I'm not. You know I'm Eleanor Anders."

"Yeah," he said. "Don't worry."

CHAPTER SIXTEEN

Karen picked Eleanor up two blocks from the police station. She'd waited in reception as long as she could and then set out walking for home within five minutes. She'd listened as the sheriff argued with the Battons, heated words and calm, sane explanations mixing like water and oil.

"What's going on?" asked Karen after Eleanor had scampered into the car. David was there and Wendy. Mr. Venn was not. "Is it about David's gun?"

"No. It's about me," she said. "I guess there's a girl from Nebraska who's gone missing. I look like her."

David went white.

"Well at least it's not about the gun," said Karen.

She took Eleanor home, not even offering to take her to the trailer. She speculated it had something to do with why David's father had not come with them to get her.

Principal Curtz took the opportunity of Jamesford High's rodeo success to have a pep assembly as a cure for the mixed reception of Zalarnik's presentation. The next day's mid-morning classes were canceled, and the rodeo participants were recognized in front of the entire school, not just the high school, but also the middle and elementary school were summoned to support Jamesford pride.

When Mr. Curtz called Eleanor up to the stage, she had to be pushed from her seat to move.

"Get up there," said Barbara. "What are you waiting for?"

"Better to get it over with," said Midge, understanding her better.

Reluctantly, Eleanor shuffled up to the stage. Mr. Curtz grasped her hands and beamed with pride as he led her to a microphone.

It was becoming her natural state of being to be terrified out of her wits but still not run away screaming.

"The first ever culinary trophy in Jamesford's history. Best dish of the county!" Mr. Curtz proclaimed to applause.

"Tell us, Eleanor," he said, coaxing her forward. "What's your secret?"

She'd been hiding behind her hair and staring at the floor, but at Mr. Curtz's urging, she looked up at the audience and blushed. So many eyes, so many faces, so much danger. There were faces that waited anxiously for her to speak, encouraging her. Her friends, Midge, Aubrey, David, Eric, and even Barbara and Robby smiled for her. There were those faces who couldn't care less and suffered through the boring assembly like any other, with whispers, texts, and iPods, squirming under the shushes from peeved teachers. These were the greatest number. But Eleanor also felt unkind eyes upon her. Jennifer stared daggers into her, and Tanner and Russell snarled. Then in the aisle, just at the door, she saw the figures of the Battons. Two adults, a small boy and a babe in arms. They were watching her.

She recalled Tabitha's voice, her weak throat, always dry and ticklish. She remembered the feeling of her tongue against the roof of her mouth and concentrated. She cleared her throat.

For the Battons' sake, she said in a distorted voice, "Real ingredients. Nothing artificial. Real butter and maple."

"Congratulations, Eleanor!" Mr. Curtz said. "I understand the yearbook committee is hunting you for the recipe. Will you share it?"

"Sure," she said.

Mr. Curtz clapped his hands to draw applause as Eleanor faded upstage to stand next to the other winners.

Eleanor wondered at the sound she'd made. She'd concocted a new voice from the pieces of several others. She could of course mimic and replicate sounds with complete fidelity, but original sounds were something else. Once before, she had merged sounds into a unique utterance. Then it had been animal, and it had been reflexive, instinctive. She'd wanted to intimidate a clerk and had done it before she realized what was happening. This time, she'd willed it. She'd caused it. She'd wanted it, created it, and it had come. It was a breakthrough.

She thought back on the control she'd had the previous day. She'd managed to control the panic and curb her metamorphosis more easily than ever before. It had hurt, it had been hard, but she'd done it. She'd faced, in the flesh, one of the greatest fears she'd ever imagined and passed through it. It was another achievement. Not only had she shown control, but also courage and quick-wittedness.

She didn't know what it all meant. It seemed strangely unfair and rushed. She was finally making discoveries, learning to use and control her talents just as her entire life fell apart. She chided herself for not having had the courage to experiment before. Love for Tabitha and the fear of rejection from her foster mother had kept so much of her hidden. Was it her mother's death that had freed her to examine herself more closely? She'd changed emotionally after the death, after David had come, after Celeste this summer. Inside her, she identified a hunger, a yearning she had not known before and could not name. It was movement. It was more than a desire to flee and hide, it was more profound, it was abstract. It was a desire to fulfill potential. It was a new sensation, and it was somehow coupled with her pride of achievement and the recognition by her peers.

Mr. Curtz asked all the winners to step forward for another bow. Eleanor felt David slide his hand into hers and wondered how long he'd stood beside her. She'd missed his entire introduction and acclaim. A senior girl who'd ribboned in roping took her other hand, and the entire line of eight students stepped forward and gave a theatrical bow to the audience before being excused to their regular schedules.

"You okay?" David asked Eleanor as they left the stage.

"A little shook up, I guess," she said.

"I understand that. What are you going to do?"

Eleanor noticed, perhaps unkindly, the use of the singular in his question. He did not say "what are we going to do," but "you." She stopped and considered how to respond, whether to challenge him or not. She decided to let it go.

"I don't know," she said. "Did you find your gun?"

"No," he said, and his voice sank. "My dad is so angry. He wanted to hit me, but tore up the trailer instead."

"That doesn't sound like him," she said.

"Eleanor, he's a totally different person than he appears. Sure, with you, in public and all that, he's Mr. Perfect Dad, but he's not that way at home. Not that way at night or when he's drinking. He's mean. He scares me. He says I owe him a thousand dollars for the gun."

"I thought he gave it to you," she said. "That doesn't make sense."

"Tell me about it."

"It'll turn up," she said.

She searched the exits for the Battons, but they were gone. She found them with Sheriff Hannon in the school office as they walked to class. They were waiting in the chairs reserved for disciplinary cases and looked about as comfortable as kids did in those chairs.

"That's them," Eleanor whispered to David.

He paused and squinted at them. "I can see it," he said. "Same features. Damn."

Eleanor waited for the other shoe to drop all week, but it didn't come. When Halloween rolled around, she joined David and Wendy in their trick-or-treating up Jacob's Ranch. As they walked up the dirt road where Russell had attacked them the year before, they didn't speak. Russell was still surly, but he'd come to some truce with David that Eleanor didn't understand. She suspected Barbara was behind it.

Wendy's endurance was short and after only an hour she begged to go home. Halfway there, David had to carry her because her feet were so tired. Eleanor and David hardly spoke.

At the Venn house, Eleanor saw signs of recent damage; a tear in the wallpaper, a mended picture frame, a new coffee maker. She noted them at a glance. Karen was at work and Jim sat in front of the TV with a beer. He hadn't showered.

"How was the begging?" he called when they came in. "Did you get lots of candy?"

"It's not begging," David said.

"Sorry," he said, seeing Eleanor. "Just kidding." He ran his fingers through his hair and sat up a little.

"So you're really from Nebraska, eh?" he said.

Eleanor smiled. "I guess everyone has a twin somewhere. I know a man that looks like Vincent D'Onofrio. People always tell him."

"I feel bad for them," he said in a wave of emotion that made her uncomfortable. "Family is everything. I bet they hate themselves right now. Blame themselves for her missing. Wondering how things would have been different had they been there."

"I better go," Eleanor said.

"I'll walk you," said David.

Outside, Eleanor saw Odin squirm out from beneath the neighbor's trailer and limp up to her. She mewed and it responded. He purred when she picked him up but hissed when she brushed him.

"His leg is hurt," she said.

"My dad did that," David said. "He has a temper."

"He's not the only one," Eleanor said.

"What is that supposed to mean?" he said.

Eleanor put the cat down. The injury wasn't severe. The leg wasn't broken, just sore.

"You didn't need to hit Ramos," she said. "At the school. You didn't need to do that."

They walked out of the trailer park and across the street. Eleanor led the way through backyards and abandoned lots, a short-cut as the crow flies.

"My dad said that was the best thing he'd ever seen me do."

"The sentiment was correct," she said. "But you could have done it differently."

"He had it coming."

"He was drunk. He's poor and alone."

"He's a creep. Don't make excuses for him."

Eleanor sighed. She didn't like Ramos, but she'd always felt sorry for him. There were very few people in Jamesford who she thought had a harder life than she did. Ramos was one of them. She'd allowed herself to believe him to be noble beneath his rags. She could see past rags. She'd been in rags. She'd been without even rags. But this year she'd been forced to see him differently. There was a meanness in him she tried to ignore. Whether it was his fault or fate, he was definitely not a nice guy now.

"I just think it could have been done differently," she said.

He snorted. He didn't hold her hand. He hadn't touched her affectionately in a long time. She missed him and stole glances at him; his long eyelashes silhouetted against the streetlight, his hair a thick muss, his cheeks reddening from the cold. Even estranged, she found him beautiful and couldn't replace her old, bright feelings with new, dark ones. Beneath it all, she loved him. She hoped he did too. Eleanor remembered the electricity they shared when their lips touched. David had described it as a "bolt of life" up his spine. She longed for another bolt, but the distance was too great to hope for just then. Patience. There was time. For a while, at least, there was time.

"Maybe you're right," he said after a while. The sliver moon slid behind a racing cloud, the precursor to a winter storm that would settle over the town that weekend. "I liked that my dad was happy with me."

"I can see why you wouldn't want him to be unhappy," she said.

"Hey, don't say that. He's not always like that."

"Now who's making excuses?" she said.

He hesitated. He looked for her face in the darkness but she didn't turn. He gave up and went on walking. "You're probably right again," he said. "Things are all messed up."

"For both of us," she said.

Before they turned onto Cedar Street, David reached out for her hand to help her up a small embankment. His hand was warm, and Eleanor was glad to touch it. When she was up, she was glad when he didn't let go.

The lunging orange flames were so bright, reached so high, that Eleanor thought at first it was her house on fire. Only after her eyes grew accustomed to the brightness did she recognize the shape of a cross in her front yard glowing beneath the raging fire.

"Oh, God," David said.

"Not God," she said. "But surely in his name."

CHAPTER SEVENTEEN

The fire department had the blaze out before the tree went up. Whoever had put the cross there and ignited it had been conscientious enough to place it in Tabitha's flowerbed, away from the big fir. Sheriff Hannon was late to the scene; it was Halloween night. By the time he arrived at Eleanor's place, there was nothing to show for the incident besides burned flowers and blackened timber in the gutter.

David had offered to stay, but a call from Wendy sent him home in a hurry. "It's my dad," he explained.

"I'll be fine," Eleanor told him. The danger was over, the message sent.

Eleanor opened the door for the sheriff after midnight. The sheriff took his hat off and wiped his feet before coming inside.

"Real nice place you have here," he said. "You keep a clean house."

"That's what I'm told," she said. "Would you like a tomato? I'm having one. They're my last."

"I'm surprised you still have any," he said.

"From the kitchen window. The ones in the yard gave up in September."

"Yep. Been pretty dry," he said, sitting down. He took a slice of offered tomato. "Real good," he said.

Eleanor watched him eat.

"So, tell me about the trouble here tonight," he said, taking out a notebook.

"There was a cross burning in my yard when we got home from trick-or-treating. It appears it'd been lit moments before we found it."

"Good thing you stumbled on it when you did," he said. "Could have been much worse."

She shook her head. "I think whoever did it waited until they were sure I'd see it. They were waiting for me."

"You don't think this was just a Halloween prank? I mean, this kind of thing goes on all the time around here on Halloween."

"Cross burnings? I don't remember ever hearing about those."

"No," he admitted. "This is a first. But there's been plenty of things like it. We had a barn burn down on Halloween a few years ago, and plenty of windows shot out."

"You're trying to tell me not to worry, aren't you?" she said.

"Yes, Eleanor. Put if off as a bad joke. A tasteless stunt pulled by some of your school friends. I'll have a talk with Russell and his gang and see if I can suss it out that way."

"I'm not so sure," she said. "I think it was the Revealers."

"Why would you say that?"

"Miss Church is a member. She's blames me for losing her job."

"She deserved to lose her job. She nearly killed people."

"I don't think she sees it that way."

"So, if it was her, why do you think the Revealers are behind it? She might have done it herself. You don't need to make a conspiracy out of it."

Eleanor shrugged. "Just a feeling."

"These kind of things always shake you up. But it's Halloween, and it's over. If you're worried, why not stay with Karen and David at their place tonight?"

"I'll be fine here," she said.

"Suit yourself," he said. "Is there anything else you'd like to add before I make a report? Like, did you actually see Miss Church or anyone else?"

"No, I didn't see anyone. I didn't hear them over the highway, or smell them for the wind. It was blowing the wrong way."

"Smell them? No need to be flippant," he said.

"Sorry," she said. "No, I saw no one."

"Don't worry, Eleanor. Just a prank." He got up. "Thanks for the tomato. Finally ate something that isn't a hundred percent sugar tonight."

"You're welcome," she said, walking him the three steps to the door. "What about the Battons. Have they gone home?"

"Yes, they left," he said.

"Glad that's over," she said. "That was weird."

He sighed. "I'm not sure it is over, Eleanor. They still insist that you're their daughter. We showed them school records and pictures, but they're not convinced. You look just like her—have for years."

"Everyone has a twin somewhere," she said.

"Yeah, I guess so. But they're not sure."

"They should spend less time bothering me and more time looking for their daughter."

"I told them that myself. We'll see. They're upset and

heartbroken, aren't thinking right just now. They'll see the light, I'm sure."

"Thanks, Sheriff," Eleanor said.

She stayed up most the night weighing an imaginary scale between running and staying. Though the danger was incontrovertible, she reminded herself she was also not wholly unwanted. She might even be loved. It had been a tough year so far, but surely things would get better now. She only had to hold on, another day, another hour, another minute and see what options came.

There was a definite clock on her life. Celeste was gone. She wouldn't be able to borrow her again. She'd run off or been taken away. She was missing and maybe dead. Eleanor had a replica of Celeste's seventeen year-old body and it would do for two, maybe three years if she was careful with makeup, but then what?

In the morning, after maybe an hour of sleep, she stood in front of her mirror studying her face. She noticed a little scar on her chin with no clue where it had come from. She tugged at her pierced ears and wondered what Celeste had worn in them, hoops or studs, dangles perhaps. She had none herself. Never had. She looked at the bruise on her arm, black and blue as it had ever been. It showed just below the level of a short sleeve and made half her wardrobe useless.

Her body had a flair for regeneration, but it always regenerated to a preset form and that form included pierced ears, long hair, and a never-healing purple bruise.

She stared at it under the light of the bathroom's single bulb. She touched it with a finger to indicate its place. She kept it there to feel the muscle, the skin, the tissue in her mind. She imagined the bruise vanishing. She imagined what her arm, Celeste's arm, would look like without the bruise. She remembered what her arm had looked like last year. She made a variation on a theme, a subtle modification of color and texture. Pain flared beneath her finger. She pushed through it. She gritted her teeth into a smile and watched the black fade to blue to yellow to tanned-pink. She did it. It was gone.

"Yes!"

The trick was to not let it return. She imagined a tiny repairman in her cells referencing a flawed blueprint and incessantly trying to put the bruise back. She could feel the change as a warming in her arm and then with a counter-order from the supervisor, the repairman went away.

She enjoyed the silly image. Whenever a niggling worry entered her mind to upset her, she'd dispatch the little repairman to send it away. It was a senseless diversion, but it worked. She felt new power to face the troubled waters roiling around her. A physical and a mental confidence she was still not wholly used to.

The Battons were back in Jamesford later that week. They skulked around the school for an afternoon. They saw her before she saw them but didn't approach her. She went home without incident.

The rumors about who they were and what they were doing were slower to catch and run wild than the tale of the burning cross on her lawn, but soon enough, the Battons, and their purpose, were well known.

"They came in to the cafe," Eric said in science class. "They ordered the cheapest thing on the menu."

"At those prices, who could blame them," said Russell.

Eric's father owned the Buffalo Cafe. Its prices were out of range for most of Jamesford's residents. The rich folks with summer houses and art studios might go there once a month, but the authentic western atmosphere was lost on them after a while. Tourists liked it, though.

"They asked questions about Eleanor. They chatted up a waitress and a couple of vacationers. Even my dad."

"What did they say?" asked David.

"That she commutes from Nebraska every morning in her flying saucer."

They laughed. Even Eleanor found a smile creep onto her face.

"They're upset about all the crop circles," added Brian.

More laughter.

"'For as the crackling of thorns under a pot, so is the laughter of the fools,'" quoted Jennifer. "'Abhor what is evil; hold fast to what is good.'"

The class looked at her, astonished. She stared back and said, "She's evil. Don't you see it? People as far away as Nebraska see it. She is a stain. Evil surrounds her."

The laughter stopped. Jennifer's wild eyes were unsettling. Eleanor moved to say something, to display her new unwillingness to put up with this kind of thing, when Mr. Gurenno stepped in before she could.

"That's enough of that, Ms. Hutton. Go see Principal Curtz. I'll be down in a minute." When she didn't leave immediately he said. "Go now. Miss Hutton. Don't make this worse."

She left.

"She's nuts," said Brian. "Totally nuts."

"You can be religious and not rude," said Aubrey. "Fundies. Fundamentalists," she explained. "They really take things out of context. That's a quote about vanity. It doesn't even apply."

"Fundies," echoed Brian, getting back to work before Mr. Gurenno made another example of someone.

Eleanor didn't see the Batton's car the rest of that week. Friday night, she had David and Wendy over for dinner and a movie. It gave Karen and Jim a date night, and Eleanor was happy for the company.

She'd made a simple lasagna she'd perfected with Tabitha when she still had her appetite. It took half a day and used cheap ingredients; Eleanor's money wasn't stretching as far as she'd like. The sudden cold snap had found her without wood and she'd had to use pension money to augment her food budget, having spent so much on "real ingredients" for her maple spice cake—her award winning maple spice cake, she reflected.

She'd splurged on some meat for the lasagna, fresh salad, which Wendy wouldn't touch, and garlic bread which Wendy couldn't get enough of. They made popcorn and watched *Peter Pan*, one of Wendy's favorites.

David was trying. True, he'd arrived with a chaperone, but when the movie started, he put his arm around Eleanor's shoulder and didn't flinch when she cuddled closer.

At ten o'clock, Wendy was asleep when there came a knock at the door.

"Who is it?" asked David.

Eleanor paused the movie and listened.

"It's Stephanie Pearce," Eleanor said, recognizing the breathing. She got up to open the door.

"Come in, Miss Pearce," Eleanor said. "David, Wendy, and I are watching a movie. Nothing untoward is going on."

"Didn't think there was," she said, shaking snow from her hair.

Wendy's head rested on David's lap. Eleanor showed Stephanie to the kitchen while David looked on.

"Why are you here, Miss Pearce?"

"I don't know how to say this Eleanor," she said.

David muted the TV.

"Have they found a foster home for me? Is that what's happening?"

"We'll fight it," David said from the living room. "Don't worry Eleanor, we won't let you down."

"It's your mother, Eleanor," said Stephanie. Eleanor had seen her flustered before, seen her officious, put out, and even sisterly, but she'd never seen her as upset as she was today.

"What is it, Stephanie?" Eleanor said. "You're scaring me. Just tell me."

"The Battons," she said.

"Go on," Eleanor coaxed.

"They found your birth certificate in Salt Lake City."

"So?" Eleanor said. "I have a copy in the bureau."

"I don't know how to tell you this. Your mother. She might have . . ."

"Just say it already!" said David, waking Wendy. "You're killing us."

"They found a birth certificate for Eleanor Anders, but they also found a death certificate."

CHAPTER EIGHTEEN

"She lived five hours," Pearce said. "She was premature."

"So, what does this mean?" asked David. The three of them sat around the little kitchen table as Wendy fell back to sleep on the couch. Eleanor had put a kettle on for tea because it was either that or leap through a window.

"Well, it makes Tabitha look, umm, strange."

"What does it mean for Eleanor?" he pressed.

"I'm not sure."

"So my mother gave me my sister's name and birthday. It's not my fault."

"That's true."

"And she's not dead. She looks plenty alive to me," David added.

"Yeah," the social worker said. "But it's more confusion. I don't know how it'll affect your situation with Social Services. We're actually pretty good at dealing with kids without papers, so to speak. But I don't know what the Battons are going to do with it."

"What do they have to do with this?"

"They're the ones who uncovered it," she said. "They hired people to look into you, Eleanor."

"They can't still think Eleanor is Celeste? We have a town full of eyewitness that'll swear she grew up here."

"They swear you're the same girl," Stephanie said scooping sugar into her tea. "They showed me the pictures. I see what they mean. You look just like her."

"She looks like Eleanor, you mean," said David.

"Either way. They want answers."

"Twins separated at birth?" joked David.

She nodded. "Mrs. Batton was under anesthesia when she had Celeste, a C-section. She wonders if she didn't have twins and one was stolen."

"That is a pretty crazy story," Eleanor said.

"Mr. Batton said something about cloning."

"And I thought there was something to worry about," said David laughing. "I'm only sixteen and that sounds totally demented to me. Don't worry, Eleanor."

"They have a congressman," Pearce went on. "From their district in Nebraska. He's kind of a big wig and is doing them favors. He called our office and probably others."

"This is a nightmare," Eleanor said not able to join David in his dismissive attitude.

"What can they do?" David asked.

"Since Eleanor is officially an orphan, they can sue for custody if they can prove relation."

"Why would they? She doesn't want to go. What would be the point?"

"Pride? Guilt over losing Celeste maybe? I don't know, but they're serious."

"What if they can't prove I'm related to them?" asked Eleanor "What then?"

"We still have your identity issue, but the Battons legal status diminishes greatly."

"Tabitha didn't talk a lot about her past," Eleanor said. "But I know she was my mother. I know I don't mean much. I'm just a poor girl in a Wyoming backwater, but Stephanie, I never thought I'd be happy again after my mother died and lately I feel like I could be. I won't cooperate with them to take me away. I'm not done here yet. Will you help me?"

"Of course I'll help you," she said. "I've always been here to help you." Then she paused and got a faraway look in her eye. "I was meant to help you," she said softly.

When Stephanie was gone, David and Eleanor talked quietly in the kitchen.

"I think I can bluff a fingerprint test," she said to him. "I think with some practice, I could do that."

"You said they didn't have any of Celeste's fingerprints," he said. "Besides they're looking at you now, not Celeste."

"Wait. Do twins have the same fingerprints?" she said.

"I don't think so," he said. "But I'll look it up. I think they'll have to do a DNA test to prove anything."

"David I can't let that happen. I don't know what will show up in those tests, but I doubt it'll be good."

"At least it would show you aren't Celeste," he said.

"But it might. I don't know," she said. "Actually, that would make me feel better. I'm afraid it'll show me to be fish or worm or something." Emotions rose in her like a sudden tide. It was a thought she hadn't explored in a long time. While she experimented with vanishing bruises and postulated swirls at her fingertips, she'd ignored the reason she could do these things. She'd allowed herself to believe she could be human, when she was not. On deeper inspection, she allowed herself to believe that she was at least a mammal, but she had no proof of that either. It was just hope. For her own sanity, to function day to day, she fantasized that she was not a monster. Tabitha had said she was another race, not another species, but Eleanor wasn't so sure. In an effort to find out *who* she was, the Battons might stumble upon the greater mystery, the more horrible truth that Eleanor herself didn't want to know: *what* she was.

David reached out to put his arm around her, but hesitated for an instant mid-embrace as if he were afraid to touch her. It was just a beat, a pause, a stutter, and his arm did ultimately reach out and pull her close, but in that moment, Eleanor fell deep into despair and sobbed. David stroked her hair, and it slowed her descent, but only a little.

Had Stephanie been more alert, like Miss Lamb, she'd have seen a distinct lack of surprise on Eleanor's face upon hearing the news of a death certificate filed alongside her birth certificate. Of course Eleanor knew she wore the name of Tabitha's dead child. For years Eleanor had clothed herself in the name as a disguise. Thinking of her mother now, of the pain she must have gone through to lose the child, she felt honored to carry the name.

Honor was a new concept for her. She pulled herself out of her sorrow a little to note the arrival of the feeling: honor. Instinct and survival had been all she'd ever known for decades. Even as Eleanor, they'd been her support pillars. Those animal motivations, so clear and true, were wearing away into shades of grey, into human nuances of love, loyalty, and now honor. Her mind, at least, maybe even her soul, was showing signs of real humanity.

"Stephanie will tell the Battons to go to hell," David said. "Celeste will turn up soon and Jamesford will have yet another mystery."

"I don't think the town can handle any more," she said, wiping her face.

"Are you kidding? It's the only thing that gives this town any life at all."

Wendy woke up. It was late. David carried drowsy Wendy to his car and drove home after midnight. Eleanor went to bed after locking all the doors.

She arrived at school early the next Monday. She'd decided over the weekend to look at herself under a microscope. Literally. She needed to know how easily she could be found out.

She began with a saliva sample. She remembered David's from Mr. Gurenno's experiment and so, with her uncanny memory, compared her own to it. She didn't notice anything different, but saliva is not a good indicator. Easy to contaminate.

She broke a slide in the sink and stabbed her finger with a shard of glass. She smeared blood onto another slide and slid it under the lens. Red blood cells appeared. They looked normal—flattened pink Cheerios under maximum magnification.

Did this mean she could mimic down to the microscopic level or that her blood was the same as anyone's? Inconclusive. That's what she'd have written in her lab book if she were to record this experiment, which of course, she would not.

Eleanor had cleared her station before anyone else arrived. Brian was the first.

"David here yet?" he asked her.

She shook her head.

"Did you hear?" he said.

"What?"

"About that bum David smacked the other day?"

"Ramos. What about him?"

"Someone shot him over the weekend. He's dead."

Jamesford being what it was, the gossip carried the details through the high school before the day was out. Ramos' body was found outside Cowboy Bob's truck stop. He had three bullet wounds: two in the chest and one in the head. No one had heard anything, and a jogging tourist had found the body. No suspects.

"He could have been killed breaking in to someone's home and then got dumped," said Eric.

"Why would anyone do that?" Brian asked.

"Don't like police?" Eric offered.

"Maybe he stumbled upon a drug factory or a smuggling ring," offered Barbara.

"Or maybe he just pissed off the wrong guy," said Tanner. "He was a jerk."

"Did you shoot him, Venn?" asked Russell. "Maybe he insulted your sister-girlfriend and you went all postal—again."

"Well we know it wasn't you, Russell," David said. "Since he wasn't shot in the back."

"How do you know he wasn't shot in the back?" asked Midge, alarmed.

"I don't," David said.

"I heard it was close range," said Brian. "Didn't hear any-thing about the back though. I think that'd come up."

"It's terrible," said Eleanor. "He was harmless."

"I don't know about that," said Alexi. "The things that came out of his mouth."

"He stole too," said Eric. "And knocked over the garbage behind our cafe daily."

"He spread disease," added Crystal. "Fleas at least. Really, why was he even still here?"

"The Revealers," said Aubrey. "They were feeding him. Gave him clothes too."

"How do you know that?"

"They take in everybody. They dress up the homeless and have them carry signs. Didn't you see them in front of the school?"

"I wondered how they got so many people here," said Midge.

"They're creepy," said Robby. "Twisted religion."

"What? And you Indians have it right?" said Crystal "You guys were worshipping rain a hundred years ago."

"Still are," said Eleanor.

"We're not all superstitious," Robby said.

"Just most of you. When it's convenient," Eleanor said.

"What do you have against us?" Robby said.

"So now it's 'us'," said Alexi. "Robby, do you think of yourself as an Indian or a white? Who are you?"

"Good question," Eleanor said, but whether to Alexi or herself, she wasn't sure.

"When Indians are attacked by whites, I'm an Indian. When it's the other way around, I'm white."

"Indians attacking whites?" Russell said. "They taking scalps?"

"Do you really think the Shoshone don't talk about whites the way whites talk about them?"

"Not everyone," said Midge.

"No, not everyone," said Robby. "There are those who hate more than others. Which is why I'd like to know what Eleanor has against us. How about it Eleanor? You'll defend a vulgar thieving hobo, but you think Indians are all backwards and savage. I'd like to know why."

"You know why," she said.

"Tell us," said Alexi. "I want to know."

"Because they don't like *me*," she said.

"Don't lump everyone into one group," he said.

"Do you like me?" she said.

"You're all right," he said. "Never did anything to me."

"Why don't they like Eleanor?" asked Aubrey.

Robby looked around the room. The others were waiting for him to speak. Mr. Gurenno, too, had stopped his work and listened.

"The same reason some whites don't like her," he said finally. "They think she's spooky."

"She is a witch," said Jennifer. "Even they know it."

"Miss Hutton," Mr. Gurenno warned. "You're on probation, I'll remind you."

She snapped the lid on a Petri dish and turned away.

"Not all Shoshone think she's a witch," Midge said.

"And not all whites think she is one either," said Aubrey.

"This town is so full of crap," said Russell, "it's a wonder we don't drown in it coming to school."

"Amen," said Aubrey and the class laughed.

CHAPTER NINETEEN

The first real snowstorm of the year had come and gone along with two lesser cousins before Eleanor realized she'd missed the fall. She had intended to take David up the canyon trails through the groves of yellow-leafed aspen and tawny wheatgrass. They'd visit the springs where the cattails still grew and see, again, the frog pond where they had played last year. They would pilgrim to their sacred clearing, fall on their backs, and stare at the blueberry sky while cotton clouds clumped into fanciful shapes in unceasing and infinite potential. And there, when the light gleamed gold and the hills' shadows stretched across the forest, she would lean into his breath and have that kiss of him that filled her with fire and lightened her.

She stood on her porch, her schoolbooks at her feet, her key in her hand. She turned to face the sunlight and closed her eyes. She drew in the smells of the valley. They were winter smells: diesel exhaust and wood fires, snow and alfalfa flakes. No apples, no yellow autumn leaves, no frogs, or cattails, or blueberry sky. She held the image of that missed afternoon with all the clarity of a real memory for as long as she dared then released it like a falling leaf, wondering if she would ever get another chance to make it real.

A few days before Thanksgiving, Eleanor had received a phone call from Stephanie.

"I think I finally have the Battons convinced who you are," she said

"Good. So they're going to leave me alone?"

"They just want a test to see if you're related to them."

"I won't do it," Eleanor said sharply.

"It's the easiest way to clear this whole thing up."

"I don't need a doctor or a Nebraska family to tell me who I am. I know who am. I am Eleanor Anders," she said with conviction. "They have to leave me alone. I don't know them."

"I'll tell them," she said.

"What can they do about it if I refuse?"

"I don't know," she said. "If they push, we may need a lawyer."

"That takes time right? Any kind of legal thing, that takes time?"

"Could drag on forever," she said. "Maybe it's best to get it over with."

"No," she said firmly.

"Okay," she said. "Are you spending the holiday with the Venns?"

"Yes," she said. "I'll be cooking all day and before you ask, yes, I am making my cake."

"How is Mr. Venn treating you?"

"He's all right," she said "I don't see much of him." Eleanor didn't even pretend that she lived with the Venns anymore. The days of that obfuscation were long gone. Eleanor's fear of the social worker was mostly gone too. Mostly.

"The Veteran's Administration asked me to check on him," she said. "Do you know if he's found a job yet?"

"I don't think he has," she said. "Why don't you call him and ask?"

"He won't answer my calls."

Thanksgiving morning, Eleanor was at the Venn's for breakfast. Wendy and David woke up to Karen's bacon and Eleanor's scratch-made pancakes. Mr. Venn slept in.

Eleanor helped Karen start the turkey and slide it into the oven with a stuffing that was half traditional Venn recipe and half Anders'. Eleanor couldn't imagine a dressing without fruit, and with Karen's approval, doctored hers to include apples and blanched almonds.

David had been cheerful during breakfast, and politely in the way during the morning cooking. When he failed to soften the butter in the microwave, handing his mother a tray of butter soup instead of a softened stick, she sent him away with Wendy to play outside.

With the turkey in Karen's oven, Eleanor would bake the breads at her house. She found David with Wendy at a neighbor's swing set.

"Can you drive me home?" Eleanor said. "We need another oven."

"Come swing with me," he said. "Like the old days."

"You make it sound like a century ago," she said, but took the swing beside him. Wendy played with a neighbor boy helping him refit his clip-on tie under his winter coat.

"Does it seem to you that this has been a long year?"

"I was thinking it'd gone by fast," she said remembering her daydream. "But I know what you mean."

"We should go to the park and swing on those good swings."

"We could really fly on those," she said.

"Fly away maybe," he said, "like we talked about. What were we? Eagles or hawks?"

"I think you were an airplane," she said.

"Do animals have family problems?" he asked her.

Eleanor kicked and lifted her feet above the snowy ground.

"They're not complicated," she said. "The problems are easier. The rules are simpler. If something's not going to kill you, it's not a big problem."

"I was talking about families," he said.

"Same rules," she said.

David drove Eleanor home and stayed to help her cook as much as she'd let him.

"Aren't you sick of that cake yet?" he asked trying to separate egg whites over a glass bowl.

"A little," she admitted, "But your dad asked for it."

"I hope you don't think you have to do everything my dad says."

"He's never asked me to do anything."

He shrugged.

"What's going on, David? With your dad, I mean. I know your issue with me."

He sighed and looked at her dejectedly. Words framed on his lips but weren't spoken.

"Tell me about your dad," she said.

He nodded resignedly. "I found out why he's home. He was discharged for being unfit for duty."

"Is he sick?"

"Yeah, in the head. He had a suicide wish, he wanted to get killed."

"You'd think they'd like that," she said.

"No," he said.

"Finish those eggs. I want to do the rolls last so they're warm for dinner."

"How'd you learn to do all this?"

"I've been cooking for Tabitha since I was ten."

"Do you get lonely?" he asked.

"Sometimes," she said. "Even when there are people around. Especially when there are people around."

He gave her the eggs and she whipped them with deft flicks of a whisk.

"How'd he get that way?" Eleanor asked.

"I don't know," he said. "It happened before this last deployment. Something bad happened. He wasn't wounded, but he got sent home. He could have left the army then, but he didn't. He was going to, but he didn't. Then we had the fire."

"How does that fit in?"

"I'm not sure. My mom had talked him into quitting, moving off base. Opening a coffee shop or something. Then the fire. Then he couldn't get overseas fast enough."

"Was he running from the police? For the fire?"

"Maybe," he said. "But it was more. He didn't want to leave us, but he needed to get back there. Like there was something left undone."

Eleanor poured the batter into the forms and slid them into the oven.

"I gotta slow these rolls. Open the door," she said.

David did, and she put the tray of rising rolls on the back porch.

"The cold should buy us some time."

"Cool," David said.

"I've been meaning to ask you, David," Eleanor said washing her hands. "What did the sheriff say about your missing gun?"

"I didn't tell him."

"Why?"

"It's not a crime to lose something," he said. "It'll just make me look stupid, especially after I won that trophy."

Eleanor dried her hands. "I think you should tell him," she said.

"Since when do you put so much trust in authorities?"

He had a point. "I don't know," she said honestly. "I guess I've come to trust Hannon. He isn't so scary to me anymore."

"You'd think my dad, for being in the army and all that, would trust officials, but he doesn't. He's afraid of them like you used to be."

"Stephanie said she's been asked to look in on him for the VA."

"He won't let her," he said.

"She's not so scary either," she said.

He shrugged. Eleanor tossed her apron on the table. "You can go home if you want to," she said. "I can do the rest. Pick me up later."

"I'll stay here."

"Okay," she said. "I'm going to change. If the timer goes off and I don't hear it, pull the cake out of the oven."

"If the timer goes off and you don't hear it, it means you're either dead or ten miles away," he said.

They arrived back at the Venns' trailer at five o'clock with two dozen hot rolls and dessert. Karen had the turkey out of the oven and was working on the gravy. Wendy decorated the table with candy turkeys made from gumdrops and toothpicks. She placed colored name cards on the plates to organize the seating. Mr. Venn was not in evidence.

Eleanor paused in the kitchen to locate him. She caught a waft of citric aftershave and heard the light clicking of David's computer keyboard and placed him at David's desk.

"How soon do we eat?" asked David drawing a finger through the potatoes.

"Go get your father," she said swatting his hand. "We're ready."

"I'll get him," said Eleanor.

David's door was closed. Eleanor opened it softly and poked her head inside. David's father was hunched over the computer in front of a web page. His right hand directed the mouse, his left held a glass of melting ice cubes. Eleanor could smell whisky.

On the computer screen, beneath an official seal she read a list names of men she didn't know associated with places she didn't recognize.

He tipped an ice cube into his mouth and cleared his throat. Eleanor pulled the door shut before knocking.

"Jim," she called. "It's time for dinner."

"Be right out," he said thickly. "One second."

David carried the bird to the head of the table and laid out a steel fork and a carving knife. Karen primped quickly in a mirror and, after dropping spoons in the several bowls of side dishes, placed them on the table. Eleanor filled a basket with rolls and sat down.

Jim Venn staggered out of David's room. His face was red and wild. He looked at the assembly as if surprised to see them. He rubbed his eyes and then came into the room.

"What a feast," he exclaimed, snapping a napkin open on his lap.

At Karen's example, the assembly joined hands for prayer.

"Jim," Karen said. "Will you say grace?"

"No," he said. "Me and the Almighty haven't been getting on well. How about you Eleanor?"

"Not sure we're getting along either," she said.

"David?" Karen said in a way that gave him no room to say no.

"Karen, you say it," said Jim. "You should."

She bowed her head and spoke. "Dear Lord, we are thankful for this food and for the hands that prepared it. We are thankful for each other and this family. Please keep us safe and let us appreciate the things we have. Amen."

"Amen," said the table.

Jim carved the turkey while bowls and baskets were passed helter-skelter from hand to hand in all directions.

After the initial flurry of eating, where no one spoke, they settled into the paced ritual of feasting. Each dish was complimented and the cooks recognized and thanked.

"The turkey is just perfect," said Mr. Venn.

"You picked it, Jim," said Karen. "The stuffing is part Eleanor's recipe and Wendy helped me baste it. I could hardly lift it into the oven. David did that."

Eleanor recognized Karen's generous game of connecting everyone at the table with whatever dish was on display. When Wendy complimented Eleanor's rolls, she said, "It's Jim's mother's recipe. David helped with the egg whites and you put the basket together. Karen made the dough; I just baked them."

Jim relaxed and joked. Several times Eleanor saw him deliberately slow his eating. David had mentioned that the army had taught him to eat so fast he wondered if he tasted anything and Eleanor had seen short bursts of that at the beginning of the meal when his entire mound of mashed potatoes was inhaled before the cranberries got to him.

"Eleanor," Jim said dabbing a piece of roll into a gravy pool. "Why won't you take the Batton's test?"

The question surprised Eleanor. It broke the amiable mood of the dinner table like a shattered serving plate.

"Jim, is now the time?" Karen said.

"Just asking," he said.

"They called you?" Eleanor said.

"Not just them," he said. "My CO called me too."

"That's commanding officer," said Wendy through a mouth of potatoes.

"I thought you were out of the army," Eleanor said.

"He is," David said more to his father than to her. "He doesn't have to do what they tell him."

"No, I don't. But he called me about you just the same. He told me to make you take the test."

"Can you do that?" asked David.

"As Eleanor's legal guardian," Jim said, "probably."

"I thought Mom was her legal guardian," said David cooly.

"Temporary guardian," said Eleanor taking unlikely refuge in the word.

"We won't make you do anything you don't want to," said Karen.

"Unless it's for your own good," added Jim.

Eleanor shook her head. Why couldn't one evening, this one special night, be without dread?

"What did you tell him?" asked Eleanor.

Jim regarded Eleanor across the table. Karen was flustered, embarrassed and red in the face.

"Why don't you want to be tested?" he asked, instead of answering.

"I'm a private person," she said. She'd let her hair fall over her face at the first mention of the test, but she shook it back over her shoulder to meet his gaze. She meant to show courage but instinct kicked in and she memorized his features, his imperfections, scars and blemishes. She plumbed his hard eyes for an inner image she could feel more than understand. Under her probing eyes, Jim pulled back suddenly unsure.

"They're not my family," Eleanor explained. "I'm sorry about their missing girl, but I'm not her. They want me to be her."

"So, put it to bed," he said. "Have the test and they'll leave you alone."

"I don't like doctors," she said firmly.

"Have you got something to hide?" he said, ignoring Karen's pointed glare.

"I might," she said. "We all have secrets. Some we know about, some we're afraid to know. I don't see any good coming out of it. And I don't like doctors."

Mr. Venn chewed a wing and thought for a moment.

"Then don't do it," he said simply.

"And you won't make her?" asked David.

"I won't. I'm not sure I could," he said. "But it won't end here. Count on it. People like this are not above dirty tricks."

"What did you tell your CO when he called?" asked Karen.

"I told him if he wanted to boss me around, he shouldn't

have kicked me out of the army. I told him he should spend more time looking out for his soldiers than playing errand boy for a politically connected hayseed. I told him to stick it up his ass. I told him I wouldn't make Eleanor do anything she didn't want to do. I told him she was family. And that shut him up."

"You said all that? Really?" asked David.

"You act surprised," he said. "I may have said it a little louder than that, maybe I added a word here or there that I shouldn't repeat, but I said it."

"Thanks, Mr. Venn," Eleanor said.

"Jim," he said with a wink.

And after that they had Eleanor's cake for dessert.

CHAPTER TWENTY

The Battons tried many times to communicate with Eleanor. With each refusal shorter and firmer than the last, they grew ever more persistent and determined, convinced, they said, that she knew more than she was saying. Stephanie finally had an attorney write a letter to make them stop harassing her and the Venns.

Their pressures turned to the Social Services office and Stephanie in particular, who weathered it all with zealous determination. She casually laughed off their threats during her December visit—an afternoon Jim conveniently chose to look for work out of town.

"I have too much seniority and am too overworked to worry about them," she said. "Besides, I have the entire bureau behind me. Their attitude is only making us more obstinate."

The second week of December, a short article written by a freelancer in Omaha had been conveniently picked up by the wire service and appeared in Jamesford's paper along with countless others across the country.

False Hope Brings Real Questions for a Grieving Family
Celeste Batton, age seventeen, disappeared from her home near

Minden, Nebraska, on August 28th. Since then, her grieving family has searched for their daughter in vain until a tip led them to the little town of Jamesford, Wyoming, where they discovered a girl who might be their daughter's identical twin.

Celeste, an honor student at Kearney County High School, was last seen by her classmates the day she disappeared.

"She was in good spirits," said a friend. "She was excited about the future."

Celeste told her parents that she was going to spend the weekend with friends but never arrived. She cancelled by telephone, saying she didn't feel well. She has not been heard from since.

Because her family thought she was with friends, they did not notice her missing until Sunday morning when she failed to return home.

"We called everyone we could think of," said Mrs. Desiree Batton.

Police and FBI were brought in to aid in the search and a state-wide Amber Alert was issued.

"The search had been tragically futile," said a family spokesman, "until the Jamesford lead."

Jamesford, Wyoming, is a sleepy, picturesque, tourist village on the way to Yellowstone. It was recently the site of controversy when The Church of Christ Revealed, commonly called "The Revealers," staged public protests which garnered national television attention.

A friend of the Battons thought they recognized Celeste in a crowd of onlookers from a news broadcast.

Filled with hope, the family rushed to Wyoming. What they discovered there was not their missing daughter, but a striking lookalike.

"We could't believe it wasn't Celeste," said Mr. Wayne Batton. "We met her. It was our daughter down to the eyebrows and voice. We know our daughter. It was her."

But it wasn't. The girl in Jamesford is a long-time resident of the town and definitely not the Battons' missing daughter.

"We couldn't believe it wasn't her," said Mr. Batton. "We thought there was some kind of conspiracy."

The resemblance was so great that the family researched the girl only to discover that her birth certificate was falsified, raising tantalizing questions about her origin.

"We're hoping the girl will consent to a DNA test," said a family spokesman. "So we can clear up this mystery. Or at least start to."

The girl, however, has staunchly refused to cooperate with the Battons and was not available for comment.

"We hope that she'll change her mind and give us some peace," said Mrs. Batton. "Is that so much to ask?"

The search for the missing Celeste continues while the family wrestles with this new mystery.

Eleanor read the article online in the library at school during lunch. From what she'd gathered from conversations all day, she was the last one in town to read it.

She pushed her chair back and stared at the picture of Celeste on the screen. It was the same one Agent Lamb had showed her in the interview room, the same one Celeste sat for the day she disappeared, almost an exact duplicate of the one that would be in Jamesford High's yearbook this year.

The plan to keep Eleanor in Jamesford relied on the absurdity of the rumors to explain the mysteries surrounding her. The assumption was that things would get better over time; people would forget the strange things they'd seen, the terrible things they knew, and the weird stories they'd heard about the quiet, little girl with auburn hair. And they just might if nothing happened to stir it all up again. The Battons were stirring.

Eleanor felt a net closing around her. She felt that she might already be trapped in it. She was free to run. As long as she had access to a door or a window she had that escape, but she doubted whether it would lead her to freedom.

In the desert, in the night, chased by a handful of drunks with guns and torches and busy with the slaughter of the rest of her family, running had worked. She could leave school now and not come back, hop a train or stow away in a long-haul truck and turn up somewhere else. But she'd need another shape. This one was compromised. Every police station in the country had her picture, the FBI had it, newspapers ran it. It was a picture of her with Celeste's name so unless she changed, wherever she landed, she'd eventually have to face the same problems she was running from.

And here she had friends. As unlikely as it was to her who'd spent years avoiding people in an effort to avoid the very disaster she now faced, she realized she had some friends now, and some good ones too. They were not the reason everything had crumbled, that her picture went out across the country on national television, her story on the newswire. That was blind dumb luck. But they were part of the reason she was still in Jamesford.

She turned off the computer, knowing she would stay, thinking she'd already paid the price to stay—or most of it, she hoped. She knew this even as her primal self howled inside her, urging her to flee, hearing the ticking clock that heralded imminent disaster.

There was nothing in the article that her neighbors didn't already know. It stirred up old stories for a while, fortified opinions, and eventually turned to its impact on the economy.

Was this good or bad publicity for Jamesford? Was there such as thing as bad publicity? Eleanor knew there was.

The town's fascination with the article was cut short with the discovery of another body on Highway 26.

The paper said the body had been dead for several days, the victim of gunshots. He was identified as a Jamesford resident but the name wasn't released pending family notification. Nevertheless, the entire town knew it was Brett Porter before lunchtime. Porter was a hard-drinking oil worker who frequented the local bars and was often seen walking home, having just enough sense not to try to drive. Since he lived alone, he wasn't reported missing. His foreman assumed he was out on another bender and had replaced him at work rather than look for him.

Eleanor knew of Brett Porter. She'd seen him walking the same lonely roads she took at night. He wasn't as quiet as she was and his steps were never graceful but they managed to keep him upright, which was more than he deserved. She'd never spoken to him. She always thought he was on the way to joining Ramos in the street, but didn't think it would be like this. He was a mean drunk and liked to fight. Eleanor seldom saw him without some injury meted out in a brawl.

In the days that followed, several additional clues surfaced about Porter's murder. He'd had a fight with a local the night he was murdered and the police had recovered bullets from his body, something they'd not been able to do in the previous killing where the bullets had fragmented.

The first horror is a shock, the second is dread, but the more one faces the unfaceable, the more accustomed they become to it. The kids of Jamesford didn't give much thought to the new killing. Old drunks and strangers were being killed, not them. Besides, the winter dance was around the corner, and, weeks before the dance, Eleanor found herself making posters for it and helping to hang banners. Tradition held that no one could be asked to the dance before the coming Friday and Eleanor was excited for the date.

The boys kept their distance from the girls that week, huddling together conspiratorially in corners and segregated lunch tables, casting knowing glances back at the girls who pretended not to notice.

Only Russell seemed uninterested in the coming dance. He sat with Tanner, playing distractedly with his food and ignoring his friend's suggestions for creative ways to invite their dates this year.

"Horse-drawn buggy?" Tanner suggested. "Always good, and I know a guy at the Crazy-A Ranch who'll help. No? How 'bout a humongous box of chocolates, heart shaped maybe, with an invitation at the bottom?"

Russell grunted and shrugged. His thoughts were not on the dance, but somewhere else. Somewhere darker. Eleanor shuddered to think of it.

Eleanor knew from experience how Russell's moods could translate into violence. She had seen first-hand how much malice he could muster from nothing. Her thoughts ran to David. Tanner had mentioned him, promising "to put him to shame" this year. Eleanor thought back on the last weeks for something David might have done to provoke Russell. She could think of nothing new, but that gave her little peace. Russell didn't need much to provoke him. He could strike out at David for things he did last year or in third grade, or things he had never done but that Russell blamed him for anyway.

Eleanor began to worry. Part of her said she was being paranoid, but another part of her, the deeper, wiser part, suggested she was only being careful. She tried to put the pieces together and identify the threat if there was one.

Russell had been quiet all year, at least for him. He hadn't hit anyone, or been sent to Principal Curtz. He hadn't even been cautioned for his language. He might have had a run in with the sheriff, but at school, he'd been a model citizen and that was wholly unlike him. Eleanor had known him for years, and thinking about it now, she couldn't imagine how he'd changed so much so quickly. Maybe Barbara was behind it, and she wondered if she wasn't also behind his new brooding apathy. He'd been embarrassed the previous year, shown up by David's dramatic invitation to Eleanor and his lame one to Barbara. Had Barbara said something about David? Something small, something sharp, something that burrowed beneath his skin and was now working its way into his cruel reactionary imagination? Was he now summoning violence and retribution? Was Russell's monster about to emerge?

Or had it already been let out?

CHAPTER TWENTY-ONE

Two weeks before the winter dance was the first day anyone was allowed to officially ask anyone to go. It was an old tradition, and curfews were lifted to allow devoted suitors to spring the question at one minute past midnight. Eleanor went home that Friday, like many girls, excited and wondering how her beau would make the formal invitation. David had set a high bar the previous year with a pyrotechnics display that launched them as a couple into the upper echelons of Jamesford High School popularity.

David's attitude toward Eleanor was not what it had been that summer when they were inseparable, but neither was it the circumspect revulsion she'd endured from him after her visit with Penelope's grandmother. There was still a distance, but she felt him wrestling with his inner prejudices and winning. The winter dance would be the perfect moment to reunite. She hadn't kissed him in months and she longed for the electricity their chemistry sparked. And he was cute.

Eleanor sat up watching the clock more than the Western on her old TV. She'd made hot chocolate and sipped it slowly. She'd made plenty just in case.

She listened to the street in front of her house, waiting for the sounds of footsteps on the frozen snow, the crisp cracker-crunch that would tell her David was coming to invite her to the dance.

At quarter past twelve, she sat alone in silence. She picked up the telephone and listened for a tone. It was working. She went to the front curtains looking for a car, a face, a sign. There was nothing. She watched the road for ten minutes and felt the familiar stirrings of her breaking heart, the chasm opening beneath her and punishing her for having the temerity to hope and to dream. It hit her suddenly, showing how close it had always been. She was falling. She was alone. She was unloved.

A tear of self-pity rolled down her cheek and she tasted the bitter salt. She looked around her little house, the old sofa, the TV, her mother's chair, the little table in the kitchen with Tabitha's favorite white and blue teacups set upon it, waiting for no one. She mentally counted the money she had in the bank and tried to picture herself starting again.

There had been watering holes after a rain in the desert in the days of the coyote. For a while the water was clear, crisp and bright, and life was good and easy and the heat bearable. But the water would go. It would recede, growing dirty from the silt kicked up by wading animals. It would be more mud than water, then just mud, undrinkable and fetid. It would threaten to trap you, its sucking depths turned to gripping claws that would slow your flight from a predator if not hold you fast like a stump for the sun to dry your tongue and boil your insides. The thirsty things would try to find a puddle and dare the depths of the killing soil. She'd seen hundreds of hopeless, eager frogs, born to die in the sludge, drying on the cracking clay. She'd seen fawns in such mud holes, and antelope, ever quick and springy, buried to their chests and dead in the muck, tricked into trusting the water longer than they should.

Jamesford was muddy now. The water was drying up. David might still ask her to the dance, he still had two weeks after all, but the urgency was gone. Her importance in his life was diminishing. Her reason for staying, not so pure. The water was receding, silty and opaque. Muddy.

But she had nowhere to go.

She drank hot chocolate until one o'clock and then flashed on the terrible thought: Russell Liddle.

She grabbed her coat and ran from the house.

The lights were on at the Venns' trailer. She ran up to it, not pausing to listen, and burst through the door without knocking.

Karen sat alone on the sofa worried and sad, a mirror image of Eleanor an hour before. Karen looked up, lifting a finger to her lips. Eleanor came closer, knelt beside her and beseeched David's mother with a silent stare for information.

"Wendy is asleep," she said.

"David?" Eleanor said. "Where's David?"

Karen glanced at the table where a pile of rose stems lay beside a plastic bowl overflowing with red petals.

"He was about to go over to invite you to the dance," Karen said. "He was going to spell it out with red rose petals on the white snow. We were plucking roses all evening."

"Where's David now?"

"Sheriff Hannon came and got him around eleven o'clock," she said. "Jim's with him. It has something to do with the murders."

Relief flowed over her like a cool breeze. David was all right.

"Is it about David's missing gun?" she asked.

"I don't know," she said. "There was a woman from Homeland Security with her."

"Miss Lamb?" Eleanor asked.

"I don't remember her name," she said. "She asked about you."

"That was nice," said Eleanor not knowing what else to say.

"No. No, it wasn't nice. It was threatening."

"Oh," she said feeling the information coalesce like a stone in her stomach. Remembering David, she asked, "What can we do?"

"Jim said he'd call. We'll just wait here until he does."

Eleanor was anxious for action, but there was nothing for it. All she could do was sit with Karen and be with her.

"Did they arrest him?" she asked.

Karen shook her head. "Just questioning, they said."

David was kept until late the next morning. When he and Jim walked back into the trailer, Eleanor was playing with Odin and Wendy. Karen stirred a pot of porridge and had bowls of it on the table before their coats were off.

David looked worn and beaten, too tired to be afraid. Jim's jaw was set and firm. No stranger to long hours and stress, he looked sure and purposeful. He sat down and dug into his meal like he had thirty seconds to finish it. David dropped down on the floor next to Eleanor and threw his arms around her. The room went quiet for a moment. In that pause, Eleanor felt the water flow around her legs and lift her out of the mire. Then Jim began eating again, and the cat filled the room with whirring purrs.

Eleanor held David and breathed in his lingering fearful pheromones, noting, too, the scents of tobacco, cheap perfume, and bad coffee. She looked over David's shoulder and saw Karen watching them. She wore a mournful countenance of a mother losing her son, her boy growing up. David had run to Eleanor for comfort, not to her.

"Was it the gun, Jim?" she asked.

"They pulled 5.7mm caliber bullets out of the last one," he said. "Since David had a Five-Seven, Sheriff Hannon came knocking."

"David can't be the only one with a gun," Karen said. "This is Wyoming."

"It's a rare gun," he said. "No one knows of another in town and everyone knows of David's."

"You told him that it was stolen, of course?"

"Yes, but he wasn't exactly a believer. He said it was suspicious we hadn't reported it before."

"I told you," Karen said.

"Don't start," Jim said harshly.

Rebuked, Karen called to David. "There's breakfast, David. It's still warm."

Eleanor coaxed him up and walked him to the table. His eyes were ringed and bloodshot, his thick brown hair a shaggy mess. He smiled at Eleanor and then, finally at his mother. He scooped sugar into his bowl and watched it melt.

"I was going for quiet this year," he said to Eleanor. "Did Mom tell you? Roses in the snow?"

She nodded cheerfully.

"I'm going to put them out anyway," he said. "Let me just get a little nap and then you go home and we'll do this right."

"No need," she said. "I'll go to the dance with you."

"Hooray!" shrieked Wendy like it was a surprise.

"But I haven't asked you yet," he said.

"Okay," she said. "You get some sleep."

"Eat first," said Karen.

"Yes Mom."

He scooped the porridge into his mouth and closed his eyes against the bright room.

"So how'd it end up, Jim?" Karen asked.

"They didn't charge him. Never arrested him. But he is a suspect. Can you believe that? He's a suspect?"

"Because of the gun?"

"That and David pushed that bugger down at school."

"Ramos," Eleanor said.

"He threatened him too. They said David has a reputation for being hot-headed. They asked questions for hours, trying to trip up his story. It was degrading. They only released us when I demanded a lawyer."

"Mr. Venn," Eleanor asked, "Why now? Why'd they come on a Friday night? On this Friday night? What was the urgency?"

"I have an idea," Jim said slowly.

Karen sat down at the table and folded her hands nervously. Wendy had gone back to her cartoons and the cat had disappeared.

"It might have been about you, Eleanor," he said softly. "Do you know Agent Lamb, Homeland Security?" She nodded. "Yeah, David said you met her last year. She hovered around the interrogation room and dragged it all out hours longer than it needed to be. When David complained and wanted to go, Lamb would say something cryptic like 'you gotta get to your girlfriend?'"

"She told me you'd break my heart," David said, "like you were breaking the hearts of the Battons by not giving them peace and doing the DNA test."

"Several times I thought the sheriff was done with us and about to let us go, but then Lamb would call him outside, and we'd sit for thirty minutes, twiddling our thumbs, before he came back to ask us the same questions as before."

"He looked put out," said David. "I don't think it was his idea to handle it this way."

"Just following orders," Jim said in terse syllables. "Yes sir. No sir. Whatever you say, sir. Destroy the enemy, sir." He threw up an ironic salute and snapped it down sharp as a cleaver before his blank face darkened with disgust. His chin, again, was set and firm.

"Do you want me to take the test?" Eleanor asked Jim.

"No," he said. "Hell no. Not now. Not unless you want to, and then I'd say don't."

"It might make things easier," said Karen.

"I swear, woman, sometimes you just won't see the big picture," he said.

"Don't even think about it, Eleanor," David said, laying his hand on hers.

She wasn't thinking of it. She was measuring the firmness of the ground, the purity of the water. Though still murky and new bubbles of muck rose and swirled around her, it was again buoyant.

CHAPTER TWENTY-TWO

Mrs. Hart returned from her sabbatical that Monday. A new face in front of the class was not surprising, and the students at first thought she was just another substitute teacher to read the required syllabus to the students. Eleanor recognized her instantly. In fact, she knew she was back before school started. Waiting at her locker, shaking the snow from her hair, she first smelled the familiar perfume Mrs. Hart favored. It was a flash of scent, just a puff left over from when she crossed the hall earlier that morning, but she recognized it, and also the scent of her skin, her brand of lotion, hair spray and soap, the combination of which could equal nothing but her old teacher.

The kids filed into their humanities class and took their seats. Mrs. Hart was bent over a pile of handwritten notes doubtlessly left by her replacements. When the bell rang, she looked up and regarded the class.

"Good morning, everyone," she said. "We'll pick up where Mrs. Durrant left off. Open your books to chapter seventeen." And without a word of welcome or explanation, she conducted the lecture as if she'd never been gone.

She acted the same, but Eleanor saw it was an act. She sensed a brokenness in the woman who'd tormented her last year. Her eyes were different, sunk back in her face as if in constant retreat. New lines stretched around them, a shadow held them in outline. Her dress was new and she'd put on a few pounds. She spoke with her old clear voice, trained to carry to the ends of the classroom, firm inflections allowing no spaces for whispers or questions until she was ready for them, but Eleanor sensed cracks in her façade. Something was gone from her. She'd expected her teacher to return with new insight, new skills and knowledge, anxious to impart her new wisdom on her students, but it was the opposite. She wanted to be anywhere but here. Eleanor wondered what it was she'd been studying. Rumors said she was finishing her master's degree and had an eye on administration. Others said she'd gone to cross-train in science before they'd hired Mr. Gurenno. Whatever it was, Eleanor didn't think she'd enjoyed it.

Eleanor watched Mrs. Hart from the back of the class, wondering why she cared. The woman in front of her explaining the Great Depression in scripted anecdotes, was not her friend. She'd been her tormentor, but Eleanor felt an inexplicable sorrow for her. She shook her head, wondering how she'd mistaken the teacher for someone she cared about. It was that movement that attracted Mrs. Hart's gaze to Eleanor.

Their eyes met for an instant. Eleanor braced herself for a dirty look or an attack, something to renew their feud now that her mother was gone and unable to come to her aid, but it didn't come. Her eyes were too sad. They looked through her at first, her words continued as if by recording, Black Friday and the stock market crash, but her thoughts were a million miles away. They focused after a moment and took in Eleanor's changed features and long hair without caring, never altering the pace or tone of her monotonous speech.

Eleanor sighed in relief and drew in a scent that explained everything and broke her heart at once. It was subtle and small, concealed and covered up, but she was certain she'd sensed it. She exhaled and cleared her palate and then she tasted the air again, drew in the molecules, sampled them, understood them and nearly wept. Milk. Looking back at the teacher, Eleanor wondered sorrowfully where the child was and who was feeding it.

"Mrs. Hart must have gone to cooking school," said Barbara at lunch. "Did you see her butt? She must have put on thirty pounds."

"She's got no self-respect," said Alexi. "I mean really, who'd let themselves go like that?"

The girls were not sitting at Eleanor's table but she heard them just the same. So did Midge who pretended not to. She'd have given anything to have Mrs. Hart's proportions. She had fifty pounds to go before she'd be near what Alexi considered a self-respectful weight.

Aubrey ignored the catty neighbors and read a book over her lunch tray. It was just the three of them today. David was at the counselor's office. Word of his Friday night had already gone through the school and the officials were quick to offer their moral support and judge for themselves if David was dangerous.

Probably to cover up the fat jokes from the other table, Midge said, "So does that count as an invitation or is David going to do something else?"

"I counted it. We're going," Eleanor said. "How about you? Did Henry ask you?"

She nodded shyly.

"How did he ask you?" said Aubrey putting down her book.

"It's corny," she said. "He shot an arrow into my door with an invitation on it."

"Indian and Cupid. Cool," said Aubrey.

"My parents were mad," she said. "About the door. And, well, also, about the invitation."

"They don't like Henry?" said Eleanor.

She shook her head. "They're old-fashioned," she said.

"Racist you mean," said Aubrey. Midge shrugged.

"Eric sang on my doorstep," said Aubrey. "It was cute and awful at the same time. He can't sing worth a darn."

"What happened to Barbara and Russell?" asked Aubrey looking at Eleanor.

"You think I know?"

"Don't you?"

"We're not exactly bosom pals or anything."

"But you hear things," she said. Midge nodded.

"I heard," Eleanor began recalling the morning's conversations in the hall, "that Russell just rang her bell after midnight with a five dollar bouquet of grocery store flowers and mumbled something about the dance."

The girls looked at Barbara and shook their heads.

"Let me guess," said Aubrey, "She wasn't impressed."

"Not one bit. They got in an argument on her doorstep that lasted an hour. They made up though," she said. "I guess."

"So they're the lamest," said Aubrey. "Who got the best invitation?"

"I'd say the arrow's the best so far," said Eleanor.

"The rose petals are better," Midge said almost defensively.

"Or they would have been, you know, if David could have finished it."

She had to admit to herself that she was disappointed that she didn't get to see the rose petals on the snow. It ate at her all day and she felt robbed. It was unfair but instead of writing it off as just another unnecessary cruelty, that afternoon she marched up the highway to the police station.

"I'd like to see Sheriff Hannon," she announced at the reception desk. The deputy wore a knowing grin that made her feel uneasy. She set her jaw as she'd seen David's father do, and looked back at him hard. In her mind, she marveled at where she stood, admired her impulsive courage. The deputy picked up his phone and announced that Eleanor Anders was here to see the sheriff. He came right up.

"Come on back, Eleanor," he said.

"Can we stay out here? Go outside maybe?" she said, her courage flagging at the thought of locked doors and windowless rooms. The sheriff seemed to understand and drew on a jacket.

"You warm enough?" he asked her when they were a few steps outside.

"I'm good," she said. She stopped and looked around. When she was sure they were alone, she said, "I want to ask you why you did that to David?"

"Why I brought him for questioning? That's my job, Eleanor."

"You know what I mean," she said amazing herself with each syllable. "You knew what that night meant. You can't tell me it wasn't intentional."

He bit his lip and Eleanor knew David's dad had been right.

"Did you see that article in the paper about the Batton girl and you?"

"I saw it," she said.

"That's stirred up a lot of things. You haven't seen the end of it yet. The Battons are putting pressure on you everywhere they can. They want that DNA test. They think you're their lost daughter. They want to know."

Eleanor remained silent, reaffirming her refusal to comply.

"They have a friend in Congress, if you can believe it, and Shannon—Agent Lamb, is looking for a promotion. The Battons pulled strings; my hands were tied. I had to talk to David about the gun and all, but how and when it was done was not my decision."

"How do you know it was his gun? He lost his gun after the rodeo. You know that."

"So he says," he said, then seeing her reaction added, "We know that now. It's a rare caliber. I had to ask him. He should have reported it missing sooner. But even so, I'd have had to talk to him. Too many people heard him threaten Ramos."

"Are you done with him now?" she said. "You know he didn't do anything."

"I can't talk about that," he said. "It won't be over until we catch someone."

"Why won't they leave me alone?" she asked sliding onto a snow covered bench.

"I'm not sure," he said. "They're crazy in grief missing their daughter. They've latched onto you. You look just like her. Even your voice is the same, they have a video of her from last summer. I thought I was watching you when they showed it to me."

"I'm not Celeste," she said softly. "I'm Eleanor. Eleanor Anders. That's who I am. Who I want to be. Why won't they let me be that?"

"Take the test and be done with it," he suggested. "Maybe you'll find you have cousins in Nebraska. What's the worst that can happen?"

"No," she said simply. The word hung in the air in a cloud of her frozen breath until a gust of wind sent it away.

"They're not going to let up, Eleanor," he said. "They want us to press charges against you, or at least threaten to, if you won't take the test."

"For what?"

"Tabitha," he said ashamedly. "And other things. There's a lot of talk about your birth certificate. When we first found out about it, we managed to keep it quiet, but the newspaper threw it in everyone's face. It didn't name you specifically, but everyone knows now. It's a wide opening for them to do something official."

"Are you going to arrest me?"

"I don't intend to," he said. "But I don't get to make all the decisions. And there are some people in this town . . ." he trailed off and then cleared his throat. "You have people fighting for you, you know. I'm one of them. Stephanie Pearce, too. She's on a crusade for you. We don't know why they're pressing so hard, but neither do we know why you're resisting so much. Can you explain it to me? Can you tell me what's so dangerous about the test?"

Eleanor opened her mouth to say something but then swallowed the words and said instead, "Sheriff, can I ask you a favor?"

"Sure, Eleanor. What can I do?"

"Can you give me a warning? If they're coming for me? Can you give me a chance to . . . to decide?"

CHAPTER TWENTY-THREE

The day after her meeting with the sheriff, Eleanor received a letter from her bank. She opened it to find a cashier's check and a letter stating that her account had been closed due to "suspected identity fraud" as unearthed by the media. Out of courtesy, they had not seized her funds but had merely closed her account. The bank manager had sent the letter himself and put a smiley face next to his signature. The letter also said that the Department of Defense had been alerted of the possible fraud and that she'd need to contact them directly to check on the status of Tabitha Anders' pension money. Another letter was sent to the state in an effort to cut off her food stamps.

The check would pay her bills until mid-January if she was careful. But if she lost her food stamps, she'd see dunner letters before then.

She calmly went to her kitchen and took inventory. She'd been eating cheaply all her life and had gone particularly Spartan in favor of her cake ingredients of late. She needed very little to survive. It was another perk of being whatever it was she was. If she mimicked, if she changed, she'd need food in abundance. She'd go through fuel like a wildfire, but fixed in a shape she could practically starve for weeks. Such was her nature. Water was important, that she couldn't do without, but as a coyote she had survived on a mouse for a week, a squirrel for a month, a belly full of lamb for nearly half a winter on the Montana border while vengeful hunters tracked her.

After studying biology, she'd come to understand it as a nearly perfect metabolic efficiency. Whereas other creatures passed back nutrients, she could take nearly all of it. The realization placed her at once at the head and at the bottom of the food chain. When stressed, when forced to it, she was the perfect parasite, taking all and giving nothing back. But that was under dire conditions. As Eleanor, she'd always had enough food and performed the normal biological functions of a human with nearly the same regularity. Even so, her mother had said she ate like a butterfly and even David commented on her little need of food. Such was her nature that she knew she was wasting food whenever she ate more than a little. And now she would eat even less.

She wondered if she could will her body to start conserving now and decided she could. She put her can of soup back onto the shelf and drank a tall glass of water. Times were dire. Starvation started now.

Thursday, Eleanor sat at her usual desk in the back beside David, wondering how she could fit a prom dress into her budget when the principal entered the classroom followed by Robby Guide and a tall stranger. Class had not yet begun and students were milling around. Mrs. Hart shot a dark look at Mr. Curtz.

"Mrs. Hart," the principal said, stressing the Mrs. "This is Dr. Conrad Sikring from the University of Arizona. He's shadowing Robby here as part of a book on Native American assimilation. He'd like to sit in on your class for a day or two."

"Research project," Sikring corrected. "I'm a cultural anthropologist. I won't be in the way, I promise."

Eleanor elbowed David who looked up from his biology textbook and squinted at the newcomer. Dreadful understanding darkened his face like a shadow of an eclipse as he saw what Eleanor saw, the face of the professor from the back of two books David had in a suitcase hidden under his bed. Sikring was the author of *Werewolves and the Case for Shapeshifters* and *Skinwalkers*. David had bought the books the year before while investigating Eleanor.

"And who is David Venn?" Sikring said to Mrs. Hart after the principal had left hurriedly. David jumped hearing his name. Eleanor smelled his sudden sweat, heard his pulse quicken even over her own.

Mrs. Hart wore a weak mask of pleasant tolerance as she pointed to David at the back of the class. Sikring followed her finger to his desk but his eyes found Eleanor and held on her. Eleanor felt his icy stare as a chill ran down her back. She stared at Sikring and he at her. She recalled other such stares she'd had with a bear and a wolf and a man with a gun. She'd stared and waited for the glance that would signal which way to run, to advance or retreat. The moment stretched out and Eleanor sensed David move in his chair. He stood up and finally drew the professor's gaze away from Eleanor.

"Are you looking for me?" he said.

"Yes, David," he said advancing and offering his hand. "I got your letter and apologize for not responding sooner."

Sikring was tall, well over six feet. He was thin and in his fifties, if not early sixties. He had long gray hair pulled back in the Indian fashion behind his head but his sunburned light complexion and pale chestnut eyes placed him as a European. He wore jeans and weathered cowboy boots, a hand-worked leather belt with a silver and turquoise belt buckle. His shirt was clean and new with a crisp western collar held shut with a braided bola tie and another piece of turquoise jewelry. He smiled warmly but cast another glance at Eleanor as he shook David's hand.

"It was a stupid letter," David said.

"I should have responded though. Unprofessional of me. Sorry, I was distracted."

"No worries," he said.

"Is this your friend?"

Eleanor jumped as if stung by a snake. She twitched and turned out of her seat, feet on the ground, ready to run, a hiding animal who knows it's been spotted. Before she could run—and she was about to run, David leaned in to the man and whispered softly in his ear.

"Leave her alone," he said. "I'm not kidding."

The words leaked out of his mouth like dripping poison. She'd never heard such threatening tones from him before. Remembering David's temper, she worried then for the visitor.

Sikring's pleasant expression vanished, replaced with the very sensible look of fear. David's free hand balled into a fist, his other gripped Sikring's so tightly it went white.

"No. Of course not," Sikring said. "I meant no offense."

He'd given it all away. David had played it all wrong. His reaction was too strong, too revealing. It was a confession, reeking of guilt. She stood up and offered her hand to the professor.

"Hello, Dr. Sikring," she said. "I'm Eleanor Anders. You

have to forgive David. He's very protective of me. There's been some turmoil around here about me. Maybe you read about it in the paper. It's been unpleasant. We're wary of strangers."

She held his gaze so he would not look at her hand. She knew her fingernails had blackened and her palms were harder than they'd been two minutes before. It had hit her suddenly and reflexively. With any luck he wouldn't notice, or if he did, maybe he'd think she'd been gardening without gloves. In December.

He tried to study her face, but she wouldn't release his gaze and held him in a predator's stare, reversing the early arrangement. In her unblinking periphery, she noticed his freckles, the shade of the sunburn on his forehead, the false tooth, the chapped lips, the subtle identifiable marks a molecule could not give her.

"I understand," he said, clearing his throat. "I just wanted to say hello."

He nearly tripped over his feet as he left them for a seat at the front. Mrs. Hart led her class as if he weren't there. After the bell rang, he offered his services to her as a guest lecturer, perhaps explaining the nature of his research project or Indian legends, which were his specialty. Mrs. Hart shrugged noncommittally and said she'd think about it.

At lunch, Eleanor saw Sikring sitting with Robby at her usual table. It had become his usual table as well.

"I don't like this," said David.

"I want to know about your letter," she said.

He sucked his teeth and said, "Let's grab some chips and go to the library."

"Way ahead of you," she said and left the cafeteria with only a carton of milk.

Eleanor's lunches were paid for by the state as part of her food stamp program. She'd figured she could survive indefinitely on the lunch portions provided she didn't get cut off. With a carton of milk a day and a state-approved vitamin enriched lunch, she wouldn't even be tired. If only she could turn her food stamps into electric bill payments, she could last until she graduated, provided she didn't make any more cakes.

"Oh, by the way," David said as they walked. "I tried to call you. Your phone's been turned off."

"I guess I forgot to pay the bill," she lied. She'd had the service cancelled the day she received the bank's check. "Don't change the subject. Tell me about the letter."

Once in the library, they found a private table.

"I asked him the basics," David whispered. "If he'd discovered any validity to the legends about skinwalkers, if there was any proof."

"Did you mention me?" she asked.

"No. Of course not," he said. "Well, not by name. I may have said something about a friend."

"The mud is hardening," she said.

"What?" he said.

"Nothing. He never wrote you back? No contact at all?"

"Not a peep. I must have sounded like an idiot."

"What idiotic things did you say in your letter?"

He flushed. "Eleanor, you've got to understand how desperate I was. I knew you'd never tell me, even though you did once, kinda, when we were little. I knew that you'd be forever distant unless I broke through on my own. There's some truth to that, don't you think?"

She nodded. "Yeah," she said. "So what did you tell him? I have to know."

"I mentioned the coyote. I said I knew somebody who said they'd been a coyote before."

"Did you mention Dwight?"

"Who?"

"The trucker. Last Halloween?"

"Oh no," he said. "I didn't figure that out for a while."

David sneaked a potato chip into his mouth when the librarian looked away. Eleanor saved her milk for later.

"Maybe it's a coincidence," he said. "He studies Indians. The Wild River Reservation is just down the road. It makes sense."

"No. It was that stupid article," she said. "It mentioned Jamesford and a look-alike. It even had a photo. Celeste's photo—my photo. He remembered your letter, examined the postmark and pop, here he is. No. He's here for me. I feel it."

"You know, you have a way of getting paranoid."

She laughed. "I haven't been paranoid enough," she said. "Don't you smell the fuse burning?"

He didn't answer.

"Tabitha said we were all on limited time. I'll take what I can, while I can, but I don't have a lot."

"Don't talk that way," he said.

She gave him a reassuring smile. She was good at lying.

The Revealers would often buy a half hour segment of radio time to publicize their church's activities and pray for the demise of certain politicians, the burning of certain books, and the return of "old fashion religion" which always made Eleanor think of human sacrifices. Jennifer Hutton personally told Eleanor to listen to the broadcast Friday night, saying with a sneer, "It concerns you."

Eleanor sat with David in his room, an ancient transistor radio between them on the bed.

"We've prayed for this town," Lugner said over static. *"James-ford is full of good and righteous people, but they've been duped. Science has blinded them from the obvious. Something is not right in our little town."*

"Our little town?" said David. "He sounds like he was born here."

"Shhh," said Eleanor.

"There's another scientist here now. This one is just as bad as the other. He proselytizes religion as myth. Oh, there's no doubt that our red brethren were tricked into devil worship before Christianity offered them a way to salvation, but this new man suggests that the Bible—the Bible, children—is also myth. This is what freethinking leads to. People don't know where to draw the line. The devil never starts with a lie. Oogy boogy great spirit animal gods are indeed graven images. The rites of the primitives are obscene hogwash, but seeing this has blinded this scientist from recognizing the true word of God."

Karen peeked in the door, drawn by the noise. Jim was behind her.

"What's this about?" Jim said. He held a glass of amber liquor and melting ice.

"We're listening to this kook," said David.

"Is that the creep that protests military funerals?" Jim asked.

"Yeah," David said.

He sat down in David's desk chair and sipped his drink. Karen stayed at the door. The cat wandered in and leapt up on the bed purring for attention from Eleanor. It looked up at her with its one, bright eye.

"And what has brought this new evil to our little town? What

has brought this poison into our schools? I think we all know what it is," Lugner went on. *"From my pulpit we have examined the history of this cursed little town."*

"Now we're cursed?" commented David.

"We have heard the tales of ghosts and apparitions, demons and monsters, unnatural burials in unhallowed ground, poison in the food our children eat. We have read about sorcery in the newspapers, had our citizens murdered in the streets, our water tainted by foul odors, drought and pestilence, and we, yes my children, we have identified the source. Yes, we know. We are not blinded by the limits of so-called science. We have revealed the source of all this wickedness that grips our lovely Jamesford."

"'Lovely' now," said David.

"Shh," said Karen, her face anxious, her eyes wide and worried.

"I cannot name names—not on the radio, for the ungodly secular laws of this country, which we fight against daily, protect the wicked from the righteous. But we of the New Church of Christ Revealed know the name. We can speak it in our meetings, and I pray that all those listening to my voice today who are not members, who have not found the way, will come and hear the name and join us in our righteous fight against this wickedness, its source and its symptoms."

"What is he talking about?" Jim said.

"Shh," said Karen again. Jim turned, ready to chide his wife for shutting him up, but one look at her and he hushed and listened harder.

"To fight this wickedness, to draw attention and drive it out, we, the members of New Church of Christ Revealed, will stage a large, righteous, and legal protest at the upcoming Jamesford High School's Winter Dance. We do this not just because they have removed the holy name of Christmas from this celebration in the

manner of liberal political correctness, but specifically because she will be there and she is the source."

"Oh no," said Karen.

Jim looked from his wife, to his son, and then to Eleanor.

"Eleanor?" he said confused. "He's talking about Eleanor? The hell?"

"The hell," she repeated.

CHAPTER TWENTY-FOUR

Eleanor stayed close to home. Like the article that had caused so much attention, the radio broadcast left little to the imagination as to her identity. It struck Eleanor as funny that she was blamed for the drought instead of God, and for the hydraulic fluid in their water instead of the fracking operation up the canyon, but being blamed for the murders was not so amusing. Everything else, she'd seen coming.

Eleanor spent Saturday morning doing what trivial homework she had, drawing it out as long as she could. Then she cleaned the house, which always made her feel useful. David arrived just after noon.

"It's shopping day," he said. "Grab your bags."

They climbed into David's little car and drove to Sherman's Grocery.

"I don't need anything," she said as they got out. "I'm pretty stocked up, but I could use some money. Would you mind if I use my card for some of yours and you can give me the money?"

"Isn't that against the rules?" he asked.

"Yes," she said. "Does that matter?"

"Not at all," he said. "For a dress?"

"Yeah. That and . . ." she stopped herself before saying more but not soon enough.

"What is it Eleanor? Tell me."

She sighed and choked back a lie. Then she told him about the bank sending her the check and the trouble the bank manager was making for her with social services and the military. Her mother's pension money was being held "pending an investigation."

"That's why I turned off the phone," she said. "But Stephanie's on it. She's talking to a lawyer. She thinks it will all be okay, but it may take a while."

"I'm hurt, Eleanor," David said. "You told Stephanie about this before me? Before my mother?"

"You guys have enough trouble. Your dad isn't working. There's the gun thing. I know there's pressure at home. I feel the tension. I don't want to bring any more into it."

"But we're getting money because of you. It's not much but it's something. You should get that. It's a no-brainer."

"It isn't. Really. I feel like I'm sinking and making waves is the last thing I need."

"No, Eleanor. That won't do. You don't have to take the money, but you have to tell my folks. And you have to apologize for not telling me."

"I'm sorry," she said. "I was trying to help."

He took her hand. He'd gripped the shopping cart so hard he was sweating. She was about to comment on the clammy handshake when the jolt struck them.

Both their arms twitched as if shocked by a sudden but soothing electrical current. Instead of flying apart, their hands gripped each others' tighter. The sensation was not unlike their kisses had been, only weaker, blunter, but still unmistakably related.

David looked at Eleanor, searching for something within her eyes and then smiling when he found it.

"Eleanor," he said. "I see you there."

"I'm here," she said. "It's me in here. Sometimes I'm a mess, but it's me and I miss you, David."

Together, they leaned forward over the cart and kissed.

How she kept standing she would never know. A pent-up energy exploded through her body and she grew dizzy. Her hair prickled beneath the erupting gooseflesh. She closed her eyes against the pageant of colors filling her vision only to have them trace across her inner eyelids. She tasted David's lips, felt his heat, drew in his breath, and was awash in warm, amber honey.

She felt her thoughts fade, her senses take control of all her reason, and forced herself to pull away. David collapsed onto the floor in a heap, unable to catch his breath. Eleanor backed into a store shelf and knocked several cans down trying to keep her balance.

Through the buzz in her ears, Eleanor slowly made out other sounds. She remembered only vaguely that she was at the grocery store.

The sound rose in her hearing as it faded in real life. She blinked up the aisle and saw four people gawking at them, their hands gesturing wildly. She looked for danger, unsure whether her legs could carry her and then realized they were smiling. In fact, they were applauding. She recognized two of them as a young newlywed couple who still held hands when they walked together. Their eyes shone. The other people, she thought she remembered, were an old couple in their seventies who came to town once a month for provisions. They also smiled at Eleanor. Their stares were deeper, more meaningful, and saw across forty years to their own courting. The old man winked at David as he got to his feet.

"Now that was a kiss," the old man said, which prompted the young couple to steal a smooch themselves.

There were more people at the other end of the aisle. Eleanor turned to them and stared right into the face of Miss Church and two strangers Eleanor immediately knew to be Revealers.

"Tramp," the old lunch lady said. "Trash."

David stumbled to his feet. A crowd formed at both ends of the aisle.

"You old nag," said the rancher behind her. "Mind your own business."

"God will—" began one of the strangers, but a woman Eleanor couldn't see cut her off.

"God will deal with people like *you*," the unseen woman said. "The things you do in His name—shame on you. Shame!"

"Don't you know who that is?" said Miss Church, pointing to Eleanor.

"Yeah, we do," said a butcher coming out from behind his glass case to see what was happening. "That's Eleanor Anders. Sweetest little girl I ever saw grow up. Never did nothing to no one. Never bothered nobody. Unlike some people."

The crowd stared at the three. Eleanor felt David's hand slide into hers.

"Leave the young people alone," said the old rancher.

"It's time your circus pulled up stakes," said a man. "The

clown show's over. I wouldn't go near that dance if I were you, either. Could get messy."

Miss Church stuck her chin in the air and flanked by the two others, marched up the aisle past David and Eleanor, none of them even glancing at them as they left.

That night, Eleanor ate with the Venns.

"You should have seen them," said David. "The crowd was so pissed. The Revealers have definitely overstayed their welcome."

"I heard about it," Karen said. "And about your little kissy floorshow."

"Yeah, well, uhm," he stuttered.

"Parasites," said Mr. Venn. "I know this town needs tourists and Lugner's congregation is bringing in money, but threatening a school dance? Are they stupid or what?"

"Everyone in my class thinks they're dumbasses," said Wendy.

"Wendy. Language," cautioned her mother.

"There too, huh?" said David.

"I heard the mayor had a meeting today with your principal, David," said Jim. "The sheriff was there, too, and some lawyers. The whole town is pretty upset."

"They think they're dumb-asses too," said David, giving Wendy a wink.

Karen shot him a look. Jim smiled and salted his food.

"So, did you meet with the foreman?" Karen asked offhandedly, but Eleanor caught a hesitant hitch in her voice.

"Yeah," Jim said, poking his potatoes. "Nothing available right now, but he knows I'm looking. Said he'll call me if something comes up. Summer is the drilling season. Should be work come spring."

"Is money a problem, Mom?" asked David. Jim stared into his plate.

"No. We're fine. Just a little tight right now."

Eleanor gave a deep sigh and said, "Not that it affects you, but I should tell you about my situation."

She explained how the bank manager had latched onto her birth certificate revelation in the paper to close her account and stop her mother's pension.

"But I had enough saved," she said. "It's not a big deal. Stephanie said the whole thing should be fixed by January. February at the latest. I'm good that long, if I budget. And I'm good at that."

"Of all the nerve," said Jim smashing his fist into the table and tipping a water glass. "I'm going down there Monday and breaking some asses!"

"Jim!"

"Sorry," he said. "Army talk."

"Stephanie's got it handled, I think," said Eleanor. "I didn't like that bank anyway."

"That was a tiny stipend," said Karen. "And it ran out next year anyway. Of all the mean-spirited, shallow things to do."

"Is the bank manager a Revealer too?" asked Wendy.

"Must be," said David.

"Dumb-dumb."

"How tight is your budget?" asked Karen.

"I don't need to sell the house," Eleanor said, trying to make a joke. "Not that I could. Or we could. Not until this thing is settled. I'm good. Might be a little light on Christmas presents is all. I can borrow a dress for Friday."

"Oh, don't you even think of that," said Karen sternly. "Let me buy you a dress."

"No, it's okay."

"Eleanor, dear, it's time to shut up. I'm buying you a dress and that's the end of it. Okay, Jim?"

"Absolutely," he said. "Sell the car if you have to. Make it a good one."

Eleanor let David drive her home after dinner. Her head swam with new appreciation for Jamesford and the reconnection with David.

"I don't think we should . . . uhm," David said.

"No," Eleanor said. "Save it for the dance. My knees are still wobbly." And they were. A glance at David's face, unable to conceal his own glee, filled her with longing and love. She had to fight herself not to reach out and run her fingers through his thick hair, trace his profile with her fingers, and fall asleep in his arms.

"Cool," he said. "Yeah, I gotta drive."

Sunday morning there was a knock on Eleanor's door after breakfast. She'd heard a heavy car pull up in front of her house and when it didn't drive away and the engine didn't stop, she shifted toward the back door.

The knock was gentle, none too urgent, but insistent.

Eleanor calmed herself, wiped her hands on her mother's rose patterned apron she loved so much, and marched forward. She knew who was behind the door before she opened it. Eleanor recognized Dr. Zalarnik, the biologist. The massive man with a crew cut beside him she remembered from the school assembly, scanning the bleachers for snipers.

"Hello," she said. The sun shone bright in a clear sky,

reflecting brilliantly off the snow and making Eleanor squint. The two men wore sunglasses.

"Eleanor Anders? I'm Dimitri, Dimitri Zalarnik."

"I know who you are."

"It's cold out here. Can we talk inside?"

"You and your shadow?"

"You mean Mr. Gordon? No, he doesn't have to come. Wait in the car, Gordon."

The large man retreated to the car without saying a word.

"Bodyguard?" Eleanor asked. She watched the big man adjust his earpiece before sliding into the back seat of the limousine. She'd seen the outline of a gun under his coat.

"Part of the job," he said. "I have enemies. And you have some of the same ones."

Zalarnik took in the tiny house with a single glance before sitting on the couch.

"You mean Lugner?" she said.

"Yeah, what a creep, huh?" The slang was an affectation. He was trying to bond with her. "But that's not why I'm here."

Eleanor waited for him to continue, offering him no handle to grip, no small talk to warm to.

"Mr. Gurenno, your science teacher," he said as if she didn't know who her teachers were, "said you are a very bright girl. He said you have a knack for science. Did you get to use the new microscopes? Did you like them? Aren't they cool?"

"They are nice," she admitted.

"Well, between you and me," he said conspiratorially, "I'm trying to get on the good side of Jamesford—and Wyoming, for that matter. You see, I'm trying to open a laboratory here to study biology. It'll bring a lot of jobs and really help the area. I'll be able to donate all kinds of things to the school and the town. I'm already thinking of a scholarship for graduating high school students who are good at science. Doesn't that sound awesome?"

"What do you want, Mr. Zalarnik?"

"Doctor, actually," he said. "But call me Dimitri. In order for me to open this laboratory, to break ground and bring prosperity to this corner of Wyoming, I need certain permits that only the government and local authorities can give me. It goes all the way to the federal level. It's really an involved process."

"Yes?" coaxed Eleanor.

"Have you ever heard of a congressman from Nebraska called Mel Wittiker?"

"So, that's his name," said Eleanor. "You're here about Celeste Batton."

"For her family," he said. "They want you . . . uhm . . . they think that you . . ."

"I know what they want, and the answer's no."

"That's where I come in. See, I have all the equipment and everything right here in Jamesford, well actually up toward Yellowstone, where we can do the test. It's a great lab, a model of what I want to build right here, but smaller and temporary. It can sequence DNA and solve this riddle in a couple of hours. All I need from you is a sample. A hair even. Nothing at all."

"No," she said.

"Eleanor, it's very important to me, to the Battons—to Jamesford—that you let this happen. I can assure you that it won't hurt. I'll even maintain your privacy. I only need to know how distant your relation is to the Battons. I can do that. Don't you want to know?"

"You assume I'm related," she said.

"Of course I do. Everyone does. Just look at you. You're the very mirror of their missing little girl."

"Not so little," she said. "I heard she was seventeen."

"They still want her back," he said.

"And failing that, they want me?"

"Family is very important to the Battons. They're like twenty generations on that farm of theirs. They have their own graveyard and everything. They like to keep track of their people, and frankly Eleanor, you're obviously one of them."

"I want them to leave me alone. I suspect this is the same attitude that Celeste took, that's why she ran away."

"I heard she was abducted," he said.

"Did you?"

He rolled his eyes and said, "Well no, I guess not. I honestly don't know what happened to her. But that doesn't matter. Not to us. Not now. What matters is that I need favors. We all need favors. It's so easy."

"So the congressman is holding up your permits if I don't submit to these tests?"

"He won't make it easy. He's a close friend of Wayne's. That's Mr. Batton, Celeste's father."

"I've met him," she said. "And the answer is still no."

"I'm a friend. We're all friends. Won't you be my friend? I understand there's a dance coming up. You need money for flowers? Would you like to borrow my limousine? I could donate a band. A good one. I know people."

"No," she said. "You seem very kind but I've got to disappoint you. Tell them all to leave me alone."

His face darkened.

"Really Eleanor, you're being pig-headed."

"Goodbye," she said standing up and pointing to the door.

He examined the sofa and pinched a piece of lint from a buttonhole before dropping it.

"Mind if I use your bathroom before I go?"

"So you can swipe my hairbrush? Yes, I do mind. Use a hydrant," she said.

She sensed he might lunge at her then, grab a lock of hair or tear off a piece of skin, but he put a plastic smile on instead.

"Leave," she ordered him. He pulled the door open and turned one last time to look at her.

"Celeste, don't be this way," he said.

"My name is Eleanor," she said. "Remember? I'm Eleanor Anders."

"Prove it," he said.

CHAPTER TWENTY-FIVE

The town filled with lawyers. The dance committee, headed by the mayor, brought in state lawyers to look into the legality of barring the Revealers from their protest. The Revealers, led by Pastor Lugner himself, led a cadre of three black-suited attorneys up the courthouse steps to respond preemptively and threaten lawsuits that would bankrupt the town if their rights were infringed upon.

All of Jamesford watched the standoff with interest and revulsion. Though no one had said anything directly to Eleanor, no one except Jennifer Hutton that is, there was growing sentiment that the best thing was for Eleanor just to stay home, go to a movie, or order in—just stay away from the dance in the hopes that the Revealers would then do the same.

Eleanor seriously contemplated doing just that when she learned of another group of lawyers who had quietly slipped into Jamesford. The Battons and their official friend Congressman Wittiker had sent a delegation to solve the matter of Eleanor's identity before Christmas.

Eleanor learned about it in Riverton Wednesday evening

with Karen. They only had a couple of days until the dance, but Karen's work schedule hadn't allowed them a chance to shop before.

"I was thinking that maybe I shouldn't go to the dance," she blurted out as Karen draped an ivory dress over her.

"Not an option, dear," she said matter-of-factly. "I won't allow it."

"You've thought about it then?"

"Jim and I talked about it. He's taking it personally, bless his heart," she said wistfully. "You're family, he says, and he won't tolerate disrespect toward family. In this case, I agree. Besides, David wants to go. Have you seen how happy he's been all week? I don't need to tell you that he's been in a funk the last couple of months. He was coming out of it slowly, but this week he's been his old self. Let's look at the blue one again."

"The ivory is nice," Eleanor said.

"It does suit your hair. I'm thinking strapless. Are you okay with that?"

"Okay," she said.

"You can't let yourself be bullied," Karen went on comparing overlapping pinks, blues and whites against the ivory each in turn under Eleanor's neck. "I got a call from Stephanie's supervisor telling us that you need to be tested. There's a legal team here from Nebraska who're putting on pressure."

"That's it then? They're making me?"

"No," she said. "Just more threats." She sighed. "I won't lie to you, they put on the pressure pretty hard. They told Jim and me that it was within our power to compel you to do it, as guardians. But Jim offered them a few choice words I won't repeat and sent them back to the drawing board."

"That was nice of him."

"They didn't think so," she said.

"The blue's nice too," she said.

"Eleanor," Karen asked suddenly. "What are you afraid of? With the test? Do you think Jim and I will abandon you to the Battons?"

"No, Karen. It's not that. It's complicated," she said. "It's personal. It's important. I . . . I can't. I don't want to. Can we leave it at that? Please?"

"Okay," she said resignedly. "Try these on."

Eleanor took the pile of dresses into the changing room. She chose the one she liked best, the ivory one, and slipped into it first. The price tag dangled from the sleeve. She looked at it and gasped. She looked at the others. They were just as bad.

Karen watched her come out, critically evaluating the length and shape, not looking at Eleanor's face, which was white with dread.

"Karen," she said showing her the price tag. "No."

"Our treat," she said.

"I can't let you do this," she said.

"Eleanor, the entire town wants you in this dress," she said. "The good ones anyway. You owe it to them. Hold your head up girl. Be beautiful. Be yourself."

"Myself wouldn't wear this dress."

"Then be what we need you to be," she said.

That night, with a tailored strapless ivory dress, matching shoes, and a handbag that could barely accommodate a hand-kerchief and her pocket change at the same time, Eleanor entered her house and saw immediately that it'd been burgled.

If she called Sheriff Hannon, he wouldn't believe that her house had been broken into. Everything was in order, nothing obviously moved or missing, but Eleanor sensed the changes immediately. The lingering smell of sweat, male sweat, clung to the air like a paste. Her cushions were moved and as she suspected everything in her bathroom had been handled. Her own room, the loft, was strangely untouched. They hadn't bothered to climb the ladder. Her mother's room however, the master bedroom, the only real bedroom in the house, had been searched. She saw that her mother's bed had been carefully unwrapped and remade. The corners were bad. The perfume bottles were misaligned and the hairbrush was clean. When Eleanor had cleaned the room, she'd left Tabitha hairs in the brush, they were her mother's last. Now they were gone.

The room was obviously a woman's but only a fool would mistake it for a teenager's. And yet someone had. A lipstick was missing and a pair of nail clippers, which Eleanor never needed, had been taken from Tabitha' bed table. Eleanor felt a mischievous glee and laughed out loud. Coyote the trickster helped by fools. Silently, like a prayer, she thanked her dead mother for looking out for her yet again.

Thursday at lunch, Jennifer Hutton and a sophomore Eleanor didn't know sat alone in a far corner. Their backs were turned to the room. Eleanor knew that pose. She watched the other students cast angry glares at them.

David had insisted that they eat at a central table, "proud and loud" he said. Their group had outgrown their old little table. Even Russell was with them today, though he kept his eyes from David and tried several times to nonchalantly flop his arm around Barbara's shoulders.

"Where's your shadow?" said David to Robby. Sikring had followed Robby for a couple of days but he had not been in school that week.

"I don't know. I guess he got bored with me," Robby said.

"He asked me about Penelope," Barbara said. "Why would he want to know about Penelope?"

"How does he know to ask about Penelope?" said Aubrey.

"It's another ghost story," said Robby. "His specialty is myths."

"So he's collecting urban legends?" said Alexi.

"Penelope was no urban legend," said Barbara. "It really happened."

"Speaking of which," said Brian. "I'm taking her to the dance."

"Get out of here," said Barbara. "How'd you get a hold of her?"

"She called me," he said.

"That's not allowed," said Alexi.

"Sue me," he said.

"I thought you didn't like her," said Midge. "I thought none of us did."

"We liked her," said Alexi.

"I meant us others," said Midge, shrinking a bit.

Alexi squinted at her.

"She was a bitch," said Brian. "But, you know. People change. She was nice on the phone. We talked for a long time."

"Why didn't she call me?" asked Barbara.

"I don't know. We didn't talk about you," he said.

The announcement speaker triggered with a long beep that no one in the cafeteria paid any attention to. The start of a staticky announcement was lost in the din of talking teenagers. Eleanor however, picked up every word.

"Attention Jamesford High School Dancers." Static mixed with the principle's voice. "In a break from tradition, this year's Winter Dance will not be held at the Masonic Hall. In fact, it will not be held in Jamesford at all due to 'technical problems.'"

"Shh," said Eleanor to get the others to listen.

"This year's winter dance will not even be held in this country." He paused for affect.

Hushes spread through the room.

"This year, the Wild River Shoshone will host our annual dance at their Reservation Meeting Hall. Your dance tickets, available at the office if you haven't bought yours yet, will grant you access across the border. You must have a valid school ID and a ticket to go. Give yourself thirty minutes for the drive. Busses will be available from the front of the school departing every half hour for those who don't wish to drive. Curfew will be lifted for the entire evening by order of the mayor. See you there, dancers!"

Another beep popped, signaling the end of the announcement. There was a moment of quiet before the room exploded in commentary.

"That's a slick solution," said Robby. "The Council can arrest any of Lugner's people on the spot for trespassing if they try to get in. They can keep the media away too. Closest they'll get is that stretch of desert out on 26 at the turn-off. You can't even see the lights of the meeting hall from there."

"A reservation? Gross," said Alexi. "I want my money back."

"You didn't pay a penny," said David. "Bryce is paying the bill."

"A smelly Indian reservation is no place for a nice dance." said Alexi, "No offense, Robby."

"Then stop being offensive," said David.

"What?" said Robby, "You think we live in teepees? Wigwams? Grow up, Alexi."

"I've been inside the new meeting house," said Midge excitedly. "It is so cool. It used to be a barracks. It smells like pine and wood smoke and has such a high ceiling. It's a wonderful place."

"She's right," said Robby. "It's great. It makes that stupid Masonic hall look like Alexi's unswept outhouse. No offense, Alexi." She glared at him.

"So, you guys want to car pool, then?" said Brian.

"It's up to Russell," said Barbara.

"With Brian?" Russell said.

"With Penelope and Brian," she said in such a way as to give him little choice.

"Okay," he said. "Do you have my number?"

"You have a phone?" said David in mock surprise.

"Shut up, Venn," he spat back.

"Don't," said Eleanor. Her voice hit a tone that silenced the table instantly, quick as a gunshot and gritty as a growl. Not wholly human. "Just don't."

"Really," agreed Barbara.

Eleanor could not face another fight between David and Russell, but she did feel the same as Alexi about the change in venue. She was relieved to be free from the hateful Revealers and the accompanying news cameras—she had already begun to concoct ways of avoiding them—but stepping onto an Indian reservation was not much better.

For the rest of the day, she was quiet and thoughtful. She

wrestled with fear and hope alike, afraid to let either get the advantage.

She felt the town's kindness toward her, realized this dance had been moved because of her. People she didn't know, hundreds she'd never seen, thousands she'd never spoken a word to, had stood up for her if only in spirit. They could have excluded her from the dance. It would not have been hard to ostracize her and David enough to keep them away. She knew how cruel people could be, but, instead, they had done this. They'd put aside their prejudice and allowed the Jamesford Cowboys to benefit from charity offered by the Shoshone Indians. Jamesford was not overtly racist, but people are people and both sides of the reservation border had private and strong opinions about the other.

The kindness worried her. In flashes of memory that she could not be sure were real, she remembered her family receiving kindness from the community before they were slaughtered. She remembered a woman in Navajo dress carrying a colorful basket of beans and offering it to her mother. The memories were just flashes, a slideshow without connecting context. When she remembered the scene, she caught a glimpse of her mother's face wearing a warm, grateful smile and heard the traditional words of greeting and thanks pass between them. She remembered a yellow truck, dusty with red dirt, idling on a dirt road. A man stood beside the truck. She remembered his stare. She could not recall his face, only his stare as he watched. His stare was not generous, was not honest or kind. Hours later, with a belly full of boiled beans, she had fled into the night when that staring man cut her family to pieces.

Eleanor watched for those stares.

She also watched Russell Liddle. He'd been on edge. David's jab at him didn't draw the reaction it might have. Eleanor didn't like that David had provoked him, but she understood why. David had a scar on his thumb to remind him of his cruelty, even though Russell hadn't actually given it to him. She had.

Disbelieving, as if watching herself from a distance, she found herself approaching Barbara after school.

"Barbara," she said before she could stop herself. "What's up with Russell?"

She was heading toward the parking lot, doubtlessly to catch a ride with someone. Eleanor saw Crystal's little car warming up in the lot.

"Same as David," she said.

"Barbara, I know we're not friends, but—"

"Who said we're not friends?"

She was stunned. The comment had sounded genuine. She had learned to tolerate Barbara once she'd stopped flirting with David, but she felt no friendship toward her. She'd sensed a change in her old rival since the summer, but hadn't thought much of it. Could Barbara have changed so much that she could now call Eleanor her friend? Can people like Barbara Pennon really change? If so, how?

"Uhm," she stammered.

Barbara watched Crystal push snow off her hood with a hand broom. "I should really go out there and help," she said. "But I can't. I'm talking to you." Giggling, she turned to face Eleanor. "You know you might be the only one who'd understand," she said. "Can you keep a secret?"

"Better than you know," said Eleanor.

"David wasn't the only one pulled in by the cops."

"Russell? He's a suspect?" Things fell into place.

"Yeah, Russell," said Barbara. "And his dad."

"What? Why?"

"Russell's dad had a scrap with Brett Porter the night he died. They had a fistfight at a bar. Two drunks swinging like windmills, I heard. Russell's dad came out the worse for it and said some things when he left."

"Makes sense then that the sheriff would talk to him," Eleanor said, wheels turning in her mind.

"The Liddles don't like the police. Long history. I'm sure you heard about it. No secrets in this town. Russell's dad's been in prison for fighting. But the sheriff didn't have any evidence so there it stands. Russell thinks he has it in for them."

"Him or them?"

"No difference. If they arrest Russell, he's in jail. If they arrest his dad, he gets sent to The Farm down in Riverton. You know, that place you almost got sent to."

"Still might," Eleanor said, and couldn't believe that she'd confided something like that to Barbara.

"No, you've got David's family. You're set. Hey, here's Crystal," she said. "You want a ride home?"

"What? Me?"

"Unless you have a ride with David," she said.

"No," she said. "David's running secret errands."

"Probably flowers," Barbara said. "Hop in, there's room." Crystal pulled her little two-door up to the curb.

"Thanks for the help," she said sarcastically to Barbara. "My feet are freezing."

"I was talking to Eleanor," she said. "Can we give her a lift?"

Crystal looked as surprised as Eleanor felt but then said. "If it's not too far. Where do you live?"

She climbed in the back seat and directed Crystal across town. They were there in five minutes.

Kindness was dangerous, thought Eleanor, waving good-bye from her porch as the car beeped a farewell. Kindness drops your guard. Kindness opens the gates to disaster. Kindness kills.

CHAPTER TWENTY-SIX

The night of the dance, David picked Eleanor up at her house, and then drove her back to his trailer for Karen to snap photos. Jim had volunteered to help with the festivities and had already gone. Since they'd be home all night, "bored to death," as Wendy described it, Karen promised to teach her how to dance.

"How'd you learn to dance?" Wendy asked Eleanor.

"David taught me. I'm a quick learner."

"I taught you nothing," he said while his mother took candid shots from strange angles. "I just sway back and forth."

"That's pretty much dancing," said Eleanor. "If you can sway to music and not fall down, you're dancing."

"It helps to hold on to someone," said David.

"One or two more outside. In the light." Karen pushed them through the door waving her camera like director's baton. "I want to get some sky behind Eleanor's dress."

"What about my tux?" asked David.

"A tux is a black suit, is a black suit," Karen said, dropping to one knee to shoot upward at Eleanor. "A dress, a woman in a gown, is a unique thing of beauty."

"David looks nice too, Momma," said Wendy.

"I don't look as good as Eleanor," he said.

"No, you don't," agreed Wendy.

David had arranged for dinner at Eric's father's Buffalo Cafe. Eleanor saw them turn away several people while they were seated. She recognized the lady news reporter who followed Lugner around. She was explaining to the maître d' how important she was in a failing effort to get a table. Eleanor hurried past her before she could be recognized.

The cafe might have followed town tradition and catered to the kids tonight, but their prices were still geared to the well-to-do. It sat on the same block as the best art studios and was something of a boutique itself. It specialized in game meats: elk, venison, and its namesake, buffalo. It had many positive write-ups in national magazines and was a tourist attraction. Ten years in Jamesford, and Eleanor had never stepped foot in it before.

"Two buffalo burgers with fries," David ordered. "Ice tea for me and for the lady, a lemonade."

"No onions on the burger," Eleanor added.

"Same with mine," added David.

"You look nice, Eleanor," the waitress said. "You both do."

"Thanks," said David.

When the waitress left, Eleanor leaned over and whispered, "She knew my name. That creeped me out."

"It's a small town, Eleanor. You're a celebrity."

"It's a nightmare," she said. "I don't want to be a celebrity. I don't like being noticed. My life is burning down because of it."

David buttered a piece of bread and offered Eleanor half. She took it but only stared at it in her hand.

"I don't see it that way," he said. "Now don't get me wrong. I understand where you're coming from. You're afraid. I get that. But it's not all bad. Your life isn't burning down, but brightening up. It's not flames, see? But light. You're shining, not burning."

"You're sweet," she said finally tasting the bread. It was a light rye. The butter was rich and creamy. Real butter. She liked it.

"You're a wonderful, special person who's been pretending to be ordinary. You're not ordinary. Now that you've allowed yourself to be who you really are, of course you'll stand out."

"By looking like someone else."

"That's not what I mean," he said. "I mean you. Look at school. You're a magnet now. Last year, you were teased. Now you can command the lunchroom with a word. You're *The Girl*, Eleanor. I think you're more popular than Barbara Pennon."

"She said we were friends the other day. She had Crystal drive me home."

"There, you see? Everyone is attracted to you."

"It's this body," she said. "Celeste bloomed last year. Inside and out. I'm a copy."

"I don't remember Celeste baking," he said. "Did she teach you how to make the best cake in Wyoming? Or was that you?"

She squirmed in her seat.

"Or did she impart to you some magical ability to unite an entire town around her to fight against bigotry and hatred? Did she unite white man and Indian for a protected school dance?"

"None of that's me," she said.

"It's all you," he said. "You're a good person, Eleanor. I

know it. You know it. And everyone else knows it too. They sense it. People do good things for good people and you are a good person."

"We keep forgetting, David," she said. "I'm not a person."

"Poppycock," he said.

"Did you just say 'poppycock'?"

"I'm watching my language," David said embarrassed. "You know what I mean, Eleanor. Just relax. Okay? For me. Let's have a good time."

"Okay," she said as their food arrived.

It was nearly dusk when David turned his little Honda out of Jamesford and fell in behind a bus driving to the Wild River Reservation and the Jamesford High School Winter Dance. Eleanor sat in the passenger seat and longed to roll down the window and feel the wind in her hair as she had in Nebraska.

Eleanor loved the wind, even when artificial. She loved the smell of the air, the taste of it. She could read it like a book, forecast the weather, locate animals, find water, and detect danger. But it was cold outside and she was afraid of messing her hair. She had tried to curl it for an hour. It would fold and wrap around the borrowed curling iron and then flex out straight again when Eleanor took her eyes off it. She'd feel a tingling in her scalp as it repaired itself to its usual pattern. Her bruise, too, threatened to return, so she gave up trying to curl her hair and pinned it up in a knot that looked at once elegant and timeless.

David twiddled with the radio dial, searching unsuccessfully for a station that didn't play country.

"Sometimes I can pick up a college station in Riverton," he said, "if the clouds are right. There's a lot of static but at least they play songs written in this century that aren't about pick-up trucks."

He passed the bus and came to the reservation turn-off in twenty minutes. Several police cars marked the intersection, their lights flashing in sweeping pans of red and blue streaks through the cold dust. David slowed and made the turn. They passed a group of picketers on the shoulder huddled together against the cold. The newspeople who'd been sent away from the cafe stood not far off, cradling Styrofoam cups in their hands, waiting for something to happen. One of them saw the bus coming and signaled for action. The Revealers grabbed their signs and prepared to make a scene.

David passed them unnoticed and drove to a metal gate where a Shoshone Tribal Policeman waited with several school volunteers. David rolled down the window and showed his tickets. The policeman signaled another man to let them through.

"Have a nice time," he said.

Beyond the gate, the road was paved and well-maintained. Signs directed them forward and past several forks that disappeared behind hills or into the far distance. Farther on, the road dipped down a hill and skirted a wash through a grove of leafless trees and then across a broad, lonely range of open pastureland where golden grasses poked through a thin layer of pale, pristine snow.

Soon they saw the lights of the meetinghouse. It glowed from hundreds of festive Christmas bulbs strung on wires between posts and framing the windows and doors of the long wooden house. They twinkled in greens, reds, and blues while white strands hung from the roof in imitation icicles.

Signs directed them to valet parking under a canopy. A Shoshone girl took David's keys and gave him a ticket. David took Eleanor by the arm and together they walked the red carpet to the hall.

Eleanor felt eyes everywhere following her. She realized before she stepped inside that most of it was her imagination, but not all. The eyes that bothered her most, the ones that stayed on her longest, belonged to a leathery Indian man who might have been a hundred years old for all his creases and lines. He sat in a rocking chair in Indian garb as a kind of ambassador, sitting next to the standing Principal Curtz and welcoming the kids with a wave.

"I wonder who that is," Eleanor whispered to David when they were inside.

"That's Mr. Crow," he said. "He's a medicine man, if you can believe it."

"How do you know that?"

"I visited him last year," David said. "My family came out to visit."

Eleanor remembered. She'd overheard him talking about it to his mother, demanding that he be allowed to talk to Mr. Crow alone. It was during the time that he was doing his "research" on Eleanor. The same research that had helped bring them together but had also brought Sikring to Wyoming.

"Does he have a first name?" Eleanor asked.

"I think Crow is his only name. I called him mister out of respect."

"What did he tell you about me?"

"About you? Nothing. About skinwalkers, he referred me to the Navajo."

"*Nimirika?*"

"Means ogre. A myth. He said it was all myth."

The hall was warmly lit inside with more Christmas lights. The decorations that were devised for the dance at the Masonic Hall had been brought here and adapted to the new space. Eleanor could smell the pine and the wood smoke as Midge had described, but the colorful lights, streamers, garlands, big tinseled Christmas tree, table of bite-size éclairs, and a huge crystal punch bowl softened the sense of strangeness. Everywhere Eleanor looked, she saw schoolmates and chaperones. The only Indians in the hall were Henry Creek, who danced awkwardly with Midge beneath a spinning silver mirror ball, and Robby Guide, who skulked behind the éclair table, watching with an eye on the door to the lady's room, holding two plastic cups of pink punch.

Eleanor saw Mr. Gurenno and Mr. Blake acting as chaperones. Mrs. Hart was in conversation with the new sophomore algebra teacher, Mrs. Pond.

The band this year had two violins and David moaned when he saw them.

"Fiddlers," he said. "Where else in the world would you have a Winter Dance with two fiddlers?"

Eleanor found Eric and Aubrey sitting at a table, each deliberately not looking at the other.

"They're in a fight," said Eleanor nodding toward them.

"Already?" he said. "What about?"

"I don't know," she said. "But I can see it. Can't you?"

"Yeah, I guess I can now that you point it out."

"Should we go over?"

"After a dance," David said.

"I thought you hated this kind of music."

"It's slow," he said. "I can do slow."

Eleanor let David take her hand and lead her onto the dance floor. Out of the shadows, beneath the flickering lights and mirrored beams, Eleanor felt exposed and tried to duck behind her hair, but, of course, she couldn't because it was up. She felt everyone watching her, heard voices trail away and fall silent as they walked to an open space. David slid his arm around her waist and lifted her arm in an archaic gesture that made Eleanor say, "I do declare," in a perfect Scarlett O'Hara impression.

Eleanor draped her arms around David's neck. He slid his around her waist and drew her in close. She closed her eyes. The music was warm, the violin strings dampened the electric guitar buzz to a cozy and soothing sound. She allowed the music to move into her like a breath, allowed her body to react to David's like feathers on that breath. She let her mind go blank, allowed herself to relax and enjoy the moment. Her mother had wanted her to dance, bade her to dance again on her dying day, and this night she would keep that promise. She would not be a fool, but neither would she miss this. She absorbed the moment like a pebble in a pond and permitted herself not only to rejoice in it, but to dream of more to come.

She didn't know how long they danced that first dance. Her eyes were closed. The music never stopped. One song blended into the next in skillful transitions like an autumn sunset or real butter across a slice of fresh baked bread. Finally, the tempo crept ever higher and became too fast for their lingering embrace.

David cleared his throat. "Should we sit down?"

Holding hands, they walked to Aubrey's table. Eleanor's head swam as she saved that moment to her memory, like a flower in a book to be found and treasured again. She was aware of the stares and the whispers around her. She heard her name, heard David's, but pushed it out of her thoughts. She would not be distracted. Tonight, at least, she would allow herself that. For David. For Tabitha. For her.

Before they reached the table, Barbara waylaid them with the help of Alexi and Penelope. Russell held back, but Brian and Alexi's date, a handsome blond at least five years out of high school, walked up with them. Barbara's face was eager and excited; Alexi's was more reserved.

"Look at you!" exclaimed Barbara.

"What?" Eleanor said. "Did I spill something? Is my hair going crazy?"

"She means your dress," the blond man said with an accent Eleanor placed as Italian. "You are magnificent. Everyone is talking about you."

"You look spectacular," Penelope said. Eleanor almost didn't recognize her. She'd put on ten pounds, her usual gaunt features were fleshed out. Her face, so skeletal before, was round, almost plump. Instead of a thin slit, like a ripped paper, her smile was full-lipped, broad and sincere.

"It's a nice dress," Alexi said to an empty space behind Eleanor.

"How are you, Penelope?" Eleanor said.

"Better," she said.

"Your dancing was so romantic," the Italian said. "Such beauty." That drew a glare from Alexi.

"Let's go get some punch," Alexi said, and taking her un-introduced date by the arm, she walked away.

"You look nice too," said Eleanor to Barbara.

"I look like a parade float compared to you. Where did you get that dress? And who did your hair?"

"Come on, Barb," said Russell. "You coming or not?"

Barbara rolled her eyes. "You guys want a shot? Russell snuck in a flask of schnapps. It's not bad if you like cough syrup."

"No, we're good," said David.

"Me too, but Russell is nervous. See you later," she said and followed her date outside.

"Getting into another fight, David?" asked Eric when they sat down.

"Looks like you two already had one," he said.

"All I said was that Eleanor looked pretty," Eric said.

"What you said was that she was the prettiest girl in the room," Aubrey said, peeved.

"Punch?" David said to Eleanor leading her away.

They kept to themselves after that. They danced a lot, never missing a down tempo and even joining a line dance at one point. When they were tired, they retreated to a quiet corner where they could talk and watch the party.

Eleanor's gaze seldom slipped from David's face, his eyes like warm cocoa, his lips warm and alluring—a magnet to her mouth. He distracted her from her fear of the crowds and set her heart racing, and they'd blush and laugh for no reason, for every reason.

"Why is everyone looking at us?" Eleanor asked, suddenly noticing.

"They're looking at you," David said. "You're beautiful."

"It's just a dress and a hairdo," she said.

"No, it's more than that. You're prettier than I've ever seen you, and you've always been pretty."

"Thanks," she said blushing. Then she had a terrible thought. She dug a tiny mirror out of her little purse and examined her face. She was different. It was all subtle, difficult to identify even for her, but she saw it. Her eyes were bigger and brighter. Her cheeks were red and lively though she'd used no rouge. Her lips were thicker, tinted a deep natural rose that went beyond her lipstick. She noticed then that her dress fit better than it had at home or even at the restaurant or the fitting room. Her hips had widened to fill it out, her waist receded a centimeter. Her feet fit perfectly in her shoes, which no longer pinched her heels. Her hair was perfect, not a strand out of place. Her pierced ears had filled in. She'd morphed into an ideal without even noticing. It hadn't even hurt, or if it had, she hadn't noticed it. Maybe that was part of it.

She looked at her friends. The dance had been going on for hours. Everyone looked tired, they were happy, but the exertion of dancing, talking, and just being happy had mussed them up. She looked fresh as could be.

"I'm giving myself away," she said. "What is it about parties and dancing, and you, and this night that so betrays me?"

"What are you talking about?"

"You don't see it?"

"Something wrong? I see nothing wrong."

"But you sense it," she said.

"You're trying to be ordinary again," he said. "It doesn't suit you."

The music stopped.

"What's going on?" Eleanor asked, alarmed.

"I don't know," he said.

Mr. Curtz got on stage. Beside him were two Shoshone, a man and a woman.

"This is a special night," said the principal. "A new tradition formed with Jamesford and our good neighbors, the Shoshone.

To mark this new tradition, I'm going to turn the microphone over to our wonderful hosts."

A tall tan man took the microphone.

"Hello, I am Two Elk. I am an Elder of the Wild River Shoshone Nation. This is Ruth Brooks, she is much revered by us. It is our pleasure to crown this year's winter dance king and queen: David Venn and Eleanor Anders!"

Applause erupted like a sudden geyser. People around David and Eleanor stepped back to create a path from their secluded table to the stage. David's jaw fell open.

"What do we do?" Eleanor said.

"You get a dance," said Midge, appearing beside her. Eleanor hadn't seen her come up, nor had she sensed Henry Creek, who held her hand and beamed as bright as Midge.

"Go on," said Henry, pushing David to his feet.

Midge hopped up and down excitedly, as if she were the one picked.

"Midge," Eleanor whispered. "I'm afraid."

"Don't be," she said. "Have your dance. There'll be time for that later."

David extended a long flamboyant arm to the sitting Eleanor and she politely and dramatically took it. The crowd applauded again. He led her to the stage where the Shoshone Elders crowned David with a gold coronet and Eleanor with a glittering silver tiara.

"What should we play?" asked one of the fiddlers.

"Something slow," said Eleanor.

David led her to the middle of the floor. A spotlight shone on them from behind the stage.

The music began, slow and romantic. Eleanor felt it move

into her like a ghost. David guided her in his arms and wore a grin so wide Eleanor thought he'd be sore for it the next day.

Indian faces watched her from the stage, teachers from the sides, the mayor had appeared, the sheriff, and even Dr. Sikring had materialized in a side doorway. All of them watched her with appraising eyes. She was not invisible. She could never again be anonymous. With all of them watching, with the entire student body of her high school applauding her, she stepped and twirled and danced. For a pebble in a pond, pressed petals in a book, a moment to hold forever and a promise she had to keep, Eleanor lost herself in the dance.

CHAPTER TWENTY-SEVEN

They'd given her roses after their dance, and Eleanor cradled them in her arms like a child. She still wore the tiara given her by the Shoshone Elder. It was just a piece of sparkly plastic and rhinestones, but Eleanor couldn't have treasured it more if it had been from the House of Windsor. David had dispensed with his crown. He said it didn't match his outfit the way hers did and it was too tall to wear while driving anyway.

She was lost in dreams and fantasies of family and friends when they drove onto Cedar Street and saw the mob of people in front of her little house.

There was Miss Church and Mrs. Westlake among the yelling horde, threatening doom to the town if "the witch" wasn't expelled. Someone had erected another wooden cross on her lawn, but it wasn't alight. A police car with flashing lights cast unnatural red, hellish shadows across the twisted faces of the Revealers.

"This looks familiar," Eleanor said.

"I'll turn around and go to my place," David said looking for a place to turn. Cars were parked so thick her wide road was but a single lane. "My dad will know what to do."

"He's right there," Eleanor said, pointing.

Jim Venn stood with two other men on her porch facing the crowd of protestors. One wore the uniform of the Shoshone Nation, and Eleanor recognized him as the man who'd checked their ticket at the gate. The third one was an oilman Eleanor had seen before but knew nothing about. They stared down the mob with hardened contempt and rifles under their arms.

"I'm getting out," Eleanor said.

"Are you nuts?" David said.

"I'm not running," she said. "Not tonight."

She threw open the door, and still holding the roses with her tiara tucked in her perfect auburn hair, she marched to her gate.

Miss Church was the first to see her.

"Witch!" she yelled and pointed. The others turned to see.

Eleanor saw Jennifer. She saw her notice the crown and the roses. She took in Eleanor's ivory dress, strapless and perfect. She must have seen Eleanor's bearing and pride. Jennifer turned her head quickly, a quivering frown forming on her lips.

Eleanor didn't slow her step as she moved across the street and through the crowd. No one touched her as she opened her gate. She heard David running behind her while hisses and curses rose from the picketers like an obscene crescendo.

"Witch!" "Sorceress!" "Whore!"

Out of the corner of her eye, she saw a man bend down and pick up a stone. He pried it off the frozen ground, leaned back, and threw it at Eleanor. She ducked it easily without even slowing her pace.

When the stone crashed into the side fence, Jim Venn sprang past her and was on the man before he'd regained his balance from the throw. In an instant, all was a flurry of military-trained jabs and enraged, flailing blows. The attack was sudden, ferocious, and terrifying. The men from the porch ran to the melee. Screaming, the Revealers scattered in all directions.

Jim landed half a dozen blows before the Shoshone policeman had him in a headlock. Blood poured from a cut above the man's eye where Jim had landed a blow so hard Eleanor had cringed from the crunch.

"You better go now before I arrest you," said the Shoshone policeman to the man on the ground as he struggled to hold Jim back.

"What?" said the man thickly, through a split lip. He rose to his knees. Blood poured from his face like an open faucet.

"I think the man just offered you an escape," said the oil worker. "You best take it." To add emphasis, David's dad broke free and rushed at him again. He was, again, restrained by both men. He grunted like a penned and wild beast. His eyes were wild and angry, his hands were red with gore.

The man took the hint and sped away after the others, nearly tripping over the dropped signs on the sidewalk.

"I think you hurt him, Jim," said the oilman.

"Job well done, then," he said.

"Hello, Miss Anders," said the Shoshone. "Hope this didn't ruin your evening."

"Dad, what are you doing here?" said David.

"My duty," he said as the other men finally released him. "I was on 'follow the idiots' duty. Sheriff's idea. I followed them here. Saw them plant that cross, made a call, and here we are."

"Thanks," Eleanor said.

"Think nothing of it," said the oilman tipping the brim of his dirty ball cap.

The Shoshone officer had been studying her casually but carefully since the fracas broke up. "Glad I could help," he said. "You got this, Jim?"

"I do," he said. "Thanks. They won't be coming back. Not tonight."

"I don't think they will," agreed the policeman.

The two men said goodnight and left in the squad car.

"He has no jurisdiction outside the reservation," said Jim to Eleanor, "but this kind of crowd is not known for their smarts. You going to invite us in?"

"Of course," said Eleanor fumbling with the lock and bringing them inside.

"Nice," said David's father. "Really cozy."

"Why did those other men help?" Eleanor asked.

"They wanted to," Jim said. Eleanor watched as he nonchalantly checked behind furniture, turned on lights, and peeked into rooms as if he was admiring the architecture. It was a good act, but Eleanor wasn't fooled. She let him go on. One smell and a moment of silence had told Eleanor her house was empty but it was reassuring to see Jim reconnoiter it for her.

"Why?" she asked.

He looked at her crooked for a moment. "Because it was the right thing to do."

"They don't know me," she said.

"Tyler's seen you around and that big Indian fella' seemed to know you. He volunteered to help before I asked him."

"I don't understand," Eleanor said.

"That's because you're 'spicious," David said, harkening

back to a conversation they'd had years ago. "There are good people in the world."

"And you're family," said Jim looking out a side window. "Wish I'd had another thirty seconds with that rock-throwing coward."

"You did plenty, Dad," David said.

"He deserved worse."

"He missed me," Eleanor said.

"Not for lack of trying," he said. "I'll sleep on the sofa. David, you go home and tell your mom I'm staying here tonight. Don't tell her what happened. Say I'm drunk if you have to. No need to worry her."

"That's not necessary," Eleanor said.

"That's not up for discussion," said Jim, kicking off his shoes and flopping on the couch.

A look from David told her that arguing would be futile.

Eleanor walked David to the door and he pulled her outside on the porch.

"You are so beautiful," he whispered. "And I love that you don't know it."

"My shape reacted to the—" she said.

"I'm not talking about that," he said. "I'm talking about you, not your clothes. I love you, Eleanor. Thank you for putting up with me, with all this. I'm the luckiest boy in the world."

"Thanks for taking me to the dance," she said.

He took her in his arms and pulled her close. He touched her bare shoulders, sending shivers down her back. He leaned in and kissed her neck. A peck. Then another. Each one a shot filling her body with heat and longing. She felt her knees weaken, but he held her and she was safe. Their faces touched, he kissed her ear, a single soft and gentle pop that drove her fingernails into the back of his coat.

The night was chilly but they sweated. She smelled David's heat like a narcotic perfume, sweet and inviting, a scent to lose oneself.

"Eleanor," he whispered.

And she kissed him. Unable to bear more delay, more teasing, she kissed him hard and hungrily. Instantly, all was light and fire, warmth and unity. She was awash in hot honey, timeless and placeless. Tingling cellular pyrotechnics up her legs and back, arms and neck—a rejoicing flash, primal and deep, but toned in shades of affection and loyalty. Love. David's face. Her eyes shut but seeing his, deep and brown and caring. Eyes that cradled her, fought for her, and protected her. Eyes that loved her. The boy who had always loved her and she him. A pairing. She and he. They.

A distant car noise brought Eleanor back to Jamesford and after a time, she pulled away.

David caught his breath. "I'd still be there if you hadn't done that," he said. "You're stronger than I am."

"No," she said. "Just more 'spicious."

Out of the corner of her eye, she saw the curtain move and Jim duck away.

"I better go home," David said.

"Yeah," she agreed, but they stood together on the porch in each other's arms for another quarter hour.

Several times during the night, Eleanor heard Jim get up to check on noises. She recognized each one, knew they were nothing, but he dutifully checked each before returning to the couch and a restless night and Eleanor turned over in her bed. When he finally woke up at dawn, he checked each door and window again before tiptoeing to the door, pulling on his coat, and leaving.

She came down and found the note. *I know how girls like their morning privacy. See you at dinner. Love, Jim.*

She had not slept, thinking how the whole evening had been a miracle: the dance, the thwarted protest, the kiss, David—all made possible by the town's inexplicable kindnesses to her.

She felt like a robber holding Jim's note on her lap thinking of the marvelous night she'd had, the friends who'd smiled for her, been happy for her, and the strangers who'd defended her. It was too much. She did not understand or trust kindness, but she did feel a weighty debt for it, like an honor, a grand gift, an expensive, meaningful gift she'd been made to take but didn't deserve.

Her feelings were a mix of obligation and overflowing gratitude. She felt unworthy of it all. She wondered and wished for something to do to earn it. Then suddenly she thought she knew how.

Russell Liddle lived in a trailer on half an acre of weeds and crumbling cottonwood trees. Eleanor had visited it once before to deliver a message that worked surprisingly well. There were two cars buried in knee-high grass, one used to be blue, the other possibly red, but both rust-colored now. A third vehicle, a battered white Explorer, mud-caked and also rusting, she'd seen driven in town either by Russell to school or his father to bars.

They had a dog on a leash tied to a tree that spent its time in a flimsy shelter, escaping the winter cold or summer sun.

The dog was lazy and tired and didn't worry Eleanor, but she didn't know what was inside the house.

She watched it from behind the Explorer for most the morning. She saw Russell moving inside but no one else. When he settled in to a ballgame on TV, she approached the house and looked in the back windows but the curtains were drawn. She listened for a long time, but could make out nothing besides Russell and football.

She retreated to a gas station street, which had a phone booth older than her school. She dropped a quarter into it and made the call.

Russell answered. "Hello?"

"Hello, Russell," she said as Barbara. "I'm bored. Come get me."

"You're not mad anymore?"

"A little," she said. "But if I don't see you how are you going to make it up to me?"

"Okay," he said. "Movie?"

"Great," she said. "Come get me. I'm so bored."

She was taking a risk, a big one, but one that she thought she was in a unique position to take. The schnapps bottle Barbara had mentioned the night before was too close a match to the one Eric said he'd seen with the German hitchhiker before he was killed. She had a hunch about Russell, a dark brooding suspicion made much the clearer by her memories of him attacking her twice with a knife. Russell was capable of the crimes plaguing Jamesford, and she was going to repay the little town by uncovering him.

She watched Russell's Explorer drive past the station toward Barbara's house up the canyon before carefully creeping back to the trailer. She moved stealthily between the cover of trees, high weeds, and rusted cars, stopping to listen and smell the air. The air was scented with a coming storm, she felt the impending snow. Wind gusts proclaimed its coming in warm, sudden slaps that tested the trees and threw garbage across the yard. Bushes scraped on siding, pinpricks of ice stung her cheeks.

She climbed the creaking wooden steps to the trailer door. It wasn't very high; the trailer was supported on concrete blocks that had sunk into the ground from time and neglect. The trailer had a tilt.

The door was unlocked and she pulled it open and went inside. It stank of cigarettes, cooking grease, and animal fur. It was untidy: boots piled by the door, coats thrown over vinyl chairs in the kitchen nook, and piles of mail and papers toppled in heaps only to have more piled on top of the mound. If they had a vacuum, and she doubted they did, it would be useless for all the clutter on the floor. It was about what she expected: dark, dirty, and poor. She was poor, but she didn't live like this. She remembered that Russell didn't have a mother. She'd run out on him when he was very young.

She waited for her eyes to adjust to the gloom and then moved carefully. The trailer was laid out much like David's with a narrow hallway leading—or rather, tilting—toward the back of the trailer where the bedrooms would be.

A wind picked up outside. She could hear crystal snow blowing against the side of the house, glass on aluminum. The grass bent and moaned, a tree branch reached down and scratched at the roof. The last sound was the most unnerving. It was loud and ground through the house like nails on a chalkboard, a wolf at the door. It made her jump and put her teeth on edge.

Next, came a bathroom. A toothbrush and the smell of Russell's shampoo. Mismatched towels. Untidy, but not overly dirty. Someone had scrubbed the sink and scraped at the rust spots in the shallow white tub.

The next room was not so pleasant. She opened a door to what she thought would be Russell's bedroom and was overcome with the stench of meat and chemicals. Rot and formaldehyde, cloying and thick. She flicked on a light switch and the dank room glowed under a single over-bright bulb clinging to the ceiling. It illuminated a doe's head half stuffed lying atop a metal desk. The skin was pulled loosely over a Styrofoam base. Its glass, lifeless eyes were crooked and too small. An ear was half broken off. Knives, mallets, bottles, jars. Needles, threads, wire, and pliers—tools she couldn't identify—all disordered on the desk. A badger stared at her from a plaque on a wall and on the floor a cat with most of its hair gone was positioned against a carpeted scratching post in a grotesque, lifeless stretch.

She noticed a drawer of the desk partly opened. She pulled it out. It squeaked on its metal casters. Inside was a pile of ten-year-old taxidermy magazines. She carefully lifted them out and placed them on the floor to see beneath.

The wind slammed the house. The floor creaked, the walls shuttered, the branch beat upon the roof. She searched the recesses of the drawer and drew a quick breath.

At the bottom, in the back, was a familiar black metal box. It had a combination lock but the lid had been pried open. Streaks of bare metal gleamed silver at the seam where the paint had been scraped and chipped from forcing open the box. She lifted the lid. David's gun lay inside. Beside it, tucked in the corner was an open box of bullets and a roll of colorful bills—euros.

She stared at the contents, making sure she was seeing it, calming her breathing, slowing her heart, and steadying her shaking hands.

She closed the box, set it back in the drawer. She had just replaced the magazines when she sensed someone behind her.

"What are you doing here?"

She jumped, a little shriek escaping her lips.

It was Russell's father. He'd snuck in under the sound of the storm and the stench of the room

"Hello, Mr. Liddle," she said quickly. "I'm Eleanor. I was looking for Russell. He said I could—"

"He said nothing to you," he snarled. "I know *you.*"

He stepped closer. Stinking of stale beer and dirty clothes, his pants hung open and his T-shirt was a dingy rag. Three-day's growth of beard scabbed his acne-scarred face, and his smell cut through the chemical stench in the room like a razor. He glared at her with hateful, bloodshot eyes. He raised his right hand and brandished an empty bottle at Eleanor.

"You shouldn't be here," he slurred.

"Mr. Liddle," Eleanor began.

"You broke into my house," he said.

"I'm sorry," she said. "I'll go."

He glanced at the drawer. With the toe of his boot, he kicked it shut.

"Mr. Liddle—" She tried to stand, but stumbled on the clutter. She took her eyes off him for only an instant, just an instant to catch herself.

It was enough.

The bottle crashed into her temple like a hammer.

After a flash of lightning, the world darkened to pitch.

CHAPTER TWENTY-EIGHT

She was smothered, buried alive. She was choking on dirt, gasping for dust, spinning in her grave. For a while, she was sure she was dead, but then the sharp pain in her face convinced her otherwise. Dead people did not feel broken bones.

She couldn't open her eyes. She knew her right one was swollen shut by the throbs in her temple. She could feel that entire side of her face burning as it tried to repair itself; pins and needles in tender bruises. She felt her muscles tear apart and deform into writhing fingers under her skin. They stretched and grabbed at broken bones and fitted the shards back into place like puzzle pieces. When the bones touched, they fused in a brilliant burst of chemical energy that brought more pain. Then the muscles latched back on in a thousand piercing, fiery, spider bites. She whimpered a muffled moan and was smothered again. She resisted the urge to scream, afraid to suffocate.

She tried to raise her arm to feel her face and found her wrists bound behind her. She tried to force the fog from her mind even as she felt her brain piece itself back together.

She recognized the pain, but not this intensity. Her body had never been so aggressive, so hurried in its conversion. It was out of her control. A deeper instinct, a survival drive resisted every conscious command she sent to slow it, to ease into shape, lessen the pain, mediate the burning. It was as if her body thought—and here she stifled another scream—as if her body *knew*, that this was life or death.

She smelled plastic duct tape and knew how her eyes and mouth were kept shut. She also smelled blood, her blood, and tasted it on her lips beneath the thick adhesive tape. Her feet were cramped and bound at her ankles. She could turn her head after breaking the half-hardened scabs that connected it to the floor. With her fingertips, she touched the cold, slick enamel beneath her and she remembered Russell's bathroom. Yes, she was at Russell's. Russell's father had hit her with a bottle and now she was lying in her own blood in Russell's narrow tub.

The pain stilled her. Her mending-disoriented brain hallucinated. She witnessed flashes of colored lights, images of sky, tree and book, school lunch, Tabitha, a red cliff, a broken leg, then a medley of smells that couldn't possibly be there: honey, pepper, cinnamon, and wildflowers. They hit her sharp and quick like angry yellow jackets. She felt nauseous. She listened to birds and speeding cars, geysers and voices from half a century before, and stopped believing any of it.

"You alive?" She'd heard the words in her dreams. She ignored them until a boot dug into her ribs. She moaned behind the tape.

She smelled him then, the dank alcohol stink seeping out in his sweat. His breath, fetid with rotten teeth, had new alcohol on it. She felt her body pulled upright by her hair, the side of her head peeling off the bathtub floor with a thick slurp of congealing blood. Pain spread across her face like a blooming firework.

She heard the strike of a match and smelled cigarette smoke. He coughed. Outside the wind buffeted the trailer like waves crashing on rocks. The tree scratched and beat at the house like it needed to get in.

"Can't believe you're still alive," he said. "You bled plenty. Skull stoved right in. You ain't never gonna use that eye again. But I guess that won't matter." He sucked on a cigarette for a while.

"Can you understand me? Did that divot in your head take your senses? Nod if you can understand me." Eleanor nodded.

"Damn," he said. "Maybe you are a witch. That foreigner didn't take half the hit you did and he went and died."

Another long draw on a cigarette. The sound of swallowing. A belch. A new stink.

"They had it coming," he said. "You all did."

She heard the cigarette butt drop to the floor and ground under a heel. He lit another. He flicked the spent match into the tub. She felt it bounce off her shoulder and sizzle in the wet blood beneath her.

"Thinking they're better than me; talking to me like that? Me?"

Heat shot down her arms and into her fingers. She began to shake. Fear rose in her like a repressed memory—ancient and dark, mindless, ugly, and monstrous. A thing beyond terror; a form of malice and retribution she sensed and feared and so it fed upon itself.

She pulled at the cord binding her wrists, but it was too tight. It cut into her flesh as her hands became claws. She was bound too tightly. She lost feeling in her fingers, smelled fresh blood, felt the warm, wet ooze of her opened wrists flow down her back.

"You ain't breaking free," he said. She heard him drink again and then follow it up with a long drag before he blew the smoke into her face. She heard him crush another butt on the floor. "Soon as it gets dark, we'll go for a little drive. It'll all be over soon," and he kicked her in the ribs. She fell on her side but her head caught the faucet and bled again.

The panic grabbed her mind in madness and she writhed against it. An idea taking root, taking hold. Taking shape. She fought against it. Her reasoning mind shouting against a wave of animal terror. She willed herself to remain calm, ordered her body to behave. She heard Mr. Liddle get up and walk out of the room. She heard the door latch and then the sound of the TV coming to life.

She took deep breaths and commanded her limbs to obey her, not the animal, but her. She needed logic and guile, not aggression and savagery. Her hands were too weak and too big to slip the cord. She was trapped.

Mr. Liddle intended to kill her. Of this she was sure. It was life or death, but her instinct couldn't break the cord. She hadn't the muscle to tear through it, the blood to endure it. It wasn't tape that bound her. Judging from the cuts in her wrists, which her body rushed to seal, it was wire. She remember the spool of it in the sickening room before she'd been clobbered. She would not be able to break it and she was powerless without her hands. Panic rose again like a tide or a stampede. Or a summoned demon.

She forced herself to reason. If she could get out of the tub, if she could get to Sheriff Hannon or to Jim Venn, all would be well. If. If she had never come here, if she hadn't been so reckless. If she died today . . .

"Stop it!" she said beneath the gag. She knew she had only a little time and her energy reserves were dwindling.

She turned her wrists away from the cutting wire until the strand slid out of her wounds. Her flesh reopened where skin had closed over the wire. The wire out of her body, she could finally stop the bleeding. She was lightheaded. She'd surely received a concussion. She'd lost lots of blood, she knew, because she was lying in it.

She listened to the wind whip at the house while the televised football game entered the third quarter.

What could she do? What could a sixteen year-old girl do in this situation? Nothing. Celeste could do nothing. So what could a monster like her do? What could a skinwalker do? What could Eleanor do?

Eleanor was nothing, nobody. Eleanor was going to die. When Liddle returned, she would lose it all: her life, her home, her new family, Karen, David and Wendy . . .

Wendy. Wendy was young. Wendy was small. Wendy's hands and wrists were petite and flexible. Like dolls hands. She needed Wendy's hands.

The pocket in her throat held nothing to copy, no maps to any other forms, let alone the littlest Venn.

But she could think. She had learned a modicum of control. Hadn't she dismissed the bruise? Hadn't she mimicked Barbara on demand to get into this hell in the first place? She sent the little repairmen out of her mind and down her arms to alter her hands.

It was a fanciful vision of what she was trying to do, but it helped her focus. She held in her mind the image of Wendy's little hands held in hers. She studied their delicate features, their soft skin, and tiny knuckles. She saw them and wanted them. She needed them. She would make them.

Heat pooled down her arms and she was suddenly ravenous. She considered eating her tongue, but before she could, the hunger lessened and was replaced with new aches spread over her whole body. Her thighs suddenly felt bruised, her waist grew smaller, her stomach contracted, her toes curled. She was wracked by a thousand pinches. She held the image of Wendy's hands in her mind's eye and concentrated.

Because of the wind or her distraction, she hadn't heard the Explorer come back. Eleanor was only vaguely aware of the conversation in the next room.

"Where you been, boy?" Mr. Liddle said to Russell.

"Hanging out," he said.

"Did I say you could use the car?" he demanded.

"You were asleep," he said. "Whatchu need it for?"

"Got business," he said.

"What business?"

"Dammit, boy! Know your place," Mr. Liddle yelled. "Don't you mind my business. Mind your own. Hell, if your mother, whore that she was, didn't stick it to me a hundred ways from Sunday. Running off and leaving me with her bastard who can't mind his own damn business even when I'm doing him a favor. You're just like your mother. I don't know if you're like your father. I never met him. You bastard." He spoke as if reciting a litany.

"I'm just trying to help," he said.

"You ain't nothing of mine. I give you my name because I didn't know better when you were born. Don't think for a second I'd do it again," he spat. "I don't need your help. I'll expect it when I need it."

"You didn't ask for it when the sheriff talked to me."

"So, you got some sense. Bully for you. I didn't ask for it because I shouldn't have had to. You got a brain, don't you? You know that you gotta look out for yourself and sometimes that means looking out for him who feeds you. It's just dumb animal instinct. You ain't completely stupid," he said. "No, not completely."

"I don't have to stay here and listen to this," he said.

Eleanor heard a slap and the sound of papers falling over.

"Don't you talk back to me, boy. Go on get outta here. And leave the car. I need it."

"It's snowing," Russell said thickly, tears in his voice, but Eleanor doubted they were on his face.

"So take a coat."

"I'm going to Tanner's," he said.

"Go to hell for all I care," Mr. Liddle said. The door opened and slammed shut.

Little hands. Little hands. Little hands. She felt skin slough off her fingers, heard a snap of bone and the rattle of finger-nails tumbling onto the soiled enamel behind her. Her hands felt like they were in lava up to her elbows. She'd scream, or try to, if she had the energy to spare, but she hadn't. She couldn't even manage a moan. She felt every rip, tear, and cut in stereo from both arms. She felt the pain in blazing searing shots up her shoulders and into her skull and then, overflowing her nervous system, cascade down her spine until her hips ached and her legs tingled because of it.

She felt water down her face and thought she'd reopened

the wound in her eye. There was nothing to do for it if she had. Higher thinking, higher priorities. But it wasn't blood streaming out from under the tape. It was tears, thick and salty.

Small hands. Small hands. Wendy's hands.

The football game was in the final minutes. Eleanor was spent. Her muscles spasmed in waves. Her legs, back, neck, and arms each having a turn at shaking like leaves in a gale. She blacked out.

When she came to her body shivered. She could not control the shaking. She remembered where she was and wanted to scream. She'd lost concentration. The game was over. Mr. Liddle was in the next room, the room with the dead animals, shuffling about, getting things ready. Loading the gun.

She rubbed her wrists together and felt slack. She could move her arms. She pulled at her left hand and it slid a couple of inches before hitting the wire. She straightened her fingers, tucked her thumb, flattened her palms and pulled.

The wire caught on her knuckles and dug into them. She pulled harder. She gave a heaving tug and felt the skin peel off her hand like a rind, but it was free.

She pulled her hand up and felt her face. Blood had scabbed over the tape of her right eye. That eye didn't feel right. She doubted she still had it. Catching the edge of the tape, she pulled it away from her one good eye.

She blinked and saw only darkness. She was blind. In both eyes, she was blind. She pulled the tape away from her mouth. She sat up and brought her right arm around. A green flash drew her attention. It was a dim LED on a smoke alarm on the ceiling. She wasn't blind. The lights were out. She stared at the light and let the fear dissipate a little. In a moment her eye had expanded to where the little light shone bright enough that she could make out the whole of the room.

Her hands felt like they were on fire. They were grotesquely small, not quite hers, not quite Wendy's, but a combination product of her desperate imaginings. She removed the wire bracelet and dropped it in the bathtub amongst the gore. She unwound the wire that held her ankles and sat up on the edge of the tub.

Mr. Liddle closed a drawer in the next room and sat down on a squeaking chair. He'd be here any minute.

Now, she thought. *Now. Oh monster that I am, now is the moment. Give me claws. For me, for my family, for my kind, for my friends, and my Jamesford, give me weapons!*

It was a prayer that echoed in her thoughts like a ricocheting bullet dispelling the conscious control she'd demanded before. She released herself to become a beast. She released the terror she'd endured for hours and used it to summon the monster inside her, the creature who'd come unbidden and angry, bloodthirsty and cruel whenever fear drove her out of her mind.

She felt it stir. Felt the claws at her fingertips begin to come, but then stutter and falter. The creature did not come. It would not take over. She could not release the controls. Betrayed by her own composure, she began to cry but had no tears.

She needed that other to do it. She, Eleanor, could not do what had to be done. Eleanor was not violent. This was not her. Eleanor was not . . . Eleanor was . . . Eleanor could be anything she needed to be.

It wasn't fair but it was right. Before, it had come like nausea at the worst times, fighting to usurp all her faculties in the name of survival. But now the beast inside bowed to her conscious primacy.

Was the terror not great enough? Was the darkness not complete enough? Was her end not near enough?

Perhaps the creature inside her recognized no threat here. Sure, she was hurt, hungry, starving maybe, but there was no immediate predator lapping at her wounds. The thing that brought the claws didn't prepare, it reacted. If Mr. Liddle hit her again, provided he didn't knock her out in one blow as before, she had little doubt that her adrenaline would release the creature, but would it recognize the threat of a gun? She feared the thing inside her was too primitive to conceive of such a threat, particularly since she'd tamed it so often and so well.

Eleanor was in charge. Eleanor would have to do this.

She looked down at her hands, tiny, pathetic, misshaped things.

"Claws," she said. "Terror," she said. "Life or death," she said through her gritted teeth.

She drew the pattern from memory, from the time beside the creek when she nearly killed Russell, from a time before she could walk, from a time before she was born. From a time before history, she took the shape. She watched it, controlled it, studied it as her body reacted to the fear she showed it, reacted to it, and thus, with her consciousness guiding it, prepared for it. The shape came to her as if she'd sampled it. It was a copy, a permanent shape her body could not forget.

Never did she lose control. Though she shook in pain, conflagrations of heat, spasms of reordering cells, hardening bones, thickening skin, she kept her mind and her will. She was Eleanor. She was not an animal. Though she could take this shape, this composited hybrid shape of man and lion and lizard and demon, she was still Eleanor.

She filled her hands with bone and claw and they burned like fire.

She slipped into something old for just a second, but in that second she howled. It was a deep primitive scream; it said pain and anger, terror and challenge. It shook the trailer.

Mr. Liddle moved suddenly in his chair. Then she heard steps in the hallway.

She flexed her hands. They were still miniature, but the fingers were each tipped with a needle sharp claw and they felt like they were made of iron. She hunched on the floor, aimed at the door, and readied to spring.

The door opened and a hand slipped inside and flicked on the light.

Accustomed to nearly perfect darkness, the sudden brightness blinded her completely.

"What the hell?" Liddle exclaimed.

She leapt. She'd taken aim at the door before the light came on and his voice set his position in her mind as surely as if she'd put him there. So she leapt.

She was weak and the three feet from the tub to the door was almost more than her shaking legs could give her, but they performed like springs and lifted her off the floor, her arms outspread for attack at the other end.

The air filled with noise and orange light. She felt her side tear open and then hit the man in the doorway.

She knocked him back into the narrow hall. Pinning him against the wall, Eleanor slashed first with her left, then with her right hand. She felt nail catch skin and tear through it. He slid halfway down the wall.

Another explosion of blazing orange air and she felt flame bore into her leg. She slammed a palm into bone and heard the crack before Liddle's scream. Her right hand slashed crossways and below where the sound had come. Three talons caught, dug in, and opened his neck like a book. Eleanor was sprayed with blood. His screaming stopped. Air hissed from his throat like from a punctured tire and he slid down the wall to the wet floor and lay still. She listened to the thick splashing rhythm of blood squirting out of his body. It grew fainter and weaker and then stopped all at once.

Blinking her one eye until it adjusted to the dim hallway light, she could see a window over the sink in the kitchen down the hall. It was night outside.

She stood up. She looked only once at the mess at her feet and then stumbled away.

Blood dripped from two bullet wounds, one in her leg, the other under her left arm. In the kitchen she found a half-quart of milk and drank it all in one pull.

The bleeding lessoned. Her body fell into automatic pilot, repairing breaches and knitting skin as fast as the fuel would allow. She halted it.

She turned her entire attention to her hands. She willed them to return to their normal shape, Celeste's shape—Eleanor's shape. Her shape. It was her life. Her terms. If she would die, she would die Eleanor, not a primeval monster.

She ate a quarter stick of butter and the dregs of a pickle jar so quickly she nearly vomited. Blood streamed down her side. She looked around the room. What a horrible place this was she decided.

Her life, her terms. She would not die here. She would die at home, or with David, or at least outside. Not in this place.

Her hands. Please. Her hands.

Her life, her terms.

She stumbled out the door and fell off the wooden porch into fresh snow. She crawled a while without direction, just away from the trailer. Then she found her feet and staggered in the direction she thought lay home. She managed a dozen or so paces before she fell again and didn't get back up.

CHAPTER TWENTY-NINE

It was his piteous moans that drew her to the cliff. They carried down the mesa and through the canyon like a river of sadness.

She'd found a butterfly bush and was gathering the sweet orange berries for Mother in a coarse brown sack. Mother would be so happy to have them, and Father, and especially Brother, who loved anything sweet. Father said that Brother would fight a bear for honey and they'd all laugh. She'd hunted for such a bush for days and wandered far from their home, and that day she had found one, but then the cries had come.

It was bright and sunny. There'd be no rain today, no flood to crash down the *arroyo* and sweep her away like a beetle under Mother's broom. She was already far away, a little farther wouldn't matter. And she had the berries. Mother could not be so cross with her. So she followed the sad groans up the canyon to the top of the mesa and then through the low junipers to the edge of a cliff.

She could see far from the edge. She could see the Far Mountains and the Never Go Near river. She could see the road that was also Never Go Near with the cars that looked like ants marching in a row.

The sound came from beneath her. She moved to the edge, still clutching her bag of berries and scanned the rocks below for the source of the cries. She saw him in the rocks, lying upside down. His right leg was twisted oddly beneath him, pointing a way her own leg could never go. His other leg was held tight in a crook between the face of the cliff and a sheered boulder. He wore a blue-checkered shirt, smeared red with dust. He had a black braid lying over one shoulder and his tan face was cracked and blistered from the sun. He was not so old as Father, but older than she. She guessed fourteen summers, but it was a guess.

Then he yelled, "*Bikan anashwa!*" But it wasn't much of a yell, barely louder than his groaning. His voice was dry and broken, the accent foreign, but she knew what he said. He needed help.

"*Ashkii? Hastiin?*" she called down. "Are you a boy or a man?"

"*Ashkii,*" he groaned, miserably. "Can you help me, *Shideezhi?*"

"I am not your little sister," she called back, "And I am not to be seen."

"Oh please *Shideezhi*, I am so thirsty, and my bones are broken. Are we not *Diné*?

Of the same people? Will you not help *Ninaai*, your brother?"

"*Ninaai?*" she said. "You are not my brother. I have a brother. He is smaller than me."

"But are you not *Ashiihi,* of the Salt People?"

"No, I am not of that clan," she said.

"But you are Navajo—*Diné*. Help me please, little sister. I am dying. Only you can help me."

She looked down at him for a long while. He squinted against the sun and looked for her on the cliff. He called for her when she didn't speak. He made prayers and lamented for his own little sisters who'd miss him when he did not come home. And he cried for them and it broke her heart.

"I am coming, *Ashkii*," she called.

It took her several hours to get to him. She had to go back down the canyon the way she had come, then around the front of the mountain, and finally up the steep rocks to where he lay.

"*Ashkii*," she called, "Are you alive?"

He did not answer, but she saw that he was still breathing. She went to the rocks and pulled his foot free at the cost of his boot. He slid a little ways down the steep slope but not far. His broken leg was like a rope beneath him.

She carefully dragged him to the bottom. He woke up for a moment when she broke the orange berries over his lips. He looked up at her and mumbled "*Ahehee*," *Thank you,* before he passed out.

Doing as she'd seen Father do with a deer, she bound two poles together and made a draw-behind. She used the sack to bind it but saved many berries in the boy's shirt pockets. She'd need those to show how things had happened.

It was nightfall before she was near her home. She was tired from the pulling and sad that she had only a few berries left having given so many to the boy. Father rushed out of their home when she was close.

"Daughter, where have you been? Mother is out looking for you."

"I found a boy. He is hurt and broken. He needs help. Come, let's help him."

Father looked down on the boy. "What have you done, Daughter? You know we are not to be seen."

"I know," she said sheepishly. "He made me sad. He is broken and thirsty. I gave him most of the orange berries but I have still five for Brother."

"Berries will not help your mother," Father said. "Go give them to Brother and bring me the water jar."

She ran to the house and dropped the berries on Brother's lap where he sat by the fire. She grabbed a small jar and carried it outside.

"Here is the water, Father," she said. He was examining the broken leg and laying it out between sticks. "Should we not give him meat so he can heal?"

"He is not one of us," Father said, his voice strained. "He needs more than meat. He needs time."

"And water," she offered. "And sticks."

"And his own people," Father added sadly.

When Mother came home late that night, Father left the house to meet her outside. Brother and the boy slept quietly beside her in the house. Father had put his own blanket over the boy, though she offered hers up without hesitation.

Father took Mother out into the junipers before speaking to her. She listened to their distant voices but couldn't make out much of what they said. Mother was angry, that she could hear. Father tried to calm her using the quiet tones he used on Brother when he was ill-tempered or hurt.

They spoke for some time. Their voices fell into the rhythms of conversation and conspiracy. After a time, they came back into the house together. Father crawled to his bed and unfolded a winter blanket.

"Daughter," Mother said. "I know you are awake. Come outside with me."

"Mother," said Father sternly.

"It's fine," she said. "Warm the blanket for me."

Daughter looked at Father who offered a warm smile but still she was afraid, and her heart galloped in her chest. She crawled over the sleepers and then outside into the night.

The stars were so many and so bright, she could weave under their light, walk in the forest for miles and never get lost.

"Daughter," Mother said. "Sit with me."

She was at the cutting place and patted a stump beside her.

"Are you very cross with me, Mother?" she asked.

She studied her mother's face. She knew every line of it, every strand of hair, every scratch. She loved that face and she knew it loved her.

"We are not to be seen," Mother said. "It is dangerous for us to be seen."

"It's only one boy," she said. "No one else saw me. I promise."

"Others will be out looking for him. His people will come looking for him. They'll find us."

"But they can't be cross with us," she said. "We saved him. Father said he'll be all right. He might have a permanent mark, like your missing finger. A limp probably, he said, but he'll be okay. He's going to live. He wouldn't have if I'd left him there. I saved him. I did something noble."

"Daughter, how you love the little things," she said.

"What little things, Mother? I don't understand," she said. But Mother only smiled.

"Sometimes it's possible to be too kind," she said. "Let us

hope this is not one of those. You should have come and found me."

"Everything will be well," she said. "He told me he has sisters. How can his people be cross with us for saving his life? He is no criminal. They will want him back. Surely his people will be thankful."

"Is that why you saved him?" she asked.

"No, Mother. That was not the reason. I only saw that he needed saving and I alone could do it."

"It was a terrible risk you took," she said.

"But—"

"But Father agrees with you," she said. "He is glad that you saved the boy. He thinks also that his people will be very glad to see him alive. He thinks this is a good thing you've done. He is proud of you."

"And you, Mother?"

"I too am proud of you," she said giving her a kiss on the head. "But I am more wary than Father. I am more timid. I am like the rabbit, afraid of shadows and quick to run. He is like an elk, cautious but not so scared. He thinks this may be good. He thinks maybe we can see people now."

"I'm glad," she said.

"But Daughter, you must remember our ways. You must remember your teachings. We are not people. We are not Diné. Our clan is outcast. We are not to be seen and you must never tell anyone. It is a secret. Do you understand?"

"Yes, Mother," she said. "The boy thinks I'm Navajo. He thinks we're people. How is he to know we are not?"

"That is true, Daughter, but you showed today that you can forget our rules and act impulsively. You must guard against it in the future for all our sakes, not just yours."

"Yes, Mother," she said.

"I love you, Daughter. Now go sleep in the house. You must surely be tired from pulling the draw-behind."

"I made it like I saw Father do it," she said.

"It is a very good one," she said. "Now go sleep and don't wake Brother. I'm going to stay out here for a while yet."

And she went to bed.

The boy called himself Paul Goodfellow of the Salt Clan. He stayed with them for two days. The first day he was in terrible pain. He moaned and cried and had hard times chewing the medicine root that would make him feel better.

On the second day, the pain wasn't so bad and he told Father where his people were. He spoke of roads and rivers and she was afraid for Father when he said he'd go and fetch them, but he was not afraid.

"You stay and keep Mother company," he told her. "Don't let her get lonely. I'll be home soon." And he left them.

She made a stew from rabbit Mother had snared that day and stretched the fur herself without asking for any help. Mother was pensive and watched the trail that led to a road that led to another road. She said they'd come from that way.

At dinnertime, she spooned stew into bowls while Brother played with a lizard on the wall. Paul watched Mother across the house as they ate. They could have eaten outside, it was such a nice day, but to be polite they ate with their guest.

"You look so much like my aunt Ruth," he said to Mother. Mother tensed and shrank back from the fire.

"That's a queer thing to say," she said.

"But it is true," Paul said. "Aunt Ruth is dead so you cannot be her. But you look like her."

Mother got up and left the house then.

"Was I rude?" asked Paul.

"You are mistaken," Daughter said. "She is Mother. Not Aunt Ruth."

"It was not meant as an insult," he said. "Ruth was a good woman. She was killed when I was little, but I still remember her."

"Mother is alive, as you can see," she said. "You are mistaken. You bring bad luck with such talk. You should be more grateful."

"Did I not see that she is missing a finger on her hand? Aunt Ruth was missing a finger the same way."

The sound of a truck weaving the narrow trail to their home brought Daughter to her feet. She ran outside and saw then the yellow truck with the rounded front pull beside the cutting place. Father and a woman came out of one door, a man came out of the other.

"Hello," said Mother. "The boy is in the house. Let's get him away home."

And she saw the stare then. The man stared at Mother as if he were seeing a ghost and Daughter became afraid.

"Do you not want the boy? May we keep him?" Mother teased the man, her voice a little deeper than normal.

"Goodfellow," said the woman to the staring man. "Help me get your son. We are in debt to these people. Do not be rude."

Daughter held the door open as the men carried Paul to the truck. They laid him in the back and the woman crawled up beside him. Father accepted the thanks from the woman while Mother held back by their house in the dimming twilight. Father waved to them as the man drove the truck away.

Mother gave Father a grim look. Father gave her a reassuring one.

The next day the woman came back with the man and they brought a basket of beans. The truck was grimy with dust and red-orange dirt. The woman presented the gift to Mother. Mother took the beans, said the formal words of thanks, and mentioned Daughter as the one she should thank. She asked to see her, to thank her formally, but Mother said that Daughter was away hunting berries. But that was a lie. She was in the house with Brother watching through a crack in the door.

"Why did you not let me get thanks?" Daughter asked coming out of the house when they were gone.

"We are not to be seen," Mother said. "We are the coyote in the brush, catfish in the river. We cannot be seen."

"But they've already seen me," she said.

"Not so much," she said. "I was afraid they might recognize you."

"Me? How?"

"From me," Mother said tasting a bean. "Ruth may have had children. I do not know."

Daughter thought of this for a while but didn't speak.

"Best we not be seen," she said finally.

"Yes, Daughter. That is always best," Mother said. "These beans are good, wholesome, and fresh. Let's cook some tonight. Father will be pleased. It was not so bad you helped the boy."

"I knew they'd be grateful," Daughter said. "They are like us, Diné. Indians."

"They are not like us," Mother said sternly. "We are not Diné, we are not Indians."

"But Father—"

"Yes, he was Diné, but Daughter, Indians are the most dangerous to us. They remember us."

"We have done nothing to them," she said. "We saved Paul Goodfellow. Please don't worry, Mother."

Mother sighed and forced a smile onto her lips. "Take Brother to the river and bathe him," she said. "I'll start supper."

Father was pleased with the beans, though Daughter thought they were bland. He said the taste reminded him of growing up.

"I prefer orange berries from the butterfly plant," she said.

"Yes," he agreed. "Those are good. Maybe tomorrow you will show us where you found them and we'll gather more."

"I would be happy to," she said with some pride.

It was dusk, about the same time they had fetched injured Paul Goodfellow the day before. There were many trucks this time.

"Go inside, family," said Father.

Without a word, Mother picked up Brother and hurried into the house. Daughter made to follow, but curiosity got the better of her and she hid instead behind the woodpile. From the doorway, she saw mother signal for her to hide. She ducked low.

Father picked up an axe from the cutting place and stood between the trail and the house.

From three trucks came six men. They were all Diné. The man who'd taken the boy led them and stared at father in a way that made Daughter shake.

"What brings you back, Goodfellow?" said Father. "Is Paul well?"

"Skinwalker," he said before raising his gun and shooting Father in the chest. Father dropped his axe, fell to one knee and raised his arm in a gesture of greeting or begging. Another man shot his hand and Daughter saw fingers fly from it. Then the others shot. Many shots. Many, many shots. Father fell in a clump.

Mother screamed from the house. The men rushed passed Father and kicked open the door. Daughter heard Mother beating at the back of the house, pulling at the wood to make an escape. But it was too late. More shots.

A man threw Brother outside and another man with an archaic spear drove an obsidian blade into Brother's body. He wore leather robes and paint, smelled of fragrant smoke and chanted medicine as he stabbed.

Daughter hid behind the wood as long as she dared, as long as she could. She watched the butchery of her family. Not content with killing them, they had to mutilate them. They cut them into pieces, slurry for the vultures and scavengers.

They set fire to her house with lamp oil and a wooden match.

"Wait," said Goodfellow, "Where is the girl? One is missing."

The men spread out and began to search. One stepped close to her woodpile, and, spooked, she ran.

She felt the rush of air on her neck before she heard the sound. Bullets flew by her like angry wasps. She ran. She ran as hard and as fast as she could. She could hear others following her, yelling, "Don't let it get away."

She ran and hid, and she survived as an animal for half a century. Long enough for her to forget how she'd caused her family's death. It was her fault; the consequence of ignoring her own identity. She was not to be seen.

CHAPTER THIRTY

Eleanor woke from her sleep with tears in her eyes.

She was alive and awake and wished to be neither. She knew where she was. In her dreams she had heard talk and smelled antiseptic and felt punctures and probings. She did not need to open her eyes to know she was in a hospital bed.

She let the tears flow freely for a while and then reached up to wipe them but could not. She opened her eyes then and saw the leather restraints holding her wrists to the bed. She blinked. Her right eye was swollen and her vision blurred, but she could make out the room.

The room could hold two, but she was alone. A cart of glowing machines stood in the free space, wires ran from them to ports in the wall. Similar ports fed wires out of the wall to plastic leads taped to her head and chest. Tubes stuck out of her arms and the back of her hands like porcupine quills. The room was rank with the stink of plastic tubing, cleaning solvents, old vomit, and pungent unguents.

She bent over and looked at her hands. They were her hands. Except for a needle sticking in one, they were perfect.

A black patch surrounded the needle. She could smell the unctuous odor from it. A similar odor rose from her arms where the tubes were stuck. She turned her head and realized that the plastic she smelled was not under her nose but in it. She snorted, swallowed, and traced the tube down her throat into her stomach.

Her head still hurt where Mr. Liddle had smashed a bottle into it but it was her leg and side that ached the most now. She could lean forward and see the wound in her side. There was only a little hole just in her front, but, a couple of inches away, just under her arm, there was a huge, ragged tear that was held closed with tape. Inside her, she felt odd sensations, gurglings and contortions, as she imagined her internal organs repairing themselves to pattern. She was grateful her liver did not have nerve endings or she'd be screaming now.

She could not see her leg, but she felt it. A bullet had entered the front but it had not passed through like the other. She traced paths of shrapnel-shard canyons emanating from the entry point like gullies off a mesa. They drilled destruction up and down her leg, spiraling into arteries and one was still lodged in her bone.

She was weak. She was hungry. The pain of the healing was stayed by the fact she had not the resources to speed it.

She could taste the sweet alkaloids of pain medicine and knew she'd been drugged. The arm restraints told her she'd been captured. Her fear told her she was undone, and her memory told her that again, the undoing was her fault.

She laid back and listened to the machines. She heard talking in the hall, saw shapes move in front of the window in the door. She thought she heard David's voice, but it was far away and the walls muffled everything. After a while the door opened and to her surprise Dr. Sikring slipped in. He closed the door behind him and rushed to her side.

"What are you doing—" she began.

"Eleanor," he whispered urgently. "Be careful. He's on to you."

"Why—" she started.

"What are you doing in here?" said a man in the doorway. "Medical staff and family only."

"Sorry," he said. "She looked lonely. Where's her brother?"

"Are you leaving or am I throwing you out?"

"I'm leaving," Sikring said. He looked up in a corner of the ceiling. Eleanor saw there a black plastic dome indicative of a closed circuit camera. He glanced back as if making sure Eleanor had noticed it. He stopped at the door for moment and smiled back at her. "And Merry Christmas, Eleanor."

The man closed the door and looked up at the camera himself before approaching the bed. "How're you feeling?" he asked in an East Coast accent.

"How long?"

"You've been here three days," he said examining the tubes in her arms. "It's Christmas day today. Well it will be for another thirty minutes or so. Then it'll be the day after Christmas. See how that works?"

"That long?"

"Um-hmm," he grunted.

"Where's David? How'd I get here? Why am I restrained?"

"Now, you calm down," he said.

"Who are you?" she asked.

"I'm Doctor Maulitz," he said. "You're in Jamesford Hospital."

"I want to go home," she said.

"You were shot," he said. "And beaten with a bottle. You're lucky to be alive."

"I want to go home," she said.

"Tell me about any allergies you have," he said reading a clipboard.

"I want to go home."

"Did you know you're allergic to every antibiotic we have?"

"I want to go home," she said louder.

"And particularly penicillin," he said. "You could have died from that. I've never seen a more violent reaction. It was like every cell in your body attacked the medicine. Your temperature topped one-twenty. You should be dead."

"I want to go home!" she screamed.

The doctor looked up from his paper.

"I want to go home!" she screamed and this time let in a little animal, a little monster, and her voice carried like a shot.

The door opened and Sheriff Hannon came in, his hand on his holstered gun. Outside in the hall, she glimpsed Mr. Gordon, Dr. Zalarnik's bodyguard, standing by the door.

"What's going on?" the sheriff demanded.

"She's not herself," said the doctor.

"How would you know?" she said.

"It's okay, Eleanor," said Hannon. "You're safe now."

"Am I a prisoner?" she asked.

"No. No, of course not," he said.

"Then undo these straps," she said. Hannon looked at the doctor. Maulitz looked at the camera. He waited a moment and then undid the restraints.

"Do you feel well enough to tell me about it?" the sheriff said.

She stared at Maulitz.

"Leave us now, Doctor. I'll call if we need you." He turned and left the room. In the hall Mr. Gordon had disappeared.

"How'd I get here?" she asked.

"Russell Liddle brought you in Sunday night," he said.

"Russell?"

"Yeah," he said.

"What?" she said. "Does he know about his . . ."

"Yeah, he knows. He knew when he brought you in."

"He saved me?" Eleanor said.

"Looks that way," he said. "He could have saved more people if he'd come to me about his dad."

"He couldn't," Eleanor said. "Family."

"Tell me what happened, Eleanor," he said. "Did he grab you? Did Russell know about the kidnapping?"

Over the last year, she'd become fond of the sheriff and much of her fear of authority had vanished because of it. But Sikring had told her to be careful. For whatever reason, he'd reminded her of the obvious.

"I wasn't kidnapped. I was stupid. I saw Russell had a silver flask at the dance," she said. "Eric mentioned the murdered hitchhiker had one. I thought that Russell was the killer, but I didn't have any proof. I went over to his trailer and tried to find some."

"Well you did," he said. "Why didn't you come to me?"

"Would you have believed me?"

"I might have," he said. "Liddle was on our list of suspects."

"But so was David, and probably his father. Maybe even me. You'd have suspected ulterior motives."

He didn't deny it. "Tell me how it all happened."

She took a deep breath. "I'm hungry," she said to buy time.

"Doctors said you were near starved when you came in.

Strangest thing. I saw you Saturday. You looked great Saturday—that dress. But Sunday night you looked like you'd come out of a Nazi camp."

"I did?" she said.

"You don't want to talk about it?" he said, steering her back on subject.

"I saw Russell leave the trailer and figured I'd take a look. I didn't know Mr. Liddle was home. The door was open. I went in. There's a disgusting room in the trailer, with dead animals and such. I figured it was the perfect place to hide something so I looked in a few places and found David's gun under some papers."

"Did you touch the gun?"

"No," she said. "There was money there too, European money. I knew then I'd been right, well sort of."

"Crazy girl," he murmured.

"Mr. Liddle snuck up on me. I'm sure I'd have heard him if it hadn't been for the wind. He hit me with a bottle. When I woke up I was in a bathtub, taped and bound with wires."

She looked at her wrists. She was not surprised to see absolutely no sign of the wires that had cut so deeply into her flesh just a few days before. If she'd even had a scratch or a scab there now it would go far to back up her story.

"He said something about me not needing to see anymore and that we'd go for a drive when it got dark enough. He made it clear he was going to kill me," she said.

"Yes, we think he would have," he said.

"He left me and went to watch TV. I, uhm, wiggled out of the wire. I heard him and Russell argue and then Russell left. It was dark in the bathroom. I heard him coming and when he opened the door I jumped at him."

"Where'd you get the weapon?"

"It's all a blur after that," she lied. "I remember jumping at him and then waking up here. Everything else is hazy. I remember fighting with him and him shooting me. I cut him and I ran."

"What kind of weapon was it? A knife? A garden tool?"

"I don't remember," she said.

"What happened to it?"

She shook her head and said, "I want to see David. I want to see the Venns. I want to go home."

"Well," he sighed, "I'll see what I can do, but things are pretty complicated around here. Do you know Dimitri Zalarnik, that big-wig bio guy?"

"He spoke at school," she said.

"That's right," he said. "He's gotten involved somehow. Seems one of your doctors called him in. Plus there was a nurse here. She's gone now. She was a Revealer and tried to exorcise you. Seriously, exorcise you. Like in the movies. Now Lugner's stirring things up. There are other people too, not Revealers, but folks who hear things and read too much into them."

"So the town knows," she muttered.

"Knows what?" he said.

"Uhm," she said. "What do they know?"

"Well what I know is that you stopped a killer and as far as I'm concerned you're a hero."

"What do the doctors know?"

He sighed again. "They don't talk to me," he said. "But even I can see you're healing damn fast. Can you see out of your eye?"

She nodded. "A little."

"You should have seen it Sunday. It was split open. Now

you can see out of it. It's a miracle. Pieces of bullet have been falling out of your leg since you got here. Your muscles are pushing them out like a Pez dispenser—you know that candy with the cartoon heads on it, that tilt back for treats? Like that. It's got them all excited. Zalarnik's been hovering around you like you were the Messiah. The only part of you that isn't getting better is that bruise on your arm."

"So he got the DNA test?" she said.

"You mean for the Battons?"

"They hired Zalarnik to help them test me."

"Sonuva . . ." he said. "I'm writing him up on an ethics violation. He never said anything about that."

"Did he do the test?"

"I don't know," he said.

"But . . ."

"But," he sighed. "He's been here since Monday. I don't know."

"It doesn't matter now," she said closing her eyes. "I'm done."

"Those Battons won't get near you, Eleanor. If they come with an illegally obtained DNA report, they'll be arrested before they're sued. I'll see to that. Don't fret."

"It's not them, not anymore. It's you and this hospital and Zalarnik. And Sikring, yes most of all Sikring."

"You're not making sense." He took her hand gently.

"I should have stayed away. I never should have gone out," she muttered. "Jamesford's been good to me. I just wanted to give something back, Sheriff. Do you understand? I was only trying to help, but I ruined everything. Again."

CHAPTER THIRTY-ONE

"So I hear you want to leave?" said Dr. Zalarnik the next morning. It was nearly eight by the clock on the heart monitor. After Hannon left, she'd seen Dr. Maulitz twice more. He'd tried to question her, but she'd ignored him so profoundly that he'd actually slammed the door when he left the last time. She'd not seen another soul the rest of the night.

"I want to go home," she said to Zalarnik. He regarded her with eager appraising eyes, studying her with the same intensity she imagined she displayed when she was readying a change.

"Yes," he said. "You have an advocate for that apparently. Sheriff Hannon is raising a fuss. I think he'll get you released by noon. Persistent man. Strange he couldn't put that energy into finding Mr. Liddle. You'd have been saved so much trouble if he had."

"I do not give you permission to sample my genetic material for any reason," she said formally, reciting the lines she'd rehearsed all night for this inevitable meeting.

"Eleanor," he said pulling a chair beside the bed. "We're a little beyond that now, don't you think?"

There was a skid and a crash in the hallway. The door flew open. David stood there gripped around the shoulders by Mr. Gordon. The bodyguard's stony expression was an eerie counterpoint to David's frantic efforts to get away from him.

"Who do you think you are?" he screamed. Gordon pulled him back and the door swung shut.

"Let him come in," she said in tones that burned her throat. "And you leave."

Whether it was the strange tone that had carried into her words, or her unflinching predatory expression, Zalarnik pushed his chair back and stood up.

"We'll talk later," he said. "Count on it."

When Zalarnik had exited, Mr. Gordon released David in the hall.

He pushed through the door and rushed to her. He made to wrap her in a fervent embrace, desperate and relieved, but he held back assessing the many wires and tubes sticking out of her.

"Kiss me," she said.

A grin so wide he couldn't pucker properly spread over David's face as he bent over Eleanor and kissed her.

The spark made her dizzy. David stumbled back into the chair Zalarnik had left. He pulled it close and leaned in to talk to her.

"You idiot," he said. "What the hell were you thinking?"

"I wanted to help," she said. "I—what happened to you?" His left eye had a blue ring under it.

"It's nothing," he said and fell silent. She didn't press him.

"Sorry I ruined Christmas," she said.

"You didn't," he said.

Then she understood about the eye.

"Your dad?" she said.

He nodded and stared ashamedly at the floor.

"Tell me what's happening in Jamesford," she said. "What are they saying about me?" She needed to get her bearings as well as change the subject.

"They found my gun in Russell's trailer," he said. "But I guess you figured that one out. Mr. Liddle is dead. Russell is in custody."

"But Russell saved me. He drove me to the hospital."

"So that's true? I'm surprised."

"Me too," she said. "Sheriff Hannon said he knew I'd killed his father when he drove me here."

"So that's true too," he said quietly.

"I had to," she said. "It was him or me. Him or me and others too. Don't hate me." She closed her eyes, afraid of seeing the distrust in his, or worse, horror when he looked beneath her disguise and saw what she really was.

"Oh no, Eleanor," he said. "I don't think that. I'm ashamed of myself. I feel like I let you down by not being there."

"That's stupid," she said. "You didn't know."

"I should have known," he said. "I should have stayed with my dad that night after the dance. To hell with what people thought. I should have been there."

"I should have told you what I was up to," she admitted.

"Yes," he said. "Yes, you should have."

"You'd have stopped me," she said.

"I'd have tried, but I don't think I could stop you from doing anything. But I might have helped. The thought of what you went through makes me so angry. But also grateful you are who you are. I still have you."

"I didn't expect any trouble," she said. "I had a hunch and

I thought my senses would protect me. If it hadn't been for the storm . . . Don't blame yourself. It was all me."

"I feel like I let you down," he said.

"Mr. Liddle would still be alive, if I—"

"Nobody's mourning Mr. Liddle," David said.

"Russell," she said.

He sighed. "He'll be better off without him. Plus, there'll be no long ugly trial now."

"So I'm judge, jury, and executioner?"

"No, you defended yourself," he said holding her hand. "Did you know Russell thought that his dad had kidnapped you? It's what I heard. He thought his dad went out and grabbed you and planned to torture you to death as a Christmas present to him. What does that tell you about Russell and his stepdad's relationship?"

"That's horrible," she said.

"Tell me about it," he said. "I'm so glad you're alive. Plus you cleared my dad. I owe you for that too."

"Your dad?"

"I thought he was the killer," he said. "I think Mom did too."

The thought stunned her. It made sense. Looking at David's eye now and remembering Jim's rage at the rock thrower, she could see the possibility.

"Oh, David," she said. "How terrible for you. To think that your father . . ."

"But it wasn't him," he said quickly. "You settled that. It's all good."

"Tell me about Christmas."

He sighed. "Dad got drunk Monday and stayed that way through Christmas. After hearing about you, he got news that his old unit in Afghanistan was wiped out. Something like fifteen casualties. He fell apart. He went mad. He tore up the Christmas tree. Mom took Wendy to your place and hid out while I tried to calm him down. That's when I got this shiner. He railed for hours saying that he'd let them down, that he'd let you down, that he was never in the right place at the right time."

"I'm sorry," she said.

"Funny thing. I felt kinda the same. About you anyway. Seeing you Monday morning, oh God, Eleanor, you were in pieces. You were dying. I'd have given anything to trade places with you. I was dying faster than you, blaming myself. That's why I stayed back to try and help Dad. I thought I understood a little of what he was going through. But he wouldn't listen. He's broken again."

"He seemed fine to me," she said.

"He's different around you. He can defend you, if that makes any sense. He threatened to kill Russell before we found out he wasn't the one who'd hurt you. Sheriff Hannon even cuffed Dad, threatened to arrest him."

"The sheriff was there?"

"You don't think a big man like him can rail like a lunatic, destroy a Christmas tree in that little trailer, with so many neighbors, and no one would notice?"

"Merry Christmas," she said.

"Yeah."

They sat together, not talking for a while. Humming machines filled the silence like crickets in the night. Eleanor reached up to her head and removed a wire that was taped there. Then she took off another. She removed everything that wasn't directly inserted into her body. There were many.

Doctor Maulitz poked his head in the door but Eleanor

greeted him with such a cold stare that he retreated without objection.

"Was Russell in on the killings?" David asked.

"I don't think so. Mr. Liddle was the killer. Russell was . . ." she reached for words. "Russell was his son. Sort of. No, it was Mr. Liddle. He admitted it to me."

"So why are they holding Russell?"

"I don't know," she said. "I think he was the one who stole your gun, but if I had to guess, I'd say he's in jail because he has nowhere else to go."

"He saved you," David said again, shaking his head. "Russell Liddle saved Eleanor Anders after she killed his father. Sheesh, Merry Christmas."

Eleanor let the silence return, unable to comment more on Russell. She didn't understand it herself. She was always confused by kindness, and Russell was now the king of it. Eleanor could see that David weighed the debt he owed to the boy who'd been nothing but his enemy as long as he could remember. Eleanor imagined Russell in a cell alone, no family, no money, facing The Farm down in Riverton. Frightened. She imagined his stiff bearing, loud bravado, and tough talk concealing his inner terror, and couldn't help but draw parallels to herself.

"Weird things are happening here at the hospital," David whispered. "What is getting around town is that you were mortally wounded and you're healing so fast doctors can watch it before their eyes. They called in some specialists, but Zalarnik chased them all away and brought in his own. He got away with it because he's paying for all of it. Your doctor is not from Jamesford, but Boston. He works at one of Zalarnik's labs."

"That figures," she said.

"I saw you Monday morning, after they'd brought you in. You looked like hell. You were covered in blood. Your face. Oh, your face . . ."

"I'm sorry if I made you sick again." She hadn't meant it to sound so cruel and realized her mistake when he flushed.

"I am so sorry about that," he said earnestly. "Please forgive me."

"I have," she said. "I'm sorry I said that." She bent forward to kiss him on the cheek and when she touched him, the shock was warm and soothing, a promise, and a punctuation to her apology.

"Thanks," he said. "But now that you mention it, it never crossed my mind. I was upset, sure. Very upset. They gave me some pills so I'd calm down, but I never felt sick. Maybe I was too scared?"

"Maybe you've changed," she said. "Toughened up or something."

"Something," he said. He took a deep breath and let it out slow. Eleanor's stomach did a flip. She felt a confession coming.

"I had to speak up finally," he said. "You were dying and they were making it worse. I had to say something."

"What did you say?" she said.

"They were doing some things that I thought were helpful, like cleaning you up and stitching you up, but they were missing the obvious. You were hungry. You were consuming yourself to heal. I could see it. You've never told me, and I'd never seen it happen, but I knew that was what you were doing. Your muscles were decaying in front of their eyes and that's what spooked them. They were trying to blood type you and getting absolutely nowhere when what you needed was a cheeseburger. You were going to die from starvation before you died of the wounds. I told them you were starving. I told them to feed you."

"Smart boy," she said.

"They didn't listen to me at first. But I made such a ruckus they finally had to try it. That's when they put that thing in your nose. They made me go in the waiting room then, Mom holding me back from bringing you a Snickers."

"Snickers aren't my favorite," she said. "Were they out of Three Musketeers?"

He laughed. "I'll remember that."

"Do you know why they tied me down?"

"You kept pulling all these tubes out."

"Oh, is that all?" she said relieved Zalarnik hadn't ordered her capture.

"No, it's worse than that," he said quietly. "Even after your arms were bound, your body pushed the needles out anyways. Stitches wouldn't last more than an hour. They'd find them on the floor with your wound open again but knitting nicely on its own. They didn't like that, so they tried tape and that worked better. They finally found some goo that numbed your skin or tricked you somehow and finally got needles and tubes to stay inside you."

"That's not good," she said.

"It might have helped," he said.

"They're learning about me. I am not to be seen."

He nodded. He understood her sentiment if not the curious phrasing.

"I'm sure they've done all kinds of tests on me already," she said.

"I'm sure," he said.

"I've got to leave," she said.

He nodded. "Mom will be here in a minute. She can check you out," he said misinterpreting the finality of her statement.

"What about Revealers?"

"Yeah, they're picketing the hospital. There're news trucks outside so of course they're here. Hannon went on record saying you were a hero and the paper said "Prom Queen Stops Serial Killer." It got picked up across the country. It's nuts."

"I am not to be seen," she said her eyes filling with tears. "I am not to be seen."

"It'll be okay," he said holding her. "You're not alone."

But she was, and she felt her good intentions wrapping around her neck like a noose. She put on a facade of calm. She was good at facades.

David didn't leave her side until Karen arrived with Wendy in tow.

"Eleanor?" Karen gasped in the doorway, wide eyed. "Oh my . . . I don't . . . How can . . . Your eye?"

"It feels okay," Eleanor said.

"You look so much better than before. Better even than yesterday. Much, much better."

"She wants to go home, Mom," David said. "She needs to go home. Right away."

"You look terrible," said Wendy to Eleanor. "I'm so sorry for you."

"You should have seen her last weekend," said David.

"No, you shouldn't have," said Karen. "Why do you want to leave, Eleanor?"

"I have to," she said. "It's not safe here."

"Not safe?"

"Mom, trust us. We've got to get her out of here," said

David. "Quietly. The sooner, the better. You can see she's well enough to travel. Just sign the papers or whatever you have to do and let's take her home."

"But her doctor said she should stay for at least another month. He hinted about taking her to another hospital just now."

"Karen," Eleanor said. "Please. Please take me home." There was desperation in her voice, panic rising as she saw Karen's confusion. Eleanor felt strong enough to walk out of the building if she had to, but then what? She hadn't a plan beyond knowing she couldn't stay there. She needed Karen's help, a place to hide, time to think.

In the window of the door Eleanor glimpsed Mr. Gordon and knew then that her chances of clandestine escape were slim.

"Please," Eleanor said again. "Please. Please, Karen."

She couldn't remember a moment in her long life when she'd needed anything from anyone as much as she did then.

"I'll be back," Karen said resignedly. "Come on, Wendy."

Karen was gone for hours. While waiting, Eleanor demanded that all the invasive needles and tubes be removed. She made the demand through David, and then directly to Dr. Maulitz and two other doctors who argued against it. They were arguing with her when Stephanie Pearce came in with a vase of flowers for a visit.

"It's against her religion," Pearce told the doctors after they had admitted that none of the tubes were necessary to her survival. "If you don't remove them, I'll see to it that you're all sued. Patients have rights in this country."

Maulitz gave a snarky snort that alarmed everyone, even the other doctors. They removed the tubes and scrubbed her arms clean of the black, oily smudges around the needle sights. As they were finishing, Karen returned, accompanied by a nurse with a wheelchair.

"I brought you some fresh clothes," she told Eleanor.

Stephanie said her goodbye with a tearful maternal kiss on Eleanor's forehead that had to look as awkward as it felt, judging from David's expression.

David took Wendy outside to hunt for a Three Musketeers while the nurse and Karen helped Eleanor dress.

Eleanor noticed the nurse's hands were shaking. She dropped her papers twice and fumbled with her buttons.

"I can get those," Eleanor said to her.

"I'm sorry I'm so clumsy," she said and Eleanor saw her eyes were tearful.

"What's wrong?" she asked her warily.

"You're a miracle, child," the nurse said. "I'm blessed for having touched you."

"We can finish up," Karen said. "We'll call you when we're ready."

The nurse wiped her eyes then silently, and reverently, left the room.

"You're being released AMA," Karen said. "That means 'against medical advice.' It means that they won't be held responsible."

"That's fine with me," she said.

"They said there's a bullet fragment still in your leg," Karen said. "They want to schedule you for a surgery next week to remove it."

"It's on the tray," Eleanor said. "It fell out this morning."

"It just fell out?"

"I dug at it a little," she admitted.

"Out of the bone?"

"Yes. It's out. I'm not coming back," Eleanor explained. "I can't, and I'm not giving them reason to bring me back. Tell Maulitz to look on the tray. Tell Zalarnik that that bullet shard is the last thing he's getting out of me."

CHAPTER THIRTY-TWO

It upset Karen, but Eleanor demanded that she be taken to her home on Cedar Street and not the Venns' trailer.

"Jim's been living there," Karen said tentatively.

"That's fine," she said. "David told me."

Karen nodded, evidently relieved that she wouldn't have to explain more in front of Wendy.

"We can better nurse you at our home," she said. "I can take some time off work and we'll get you up again."

"I can't do that," she said conclusively.

"I don't like it," Karen said but turned the van toward Eleanor's house.

"Thanks, Karen," said Eleanor. "You've been more than understanding."

When they crossed onto Cedar, Eleanor saw her little white picket fence was festooned with yellow ribbons and flowers. The house was dark but David's car, which Jim had borrowed, was parked in front.

"What's all that?" Eleanor asked. Her right eye was still blurry and tinged in pink.

"Pretty," said Wendy climbing out of the van.

"Did you guys do this?" Eleanor asked.

"No," said David. "Maybe it was Dad."

"It was a bunch of school kids and a couple of adults." Jim Venn came out from behind the house. "I nearly chased them off thinking they were those church nuts."

"What does it mean?" Eleanor asked.

"It means come home soon," said Wendy. "That's what the yellow ribbons mean. We put them out for Daddy when he was gone. Hi, Daddy!"

"Hi, sweetheart." Wendy trotted up to him and he picked her up and hugged her. Jim hadn't shaved in days and his clothes were a mess.

"Welcome home, Eleanor," he said. "You don't look so bad. I was told it was much worse."

David spoke before anyone could offer an explanation. "Let's get her inside," he said.

She could have walked on her own, but Eleanor let David and Jim carry her inside. They were rougher than the hospital staff had been, but they carried her across the snow and up her porch, and finally deposited her on the couch without opening any wounds or making her call for a pain pill.

"Do you remember who put the ribbons on?" she asked.

"Well, there was a plump girl with a big Shoshone fellow that did some ribbons. The flowers have been appearing the last day or so. Lots of people dropping them off. Kids and grown-ups both."

"Midge," Eleanor said. "I should call her."

"I'm not leaving here again," David announced. "I'm here until Eleanor is well again."

"No," Karen said.

"I'm staying too," said Jim.

"It'll be okay, Mom," said David. "Won't it, Dad? No drinking. Eleanor has a rule about it in her house." She didn't, but Eleanor didn't correct him.

"Oh, yes, of course," he said. "I'll get rid of it right away."

"Actually," Eleanor said. "I'd rather be alone."

"That's not going to happen," David said decisively. "Not a chance."

"Really, I'll be fine," she said.

"No," said Jim firmly.

"Okay, you can stay at night," she said. "But I really feel like being alone."

Jim shook his head. "I'll stay at night, but during the day, one of us is here with you until you're on your feet."

Eleanor made to stand up, but David pushed her back on the couch with a gentle shove. "Don't," he said. "You're pissing me off. Lay there and tell me what you need."

Eleanor didn't want to come right out and say it. She was afraid for herself but she was also afraid for the Venns. They did not know what they were getting into, what they were already into. She didn't either, but she had more information than they had and she was terrified. If they'd leave her alone, she could heal quicker and then escape while there was still time and not have to involve her adopted family any more. But she was tired and hungry. Her eye was blurry, and a slow, deep ache was beginning in her side.

"Okay," she said. "I'm hungry. David knows what I like." David nodded understanding. "And vitamins. Don't forget those."

"Don't worry about a thing," said Karen.

That night, David moved in to her loft room, and at Karen's insistence, Eleanor's things were brought down to the master bedroom.

"I appreciate why you haven't made this your room," Karen said. "But if Tabitha were here, she'd want you to sleep here while you heal."

Jim was to sleep on the couch, but that first night he kept a sleepless vigil in front of the window. Though he tried to conceal it, he'd brought his rifle with him and kept it close under the sofa. He stayed until after lunch when he drove back to the trailer for a nap.

"This works out fine," David said. "Dad can stay in my room without worrying Wendy."

"Didn't she see his breakdown?" Eleanor asked.

"Yeah, she saw most of it. But she's little. And, to be honest, she'd seen it before."

That afternoon, more people came by the house. Eleanor listened to them from the kitchen as she devoured ham steaks and drank gallons of milk. David watched from the window.

"I think that's Mrs. Westlake," said David in alarm. "It *is* her."

"This can't be good," she said.

"No, wait. She's laying flowers. She's kneeling. Right there in the snow, she's kneeling and praying."

"For my destruction no doubt," she said.

"I don't think so," he said. "She looks . . . well, she looks . . . not angry."

Mrs. Westlake's strange devotions were repeated several more times that day by others, David reported. Many he did not even recognize.

Just at twilight, Karen's van pulled up. Jim hopped out and retrieved a three-foot Christmas tree from the back. Karen called for David and together they brought in turkey and potatoes, dressing and gravy. Wendy made two trips to bring in all the presents.

"Since you didn't get a Christmas, we brought you one," exclaimed Wendy.

"Are all those presents for me?"

"Yes," she said.

"Oh," Eleanor said from the couch. "I didn't have time to—"

"Good," said Jim. "We'd be mad if you had gotten us anything."

"Not another word about it," cautioned Karen.

They feasted that night while the little tree sparkled and blinked on her old secondhand coffee table. Eleanor hadn't had a Christmas tree in years and felt now how much she'd missed them.

After dinner, Eleanor opened her gifts. She'd mentioned before how she loved puzzles and games and they'd picked up some good ones for her.

"You have to teach us how to play this one," Wendy said holding up a box with cartoon farmers on it. "It says up to eight people can play it. I want to try."

"Those wood puzzles are a regift," admitted Jim. "Darned if I could solve them. You have a go at them."

Eleanor was overwhelmed and felt uncomfortably indebted by the end of the night. She tried to hide her trepidation behind warm, thankful smiles and pleasant conversation, which never led back to her ordeal or her recovery. She was thankful for that as well, and added it to the list of kindnesses she'd be unable to repay and that she'd surely suffer for later.

The evening ended before eleven so Eleanor could rest. After storing the leftovers and tucking her into bed with a single electrifying peck on the lips, David climbed up to the loft. Jim took his usual station at the window and Eleanor fell asleep confused and frightened, but hiding it well.

During the days that followed, Eleanor's house became a kind of cloister during the good times, and a fortified stronghold during the bad.

In the quiet times, Eleanor concentrated on healing. She ate all she could and then took hot baths. She chewed vitamins while her body did what it had to do, urged on by Eleanor's own will to have it done as fast as possible. She found that the pain pills, though effective, slowed her healing. The pain was required, it seemed, for her supernatural regeneration. It was a miserable time for her, but she preferred physical pain to the other kind.

Word spread quickly that Eleanor was home, that the lights in her little house were not just Jim Venn kicked out of his trailer after a Christmas fight, but Eleanor Anders herself back at home.

Eleanor was still amazed at the well-wishers who brought flowers and cards and decorated her fence with ribbons. It was an unreal continuation of the dance, and she didn't know what it meant. She was particularly troubled by the strangers who treated her place like it was a holy shrine. Some would light candles, others knelt and prayed, invoking her name in their supplications for health and love, redemption and forgiveness. Several deposited holy icons of different faiths at her gate. There were statues of the Virgin Mary, ornate dream catchers, and Tibetan prayer flags. Besides littering her yard and baffling her, they were respectful and left her alone.

The Revealers were not so considerate. They began a short-lived, round-the-clock vigil a few days after Eleanor came home. The news crews followed them and Lugner himself stood outside of Eleanor's house and talked to them. He waved a Bible in one hand while his breath caught on the frost, making him look like he was breathing brimstone. Eleanor couldn't watch.

Several news agencies tried to get an interview with Eleanor, but she declined them all. Some were pushier than others and once Jim "accidentally" broke a News 6 camera when he tripped into and flattened a cameraman aiming it through the porch front window.

Eventually, David called Sheriff Hannon and he ran everyone off at dusk, citing curfew laws. The next day, city construction equipment was set up on both ends of Cedar Street with signs declaring that only local traffic was allowed. No city workers ever appeared and nothing was ever actually done, but a stationed deputy in a police car kept much of the unwanted non-locals away while Eleanor recovered.

New Year's Eve, the police were stretched thin and Cedar Street was left to itself. Eleanor sat on the porch, huddled under a blanket with Wendy and Karen, while David and Jim, laughing, lit rockets in the road.

Eleanor saw them first, a tall man walking slowly with a dog on a leash. She'd heard no car and she did not recognize him as anyone from the neighborhood. In the flash of an exploding firework, she recognized the gray braid.

Karen followed her stare and then Jim and David, and finally Wendy looked up the street as the man approached.

"Good evening," he said. "And Happy New Year."

"Happy New Year," said Wendy.

"Who are you?" asked Jim stepping up to him.

"I'm Conrad," he said.

"Dr. Sikring," said Eleanor.

"Please Eleanor," he said approaching the gate. "Call me Conrad. I want to be your friend."

"What do you want?" asked David.

"To wish you a Happy New Year," he said.

"Thanks," said Wendy. "Same to you."

"Thank you," he said warmly.

"Cold night for a walk isn't it?" said Jim.

"My new dog needed some air," he said kneeling beside a huge grey hound.

"What kind of dog is that?" asked Karen.

"She's an Irish wolfhound. This one's an adult. Over a hundred pounds. She's big isn't she?"

"What's her name?"

"I don't know," he said stroking the dog's back. "I haven't named her yet."

Eleanor stared at the dog. It stared back at her. Its head was huge, its maw sloppy with spit. It was large enough to snap a man's neck like a pretzel. Under the stars, it reminded her of The Hound of The Baskervilles.

"Would you like to see my dog, Eleanor?" he asked. The dog tugged on its lead and nearly pulled him over. David moved toward the porch to intercept it if it broke free, though what he would do to stop the animal if it was intent on getting to Eleanor, she couldn't imagine.

When she was a coyote, Eleanor was unable to join packs of other coyotes. Their senses were too good to be fooled by her for long. She knew her scent was never quite right, her actions never quite feral enough. They tolerated her at a distance, but they knew she was not one of them.

Hunters, wolves, dogs, and even eagles vexed her across five states. Hunters were the most deadly, but had one chance only before she could outrun them. Eagles were the same, but dogs, be they wolves or bored domestic pets who killed for sport, could track her. They could smell her, differentiate her scent from a thousand others. They could see through her. She looked at Sikring's huge grey beast, slobbering stupidly, and wondered if even then the dog knew that she was not human, and if so, what had it been trained to do about it.

"An adult dog without a name?" said Jim.

"I just bought it."

"You bought an adult dog?" said Karen. "Why not a puppy?"

"This is a rare breed," he said. "Big and beautiful, don't you think?"

"Is she nice?" asked Wendy.

"Sweet as candy," he said.

"Expensive?" asked Jim.

"In dollars, yes, but it depends what you're trying to buy."

"This is a private party," Eleanor said.

"Don't be rude," said Karen.

"It's okay," said Sikring. "Trust is earned."

"And not purchased," said Eleanor.

"Yes, that's how it goes," he said.

"Goodbye," said Eleanor.

"Good evening all," Sikring said zipping up his coat against the frosty air. With the dog pulling him onward, he turned around and headed back to town.

"Wendy, come light this one," said Jim. She ran down the steps to the street excitedly. Karen leaned in to Eleanor and whispered.

"Who was that exactly?" she asked.

"A man who scares me."

CHAPTER THIRTY-THREE

The next day, New Year's Day, a car pulled up in front of the house late in the afternoon. Jim was at the trailer for some sleep, and David had just left to fetch some groceries. Eleanor was alone for the first time since she'd been home.

She recognized the limousine and the man driving it, Mr. Gordon. She expected to see Dr. Zalarnik step out of the back seat, but Agent Lamb was a surprise, as was Mr. Poulson, Lamb's superior at Homeland Security when she met him last year.

They noticed her watching them from her window. Lamb waved hello. Eleanor went through the kitchen and unlocked the back door. She stayed there listening to them knock and weighing her options. When they didn't kick in the door but only insistently rang the bell, she figured she still had some time.

She collected her crutches. All her injuries were healed but tottering around on the borrowed sticks made for a good act. She was as perfect and whole as she'd ever been as Celeste-at-seventeen. She'd left the bruise on her arm since the hospital, for effect. She considered wearing an eye patch but her need to see overruled that bit of theatre.

She hobbled to the door and unlocked the latch.

"Hello," she said.

The sun was bright in a crisp, blue sky. Their faces were red from standing in the cold and their breath came in white puffs of frost. Mr. Poulson had his hands in his pockets, while Lamb's were crossed. Zalarnik wore gloves.

"Hello, Eleanor," said Zalarnik.

"Hello, Dimitri," she said. "Hello, Agents Lamb and Poulson."

"So you remember me," said Poulson offering his hand. She remembered him as a reasonable man, not unkind, not stupid. Efficient. That did not mean he was her friend. She knew that neither he nor Agent Lamb were here on her behalf. She didn't take the offered hand.

"Are you going to invite us in?" asked Zalarnik.

"Do I have to?"

"Told you," said Lamb under her breath.

Poulson spoke. "No, of course not," he said. "But it would make talking easier for all of us. We're freezing out here and it can't be good to stand there on those crutches. I understand you were gravely injured."

"I don't feel comfortable letting you all inside. I'm alone," she said.

"We know," said Zalarnik. "I thought it would be better if we talked in private."

When she didn't move, Zalarnik went on.

"You know Shannon is a Homeland Security agent," he said. "She's one of the good guys. And Alan here is now with the NSA, National Security Agency."

"Are you here to arrest me? Take me to Nebraska?"

"Heavens no," said Poulson.

"I'll tell you what, Eleanor," said Zalarnik. "I'll just come in. I can tell you what needs to be said and there's no need to make these two stand out in the cold if you won't invite them in. How's that?"

Closing the door on them would only postpone things. Besides, she was curious. They'd come to tell her something or ask her something and what that was would tell her much about her situation and her future. She had to know.

She didn't like standing so close to Zalarnik. She could see that he was examining her, studying her eye for trauma, studying her stance for actual injury. Inside at least, she could put some distance between them and lower the lighting. The day was so bright she felt like she was on stage.

"Okay, Dimitri. You can come in," she said.

She hopped back a pace on her right leg and let out a low groan for effect. The others returned to the car, Mr. Gordon opening the door for them, expressionless behind his black sunglasses. Silently, Zalarnik came inside and sat on the sofa as before. No, not as before. He was not here to beg now. This time he was here to dictate. She could see it in his bearing.

She limped around to her mother's chair and sat down with another theatrical groan. Zalarnik took in the room. He noticed the folded pile of bedding at the end of the couch.

"Having a sleep-over?" he asked.

"Tell the Battons to lay off. I'm not their daughter."

"I already have," he said. "I told them the news before Christmas."

"So you did the test anyway."

"Oh yes," he said.

"And discovered I wasn't Celeste."

"No," he said. "Actually, once we got your real material, we discovered you were a perfect match. No question about it."

Eleanor shook her head. "Then what about the Battons?"

"I sent the samples to our Massachusetts lab for verification. The sample we tested here was so perfectly matched that I couldn't be sure we hadn't cross-contaminated our control. Besides, verification is the basis of science. I wanted to be totally certain before we took things further."

"How conscientious of you," Eleanor said. "What did your Massachusetts lab have to tell you?"

"The samples we sent them didn't match Celeste at all. They had degraded so profoundly that they were unable to collect enough DNA under conventional means. They had to turn to more advanced techniques, and even that proved tricky. In the end, they found that the cells they had didn't have DNA in them at all. At least not as we know it."

"Blame it on the Federal Express," she said.

"I looked at the samples we still had here. You know about my field lab up the road? Yes, I told you about that. Well, guess what? All the samples there had degraded too. It's unheard of. Really strange. All the tests were weird. They made no sense."

"It's a poor musician who blames his instrument," she said.

"Then there was the regeneration in the hospital. Again, unlike anything I or science have ever seen."

"Aren't those the same things?" she asked. "Aren't you the expert?"

"I know you're trying to goad me, Eleanor," he said. "But there is some truth to that. I am an expert in my field. I brought in Dr. Maulitz to have a look at you too. He didn't have words to describe what was happening."

"He wouldn't have been good at using them if he'd found any," she said. "He's a rude jerk."

"You're right. Too much lab and not enough bedsides," said Zalarnik. Eleanor wished he would get angry, that he'd show her something she could fight against. His calm, friendly manner made him more menacing to her than Mr. Liddle had been.

"You know you're special, Eleanor," he said. "You're the most special person on the planet. I'm not exaggerating."

"Go away," she said.

"Let me finish," he said, leaning back, "then I'll go, and I hope you'll come with me."

She mentally plotted a course out the back: out the chair, over the table, through the door and away.

"Biologically speaking, you're a miracle, Eleanor. Every cell in your body is a stem cell, or rather, is like a stem cell. Each one has the potential to be any other kind of cell, but unlike ordinary stem cells, they're not fixed. They can change back or into something else. It's amazing."

"Go away now," she said.

"You know about stem cells? Have you heard about genetic therapy?"

She shook her head rather than speak the lie.

"Mr. Gurenno never talked about it? Probably too controversial," he said. "Suffice it to say that this avenue of medical research promises everything you can ever imagine science and medicine doing: curing cancer, regenerating organs, prolonging life. These are the things we might be able to do with current cell lines, but with yours . . . with yours Eleanor, there's no telling what could happen."

His excitement had rushed to his face, his ears were red,

his checks flush, and his eyes stared past her into a future she knew would mean her destruction.

"You have my cells," she said. "You stole some. What do you need with me?"

"Cells don't live forever. Even yours degrade. Faster than you'd think. We need the source to study them. Harvest a strain that we can use. Plus I'd like to know more about your physiology, like that recess in your neck and the soft-matter gland inside your head." He leaned forward as if trying to get a look at something in her skull.

"Are you Celeste Batton?" he asked.

She didn't answer.

"If you aren't, why are you her exact duplicate? How can you be two places at once? How are you related? Do you know these answers? Will you tell me? Do you want to know?"

"No," she said.

"Eleanor, do you know what the most profitable industry is in America? Pharmaceuticals. The things I can make out of you would make you the richest woman in the world. Hell, I'll tell you what, I'll go with 70/30 with you, seventy percent to you. I'll even give you a million dollar signing bonus right here and now. All you have to do is agree to come with me, recant the Venns' guardianship and be rich. Make them rich too. It's a win-win-win. You might be the savior of the human race, Eleanor, but you can definitely be the savior of your friends."

"No," she said.

He sighed. "Two million dollars? Ten?" He leaned forward, he looked at her with intense and zealous eyes. They reminded her of the Revealers, so certain in their beliefs they burned with purpose.

"Do you know what's been happening out there while

you've been holed up in here?" he asked her. "The press is going mad talking about you. 'Prom Queen Vigilante' was just the first headline. Some nurse at the hospital came out telling stories of your regeneration. I caught her pouring holy water over you. Those stories have Lugner's band in a serious frenzy. They already had you pegged as a witch. Now you're the devil himself to them. Others see it the other way. With these new stories, people are now proclaiming you a saint—or more. Fights have broken out. A religious war with you at the center is threatening to destroy this town."

"It's all rumors," she said. "They'll die off. Eventually."

"I don't know about that," he said. "Not while you're right here under their noses. You know even the Indians are up in arms about you? Some say you have to die, others say they'll die protecting you. Jamesford is going crazy and it's all because of you."

"I didn't know any of this," she said.

"That's because your friends are sheltering you, but it's time to wake up and smell the scandal, Eleanor. Is it Eleanor or Celeste? Give me that much," he said.

"I am Eleanor Anders," she said.

"Okay, Eleanor. Those are the things that are happening without any official mandate or pressure. Sure the Battons are gone at present, but now the government is interested. You could be a threat or a national treasure."

"You mean natural resource," said Eleanor. "How'd the government become interested? Was it Lamb?"

"I called them in," he said. "This is bigger than us. The government wants to know more. This whole thing might just get so big that even I can't help you."

"What would they do?"

"Don't know," he said. "But I know they have secret testing labs hidden all over the world. Black Ops and all that. Do you speak Polish? Ever been to Cuba?"

"How's that any different from your offer?" she asked.

"You'll be up the road from David," he said. "Think about them, the Venns. Do you think they're having an easy time? Can you imagine how much worse things can get for them? Will get for them?"

"I'm Eleanor Anders," she said. "I live on Cedar Street in Jamesford, Wyoming. Last year I got my driver's license and my mother died."

"And you buried her illegally. Yeah, I heard about that. She's up in Sunset Lawns now, right? We'll need to dig her up of course."

"You wouldn't," Eleanor said.

"Will you agree to come with me?" She didn't move a muscle.

"Eleanor," Zalarnik said softly, "Think of your mother. She died of cancer. You might have the cure to cancer within you right now. All we have to do is coax it out."

"I have friends," she said. "You're trying to scare me because you've caught me alone, but I have friends. I might even be loved by some of them. There are laws, procedures. I have rights."

"That's why I'm here being reasonable," he said, impatience finally finding its way into his voice. "But things can happen within laws, and laws can be broken. Things can happen that no amount of court time can ever rectify. People get hurt by hit-and-run drivers, others go missing. Anyone can be arrested. Even if they're acquitted, it's devastating. How can you replace the lost time, money, and reputation? Lives—whole families are ruined forever."

"Thank you," she said.

"Why?"

"Because now I see what you are," she said.

Like a shadow passing off his face, he brightened.

"Don't think I'd do anything like that, Eleanor. Not me," he said. "But remember that I'm not the only one involved here. Revealers and the NSA, hell, maybe Mr. Liddle had friends who want revenge. Not everyone in Jamesford likes you, Eleanor, recent dances excepted. Don't overestimate your position."

"I doubt I could," she said. "You've said what you came to say. Now go."

"Be a shame if some harm comes to David," he said as if to himself. "Lots of dangerous people around you right now. And little Wendy, what a shame that would be."

She leaned forward, her body sliding lithely like a serpent. She felt her eyes grow large, felt them widen and stare unblinkingly at the scientist. Her neck stretched a centimeter; she felt the heat, felt the pull. Her hands hardened and clutched the chair arms in a strangling grip. Her voice fell into a guttural parody of her usual speech.

"Don't you dare threaten me," she growled in a register just inside human hearing. "If anything happens to David, or Wendy, Jim, Karen or even the cat, I'll hold you responsible. I'll come after you."

Her words were like wisps of burning fuse, low, hissing, and dangerous. Zalarnik's face drained of color. His confidence was shaken, his position undermined. He stared at her, afraid. She could smell it. She liked him scared. He needed to be scared. She had more than enough fear to go around and he deserved some. Worse, she knew she meant it. If anything happened to David or his family, she'd go crazy. Imagining what she would do—what she could do—frightened her.

"I'm . . . I'm not saying . . ." he stuttered. "It's not me. I'm a spokesman. I'm just saying . . . I mean there are forces out there . . . it's explosive. You can see that. It's not me. You can't hold me responsible. I'm trying to help."

Eleanor leaned back in her chair and felt her muscles relax, her hands soften, her irises shrink. The pain of it soothed her. "I think I told you to leave."

"Okay," he said. "I'm going to let you think about it. I'm not a bad guy. You could do much worse in a partner than me. He extended his hand to her. It was trembling.

She studied his earnest sweating face and took his hand.

"Ouch," he cried when they pulled apart. "What was that?"

"Sorry," she said. "My fingernail must have caught your palm. Sorry if I scratched you."

He looked down at the red line across his hand and then suspiciously at Eleanor. "No harm done," he said forcing a friendly grin. "Cut your nails. And get feeling better."

He deliberately left a business card on the table beside the little Christmas tree and closed the door behind him as he left.

Eleanor watched the car drive away. Looking out her mother's favorite window she watched the empty street for a while thinking about her options and sucking on her finger.

CHAPTER THIRTY-FOUR

"What happened, Eleanor?" David said. "What's going on?"

"I got scared," she said.

"What scared you?"

"I'm not ready to talk about it," she said. "I need some time."

She could tell he didn't like being put off, but he left her alone. He carried in the groceries and together they put them away.

"Hey, guess what I saw at the grocery," David said. "A jar full of money with your picture on it. Someone's organized a fundraising campaign for you."

"Why?"

"For medical bills, I suspect," he said, not understanding the depth of her question, "Or maybe food or legal stuff. Whatever you need."

"My picture was on it?"

"Uh, I think they used the one of Celeste from the paper," he said. "But the money was for you. Occupational hazard, huh?" He smirked, but, of course, Eleanor wasn't in a kidding mood. "You want some buttermilk? I stocked up big time."

"No, I'm not hungry," she said.

"So you're all better now? All the way through?"

"I've fixed everything I can," she said. "Was there lots of money in the jar?"

"There was at the register I was at," he said. "I can't speak to the others or the other shops."

"What? They're all over town?"

"Yeah, and people are putting their change in to help you."

"That's . . ." she searched for words. "Really nice," she said.

"You have friends, Eleanor," David said. "You're not alone. Don't ever forget that."

David's simple words touched her like a warm embrace. She thought of people she didn't know putting pennies into a jar for her and felt grateful and empowered. "I'll try not to," she said.

Saturday, Eleanor was at the Venns' for a marathon of college football games. Karen had made a seven-layer dip and chocolate chip cookies for the party. Jim sat in front of the TV drinking beer out of cans and slowly sliding into brooding silence with each passing quarter. Eleanor sat with the others playing one of the games she'd gotten for Christmas. It was a quiet and cozy day. Outside, occasional snow flurries found their circuitous way to the ground like idle thoughts on a weekend. Eleanor felt welcomed and at home.

During halftime of the second game over sandwiches, she finally gave them an account of her ordeal in Russell's trailer. She kept it as non-graphic as possible and even then Karen tried to send Wendy out of the room, but Eleanor's spirits were high and she made it sound like an action adventure and not the horror it really was. When she came to the part when Mr. Liddle died, she said only "Things got confused then. I remember wrestling with him and him shooting me. Then I woke up in the hospital."

To David she'd already told the entire tale, leaving nothing out, even saying at one point, "I slit him open with my claws in Wendy's hands." She'd told him days before and had expected the stark and vivid imagery to weaken his stomach and his resolve, but to her delight, he'd commented only on how talented and quick-witted she was.

"I don't think I'd have had the courage to do anything more than cry," he had said. "You're so strong."

She'd looked at him hard and long then, trying to tell if he really meant that, really felt it, or if he was saying it because that was what he thought he needed to say. He really felt it. He was proud of her, and she felt his admiration like heat on her face. It was that heat that had kept her in the kitchen after Zalarnik's visit and allowed her to tell the story now.

"You're one tough cookie," Jim said. He'd eaten a sandwich while listening and it cut through some of his beer. Still, Eleanor saw melancholy in his eyes. "That's whatcha gotta do," he said. "No use feeling sorry for yourself. You gotta fight."

By the silence, Eleanor imagined that David's family heard deeper meaning in his words than she had.

"You were so brave," said Wendy. "Was it really dark in that room?"

"It was pretty dark," Eleanor said.

"But you weren't afraid," Wendy said. "You were smart and escaped."

Eleanor wasn't proud of that night. She was about to tell Wendy that she wasn't smart, but a fool for getting into that situation in the first place when Karen spoke.

"Have you always healed so fast?" she asked.

"Yes," she said. She could see the answer didn't wholly satisfy. When Eleanor didn't elaborate, Karen began to ask another question, but let it drop.

Eleanor heard a car outside. She heard it cut its engine in front of the Venns' trailer.

"There's someone here," she said. "Someone's coming." The way she said it betrayed her alarm. Jim reached under the sofa and withdrew a black pistol. Karen grabbed Wendy and moved into the hall. David stood in front of Eleanor. The bell rang.

Holding his pistol, Jim went to the door.

"Two of them," Eleanor said raising as many fingers. Jim didn't ask her how she knew that.

"Who's there?" he called.

"It's Sheriff Hannon."

"You got papers?" Jim called through the door.

"What? No," Hannon said irritated. "Don't be so jumpy, Jim, it's a social call. I have Principal Curtz here with me."

David's dad slid his pistol into his waistband behind his back and covered it with his shirt, then he opened the door a crack and looked out. He undid the chain and let them in.

David relaxed, but not Eleanor. She didn't like the Venns' trailer. There was only one door.

"Sorry to bother you folks," the sheriff said.

"Sorry, we're so jumpy," said Jim trying to blink the alcohol out of his eyes.

"Well, I guess I can't blame you," Hannon said shaking hands. "We've got some things to discuss."

"About me?" asked Eleanor.

"Yes," said Principal Curtz. "May we sit down?"

With angry protests and promises of early cake if she behaved, Wendy was sent to her room to play. Everyone found a seat. The TV was muted, but not turned off. Eleanor was glad of that; it made the meeting less dire and menacing, somehow.

"My, you've really healed up," said the sheriff.

"What's this about?" Eleanor asked.

"Before I explain our reasons," said the principal, "let me first make the suggestion. We think it would be best if you didn't come back to school after winter break. At least not right away. We can arrange for all you assignments to be brought to your home. It won't jeopardize your graduation."

"For how long?" asked Eleanor.

"'Why' is the real question," said David. "What did she do to get suspended?"

"Nothing," Curtz said. "This isn't disciplinary. It's quite the opposite. Eleanor is such a celebrity that we can't ensure her safety at Jamesford High."

Eleanor didn't look surprised, but the others did.

"Both the school and my office have been bombarded with calls," the sheriff said. "They're not all threats, but there are some."

"What do the callers say?" asked Eleanor.

"Oh nothing you should care about," said Curtz.

"Tell me," Eleanor said. "I want to know."

"I'm not sure I do," said Karen, ashen-faced.

"Well," said the sheriff, "there are the cranks who say you're a witch. They've threatened violence against the school and you in particular. We fully expect the school to be picketed by the members of the Church of Christ Revealed."

"New Church of Christ Revealed," corrected Eleanor.

"Yes. New," he said. "They've called the news. They'll be there to disrupt things. It could get ugly. It will get ugly."

"You've handled them before," said David.

"If it were only them, I wouldn't be worried," Hannon said. "But Eleanor has a fan club who've promised to protect her. They have no leader, but they sound as zealous as the Revealers, but not in hating you. In, uhm, liking you."

Everyone exchanged confused looks.

"I could keep them away from your house under municipal repair trespassing laws, but Lugner went and got a permit to be near the school. We couldn't stop it in time. He planned ahead; applied for the permit to picket the school the day we announced the dance was moved to the Rez."

"Another problem we're having is with the parents," put in Mr. Curtz. "We've had several families threaten to take their kids out of school if you attend."

"Because they think I'm evil?" asked Eleanor.

"A couple are superstitious," he said, "them I don't care about. No getting through to them. I've been hearing from them since Lugner's bigots came to town. Excuse my language. No, the ones I care about are the ones who think that things will get out of hand at the school. The threats against you and the school have leaked out. Violence at the school was mentioned. They're afraid for their own kids. Crossfire."

"What? You think someone's going to shoot up the place?" asked David incredulously.

"That's what we're afraid of," said Sheriff Hannon.

"Of course nothing like that will happen, but it puts pressure—tension—into the school that could affect learning," added the principal.

"So how long?" Eleanor said.

"A week or so," said Mr. Curtz, "until this blows over."

"Might be a couple of weeks," Hannon said. "It depends on how hard the Revealers fight."

"What does that mean?" said Jim.

Hannon shook his head. "Jamesford has had a belly full of Lugner and his creeps. We're evicting them. We're chasing the whole lot of them out of town, and out of Wyoming if we can. Once they're gone we'll have maybe a half dozen converts. With any luck, they'll go with them; darken some other town with their traveling circus."

"How can you evict them?" asked Eleanor.

"They're already up to a hundred eighty-five tickets for trespassing, disturbing the peace, inciting a riot and spitting on the sidewalk. That's before the attorneys weigh in next week. They went too far with the dance. Pissed everyone off. Now threatening the school, that'll mean prison if we can trace it. In any event, they will be out of here soon. Count on it."

"Good," said Jim. "Fight the bastards."

"Once the Revealers are gone, things should settle back to normal," said Curtz. "If anyone wants to stay away from school then, well, we have truancy laws for that, don't we, Sheriff?"

"You really want them back?" he said.

"I don't blame the kids. I blame the parents."

"Stupid people refusing to go to school," said David. "Makes sense."

"They're blaming Eleanor for everything they can think of," Hannon said.

"They think I'm a witch," she said.

"Yeah," he said. "But keep in mind we're talking about a certain part of the population that I like to call 'morons.' There may be a more scientific name for them, but mine works."

"I was told the Shoshone are talking about me too." Eleanor said. "Is that true?"

"Yes," said the sheriff. "There are some Shoshone now who're also buying into the crap. Sikring said they're using old stories and trying to apply them to you. It's split the reservation like it's split Jamesford. Everyone's got an opinion. Nobody seems to have enough business of their own to mind. But don't fret about that. They're plenty down there who like you, like you a lot. Same as up here."

"Sikring? What's he been up to?"

"He bought a dog," the sheriff said. "Big old thing."

"We saw it," said David.

"He's a queer fellow," Hannon said.

"What does he say about me?" asked Eleanor.

"Why do you care?" asked Karen. Eleanor ignored her.

"He doesn't say much. He's excited about things. I think he's going to write a paper on how gossip gets out of control in small backwater towns. He'll get a Nobel Prize for it. I like him though."

"So what do you say, Eleanor?" said Curtz. "You do a little homeschooling for a week or so? Would that be okay?"

"Are you're asking me or telling me?" she asked.

"I'm asking you," he said.

"It's up to you, Eleanor," the sheriff said. "And you folks," he added, looking at the Venns. "We won't stop you if you want to go back. If you want to, go ahead. It might be for the best. Have it out once and for all. Might be just the tonic."

"But I'd rather not have it at the school," said Mr. Curtz, looking at the sheriff. "We have other, less tumultuous options. Options that won't give Lugner his photo-op or make the town look bad."

Everyone watched Eleanor. She looked at Karen and then at Jim in turn, wanting to hear their input, to see whether they'd exert their guardianship and order her to do one thing or another. But they didn't. Another kindness.

"It's the least I can do," she said. "I'm in your debt."

CHAPTER THIRTY-FIVE

Eleanor caught glimpses of the protests on the Venns' television and heard cries and shouts carry all the way from the school to her house on Cedar Street. David delivered her homework through a gauntlet of police cars and clusters of people milling around at the ends of her street. There weren't many at first. The news crews were at the school, where she was supposed to be, but by the end of the week David had to be escorted through the crowds.

From her window in the loft, she could see them. Some held the hateful signs of the Revealers proclaiming God's hatred of this group or that, not specifically against her, just there for the media coverage. Some were more personal and she read, "Suffer Not a Witch" and the more direct, "Eleanor, leave while you still can." They were disturbing, but the placards that gave her the most worry were of a different temperament entirely: "Eleanor, Save Us," and "He sent us a girl this time."

An assemblage of Catholic clerics asked to visit her. She declined. Andy Crow, Elder and Medicine Man from the Wild River Shoshone asked to come and bless her house. Again, she refused.

By the second week of school, the crowds had pushed beyond the ends of the street and stood in front of her house from seven in the morning to ten at night when the police, citing curfew laws, would chase them away. The circus that was her celebrity was not abating as the sheriff had promised, but growing in fervor. The national news had gotten hold of the story. Someone had leaked a before-and-after picture, showing Eleanor the night she was admitted to the hospital and one taken of her the day she left four days later, only a day after she came out of her three-day coma. CNN asked for an interview, promising to pay handsomely for an hour of her time. She declined.

Tuesday evening, Stephanie drove her little Volkswagen up to her house with the help of state police, sent to Jamesford from Cheyenne. They pushed the crowds back under the blazing halogen lights of the news cameras and escorted the social worker to Eleanor's door. Jim let her in.

"Oh my," she said once inside. "What a zoo."

"Hello, Stephanie," Eleanor said. "Welcome to my prison. We'll clean up tomorrow."

"It's not as bad as all that is it?" she said sitting down. Even on a cold January evening, the exertion of walking up the steps had winded the big woman and she dabbed sweat from her forehead with a tissue from her purse.

"It kinda is," Eleanor said.

"The news crews will leave as soon as something else happens," she said. "The Revealers will be booted out of town as soon as the cameras are gone. The sheriff told me so."

David stood next to Eleanor, who sat regally in her mother's chair. Jim stayed by the door, his eyes scanning the crowd.

"Why have you come?" Eleanor asked.

"Social Services is set to hold a closed-door hearing about you this Thursday."

"This is the first we've heard of it," said Jim.

"It's why I'm here," she said. "It's rushed because of the situation."

"What's going to happen?"

"Well," she said. "We've sought permanent guardianship for you with Jim and Karen. It'll finally be settled."

"Why now? As if I have to ask," said David.

"Social services is getting bombarded with calls. I think they just want it off their plate. Once they hand over guardianship, Jim will get to tell them to go away. And since he's a private citizen, they'll have to."

"So the hearing is a good thing?" said Eleanor.

"Absolutely," she said.

"I'm scared," Eleanor said.

"I know, darling, but don't be. This town loves you."

"Doesn't look like it," she said. "Why can't they just leave me alone?"

"It'll get better. Just be patient," she looked at David and surely read the weariness there. "We have over twenty thousand dollars collected for you. Did you know that? People are mailing checks from all over."

Eleanor shook her head.

"The merchants say this has been the best week of their careers, better even than the fourth of July. The town's booming."

"Because of me."

"Yeah. The stories bring them in," she said. "Some are really quite amazing. I've been contacted by agents looking for you.

Hollywood agents, can you believe it, Eleanor? You could really cash in on this. This is your golden ticket."

"What? Like a movie?" said Eleanor.

"Eleanor, you're beautiful and brave and strong. You're everything every girl wants to be. I know it's hard right now, but think of it: within twenty-four hours you united the whites and the Indians, were crowned the most beautiful girl in town, and stopped a killer while escaping certain death. Eleanor, it's an amazing story. An uplifting story. It's your story. People are eating it up."

"Tabloids?" asked David.

"Oh, yes," said Stephanie.

"It's horrible," said Eleanor.

"It'll work out. You know why I think so? Because of who you are. You are the strongest girl I ever met. No. You're the strongest *person* I ever met—ever. And you're blessed. Your mother is looking over you." And here she paused in a shared secret with Eleanor. "After the hearing, you can negotiate for a book deal or something and be set. The town of Jamesford will benefit for decades. You're a Godsend, Eleanor, for everyone."

"I am not to be seen," she muttered.

"A little late for that," Stephanie giggled. She would not be put off from her excitement by the dour mood of the house. "Oh, and the wedding we'll throw for you two," she said smiling at David so broadly it made him blush.

After she left, Eleanor sat with David and his father eating dinner. The crowds had thinned, the malevolent ones had gone home and only a small group of onlookers remained, singing a quiet hymn outside like a lullaby.

"It's time I knew a little more," Jim said suddenly. "What's really going on here?"

David and Eleanor exchanged looks. Jim waited. He hadn't had a drink in a week, and even Eleanor had noticed a change in him. He was no longer as ill-tempered and melancholy. He'd found a noble purpose in defending her and had become a soldier again. He'd fortified her little house like a bunker. The rifle was no longer hidden under the couch but stood by the door, loaded and ready. He kept a pistol in his belt at all times and showed them where another was kept in a drawer. He'd been all business and hadn't questioned the reasons for his purpose before now. A purpose had been enough.

"Stupid crazy rumors, Dad," said David. "You see what's happening."

"Is that all there is here, Eleanor?" he asked her.

She'd trusted three people with her secret in her entire life, Tabitha, who had died, Celeste, who was missing, and David, who'd just lied to his father for her. She was not good with trusting. She was too vulnerable, her secrets too extraordinary to share. She was not to be seen. But she felt like a liar and felt an indebtedness that could only be repaid with some kind of honesty to someone, somewhere. Each penny of twenty thousand dollars was a debt she could only repay in trust.

"It's worse than even David knows," Eleanor said.

"What?" said David.

"While I was at the hospital, Dr. Zalarnik had a chance to examine me in detail. What he discovered, what he saw, what many saw, was that I am not what I appear to be." She took a breath and forced herself to continue, editing her speech one thought at a time. Unwilling to admit she was a monster, she focused on the threat.

"Zalarnik knows, David," she said. "He doesn't know what

he knows, but he does. He hasn't put a name to me, but he knows."

"What does he know?" Jim asked.

"I'm not human, Jim."

"Bullshit," he said.

She pulled up her sleeve to reveal the omnipresent bruise on her arm. She closed her eyes and fed it heat. In a moment it faded and was gone.

"My healing is just part of it," she said.

"You are human, Eleanor," said David angrily. "An evolved human."

"Maybe, but I'm different enough to be a 'threat or a treasure.' Zalarnik—and he's not the only one—sees me as one of Mr. Gurenno's frogs."

David swallowed. Jim stared at Eleanor for a long while. Eleanor watched him carefully, trying to predict his actions, ready to interpret the next words spoken, honest or deceitful, as a declaration of intent and the path to her future.

"I'm sick of this town anyway," he finally said pouring more steak sauce on his plate. "Hell, I'm sick of this country. I have a buddy in Canada. We'll head up north in the spring." He cut a piece of meat and smacked it with pleasure. When the others didn't eat again, he leaned forward and looked at each in turn.

"I'm not going to abandon you," he said. "Either of you. I haven't been a great dad. I know that, David. I don't know how to be father, but I do know how to fight and I'll see this through no matter what. For you. For me. For my family. It's my obligation—my privilege—to do it.

"David thinks the world of you, Eleanor, and though I don't always show it, I think the world of him. His mother told me that he'd leave us if we didn't protect you. I believe it, and I see why. You're a good person, Eleanor. Pearce was right; you're everything a girl could want to be. Everything a boy could want. Everything a father would want for his son. I don't care if you're human or a cat or dog or the Loch Ness Monster, you're my family and I won't leave you in the lurch. I won't betray you. I won't retreat."

With the street singers' hymn underlining his speech, his words had a beatific quality that moved her. Eleanor added another measure of debt and confusion to her already over-flowing emotional burden.

The next day, the night before the hearing, Eleanor was woken up by a car pulling in front of her house. She pulled on a robe and stepped out of her room to watch the door. Jim was already at the window holding the rifle and peering out at the street. David slept upstairs.

Eleanor tiptoed to the window and looked outside. It was Karen's van. She got out and waved at the window, Jim waved back. The side door slid open and Eleanor gasped. Conrad Sikring stepped out. Beside him was the gray hound he'd had before.

Then from around the van, having exited from the far side, she saw a figure in a heavy down coat. The hood was up and pulled closed and Eleanor couldn't see the face. The figure took the dog from Sikring and together with Karen approached the door. Sikring held back, lit a cigarette and watched them go.

"What's going on?" Eleanor said.

"Let's find out," said Jim, opening the door.

"Karen," he said. "What's . . ."

"May I see her?" came a new but familiar voice. "Alone?"

"Step out here with me, Jim," Karen said.

Mr. Venn looked back at Eleanor and then at the stranger under the hood. The dog sniffed the doorjamb and peered inside the dark house.

"Is that dog dangerous?" he asked.

"No. He's a sweetie," came the reply.

"I'll be right outside, Eleanor," said Mr. Venn moving aside to let the stranger with the dog in. "Right outside," he said, and pulled the door shut behind him.

"Turn on a light, Eleanor. I want to see you."

The stranger threw back her hood revealing a cropped mane of jet-black hair and showed what Eleanor had already surmised. She hung her coat on a hook and tied the dog to the doorknob.

"How've you been, Eleanor?" she said sitting on the sofa.

"It's been a rough year," she said. "How've you been, Celeste?"

CHAPTER THIRTY-SIX

"I saw the ad in New Orleans," said Celeste. "Well, actually a friend of mine pointed it out to me. She's the kind of girl who reads the personals. It was a simple message and I guess it'd run in every big newspaper for weeks. It said "Celeste, Eleanor needs you. Contact Conrad at this number.""

"Conrad being Conrad Sikring?"

"Yes," she said. "But I found it too late. I didn't mean to get you into so much trouble."

"It's not your fault," she said. "I was unlucky. And stupid."

"Still, I'm sorry. It was my dumb parents that got you into this."

"What happened to you?" Eleanor asked.

"I got sick of it and left. My parents were being unreasonable and I'd had enough of it. They'd planned out my entire life from birth to death. They'd show me my burial plot every Memorial Day like it was a coming trip to Disneyland. They'd lined up a group of three possible husbands and wanted to discuss each with me. It was a joke. I didn't want that life."

"What kind of life do you want?"

"I don't know. I may never know, or maybe that is what

kind of life I want; one where I never know, one with surprise and adventure. Back on the farm, my life was another
crop cycle. When I got the chance to go with Jack, I jumped
at it. I had to."

"Jack is your boyfriend?"

"Sorta. He's my friend. He's the gypsy I told you about, goes
from place to place in a little camper. There's a lot of nomadic
folks like that. They build communities for a couple of weeks,
months maybe, and then pull them down and move on. It's
another cycle of sorts, but more interesting."

"Your parents were under the impression that you were
kidnapped."

"They lie. I left a note. I suspect they had to lie to get the
kind of attention they needed, help from their political friends
and the cops. They lie and they don't like being wrong."

"You should talk to them," Eleanor said. "They're still your
family."

"I will," she said. "I would have if it would have helped you,
but like I said, I found out too late. They're not the problem
anymore. Conrad told me what's been happening. Things are
really weird around you now."

"You've changed your hair," Eleanor said, admiring the
straight black bangs.

"You like it?"

"It's different," she said. "Looks good. Maybe I'll try it."

"Go ahead," she said and Eleanor heard the deeper invitation. She admired her clothes, cast-offs like her own, but
cutting-edge stylish. Her makeup was more pronounced than
she'd ever dared or ever imagined on that face. She'd pierced
her ears again: three studs on one ear, two on the other. She
wore a ring on each finger. It was a good look, eclectic and

cool, a complete urban contrast to the simple rural appearance she usually had.

"What does Sikring know? What did he tell you about me?"

"At first I thought he was your confidant," Celeste said. "He talked as if he knew all about you and your powers, but I quickly figured out that he was only guessing. I didn't tell him anything. I said only that I wanted to help you, which I guess implied I knew who you were. Beyond that I've been pretty quiet. Mrs. Venn's pretty upset, but didn't say anything."

"You know what Sikring studies?"

"Indian legends," she said. "Is that you?"

"An Indian or a legend?" she asked.

"I saw the crowds outside, I'd say you're already a legend, but I always wondered where you came from."

"I don't know where I came from. I remember I once had a family who were Navajo, or at least they looked Indian and spoke Navajo. They were all killed. Since then I've been a coyote and you—your doppelganger."

"I don't mind," she said. "It's why I'm here. To give you another 'dose.'" She laughed. It was a girlish giggle, incongruous with her mature and urbane appearance.

"You haven't changed so much," Eleanor said. "So Sikring knows I need a 'dose,' and he sent you here for that?"

"No," she said. "Or, I don't know. He said only that you needed help. He told me what was happening and asked if I thought I could do anything. I think he originally thought I'd come forward as Celeste and pull the heat off you. I'm not sure what he expects me to do now."

Then it dawned on her. "I think he expects me to kill you," Eleanor said.

"What?"

"It's what my kind does," she said. "Usually. The legends say that we steal a shape, kill the original and then take their place. He's putting you on the altar to see what I'll do."

"You're joking," she said.

Eleanor shook her head. "But I don't want your life," she said. "I want my life."

"I didn't want my life either," Celeste said. "The only thing I felt bad about when I left, even more than leaving my brother and sister and appaloosa, was you. I figured to contact you in a couple of months, closer to summer and meet up with you. I was glad you'd told me where to look for you. I didn't want to lose you. Could you really kill me?"

"No," said Eleanor, hoping it was true.

"Did you really fight a serial killer?"

She nodded.

"And you were shot?"

Another nod.

"And came back from the dead and healed yourself by Christmas?"

"I heal quick, but I was never dead. I can die," she said. "My kind can die. I'm sure of that."

"Are you religious?"

"No," Eleanor said. "Why?"

"Some people are calling you . . . well they say it's a miracle. How you survived, what you did and all. They're linking it with your crown and putting all kinds of symbolism to it," she said.

"People see what they want to see," Eleanor said. "Usually it works in my favor."

"So you're not . . ."

"No," she said. "I can be many things, but that I am not."

Celeste didn't seem so sure.

"Isn't it weird to be talking to ourself like this?" Celeste said.

"David said kind of the same thing."

"So, you have changed into other people too? You said you could, but I thought it was only me you actually ever did."

"No," Eleanor admitted. "I've had to be others too."

Celeste looked disappointed.

"I've loved being you," Eleanor said. "This last time I became you, I think because I talked to you, I got more than your long hair and hips. I got something of your wanderlust. I got some of your courage."

"I've no courage."

"Of course you do. You leaving proves it. I got some of that. A lot of it."

"I'm not going to take blame or credit for you, Eleanor. You underestimate yourself," she said. "You look like me. I look like you, but we're different."

"Only because I never got to know you well enough to copy you more accurately," she said.

Celeste leaned back in the sofa and shook her head. Then with a sigh, she said, "You're wrong, Eleanor, but okay, I'll leave it. I've come to help you. What do you want to do?"

"I want to stay in Jamesford. I like my life here, the good parts of it anyway."

"Okay," she said. "I can understand that. But see? We're different right there. Faced with trouble, you want to stay. Faced with easy, I left. I didn't have a plan. I just knew I had to go. Jack once told me that sometimes it's time to leave even when you have no destination. That's what I felt in my life. You feel the other way. We may look alike, but we're not alike. You're stronger than me. I admire that."

"Maybe I'm just afraid of change," Eleanor said.

Celeste laughed. "You? Afraid of change?"

Eleanor didn't laugh. "Think about it," she said. "I can change into anything, but then it stops. Look at my arm. See this bruise? I wear it because you had it that night at the farm. I'm a still photograph, a statue. You change. You evolve. I copy."

Celeste stared at the bruise and touched her own unblemished arm. She took a deep breath.

"I came here to help," she said. "Stop being so negative. You're not a statue. You are an individual. Stop putting so much emphasis on looks. Don't be so shallow."

Eleanor thought of the girls at her school and how she hated them for doing the same thing Celeste had caught her doing.

"Okay," Eleanor said with little enthusiasm.

"You grow up poor?" Celeste asked after a while. "That shaped you, I bet."

"It did," she admitted.

"And now you're going to be wealthy. Books, movies, a talk show I bet. You could even start a cult, if you wanted," she said. "Just kidding. But really, Eleanor, you have a wonderful future. I'm envious."

"It's built on a lie," she said.

Celeste didn't understand. How could she? She hadn't seen the results of being discovered.

"It'll all come crashing down," Eleanor said miserably.

"Why? You've done nothing wrong," Celeste said.

"I need to hide," Eleanor mumbled. "Forces are arraying themselves against me. Preachers and townsfolk, corporations and governments have noticed me. I need to hide."

"So hide in plain sight," Celeste said. "Stop hiding in this house and go outside and let them see you."

"No," she said. "What if they snatch me off the street or something?"

"You're paranoid. You've done nothing wrong. You're a hero, not a villain."

"Doesn't matter," she said. Eleanor thought of how Zalarnik wanted to harvest her cells and remembered Mr. Gurenno justifying the extinction of an entire species if it bettered mankind.

Celeste said, "It's easy to kidnap someone who's hiding all the time, Eleanor. No one will miss them. Something quite different to kidnap a celebrity."

"You really think so?" Eleanor said.

"Of course," she said. "You need a publicist, that's all. Someone to publicize you, how and when you want to—someone to show you off. You don't need to do another thing your whole life. Prom Queen kills murderer is a story of a lifetime. Cash in and do what you want."

Celeste's enthusiasm was contagious.

"And I'll be around to help," Celeste said. "I want to help. I'll even work for you, we can do charity events. I can appear in Rome at a fashion show with Jack while you and David are cruising the Bahamas. We don't even need to hide. Everyone already knows we look alike."

"I haven't been living a lie?" Eleanor asked.

"How can anyone live a lie? You're living, that's all. Am I living a lie for being a white girl in America? Am I living a lie by cutting my hair so it's attractive? Or not eating at McDonald's every day to stay thin? Am I manipulating people into liking me by controlling my looks? Of course I am. Everyone is. There's no lie in that. It's being human. It's being social. You're just better at it than most."

"I'm not human," Eleanor said.

"You look human to me," she said.

Eleanor wanted to argue, had arguments prepared, but she left them unsaid. Celeste had brought new perspective.

"Conrad says there's a hearing this week and David's parents get custody of you. You only have to chill until you're eighteen and then do what you want. The law's on your side. The Venns will support you. I know they will."

"How do I explain that I look like you?"

"Don't," she said simply. "The world needs mystery. If it bothers you, dye your hair. I think a bright red would be cool."

"Too flashy," said Eleanor.

"I'd like it," Celeste said.

Eleanor smiled. "What's with the dog?"

"Oh, Conrad said that's a gift. He's giving him to you."

"Did he say why?"

"No," Celeste said looking at the animal lying on the floor. "He said that he had a better chance of you accepting the gift if I gave it to you. He doesn't think you trust him."

"He's right," Eleanor said.

"He told me to tell you he's finally given it a name," said Celeste.

"What is it?"

"*Ye-Tsan,*" said Celeste. "I think it's Chinese."

"It's not," said Eleanor. "It's Diné, Navajo. It means 'run away.'"

CHAPTER THIRTY-SEVEN

Eleanor kissed Celeste at the door before she threw her hood back over her head and walked to the car. Sikring stood outside by the van finishing a cigarette. He watched Eleanor in the doorway. When Celeste arrived, he opened the door for her and got inside himself before Karen drove them all away.

Jim appeared out of the shadows and came inside. Eleanor read an email address Celeste had given her, memorized it and then tore up the paper.

"David wake up?" he asked.

"No," said Eleanor.

"You want to talk about it?" he asked.

"No," she said.

"Will you? One day?"

"I don't know," she said. "Does it matter?"

He considered it for a moment. "No," he said. "People are allowed their secrets. Some things, good or bad, need never be shared. Should never be shared. You go get some sleep Eleanor. I'll guard the house while you do."

And Eleanor did sleep that night. Seeing Celeste and talking with her had given her a new hope. She'd called her strong, but Eleanor knew Celeste was the stronger. She had the optimism that would carry her further than she could ever imagine. She had courage, compassion, and poise that Eleanor hoped she'd grow into herself. If she were always just to be a copy, she could do worse than be a copy of Celeste Batton, her friend.

David demanded to have the details the next day and Eleanor filled him in, catching again some of the excitement the midnight visit had left her with.

"I wish I'd met her," David said. "Or maybe I already have."

"You haven't," Eleanor said.

"I'm just kidding," he said.

"That's what she gave me," Eleanor said. "She showed me that I'm not just a copy."

"Shame on you ever thinking that you were."

"Let's go for a walk," she said.

Eleanor checked to see that the crowds weren't watching the back of the house and led David over the back fence and across the neighbor's lot without being noticed. The cold had kept all but the most dedicated onlookers away. Only a dozen or so stood vigil with candles of hope or placards of hatred. It was too cold even to bicker so the two sides just glared at each other.

Eleanor didn't mind the cold. She could tolerate it much better than anyone she knew and today she was warmed with a special inner heat that made even the winter wind seem like a caring caress.

She threw snowballs at David, and he returned the favor. He threw better than she did, but she dodged better, so it was a tie. Outside of town, climbing the trail along the river to the clearing they both loved, Eleanor threw herself into a virgin patch of snow and made a snow angel. David dove in beside her and made his own. Eleanor jumped to his other side and made another. They made half a dozen. When they were finally chilled and worn out, Eleanor stood up and said, "Look, it's like a string of cut paper dolls. Each holding hands with the other."

"Friends," David said. "You have them."

"You see through me," she said.

"I love you," he said.

Too cold now to continue up the canyon, they wandered back to town holding hands. They arrived at David's trailer shortly before dusk. Jim was still asleep.

"You're in a good mood," said Karen to Eleanor.

"I am."

"So you did know Celeste after all," she said coldly.

"Yeah," Eleanor said. Karen waited for more.

"It's all good, Mom," said David.

Karen was haggard and worried. Eleanor could tell that David's mother was sick of secrets. She was tired and frightful. She'd had enough.

"You can see that Celeste and I aren't the same person," Eleanor offered. "We just look alike. I couldn't have helped them find her."

"Some protestors came into the grocery today," she said. "I got pulled off cashier and sent to the back when they started yelling at me."

"That's terrible, Mom," David said.

"I think they're going to fire me," she said and the words hung in the air like smoke.

"Dad said we should move," David said.

"He hasn't told me anything about it," Karen said. "You three now in conspiracy? I'm the last to know? I'm the only one trying to make a life for us and I'm kept in the dark? I'm lied to? I'm put in danger and expected to just put up with it?" She was crying now. "I can't take it anymore. I'm at the end."

"Mom, I'm sorry," David said coming to her side.

"It's not your fault," she said. "It's hers!"

Eleanor froze.

"There's some truth to what everyone says about you," she said. "I know there is. You've bewitched us all."

"Mom," said David. "You don't mean that."

"I do! . . . And I don't," she said crying into her hands. "I never see my son or my husband. I'm an outcast for taking in an orphan. Hated by Christians for doing the Christian thing. How was I to know? But I could have known. I could have been told. You knew all this was going to happen, didn't you, Eleanor? You saw this."

"I didn't," Eleanor said. "I swear I didn't."

"But you know more than you're telling. More than you're telling me at least. David knows, I bet. And Jim's no fool. Wendy probably knows too. Hell, that stupid one-eye cat knows more truth about you than I do. Eleanor, when are you going to tell me? Don't I have a right to know what you've dragged my family into?"

"Mom," said David.

"Shut up, David," she said. "I'm talking to Eleanor. I want to know now before my life's ripped up any more. Before Jim drags us away from our home for you, before the police kick down my door, or someone burns a cross on my lawn. You owe me that. You owe me."

Eleanor crumbled into a chair. Jim came out of David's room in a pair of pajama bottoms. He stood quietly against the wall and surveyed the room. Karen stared at Eleanor, tears running down her face unhindered.

"You're right," Eleanor said. "You most of all should know, Karen. I should have told you. I'm not good at trusting. I'm not used to it. I've learned the hard way not to, but you're right. I owe you."

And Eleanor told her story to the Venns. The afternoon sun dropped below the horizon. The sky glowed tangerine, then red, and then dark before she was done. She began at the beginning, sharing the memory she'd only just recovered: the boy with the broken leg, the beans, and the desert massacre. She described the coyote and the trek north, which took more seasons than she could count. She explained, as best she could, for she had no words to describe her feelings as they were in that state, the overwhelming loneliness and sorrow that haunted her and now remembered why. She told about forgetting, how she had lost her family's names in an effort to rid herself of the recollection of her terrible crime of kindness, and how in an effort to regain them, she'd gone into the campsite.

"It drove me to a little girl," she said. "I was so lucky. I met Celeste."

No one said a word or asked a question or interrupted her as she explained how she found Tabitha by the lake after kissing Celeste, and how they had saved each other. She told how they knew to hide her, to conceal what she was so Eleanor could taste some of life and not be found out and destroyed.

"Every second since Tabitha's death has been a borrowed

moment," Eleanor said. "David convinced me that I could keep going here. He convinced you, Karen, and for the love of your son, we both tried to make it work. I screwed up when I was on TV. That's what started it all. Bad luck."

Wendy came in the door then, tired and hungry. "When's dinner?" she demanded and turned on the television before taking her coat off. Eleanor hadn't finished her story. She hadn't told them about her recent changes, about her visits to Celeste, about Dwight the trucker, Penelope, or Tabitha. Nor did she tell them about Zalarnik's visit or Celeste's last night. Those things she'd leave for another time. This was more than enough for one night.

Eleanor looked at the family. She half expected someone to start laughing, to say something like "great, now pull the other one, you joker," but no one did. She almost wished they wouldn't believe her. She'd never told this much of her story to anyone before. Not even David.

"I should get home now," she said. "Tomorrow's the custody hearing. If you don't want to go through with it any more, I'll understand."

"No one's saying that," Jim said.

"We'll talk about it, Jim," said Karen.

Eleanor nodded. "I only need a couple of years. Just until the age of emancipation: eighteen, in Wyoming."

"That's not true," said Karen. "We don't know how old you are."

"I'm sixteen," she said. "I'm Eleanor Anders. Tabitha Anders' daughter. That's who I am."

"David, you take Eleanor home," Jim said. "I'll be over directly."

They didn't talk much on the walk back, but they did hold hands. Eleanor felt strangely light as if she had help carrying a heavy load.

"The killing. The massacre. That kind of thing can't happen anymore," David said breaking the silence. "Not anymore."

"No," she said.

The next day, Eleanor sat at a crowded conference table in the strip mall office of the Jamesford Social Services building. David and Karen were on either side of her. Jim was home with Wendy. Karen squeezed Eleanor's hand under the table and Eleanor wanted to hug her.

Stephanie Pearce sat next to them and across the table were three people Eleanor had never seen before. They were introduced in turn as varying levels of Social Service bureaucracy, none of whom were from Jamesford. One had come from Cheyenne, the other two from Riverton. At the end, between the two groups, sat Sheriff Hannon and Principal Curtz.

Reporters assembled outside the building. The meeting was closed-door, and though nothing had been done to alert the press, word had leaked out. With the cameras came the Revealers and Lugner himself led the loud prayers outside. Another group, still without a leader, kept them from getting too close and spoke of Eleanor in hushed and reverent tones. She had glimpsed the crowds and saw Shoshone on both sides of the divide. Priests and rabbis in their finery stood stomping their feet against the cold as they stood vigil outside the building, as if waiting to hear about a condemned man's last clemency hearing or the election of a new pontiff.

Eleanor was terrified, but still she carried on. Everything she'd feared had come to pass, and so far at least, she'd withstood it all. The world had changed. Everything changes. She was living proof of that. She thought of her three mothers as different points of a single triangle pointing to the three directions of notoriety.

Her Indian mother, whom she still remembered only as "Mother," had wanted to hide her. Tabitha, her second mother, had wanted to keep in the shadows but still be part of life's dance. With Karen she found herself at another place, out front and in the spotlight, seen by all, and thanks to Celeste's words, feeling safer for it.

"This won't be a long meeting," said Mr. Stanzen, the director from Cheyenne. "This is a formality to announce the custody committee's findings." He opened a thick file and laid it out in front of him.

"Is Ms. Pearce here?"

"Hello," she waved from her side of the table.

"You've been working with Eleanor Anders for nearly ten years, have you not?"

"Yes, ever since Tabitha Anders requested our help. She had terminal cancer. We took an interest in the family then."

"Did you know that Eleanor was not Mrs. Anders' biological daughter?"

"What? No, I don't think anyone knew," she said.

"It was a surprise," said David. "Even to Eleanor."

"Ms. Pearce, you have been an outspoken advocate for Eleanor during her troubled childhood and especially this year. We can tell you really care about the girl."

"Thank you," she said. "I do."

"And Mrs. Venn, I understand you have petitioned the committee for full custody of Eleanor until her age of emancipation. Is that correct?"

"Yes it is, your honor," said Karen.

"I'm not a judge," Mr. Stanzen said. "You can call me Mr. Stanzen. Have you had any problems with Eleanor? Any disciplinary problems?"

"Only problems from Eleanor have come from the outside," she said. "She's been a model teenager."

"Quite," said Mr. Stanzen. "But have you been a model parent?"

"What?"

"You removed Eleanor from the hospital against medical advice after she was severely injured," Mr. Stanzen said. "You allow her to live alone in a separate residence, a house which lies over two miles distance from yours."

"It's much closer than that," said David.

"You have accepted money from the Division for fostering a child who isn't even under your own roof. Some might say such behavior borders on fraud. Similarly, Eleanor has been receiving money from Tabitha Anders' estate as a daughter, while in fact she is not."

"She didn't know that," said Stephanie, the color bleeding from her face.

"Eleanor may be a model teenager, but what kind of teenager buries a body in their back yard? Eleanor faces felony charges for indecent disposal of a body."

"There've been no charges," interrupted the sheriff.

"I'm told that the District Attorney may yet file those charges. He's awaiting for the dispensation of this committee's findings before he makes a final decision."

"Could you say that with any more bureaucratic double-speak?" Hannon said sarcastically.

Another committee member opened a folder. Before he turned the page Eleanor noticed an official seal and under it, in red letters was stamped "NSA Top Secret".

"Don't forget," said the committeeman. "It is common knowledge that David Venn and Ms. Anders are 'going out,' and that you, Mrs. Venn, have done nothing to prevent them from dating. It's a scandal and not a healthy environment at all. It's indecent."

"I understand your husband is serving overseas," said the third man.

"No, he's been discharged," corrected Mr. Stanzen. "Psychological discharge. PTSD, potentially dangerous."

"You rotten—" began Karen.

"You shouldn't have taken Eleanor out of the hospital," said Mr. Stanzen. "We've received information that Eleanor might be very sick. Though her diagnosis is incomplete, Dr. Maulitz suspects she may have a life-threatening illness. She needs special care."

"You have a high-risk family," said a councilman to his papers, "The tumult surrounding Eleanor, be it her fault or no, can't be healthy for your family—your real family."

"Don't tell me what's good for my family," she said.

"It's our job," said Mr. Stanzen smugly.

"We'll appeal," said Stephanie.

"We haven't stated our determination yet," said Mr. Stanzen.

"Do it and get it over with you evil, cowardly men," said Karen.

"I had some trepidation about this, but now I don't," said. Mr. Stanzen. "The girl known as Eleanor Anders is to be removed from the Venns' guardianship and put into protective state custody until such time as more suitable and permanent arrangements for her well-being can be made."

"We'll appeal," said Stephanie. "I know how. We'll file immediately."

"It's out of our hands now," said Mr. Stanzen.

"Miss Anders, have your affairs in order by Monday at eight in the morning. You'll be picked up then." Without looking at anyone, the three got up and left the room.

"I can get this stayed tomorrow," said Stephanie. "Saturday at the latest. You're not going anywhere."

Before Eleanor could say a word or melt to the ground, she found herself in Karen's arms. Then David joined his around them both, then Stephanie. Their embrace held her up.

"It'll be okay," said Karen.

Stephanie followed them home and came inside for a coffee while Jim was told about the meeting.

"Word about this will be out by tomorrow," said Stephanie. "People will be upset. No one likes seeing a family broken up. They'll see it's political."

"I'm surprised," said Jim.

"I wish I were," said Eleanor. She held Odin on her lap. The one-eyed tom purred loudly and contentedly as she rubbed his belly. "I expected disaster."

"You always do," David said. "What would Celeste say?"

"Celeste?" asked Stephanie.

"Inside joke," said David.

The phone rang. Jim answered it.

"This is just a little detour," Stephanie said. "It'll take some time, but we'll get through it. These things always go slow. We'll make them prove everything. Nothing will change until they do. Things will stay as they are until the whole thing is brought before a real judge. We can tie it up for at least a year, maybe two."

"Until I'm eighteen?"

"Oh, yes. We can do that," she said smiling.

Sitting alone at the table, withdrawn from the others, Eleanor saw Karen wrap her arms around herself like a blanket. She listened to Karen's breathing, broken and shallow. She could smell the worry on her in salt and sweat, pheromones of fear she knew all too well. Karen's eyes darted and searched the room, landing on Jim and David and Stephanie in turn.

"Eleanor," Jim said offering her the phone, "It's Sheriff Hannon."

Eleanor put the receiver to her ear.

"Remember that favor you asked?" Hannon said.

"Yes."

"They're coming for you tomorrow," he said.

CHAPTER THIRTY-EIGHT

Stephanie rushed out, eager to wake an attorney she knew in Dubois. "He'll eat this up," she said excitedly. "Don't worry, Eleanor."

"They can't get you if you're out of town," said Jim. "We were told Monday. No need to break up our long-standing camping plans." He winked.

"What's their hurry?" Karen said.

"Possession is nine-tenths of the law," said David.

"They're trying to avoid a scene," Jim said. "Makes sense." The soldier in him took over and he ordered his family to task with critical efficiency. "David, pack the car. We'll be gone five days at least. Karen, you'll stay here with Wendy, be our eyes and ears. Eleanor, what do you need?"

"Clothes," she said. "And food. I think I'll need food."

"I stocked Eleanor's fridge," David said. "Some of it is still in sacks. Easy to get."

"Okay, I'll take Eleanor to her place," said Jim. "We'll be back here in thirty minutes. Be ready to go."

Eleanor followed Jim outside and they drove David's car at

speed to Eleanor's house. It was past midnight and the street was deserted.

"What about the dog?" Eleanor asked seeing Sikring's gift sitting on her porch on a blanket.

"I'll have Karen take care of it."

Eleanor trotted up the porch and opened the door. The dog rushed past her to get inside. "Sorry," she apologized to the cold animal. "I got busy."

Up in the loft, Eleanor rummaged through her meager collection of shirts and pants and stuffed them into a pillowcase. She glanced at her cooking trophy and silver tiara set on the bureau like a shrine. She stared at them, transfixed for a moment, lost in thinking of what-might-have-beens, but grateful for what she'd had. Below she could hear Jim rifling her cabinets.

"Protein," she shouted down.

"Do you have a cooler?" he called up. "Nevermind. We've got one."

Eleanor worked in the dark. Out of the corner of her eye, she saw the red light and thought she'd imagined it. She turned to the window and saw her curtains blink red and then blue. Then she heard the cars outside.

"Jim," she yelled and sprinted to the ladder.

Jim was at the window holding his rifle under one arm, peeking through the curtains. "Two cars," he said. "Not sheriff. State police."

"Goodbye, Jim," Eleanor said and dashed for the back door.

Her body was alight with adrenaline. Her hands shook as she turned the bolt and threw open the door. Her legs bent to sprint across the yard, jump the fence and disappear into the woods. Then north out of town, through Yellowstone to Canada where she could be cold and hungry and lonely, but alive.

She screamed when she saw the man come over the fence. She startled him in return and he dropped his rifle before jumping down.

Jim appeared at her side and pulled her into the house. He heaved his gun to his arm and took aim. He fired three quick shots. The policeman scampered back against the fence. His rifle exploded into pieces on the ground, the stock split in half, black plastic splinters flying over the white snow.

"Git," Jim told him.

The man flopped over the fence and ran away.

The dog barked wildly. Lights flickered on in nearby houses.

Jim pulled the door shut and locked it. He pressed a chair against the handle before drawing the curtains tight.

Eleanor ran to the front of the house. She found Jim's pistol on the table and picked it up. It was heavy and ugly. She didn't like it at all. She held it a moment as if waiting for it to decide, then she put it back.

"I think we can make it out back if we go now," Jim whispered.

"No," Eleanor said. "I heard at least three others that way. There're six out front."

"How'd they get here so fast?" said Jim reloading his gun with a deft flick of his wrist. "Were they watching us?"

Ye-Tsan, the Irish wolfhound, pushed its muzzle against the glass and peered out the front window. It barked at the police outside.

"What are they doing?" Jim asked from the kitchen.

"They've drawn guns," Eleanor told him. "They're behind their cars pointing them at the house."

"Standoff," Jim said. "We'll have to wait for the cavalry."

"Who's the cavalry?" Eleanor asked.

"Jamesford," he said. "Hannon, the press, NASA—everybody." Jim pulled the coffee table into the middle of the house, toppling the dying Christmas tree in a cloud of needles and shattering globes. He piled it with bullets. The house was small. From his vantage point he could see the whole front of the house, the door, the window, the sides, and over his shoulder, the back door through the kitchen. The side windows were small and Eleanor knew it would be impossible for a man to get through one of them. She'd imagined herself squirming through one of those countless times at just such a moment as this, but knew that this year, thanks to Celeste's growth, that was out of the question. They might as well have been walls.

"They're moving at the front," Eleanor said.

Jim came up. He cracked the door open, pushed his rifle out and fired twice into a police car, shattering its windshield. Another five quick snaps from Jim's rifle and Eleanor heard tires deflate and headlights splinter and sizzle in the cold while men ran scared across the frozen road.

"That'll teach them to stay away," he said, slamming the door. He skipped back to his table and reloaded. "They won't dare come in now."

He had a wild look in his eyes that told Eleanor that he did not expect to get out of her house alive, and worse, he did not want to. It was a distant stare into an emptiness half a world away—to a sun-bleached desert that Eleanor knew held him still.

"I have to get away, Jim. I have to escape," she said.

"No," he said. "No running. You can't run away. Better to die fighting than die slowly."

"Jim, this isn't the war," she said.

"Isn't it?" he said. "What's the difference? If I die here, defending my friends, I'll die once. If I run, I'll die here and then there again. A million times. A million deaths. Not again. Cowards live, but live the life of cowards. I'll defend this house to the end. I'll defend you until the end. It's what I have to do."

The house was still; the street was quiet. Police lights cast ghostly, bloody shadows through the window curtains, belying the sudden calm.

"Jim," Eleanor begged.

"Cavalry's coming," he said almost coming to himself again. "When they see what's happening here, we'll win. We'll fight this thing. Then we go. After we've won."

But Eleanor knew the moment Jim fired in the backyard, expertly destroying the policeman's rifle, that their plan was over. There was no way Eleanor would be allowed to remain with the Venns. Not after Jim fired his gun. The standoff could end one of two ways: bad or worse.

It came down on her in a rush. The borrowed time all spent, the bill come due this night. She was trapped, caught. Undone.

She fell to her knees under the weight of it. Her hands gripped her head as if it were about to explode from rage and disappointment. Suddenly she threw her arms back. She craned her neck and looked up at the ceiling, her mind seeing past the roof onto the stars, into the face of the cruel universe, which again was taking from her everything she loved. She howled like a wild animal, like a caged and wounded animal. Ye-Tsan joined in the howl and the windows shook. Together they screamed at the universe until Eleanor had not the breath to continue it and she fell in a clump on the floor. Ye-Tsan ran over to her and licked her face.

She looked at the dog, the hair parted on its muzzle, the ugly face of a strange beast, so primitive, so near wild that she felt kindred to it.

The howl had sobered Jim enough and he watched her wide-eyed and alert.

"I'm so sorry, Eleanor," he admitted. "I don't know what to do."

"I was a fool to think I could continue this. Last year I wanted to run and I stayed, now all I want to do is stay, but I must run. I have to run. Jim, I can't get caught. You're going to have to let me go. Tell David I'll come back when I can, but I can't get caught. I can't."

"I understand," he said.

"I know it's all my fault. It's always been my fault. I'm a fool and a liar and a thief. It is only justice, but I can't accept it, such is the monster I am. I should let it come for me. I should surrender, let them take me, poke me and analyze me. I've lived a long time. I should be ready to let go, but I can't. I can't. I can't fight and win. I'm a coward, Jim. I have to live. My life is all I have, all I've ever been able to keep, as base and monstrous as it is, it's all I've got!"

She'd been screaming, reaching tones and volumes that alarmed David's father and sent the Irish hound hiding behind the sofa.

"I'm running," she said. "But I can't like this."

"What do you have in mind?"

"I need time," she said. "Buy me some time."

"How much?"

"I don't know," she said. "Six hours, maybe more."

"I can do that," he said. "I will do that."

"Okay," she said. "Here's the plan. But first, tell me. Are you squeamish?"

At dawn, the sun broke over the horizon and lit the Anders house on Cedar Street in muddy yellow light. Half the town of Jamesford fought to get closer to the house just beyond the police lines of tan and brown uniformed state troopers. All the players had arrived: the sheriff, the Shoshone, Lugner and his Revealers, townsfolk for and against Eleanor, school friends and priests and, of course, the Venns.

Eleanor was in agony. She'd changed as quickly as she could, but the mass difference was so great, so painfully different, that she'd wanted to die for most of the nine hours it had taken. She'd been unable to keep from screaming several times and had faint recollections of Jim rushing into the bathroom to see that everything was all right. At first, she saw he wore David's face of disbelief and horror, but it passed as suddenly as it appeared and was replaced by another expression. She didn't know what it was, what it meant, for a long time. The pain wouldn't let her think, but she kept at it, trying to decipher the look on Jim's face. It gave her mind, her pain-throttled mind something to do besides feel her bones bend and break, her skin slough off and her muscles contort in debilitating contractions while swimming in the soup of her own discarded flesh. Then, shortly before dawn, as she'd lost the power of speech, she knew what the look had been: wonder.

She could hear voices outside. She was dizzy and still unsure on her feet. She lay still and listened, wishing she could sleep for a while but knowing she could not. This had to end soon.

She could hear the voices rise with the light. People—angry people demanding that something be done.

She heard Sheriff Hannon talking to the mob, telling them to go home. She heard him tell reporters to stay back. She thought she heard him arguing heatedly with Agent Lamb.

"Give me a chance to negotiate," he pleaded. "And do we really need snipers?"

Lamb was uncharacteristically succinct. "Get out of my way or I'll have you arrested," she said.

She heard Reverend Lugner cursing the house and all the evil within it, ordering, if not begging the authorities to destroy the house now and everything in it while they still could "Let not the Evil Escape!" he howled.

She thought she heard Zalarnik's voice, but she couldn't be sure. It was coming over a radio and the static made it difficult to tell.

She rolled over and shook her head. Jim looked at her and his face lit up in wonder again. It was a warm, marvelous expression but also sorrowful and afraid.

"I've seen a miracle," he said softly, emotion cracking his voice. "Thank you."

Suddenly her loft window exploded in glass and fire. She smelled the gasoline before it erupted. Screams came from outside, shouts, orders. Someone fired a gun.

Her loft was ablaze. The house filled with smoke. She listened to the fire suck the air out of the space, igniting her bed, lapping at her roof. She listened to her room burn.

She was ready. She nuzzled Jim's leg and he carefully petted her back. Keeping low, he crept to the front door and opened it. She made ready to run.

Outside the crowd saw a large Irish wolfhound run from

the house. It hesitated on the porch and then bolted through the open gate and into the street. Smoke poured out the front door like water from a cracked vase.

The dog ran sideways in front of the watching police and headed for the crowd. All at once a shot rang out and the dog spun around, a high-pitched yelp escaping it's torn jaw.

"No!" screamed a voice from the crowd.

Another shot and the dog's body lurched to the left as the bullet exploded in its flank.

David broke through the cordon of police and sprinted to the heaving dog. "No!" He screamed. "Murderers!" More gunfire.

Seeing his son alone in the street hovering over the dying animal, snow exploding around him from unseen shooters, Jim ran out of the house. He broke out of the smoke like a meteor, and ran to his boy still clutching his rifle.

Surprised by his sudden appearance, the police opened fire. The first volley missed him, burrowing into the snow, splitting the white fence posts in sudden snapping pops. Many found the house, exploding the front window, splintering furniture, punching holes in the fridge. Flames, hungry for air, burst out the newly broken window. Noxious smoke rose in a billowing black column into the morning winter sky.

The shooting continued. All at once, bullets hit Jim in the legs, his chest and neck. He fell forward in a cartwheel, stumbling across the dried flowerbed and falling over the low fence onto the sidewalk.

Karen screamed. It pierced the air and drew other screams, shouts and cries. Sheriff Hannon raced from behind a car, his hands up. He spoke in slow motion or so it seemed to Eleanor.

It was all so horrible. Her lungs were on fire. She was dying. She coughed and spit and wanted to give it all up then.

Firemen raced to the house but they couldn't get near for the heat. Zalarnik stood with a group of men in space suits trying to approach the building, but they were kept back.

Emergency personnel pushed their way through the crowd as reporters yelled to be heard over their cacophony of cries and curses.

"She's still in there!" someone yelled. "Where's Eleanor?"

"God be praised! The Devil is dead!" Lugner said and smiled on camera. An instant later, a flying bottle split open his forehead. Pandemonium erupted as a group of Shoshone fell into the Revealers, war cries against curses, fists against placards.

David knelt over the bleeding dog. Blood pooled beneath them in an expanding circle of red against the fresh white snow.

"Help! Help! Save her! Save her!" he cried.

A policeman flew at him from behind one of the patrol cars. Without slowing, he plowed into David at full speed, tackling him blindside on the frozen road. Eleanor heard a loud and horrible crack, and David stopped moving.

She watched his still body under the protective policeman and replayed the sound in her mind. It was fractured bone, a noise she knew well. Splintering agony, a thing she'd endured many times, a horror she could survive, but one David might not.

Karen didn't see it. She had run to Jim. Another policeman appeared and pulled her away. She screamed, fought and kicked at them reaching out for her husband. Wendy stood between the dog and her father, her screaming mother and her unmoving brother. She looked at it all in silent shock. Finally, she sat down in the road and cried.

Midge, Aubrey, and Barbara watched with Eric and Brian. Their eyes were fixed on the conflagration. The heat of the burning house reddened their faces, but they did not back away.

It was as it was. Kindness repaid with death. She'd been foolish. She'd been seen. She'd ruined everything and because the universe is cruel she was kept alive again to know what she'd done, to live with it and try to forget it if she could.

She watched smoke pour out of the side bathroom window from where she had jumped. Her lungs burned from the toxic smoke of the life she had tried to make in Jamesford. She'd jumped out of the house just moments before it crashed in on itself in a pillar of orange fire. Her house—her life—nothing but a column of sooty, poisonous smoke. All at once, as her paws hit the melting snow, she remembered her crown and her cakes, her mother and their chair, the tomatoes and the games, and the simple luxury of feeling safe and loved for a while. She'd have cried if she could have. But cats cannot cry, and she had but one eye besides.

With that one eye, she had again beheld the destruction of her family. She was familiar with the scene. It was a variation on a theme. A near copy. She knew copies.

She turned and trotted away. Driven and afraid, her paws already cold from the snow, instinct took over.

She hadn't heard him for the rush of the falling house, hadn't smelled him for the smoke of her ruined life, hadn't sensed him for the horrors in her mind.

He lifted her off the ground by the nape of her neck.

Conrad Sikring looked her right in the face.
"Hello, Eleanor," he said. "I've got you."
And she could do nothing but bare her teeth and howl.

ACKNOWLEDGEMENTS

I'd like to thank, first, the readers and fans who've embraced the flawed and frightened Eleanor. Thank you so much for your time and trust, understanding and enthusiasm. I have been stunned by your response, grateful beyond words, which is something for me.

I must remember my mother, my alpha reader and biggest fan; a light in the gloom of rejection, a cheerleader in a crowd of doubters. Love you!

At Jolly Fish Press, a big thanks to TJ da Roza, my editor, who got it, and embraced the starkness to better feed the undercurrents; a trusted partner and friend, joined at the pen in the telling of tales. My publisher, Chris Loke, the heart of the operation, is a constant font of optimism and patience. Thank you for your continued faith in me and my career and for another breathtaking cover.

This book is dedicated to a family in Denmark who, like the Venns, took in a stranger only to have him entirely upset their lives. My gratitude and apologies cannot be overstated. *Tak for alt.*

And finally, my thanks, again, to Eleanor, my strange, fearful daughter who lets me tell her story. She is metaphor and muse on this strange trip we take together, as real and dear to my heart as the memory of a cherished, childhood friend.

JOHNNY WORTHEN is a nationally acclaimed, award winning author of books and stories. A son of the Wasatch Mountains, he graduated with a BA in English and MA in American studies from the University of Utah. With this basis in literary and cultural criticism plus a lifetime of scars, he writes upmarket, multi-genre fiction seeking truth in narrative. When not presenting at conferences or attending conventions, Johnny is most likely hard at work at his keyboard somewhere in Sandy, Utah with his wife, two sons and cat, guaranteeing at least one fan by writing what he likes to read.